the hounds of avalon
the dark age

the hounds of avalon

MARK
CHADBOURN

GOLLANCZ
LONDON

First published in Great Britain in 2005 by
Gollancz
An imprint of the Orion Publishing Group
Orion House, 5 Upper St Martin's Lane, London WC2H 9EA

1 3 5 7 9 10 8 6 4 2

A CIP catalogue record for this book is
available from the British Library

ISBN 0575072776 (cased)
ISBN 0575072784 (trade paperback)

Typeset by Deltatype Ltd, Birkenhead, Merseyside

Printed in Great Britain by Clays Ltd, St Ives plc

www.orionbooks.co.uk

For more information about the author and his work,
please visit www.markchadbourn.net

acknowledgements

Ben Moxon for his erudite advice on horses and how
they cope with the cold. All the other regular visitors to
the Mark Chadbourn message boards. John McLaughlin
and Charlotte Bruton.

For Betsy, Joe and Eve

contents

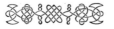

chronicles of
the fallen world

One night, the world we knew slipped quietly away. Humanity awoke to find itself in a place mysteriously changed. Fabulous Beasts soared over the cities, their fiery breath reddening the clouds. Supernatural creatures stalked the countryside – imps and shape-shifters, blood-sucking revenants, men who became wolves, or wolves who became men, sea serpents and strange beasts whose roars filled the night with ice; and more, too many to comprehend. Magic was alive and in everything.

No one had any idea why it happened – by order of some Higher Power, or a random, meaningless result of the shifting seasons of Existence – but the shock was too great for society. All faith was lost in the things people had counted on to keep them safe – the politicians, the law, the old religions. None of it mattered in a world where things beyond reason could sweep out of the night to destroy lives in the blink of an eye.

Above all were the gods – miraculous beings emerging from hazy race memories and the depths of ancient mythologies, so far beyond us that we were reduced to the level of beasts, frightened and powerless. They had been here before, long, long ago, responsible for our wildest dreams and darkest nightmares, but now they were back they were determined to stay for ever. In the days after their arrival, as the world became a land of myth, these gods battled for supremacy in a terrible conflict that shattered civilisation. Death and destruction lay everywhere.

Blinking and cowed, the survivors emerged from the chaos of

this Age of Misrule into a world substantially changed, the familiar patterns of life gone: communications devastated, anarchy raging across the land, society thrown into a new Dark Age where superstition held sway. Existence itself had been transformed: magic and technology now worked side by side. There were new rules to observe, new boundaries to obey, and mankind was no longer at the top of the evolutionary tree.

A time of wonder and terror, miracles and torment, in which man's survival was no longer guaranteed.

chapter one

can't get there from here

'These are the times that try men's souls.' Thomas Paine

The final days of the human race started as they would end, with sapphire lightning bolts lashing back and forth across a stark hall. It appeared to the assembled group that a furious electrical storm was raging within the room, the air suffused with the smell of burned iron. Eyes shielded from the glare by sunglasses, the four men and one woman stood in awe behind the Plexiglas screen. They had the universe in their hands and they knew it.

Standing at the back of the group was Hal Campbell, at first ignored, now forgotten. Twenty-eight years old, bag-carrier, coffee-maker, officially titled chief clerk to the Ministry of Defence. Bookish, quiet and always watchful, sometimes Hal was happy in the obscurity with which nature had blanketed him; at others, he yearned to be involved in the great affairs he saw around him every day. But he knew it would never happen; there was no bigger barrier to this than his character, which shunned risk, wallowed in nostalgia, was overly sentimental and romantic and found security in the routine. After seven years climbing the career ladder in a world of quiet voices and filing cabinets, he knew he had now reached as high as he could go.

Another bolt of energy almost crashed against the Plexiglas window and the front line of viewers took a step back as one, before laughing nervously. Hal observed their faces, transformed into fantastic visages by the shifting shadows of the flashing blue light.

At the front, exuding authority, was the General. He was known simply by that title as if there was only one, but his full name was Clive Parsifal Morgan. Though in his late fifties, he still maintained the boyish, floppy haircut and superior demeanour he had developed at public school, honed at Welbeck College, turned into a fine art at Sandhurst. 'He's coming,' he said simply.

'How can you tell? I can't see anything past all that damned flashing.' David Reid pressed his sunglasses against the bridge of his nose and leaned towards the protective window. As he did so, his jacket fell open and Hal caught a glimpse of Reid's handgun in its holster. Slicked-back black hair, piercing blue eyes, expensive dark suit.

Still thinks he's James Bond, Hal thought

Next to Reid, Catherine Manning stood icily aloof. Hal knew she'd been an investment banker in the City before the Fall; not much call for her occupation since the crash, but somehow she'd managed to find a place in the re-formed Government. Hal was impressed by her always impeccable appearance, long black hair gleaming, lips and eyes made-up despite the increasing rarity of any beauty products. She wore a smart pinstripe jacket and skirt, and standing next to Reid, Hal noted how alike they were in manner and dress.

The final observer was the Government's chief scientist, Dennis Kirkham. Hal knew little about his past, but Kirkham was certainly well respected in current Government circles. He was a grey-faced man, quiet and intense, his thick glasses magnifying an unblinking stare that made Hal uneasy.

All eyes were fixed on the giant bluestone that dominated the hall. Proud and inspiring even torn from its context, it was still covered in lichen and clods of earth from Stonehenge. Hal couldn't help feeling a twinge of sadness to see it there. For around 4,000 years it had stood guard over Salisbury Plain, but once the higher authorities had decided that they had another use for it, it had been uprooted and transported unceremoniously to its new location.

His attention was suddenly jerked from the megalith to the depths of the light display. In the infinite blue, he could have sworn he fleetingly saw a face looking back at him. Even more disturbing, it appeared to have his own features. Hal knew it was just a trick of the coruscating energy at play, but even so it left him with cold sweat trickling down his back.

'He's there, I tell you.' The General tapped forcefully on the Plexiglas shield. 'Can't you see his outline coming through? Over there?'

Everyone turned their attention to the few pieces of electrical equipment that had been used to jump-start the bluestone's residual energy. The red and green lights of a computer terminal were just visible through the sizzling blue glare.

Hal still couldn't see anything, but Catherine Manning had become animated. 'Yes – I see him! He's made it!'

'Let's not get too excited yet,' Kirkham cautioned, his face set. Of all of them, he was the one who most understood the risks. Hal recalled Kirkham's briefing when Glenning had been selected. They had laughingly dubbed Glenning 'the Psychonaut', a name that had since buckled under the weight of its own accumulated mythology.

'The chances are you may not be coming back,' Kirkham had warned Glenning as they stood before the lecture hall whiteboard covered with Kirkham's convoluted diagrams. 'The knowledge encoded in all the old stories makes it quite clear what will happen to mortals who venture where they shouldn't.'

Hal was jolted from his memory by a shimmer of blue light in the shape of a man near the spot the General had indicated.

'Yes!' Catherine said, her fists bunched in triumph.

'Phasing in,' Kirkham muttered to himself. He checked the set of monitors on the desk next to him. 'Ozone level high. Ultrasound. EMF spiking. This is it.'

'So you don't have to be at one of the nodes after all,' Reid mused. 'As long as you can manipulate that energy, you can do it anywhere. Think of the implications.'

'Yes, just think,' the General said sardonically, 'all you need is a four-ton megalith strapped to your back.'

A soundless explosion of blue light forced them to shield their eyes despite their sunglasses. When it cleared, the crackling bolts of lightning had gone and Glenning was standing near the bluestone, still wearing his RAF thermal flight suit. Hal could instantly see that something was wrong. The pilot was shaky on his feet, disoriented, his skin as pale as snow. But it was his eyes that would haunt Hal in the coming months. Buried in their depths was a terror so vast that it appeared to be consuming Glenning from within. This was a man who had personally seen the very depths of hell, someone who knew that his life was already over and that what was to come would be worse.

Glenning stared at them all through the Plexiglas window and desperation carved its way into his face. He reached out one arm, opened his mouth to plead, and then he simply . . . disintegrated. It was as though, Hal mused later, he had been a statue carved out of sand, collapsing under its own weight. A pile of grey dust was all that remained in the sterile atmosphere of the hall.

Hal couldn't quite believe what he had seen. One second Glenning had been there, living and breathing and human, and then, unbelievably, he wasn't. Hal's mind rebelled at what his eyes were telling it. Gradually, though, his incredulity became dismay at the loss of a man in such an inhuman way.

'Another failure,' Kirkham said levelly, checking his monitors.

Jubilation drained from Catherine Manning's face, leaving behind a sickened horror. 'Oh my God,' she said, her voice dry. 'What's happened to him?'

'The only way we're ever going to cross over is by defeating that fatal flaw in our make-up that self-destructs whenever we try to pass through the barrier,' Kirkham continued, ignoring the question.

'We know that some people can do it,' the General said. 'We need to find out what they've got that we haven't.'

'Gladly,' Kirkham said, 'if we had one I could examine.'

'What about Glenning?' Hal couldn't take his eyes off the pile of dust.

'Yes, poor bastard,' Reid replied. 'Somebody is going to have to tell his wife.'

In his office filled with antique furniture and books that had not been opened for many a year, the General lit a small black cigar and offered the others whisky from a crystal decanter. Hal distributed the drinks on a tarnished silver tray.

'I don't believe we can afford to wait any longer, General,' Reid said once they were all seated around the large desk. Hal retired to a shadowy corner, invisible but watching.

'I agree.' The General swirled the amber liquid in his glass and then inhaled the honeyed fragrance. 'Thought so for a while now, to be honest. But as you know, the PM is a cautious man.'

'There's no great urgency,' Catherine Manning said. 'They've left us alone in recent months. In fact, intelligence hasn't reported any sightings of them anywhere.' She looked to Reid for confirmation.

'Make no mistake, the Tuatha Dé Danann are still out there.' Reid had a file filled with the latest briefings from his men and women out in the communities. 'And the things that came along with the old gods are certainly still a threat. Villages in the Yorkshire Dales being terrorised by some creature that turns people to stone. Something with blades for hands cutting people up in Liverpool. The National Parks, the fells and fens – whole swathes of the country inaccessible unless you've got a squadron of heavily armed men—'

'The Tuatha Dé Danann are the root of it all,' the General said firmly. 'Without them, none of these other things would be here.'

'But we're still not adequately equipped to fight them,' Manning protested. 'How can we be expected to go up against gods—'

'They are not gods,' the General stressed. 'Uneducated, barbaric peasants centuries ago might have thought them gods when the Tuatha Dé Danann first ventured here, but we're above such primitive nonsense. Yes, they have immense power. Yes, they can do things beyond our current understanding. But they are *not* gods. And they can be defeated. We have to use our intelligence, our resilience and the other abilities given to us by Himself. The real God?'

Manning sipped her drink quietly, but Hal could tell that she was not convinced.

The General turned to Kirkham. 'Review what we know.'

'Einstein postulated the idea of a parallel universe . . . other dimensions. Of course, they've always existed in myth. The home of the gods. Asgard. Avalon. Now we know, in this as in so many other ways, that the old stories have a greater degree of truth in them than we suspected. But the roots are also there in solid science—'

'You're not about to go off on one of your interminable

incomprehensible rambles, are you?' Reid said wearily. The General waved him quiet.

Kirkham was unperturbed by the interruption. 'It all comes down to String Theory. Complicated physics, I know, but bear with me. In nineteen ninety-five, Edward Witten at the Princeton Institute for Advanced Study came up with what he called M-Theory, which implies the existence of higher dimensional shapes called membranes, or branes for short.' Kirkham, as always, was not about to be rushed – or deterred. 'Branes can be as large as a universe. Indeed, a brane might even *be* a universe, and we could be living in one right now.'

'And the point is?' Reid enquired rudely.

'The point is that reality is not as clear cut as we were taught growing up. Witten described string theory as "twenty-first-century physics that fell by chance into the twentieth century". We're at the cutting edge of science here. Is the Otherworld of Celtic mythology another brane? Are the gods the inhabitants of that brane, as we are of this one? Is it possible to *leak* between the two in the same way that M-Theory suggests happens to excess gravity strength?'

'Bottom line: you still believe we can find a way through to their homeland?' the General asked.

'We know that the Tuatha Dé Danann can cross over at will,' Kirkham replied. 'We also know that some human beings can pass back and forth, albeit only at certain locations. The mechanism is not clear at the moment, but with enough time and resources—'

'You'll get all the resources you require,' the General said. 'Time is a different matter. The Tuatha Dé Danann may have left us alone since the Battle of London, but we have still been invaded. The country is under enemy control, and we have no idea when they will attempt to begin cleansing. We've waited long enough already.'

'Sir?' Hal ventured. The others looked up sharply – they'd forgotten he was still there. 'Shouldn't we be working alongside those who fought off the original invasion at the Fall ... the Brothers and Sisters of Dragons? From the intelligence we've gathered, we know they can cross over without any harm.'

'I've been asking for one of them to question for a long while,' Kirkham said to the group, his frustration plain.

'Are we sure they're not just urban legends?' Manning asked. 'I mean, five men and women – in what, their twenties? – who somehow mysteriously banded together and stopped the invasion from crushing us completely?'

'How do you think the invasion was stopped at the Fall?' the General said. 'It wasn't us. Our forces were paralysed . . . decimated. Why did the gods decide to sneak off into the woodwork after the Battle of London, when they'd already demonstrated that they could wipe us out any time they wanted?'

'Yes, but five people,' Manning continued incredulously. 'I've heard the stories the same as you—'

'Oh, they exist all right,' Reid said. 'We had two under surveillance at Salisbury, but they've since eluded us. The Five who fought at the fall were Jack Churchill, an archaeologist; Ruth Gallagher, a lawyer; Ryan Veitch, a career criminal; and Laura DuSantiago and someone who went by the name of Shavi, two aimless drifters, no more than that as far as we can tell. Not exactly hero material, is it? They were empowered in some way by that blue energy we saw down in the lab.'

Kirkham nodded in agreement. 'Can't explain that at all. It seems to have come with the Fall.'

'After the Battle of London,' Reid continued, 'the ones who survived disbanded, drifted off. The information I have is that a new Five is now in the process of being formed – the two we were observing in Salisbury were the first of the new group.' He paused, choosing his words carefully. 'Apparently that blue energy is supposed to . . . choose these . . . champions. Seems to have a thing about the number five, too.'

Manning snorted at the implication in Reid's words.

'What about the original Five?' the General said.

'Two of them are believed dead,' Reid replied. 'The two women are missing. The fifth is located at some college for mystical loons in Glastonbury.'

'So why haven't you picked him up if you know where he is?' Manning asked. Hal noted her barely restrained pleasure at Reid's discomfort.

Reid set his jaw. 'We've sent out several operatives to contact the individual, but none has returned.'

The General sat back in his chair, smoking thoughtfully. 'This new group . . . there're just two of them so far?'

'There's been no sign of any others as yet,' Reid confirmed. 'We've got people stationed at all the liminal zones – the standing stones, the henges, the ancient sacred sites – just in case anyone attempts to cross over. I've heard nothing.'

'What is all this nonsense?' Manning asked. 'Five champions? Somehow I can deal with the notion of an invasion of extraterrestrial biological entities, but this . . . it's like living in a bloody fairy tale.'

'Come on,' Reid said impatiently. 'No one knows what we're really dealing with here. Suddenly there are all these new rules.'

'We need to get hold of those two you were observing in Salisbury immediately,' the General said.

'Yes, sir.' Reid shifted uncomfortably in his chair; clearly he didn't think it was going to be as easy as the General was implying.

'Finally,' Manning said. 'If these Brothers and Sisters of Dragons do know how to cross over, perhaps we can actually show the Tuatha Dé Danann that we've got some teeth.'

'That is my intention, Ms Manning,' the General said. 'I'm going to the PM with a new proposal. We've had our heads down for far too long. This is the time for action.' He turned to Hal. 'Mister Campbell? Find Hunter. He should put a team together immediately.'

'I'll tell him at once, sir.' Hal slipped out quietly, anticipation mingling with queasy apprehension. This was it, then: the war was finally about to be launched.

The Oxford night was balmy as the heat of the June day gradually leaked away. Hal made his way from the Ministry of Defence offices and staff apartments at Magdalen College into the cool dark of the ancient Deer Park. It was a walk he took every night to clear his head. He loved Magdalen – its near-six-hundred-year history, the Great Tower, the chapel, the cloisters, so beautiful in the snow – but sometimes the tiny rooms and ancient corridors grew claustrophobic: too much gossip, too much back-stabbing, too many rumours.

Whichever way he looked at it, though, Oxford was still better than London. All the old colleges now housed the Government departments that had fled the capital during the Fall. They still inhabited the same grandeur they had all enjoyed in Whitehall and the Palace of Westminster, but it felt like a fresh start; and that was a good thing.

As he slipped off his shoes to feel the deer-cropped grass, the shock of Glenning's death finally hit him hard and he took a deep, juddering breath, throwing his head back to stare at the sky. The stars were comforting, but after all they had been through so were the city's streetlights and the golden electric lamps that still blazed in many of the windows around the college.

'Amazing, isn't it?'

Startled, Hal spun around to find Samantha standing behind him, hands on hips, smiling in the way that always made his spine tingle. Her ash-blonde hair was tied back with an elastic band and she was dressed in a well-worn T-shirt and a pair of tracksuit trousers. The sweat of her run still gleamed on her forehead.

'You're jumpy,' she said, laughing.

'Had a bit of a shock earlier.' Hal took another deep breath to calm his thumping heart.

'And I don't suppose you can tell me about it. Ultra top secret, as usual.'

'You know how it is.' Hal shifted uncomfortably; he wished he *could* tell her. Glenning's death was one thing he desperately needed to get off his chest.

'It is amazing, though, isn't it?' Samantha moved closer to Hal, and he was suddenly aware of the not-unpleasant aroma of her sweat mixed with the fragrance of whatever perfume, shampoo or other aromatic she used. 'Electric lights. A few years back, you'd never have thought what a wonder they would be.'

'They still are for most of the country. Mustn't forget we're only blessed with them here because it's the new seat of Government—'

Samantha laughed again.

'What?' Hal's cheeks coloured.

'*Blessed with them*, indeed. You talk so strangely sometimes.' She was still smiling when she slipped an arm around his waist and gave him a gentle squeeze. A different kind of heat ran into Hal's face. 'Don't get me wrong – I love it. You're a breath of fresh air around here, Hal.'

Hal would have liked to respond – with an arm around her waist, perhaps a kiss – but it wasn't the time. It never was, and a part of him wondered if it ever would be.

'Any idea where Hunter is holed up?' he asked, changing the subject.

Samantha rolled her eyes. 'Let's draw up a list of the worst dives in Oxford and I'll guarantee he's in one of them. He's banned from all the good places. I heard he was thrown out of Stanyard's last week.'

Hal nodded. 'Caught in one of the toilet cubicles with a girl . . . by her boyfriend. Between them they wrecked the place before the landlord managed to toss them out.'

'And the Government wouldn't be here if not for his strong right arm,' Samantha said sarcastically. 'That's what he tells all those floozies. And they all fall for it.'

'You don't like him very much, do you?'

'I loathe him. And I can't understand why you're his friend. Not in a million years. What have you ever got in common?'

'I ask myself that some days.' Hal glanced up just as a shooting star burned its path across the arc of sky visible above the city lights. 'See that?' he said. 'It's an omen.'

Samantha grew serious. 'The fight-back starts soon?'

'You know I can't answer that.' Hal looked towards the dark, unruly city beyond the grand, historic colleges. 'I'd better find Hunter, drag him out of whatever mess he's got himself into this time.'

'OK, Hal. I'll see you tomorrow.' Samantha gave him another warm smile before jogging off. Hal watched her until she disappeared into the shadows. A braver man would already have made his move, but Hal couldn't until he was sure one hundred per cent that she wouldn't say no. Deep in his head, he'd always considered himself a romantic, a counterbalance to a life lived in the dusty here-and-now to which he had been consigned; or rather, to which he had consigned himself. And he'd known pretty early on in their friendship that Samantha was the only one who could truly make him happy; not love at first sight, exactly, but near as dammit.

The first time Hal had seen her, she had been giving her lunchtime sandwich to a young girl begging on the side of the street. When Hal mentioned it to her later, Samantha had denied her act of charity, which had only intrigued him more. But the one moment – the one shining moment that had changed everything for him – had been in some dingy bar after work when, drunk and argumentative, she'd clubbed Hunter around the head and then, minutes later, given an a cappella version of 'California Dreamin'' that had sent shivers down his spine. There was no reason why it should have affected him so deeply; but it had been an alchemical experience, fuelled by magic and mystery in the banal crucible of everyday existence.

He would never forget how she'd made that gold from the base lead of his life; it was too valuable ever to risk losing.

The brothel on St Michael's Street had become a thriving if frowned-upon establishment ever since the new Government had moved to Oxford and saved the city from ruin. From the outside, the building looked abandoned, but the majority of Government employees knew its location, and for many of the men in the lower ranks it provided a welcome release from the numerous pressures of trying to lead a country thrown back to the Dark Ages.

Hal knocked discreetly on the unmarked door, which was opened by an elderly lady with an ice-cream-cone mound of white hair piled on her head and a little too much make-up on her face. 'Is Hunter here, Mrs Damask?' he asked.

'Yes, Jeffrey's inside,' Mrs Damask replied in her lyrical Scottish brogue. 'Would you like to wait for him?'

'You know he doesn't like to be called Jeffrey,' Hal said as he entered the baroque entrance hall with its atmosphere of incense and classical music playing quietly in the background.

'And that's why we call him it,' Mrs Damask whispered with a conspiratorial wink.

She led Hal up three flights of stairs to a long corridor with doors on either side; various human noises of pleasure and pain emerged from behind several of them. Mrs Damask motioned to a row of chairs where Hal could wait. Once she had gone, Hal listened self-consciously at Hunter's door and when he was sure there was no activity within, he knocked quietly. There was a grunt that Hal knew to be a signal of admission.

Hunter was lounging in the middle of a king-size bed beneath black silk sheets, smoking from a large hookah that bubbled on the bedside table. There were two blondes with him, twins from the look of it, probably in their late teens. Both were sleepy and clearly worn out.

'Want a go at my sloppy seconds?' Hunter asked lazily. Hal always thought he looked like Errol Flynn in *Captain Blood*: the heavy gold earring, the long black hair tied back with a black ribbon, the devilish goatee. No Government operative would have been allowed such self-expression in any other time, and few even in these dark days. But Hunter had special dispensation. *You can get away with murder when you're good at what you do*, Hal thought.

'You really are disgusting,' he said.

Hunter saw the serious intent in Hal's face and tapped the girls on the shoulder, waving them out of the door. Not bothering to hide their nakedness, they skipped out with a giggle and a backward glance at Hunter.

Hunter noted Hal's disapproval with weary disdain. 'In times like this, you've got to celebrate life, have some fun. But you wouldn't understand that – you like wallowing in your misery.' He swung his legs out of bed and started to pull on his clothes before pausing with a wrinkled nose. 'I need a shower.'

'The General wants you to put a team together for a retrieval—'

'That swaggering git always wants something when it's my night off.'

'They're going after a couple of those Brothers and Sisters of Dragons.'

Hunter raised an eyebrow. 'Finally. I was starting to think they were scared of them or something.'

'They're beginning to feel backed into a corner. Glenning didn't make it.'

'He was a stupid bastard for volunteering.' Hunter paced across the sumptuous rugs, stretching his lithe body. A large black tattoo of a snake rose up his spine from somewhere below the waistband of his trousers to the nape of his neck, slithering as the muscles beneath it rippled.

'How can you be so hard-hearted?' Hal protested. 'Glenning sacrificed himself for the sake of the country.'

Hunter stared at Hal in disbelief. 'Don't start falling for the propaganda. It's not good for your health.' He pulled on a loose-fitting red silk shirt that masked his hardness with a dandyish air.

'Glenning was a drone who jumped through hoops whenever anyone higher up the pecking order shouted at him. That mission was always going to fail. You know that.'

'Someone has to try—'

'Yeah?' Hunter shrugged. 'Why?'

'We're at war, fighting for the existence of civilisation . . . everything we've achieved—'

'And what have we achieved, exactly?'

'There's no talking to you when you're in this mood.' Hal marched to the antique sideboard and poured himself a glass of vintage wine from a crystal decanter. 'It shows our resilience as a race that we're still clinging on after all we've endured in recent times. The basic rules of science shown up for what they are – just one way of looking at the world, and not the most important by a long way. Society turned on its head—'

'You say all that as if it's a bad thing.' Hunter flopped on to the edge of the bed and pulled on his boots.

'It's amazing that we've managed to establish a new Government here in Oxford after what happened in London. We've even got the power back on, instituted some semblance of normality. A year ago, no one would ever have thought that would have been possible.'

'You said it yourself – we're clinging on. What's the point in trying to hang on to the old days? They're gone. The way we lived, the things we believed in . . . they're all part of the past. We've been presented with a whole new set of possibilities. We should be reinventing ourselves to live now . . . to create a better world, not just repeat all the old mistakes simply because it makes us feel comfortable.'

'It's not that—'

'Yes, it is. We're all terrified of change – especially the big change, death – so we try to pretend that there's some permanence in this world that change can't influence. It's all metaphors and symbols. I thought you were the smart one in this friendship. You know that nothing has meaning on the surface. The surface is just a clue to what's locked underneath—'

'I didn't come here for a philosophical discussion.' Hal drained the wine in one go.

'There's no talking to you when you're in this mood,' Hunter mocked, but gently. 'We've got the chance for a good thing here, but we'll never see the benefits. Do you know why? Human nature. Forget the gods and the monsters – we're our own worst enemies. It's hard-wired into us. Someone will come along to fuck things up for the majority, just to get a shot at making more money or gaining more power for themselves. Wait and see.'

'Why do you do this, Hunter?' Hal said, hitting back in the only way he knew how.

'What?'

'All the women, the drink, the drugs . . . You're just trying to run away from who you are. Can't face life as the big, scary Hunter. It's childish, you know.'

'Yep.'

Hal sighed. 'Don't you have any self-awareness?'

'Nope.'

'That's it, isn't it,' Hal said morosely. 'I do all the thinking and you do all the doing.' He sagged on to the edge of the bed.

Hunter laughed and clapped him heartily across the shoulders. 'Come on, let's get tooled up.'

While Hunter went to his flat to get a shower, Hal wandered the maze of quiet streets in the ancient quarter between Cornmarket and Longwall Streets. In the long shadows cast by the Divinity School and the Bodleian Library, it was possible to imagine he was back before the Fall and that sooner or later he would bump into some students making their way home after a late-night party.

As he rounded on to Catte Street and approached the Radcliffe Camera, he was met by a strange sight. Although it was night, four thrushes sat side by side on a wrought-iron fence, silent and immobile, while a fifth hopped around in a circle on the pavement. Hal came to a halt, curious at the bird's antics, but he was even more surprised when the bird on the pavement appeared to notice him. It hopped up to his foot and stopped before raising its head to stare at him. Hal looked from the strange visitor to the four birds on the fence and back; all of them were staring at him, or so it seemed. He waited for the bird at his feet to fly off, even shook his leg slightly to encourage it, but the longer it remained, the more his curiosity gave way to an unsettled feeling. In the end, he walked off himself. Ten yards away he glanced back. The birds were still where he'd left them, but they had turned to watch his departure.

Hal laughed it off, but the unnerving sensation clung to him like autumn fog. Soon after, it was compounded. On the first storey of a building on the High Street, five windows in a row were lit, but one had a blind half-pulled down. Further on, four bicycles leaned against a wall, while a fifth lay on its side in the gutter.

Coincidence, his rational mind insisted, yet an age-old instinctive part of him couldn't help feeling slightly uneasy at this pattern manifesting itself in the most mundane things. His mind conjured an image of the universe as one living creature, breathing slowly like a man at rest, an entity that had, at that moment, chosen to notice him in particular, and to communicate some incomprehensible but vital message to him alone. Shaking his head at the odd turn his thoughts had taken, he continued along the main thoroughfare.

Suddenly, a man lurched out of a darkened alley. His tattered clothes were filthy from a life lived on the streets, his skin so black with ingrained dirt that his eyes stared out wide and white, his hair and beard a matted mane of mud-stained grey and black. He reeked of engine oil and urine.

Hal stepped back, instantly on his guard. The man held out one filthy hand, fingers splayed. Four stood erect; the thumb was missing, a ragged sore seeping at the joint.

Involuntarily, Hal ran, not stopping until the comforting lights of Magdalen burned off his fear. He told himself how stupid he'd been, but nothing would have convinced him to return to the dark maze of ageless streets that night.

Hunter sat at the back of the auditorium, alert and serious. Hal knew it was only a front for his superiors. Six other men were scattered around the rows, waiting silently, all of them former SAS or SBS. Their cold inhumanity scared Hal; they were prepared to do things no normal member of society would consider. Hunter always insisted Hal go easy on them: he was allowed to sleep peacefully because men like them existed. Hal could see the logic of that argument, but in truth he didn't think Hunter really liked any of them either.

The General stood at the front, relaxed and confident. Hal knew that the military had been pushing for more direct involvement in day-to-day events for a while, but they had always been restrained by the intelligence corps and the politicians who feared showing the Government's hand too soon. But the power base appeared to be shifting in the eternally baffling, subtle machinations that thrived in the shadowy corridors of the Government headquarters.

'Some background,' the General began. 'The mission on which you are about to embark is to seek out and capture one of the group known as the Brothers and Sisters of Dragons. You will recall the first stories of their appearance at the time of the Fall. We discounted them as rumours and concentrated on a traditional response to the threat facing us.' His face grew grim. 'A mistake. The Brothers and Sisters of Dragons were instrumental in preventing a catastrophic defeat. The powers arrayed against us were held back. Some – the worst – fled after the Battle of London. Others adopted a watching brief, but are still a threat.'

'They did us a favour,' said a man at the front, his face marred by severe acne scars.

'Our advisors tell us that they are some kind of champions chosen by the . . . forces that are active in the world at present.' Hal could see that the General was uncomfortable dealing with concepts that were alien to him. *Forces. Gods. Magic.* 'They are empowered by some kind of subtle energy that runs through the planet. It gives them certain abilities . . .' His voice trailed off.

'Maybe it doesn't.' Hunter smiled a wry smile. 'Maybe they're just better than everyone else. You don't have to be Special Forces to be a *champion.*'

The General stifled a hint of irritation and continued, 'One of the abilities they do have is to cross the barrier that separates us from our enemy's homeland. If we want to strike at them where it hurts, *we* need that ability. Our advisors suggest this energy may be intelligent in some way, that these champions appear where or when they're most needed. Take that as you will. Sounds like a load of bunkum to me, but it doesn't have any impact on the mission at hand. All you need to know is that a new group of Five is being formed. Two have so far been identified.'

'How dangerous are they?' the acne man asked. 'The Five who fought at the Battle of London sound like nutters.'

'Dangerous is a good word for them, Grieg. Particularly so in the case of these two,' the General replied. 'The first one goes by the name of Mallory, Christian name unknown. He's a mercenary. Most recently, he sold himself to the Church.'

A sneering murmur ran through the assembled men except Hunter and Hal, who listened intently.

'Don't make assumptions or you'll pay the price,' the General warned. The Church – what remains of it – is based in Salisbury Cathedral, where they're training up a new bunch of Knights Templar. Forget your history. These are fighting men. Hard. Well suited to the times we live in. Well trained in swordplay, archery, survival techniques. And they had a good teacher: Blaine.'

'*The* Blaine?' Grieg asked.

The General nodded. 'Indeed. Bloody Blaine of Belfast. So don't underestimate Mallory. If you don't have your wits about you, you'll be dead before you're within three feet of him.'

'Is he travelling with the other one?' Hunter asked.

'Yes. A woman.' The General checked his notes. 'Sophie Tallent. Special abilities: she can manipulate that subtle energy in some way, has certain supernatural powers . . .'

Hal found himself wondering what chance they had if the military couldn't accept the profound changes that had taken place across the world. The supernatural was a fact of life: strange creatures, bizarre powers, hidden rules. Everyone knew it; they'd all seen the signs – much of the evidence lay in the cells of the high-security wing below Brasenose College, not far from the lab where Glenning had died.

'Are they lying low?' Hunter's face had a strange expression that Hal couldn't quite read.

'They don't realise that we're aware of them,' the General replied, 'let alone searching for them. They should be relatively easy to locate. Our last reconnaissance placed them somewhere in the vicinity of Sparkford in Somerset. It appears they're searching for something, though without much luck so far.'

'Can we use the chopper?'

Hal flinched at Hunter's request. With no new fuel being produced, vehicle use was rarely sanctioned, but the General acceded without hesitation. Hunter winked at Hal.

'Get them back here as quickly as you can. Get them back in a state we can use,' the General said firmly. 'And don't come back empty-handed.'

Outside Magdalen's main college buildings, Hal waited for Hunter in St John's Quadrangle, in the shadow of the porter's lodge. Hunter had stayed behind after the General's departure to brief his men, which Hal knew usually meant threatening them with genital removal in the event of failure. Hunter called it *motivational therapy*; Hal wasn't wholly sure it was a joke.

'I've got a funny feeling about the way things are going at the moment,' Hal said when Hunter emerged.

For once, Hunter's response wasn't glib. 'We're at a turning point, no mistaking.' He forced a grin. 'Let's hope the leadership are up to what's expected of them.'

'You don't have much time for anyone, do you?'

'Not really. That way you never feel let down.' He cracked his knuckles uneasily. 'I can't get this damned REM song out of my head.'

'The one about the end of the world?'

'You'd think, wouldn't you? No, another one, an older one.'

Hunter paused as Samantha emerged from the buildings that housed the staff living quarters. She'd showered after her run and her hair was still damp. Her face lit up with an open smile when she saw Hal, but became instantly guarded when her eyes fell on Hunter.

'Hmm. Fresh and squeaky clean,' he said as she approached.

Samantha's eyes flashed. 'I gather you're about to depart on an extremely dangerous, possibly lethal mission. Don't hang around here on my behalf.'

'Samantha, you're the reason I'll be back. You give my life meaning.' He winked at Hal. 'See you, mate. Put the champagne on ice.'

Samantha watched until Hunter had disappeared from view, and then turned to Hal and said, 'He gives sleazy a bad name.'

'You know you like him really,' Hal joked and was surprised by Samantha's indignation.

'How can you say that?' Her tone was unduly sharp.

'I was just—'

'Well, don't.' She softened. 'Listen, have you heard the latest gossip?' Hal allowed himself to be dragged conspiratorially into an alcove. 'The security forces have captured a god.'

'What?' Hal said, suddenly uneasy, although he didn't quite know why. 'I don't believe it.'

'It's true. They used some super-secret weapon, apparently. Anyway, he's been brought in for interrogation—'

'Brought here? Is that wise?'

Samantha looked at him, puzzled.

'I know we've got secure cells—'

'They're already holding some powerful things down there,' Samantha said.

'I know. But not a god. How can they contain a power like that?'

'He's not a *real* god—'

'You know what they did to London. Besides, even if we could hold it, that's got to attract the attention of all its kind. Do we really want all that coming down on our heads?'

A flicker of disappointment crossed Samantha's face. It stung Hal harder than he would have expected. 'We're at war, Hal,' she said gently. 'We have to take risks, for the sake of everyone.' She gave his arm a reassuring squeeze, as if he was scared for his own safety. 'Don't worry. If I hear any more I'll let you know.' She flashed him a smile and headed towards the refectory for a late-night meal.

Hal stood in the silent quadrangle for a long moment, turning over what she had said. He wished Hunter was still around; he needed to discuss it with someone. It was too big to deal with himself. But there was no one else and, with a mounting sense of disquiet, he headed out into the night.

After everything that had happened that evening, Hal felt distinctly out of sorts. Glenning's death had shaken him profoundly, and the random numerical manifestations of five minus one still haunted him. He tried to pretend that his mind had only noticed the similar numbers because it was already troubled, but he couldn't shake an overwhelming feeling that it meant something, although he couldn't begin to divine what.

Yet he found no ease in the moon-shadows of the Deer Park. The night was too hot and appeared to be growing warmer by the minute; his sweat-sodden shirt clung to his back. But it wasn't the temperature that continued to turn the screw on his psyche. With mounting disorientation, he looked around at the cityscape visible beyond the ancient rooftops. It was like looking at the city through a heat haze: a transparent curtain of shimmering sapphire light rippled back and forth, and through it Oxford appeared transformed. The medieval buildings and their modern counterparts merged and flowed into more fantastic structures: towers reached up into the night, some constructed from gleaming blue-white stone, others seemingly of brass and gold; lofty-roofed halls and gargoyle-riven battlements; arching bridges; steeples and spires and domes.

The illusion came and went with every eye-blink, fantasy and reality, reality and fantasy, so that in the end he couldn't tell on which side of the line he stood. With it came a tingling in his fingers and toes, energy drawn from the ground itself, curling up his spine like the snake that slithered across Hunter's back. Hal's breath was taken away with wonder, while his rational mind ran wild in search of understanding.

Yet he was distracted after only a few seconds by a figure emerging from the haze as if it was slowly gaining solidity from a phantom existence. It was a giant of a man at least eight feet tall. His long black hair and beard and the dark coals of his eyes reminded Hal oddly of the disfigured tramp he had seen earlier that evening. Though his height was daunting, it was the man's clothes that instantly set him apart. He wore a rough brown shift fastened at the waist by a broad belt. His left forearm was bound with a thong, from which several malicious-looking hooks gleamed.

Hal thought it prudent to retreat to the safety of the buildings as quickly as possible, but was sickened to discover that his legs wouldn't obey his thoughts. Yet despite the stranger's foreboding appearance, Hal felt no sense of threat. Instead, it was almost as if he was in a dream, watching the scene through someone else's eyes.

'I have searched for you across the worlds, for time upon time upon time,' the giant began, 'and now I find myself summoned to the place where you stand. Existence weaves a pattern that none of us can see.'

'Who are you?' Hal asked. The taste of iron filings numbed his mouth.

'I am the Caretaker. I am the lamplighter. In the darkest of the dark, I ensure that a single flame burns. In the midst of chaos, I ensure that the home is kept safe and secure.'

Something supernatural, Hal's sluggish brain thought. *One of the gods?*

'Are you causing all this?' Hal gestured towards the shimmering phantom city that kept overlaying itself on the Oxford skyline.

'No. But it is serendipitous.'

Slowly, the Caretaker's words wormed their way into Hal's consciousness. 'You're looking for me?'

'I come with a warning of greatest import: something has noticed you.'

'What?' Hal's mind fumbled for meaning.

The Caretaker raised one huge hand and pointed up to the sprinkling of stars. 'Out there, on the edge of Existence. It has seen you . . . and it is coming.'

Hal stared dumbly into the deep black depths of space. 'What's coming?'

The blue haze began to fade and the true outline of Oxford started to emerge into sharp relief once more. When Hal looked back at the Caretaker, the giant had retreated several paces, though Hal had not been aware of him walking away.

'It will be here soon now . . . very soon,' the Caretaker continued in a low, echoing voice. 'It may even be here already. You must be prepared. The Brothers and Sisters of Dragons must be united. But know this: one of the Five has already fallen. And without the correct number their effectiveness is dimmed.' He stared towards the few lamps still burning in the windows of Magdalen. 'There is little hope. Soon even the last light may be extinguished. And then my job shall be done.'

The Caretaker continued to fade, drifting across the grass, becoming more insubstantial the further from Hal he got.

'War . . .' The giant's words were breaking up. 'There will come an ending.'

'Why are you telling me this?' Hal called.

The Caretaker's response was lost to the night breeze. A second later, he vanished and the blue haze along with him. Reality was hard and fast all around. But inside Hal the dread that had been mounting all night had now crystallised.

He had been noticed. And *something was coming.*

23

the call of ancient days

'The philosophers have only interpreted the world in various ways; the point, however, is to change it.' Karl Marx

'Give us the sword.'

The skinhead wore a fixed, dead stare, but it was the shotgun the thug was pointing casually that held Mallory's attention. In the distance, smoke from the burning village clouded the blue sky.

'It's not very fair, is it?' Mallory said. 'Sword . . . shotgun . . .'

'You should have thought of that when you were choosing your weapon.' The skinhead let out a gurgling laugh, then looked around at his gang as if he had said something clever. The gang clustered closer, smelling blood.

Physically, Mallory and the thug couldn't have been more different: Mallory, with his shoulder-length brown hair and calm, intelligent eyes; the skinhead, clearly unintelligent, his arms a mass of tattoos – the flag of St George, a skull and crossbones, the names of girls who had long since faded from his memory. But Mallory's attention was drawn by the one thing he shared with his opponent: a uniform. Mallory still wore his distinctive Knight Templar garb of a black shirt with the red Templar cross against a white square on the breast and right shoulder. The skinhead's black shirt had a large red 'V' running from shoulders to waist.

'What *is* that?' Mallory said, nodding at the T-shirt. 'I'm seeing it all over.' And the insignia wasn't just on the clothing of the gang members who were increasingly visible around the countryside; it was also painted on walls, abandoned cars, doors – graffiti with an odd air of menace.

'He's killing time,' one of the other gang members said. 'Just kill him instead.' More laughter ensued, but Mallory's calm in the face of his impending death was clearly destabilising the group.

A strange expression briefly obscured the brutality in the skinhead's face; Mallory decided it was almost like awe. 'We're followers of the Lost One,' the thug said. The others grew sombre, nodding in agreement.

Mallory considered a glib response, then decided it probably wouldn't be in his best interests. 'Who's that, then?'

'The Lost One,' the leader said again, vehemently this time. 'He disappeared in the Battle of London. His name is Veitch . . . Ryan Veitch.'

Mallory recognised the name instantly. 'The traitor.' One of the five Brothers and Sisters of Dragons who preceded him. They hadn't been heard from since the Fall, but their presence still loomed large over the population; Mallory heard their names wherever he went.

The leader ignored the implication in Mallory's words – denial or acceptance, Mallory wasn't sure which. 'He was the one who saved us, not the other four. When he comes back to us, he'll lead us out of this mess we're in.'

'He's dead,' Mallory said. 'He's not coming back – or so the stories say.'

'The stories are wrong! No one's seen a body! He showed us how to act, how to survive – you do what you have to. And that's what we're doing.'

'Just get his sword and have done with it,' another gang member prompted.

Mallory gripped the hilt of his weapon more tightly, though he had no idea what he could do against a shotgun and fifteen brutes armed with knives, razors and clubs. 'You know, this isn't just any sword,' he said. Mallory turned the blade so that they could see the faint blue glow emanating from the steel itself and the dragons carved into the handle. 'It comes from the Otherworld—'

The leader hesitated; the others grew uneasy. Sensing that he had them, Mallory continued quickly, remembering the words of the god who had given it to him. 'It's one of the three great swords.

The first is the sword of Nuada Airgetlamh – you know that one, right?' Mallory didn't even know it himself, but his confidence convinced the leader to nod. 'The second is lost, believed corrupted. We won't be seeing that one again. But this one . . . this is Llyrwyn. And, well, basically, mate, you don't stand a chance.'

Mallory wished he was telling the truth, but while the sword endowed him with a degree of prowess, it certainly wasn't powerful enough to take out the whole group. The gang had grown edgy – like most people since the Fall, they had quickly learned to assimilate the supernatural and the terrible dangers that surrounded it – but Mallory knew it would only be a matter of time before they tested his bragging. He braced himself, ready at least to take off the leader's smirking head; a small spot of joy before he died.

A sound like the billowing of a tarpaulin disturbed all of them. As the gang looked around for the source of the noise, a shadow swept across the green fields and descended on them. Mallory saw what it was before any of them, and he just had time to throw himself to the ground and cover his head before a murder of crows blazed out of the sky to attack the gang.

Blood spattered all around. The birds darted in, tearing flesh with beak and talon, their dark wings smashing against faces and throats. The gang scattered, some screaming with eyes missing, others terrified and cursing. The corvids didn't relent until only Mallory remained in the centre of the lane. As quickly as they had come, they flapped away to lose themselves in the fields and trees.

As Mallory scrambled to his feet, he looked around for the familiar face. And there she was, her long brown hair flowing behind her as she strode through the tall grass of the nearest field, her eyes blazing, her hippie dress swirling with the determined motion of her legs. Mallory could see her irritation, but the fire in her only made her more attractive to him.

'You are such a moron,' Sophie snapped when she reached the stile.

'Me? I could have lost an eye in that bird attack.'

'A "thank you" would be nice for saving your worthless life.' She stepped lithely over the stile. 'I told you to approach the village with caution.'

'Sorry. I forgot you were queen of the whole bloody world.'

'Stupid bugger.'

Mallory grabbed her; she play-resisted before overpowering him with a passionate kiss.

'But you still haven't got this role thing down,' Mallory said when they broke. 'I'm the knight, the trained killing machine – I'm the one who's supposed to be protecting you.'

'In your dreams.' Her warm smile eased the dull throb of the aches and pains he had developed on their long, hard journey from Salisbury – battles with looters and self-styled law-enforcement officers, potential rapists and horse-stealers, and all the nightmarish things that crawled out of the dark in the lonely stretches of countryside they'd crossed. Oddly, he found it easier to deal with all the supernatural predators than with seeing his fellow man preparing to commit some inhuman act.

'They weren't your average looters,' she said.

Mallory stared past her to the now furiously burning village. 'I didn't think they were. We've seen them all over. I thought they were just some sort of movement – like the Celtic Nation – trying to fill the void in society. But that V on their shirts – you know what it stands for? Veitch.'

Sophie stiffened in his arms, kept her face pressed into his shoulder. 'Ryan Veitch?'

'It's like they worship him . . . some sort of saviour who's going to come back and make everything all right.'

Sophie pushed herself away from him, uneasy now. 'There are myths building up around all of the Five.'

'But the wrong ones are building up around Veitch. He was the traitor, sold all the others out. Jack Churchill, the leader, died because of what Veitch did. These morons think that's some kind of plan for living.'

'Then that only shows what a responsibility we have. Existence, the universe . . . God, the Goddess . . . whatever you want to call it – it selects five people to be the champions of life at any one time. Five people from all the multitude. The last Five saved us from extinction after the Fall—'

'And now we've got the job.'

Sophie heard the familiar note in his voice. 'You still don't want it?'

'It's not as if I have a choice. But it would have been nice to have been asked.'

Salisbury still preyed on Mallory's mind even though he had left it behind six months ago. His time there at the cathedral had been one of hardship and suffering, as the Church desperately attempted to cling on in a world that had grown largely immune to its teachings. When he had arrived at the cathedral gates, a mercenary looking for employment in the newly formed Knights Templar, Mallory hadn't believed in anything. The Church leaders had accepted him eagerly, and his training had made him hard, but he had still been directionless. It was his meeting with Sophie and his recognition of his feelings for her that had given meaning to his life. Sophie was not only his moral compass in a world where the distinction between right and wrong was increasingly blurred, but also the sole thing that mattered to him. He knew that she loved him, but he suspected that she had no idea how much he loved and needed her in return.

Discovering that they were a Brother and Sister of Dragons had only strengthened the bond between them. They were united by some great power that coursed through the earth and everything on it, a blazing blue energy that had entered both of them. Mallory didn't care that it meant they were both champions of life. To him, it was a sign that he and Sophie were meant to be.

And so he had agreed to follow her when she had insisted on embarking on a quest to find the remaining Brothers and Sisters of Dragons and to discover what their destiny really was. She spoke of responsibilities and obligations and a higher calling. Mallory only heard her voice.

But despite the inner peace he was feeling for the first time in his life, Mallory knew that all was not right. The emptiness in his life that Sophie had filled still echoed somewhere in the deepest part of him. It was characterised by an image that haunted his nights and was always there on the periphery of his thoughts during the day: a flash of fire in the dark. He knew in some way that it signified his death, but rather than being a premonition, it appeared to be some fragmented memory. How could that be?

Sophie had helped him come to terms with it at Salisbury, and for a while he thought he had put it behind him. But in recent weeks it had returned in force, the ghost that refused to let him forget but would not let him remember, either.

Fire in the dark, and death. What did it mean? Why wouldn't it leave him alone to enjoy Sophie's love and his life with her? What was the terrible secret that he knew lay just behind that unsettling image?

In the late afternoon sun, Cadbury Hill cast an enormous shadow across the Somerset lowlands. Majestic in scale, the terraces and cuttings of the Iron Age hill-fort hinted at hidden mysteries, artificiality layered over the natural so that it was impossible to see where one ended and the other began. Mallory and Sophie stood on the edge of the umbra and surveyed the wooded slopes where birdsong echoed pleasingly. Wild flowers grew all around – wood spurge and spurge laurel – the scent of summer promise.

'It's bigger than I thought it would be,' Mallory said.

'You can see why it's been identified with Camelot for more than six hundred years,' Sophie replied. 'It inspired the medieval romances of Lancelot and Guinevere, Galahad and the Holy Grail. Can't you feel it? There's something in the air itself, as if it's radiating out of the heart of the hill.'

'So it's the right place?'

'It has to be.' Sophie took a deep, soothing breath, finally happy to be at the destination that had plagued her ever since they had left Salisbury at Christmas. The first hint had come in a dream, an imposing hill in a green landscape, a crow telling her to take heed. It had all the hallmarks of a communication from the Invisible World and the image had stayed with her potently for days. When she had used her Craft to commune with the Higher Powers for answers, the response had been cryptic and teasing, as always. But as the weeks and months passed, the clues had mounted, finally leading them here.

'It's not just the feeling,' she continued. 'The mythic symbolism is perfect. We know that the Arthurian legends are a code. They all identify places of power where the walls that divide dimensions are thin, where there's a doorway to the Otherworld . . . T'ir n'a n'Og.'

'The Land of Always Summer. You see, I *was* listening when you were telling me about your crazy religious beliefs.'

'King Arthur is a code for—'

'The energy that runs through all things. The Blue Fire,' Mallory chanted with mock-weariness. 'The Pendragon Spirit.'

Mallory tried to pretend it was all a joke, but he'd seen the evidence of the power, felt its euphoric effect. It was the thing that linked the Brothers and Sisters of Dragons across millennia and though he would never have mentioned it to Sophie, he was humbled to be a part of it.

'So what exactly are we looking for?' he asked.

'Something important. Something that ties in to the whole reason why we were chosen.' Her eyes were filled with passion and just the briefest hint of apprehension.

They spent the next half-hour fighting their way through the wildly overgrown lower reaches of the hill. It didn't look as though anyone had been there since the Fall. The largest butterflies Mallory had ever seen in his life flitted in and out of the trees, and there was an abundance of wildlife – rabbits that were almost tame, even a fox slinking like a russet ghost through the vegetation's shadows.

'Can you see anything yet?' Sophie asked him as he hacked through the undergrowth.

'It's hard to concentrate when I'm having to chop and thrust every six feet.' Mallory paused to rest on his sword. 'Just give me a minute to catch my breath.'

Once he had rested, he tried again, just as she had been teaching him during the last six months. The perception wasn't easy to reach, or to sustain – Sophie had described it as 'like looking at a Magic Eye picture' – but when he did finally achieve it, he was shocked by what he saw.

Lines of shimmering blue appeared on the ground as if power cables were glowing just beneath the surface. They ran backwards and forwards in a grid pattern across the whole of the hill, and on the flat summit he could just make out a spike rising up to the clouds like a gigantic radio antenna.

'Bloody hell,' he said, awed.

'It's like a giant battery.' Sophie took his hand and tugged him to the left. 'This way.'

As they carved their way through brambles and long grass with renewed vigour, Mallory said, 'OK, but why this place, of all the Arthurian locations?'

'Because this is one of the most special. Legend says it's hollow, like the one at Glastonbury Tor, which is unquestionably special. At the summer solstice, it's supposed to turn into glass so that you can see all the secret caves inside.'

'Aha. And it would be . . . what? A coincidence that we just happen to be here at the solstice?'

She smiled enigmatically.

'And what's supposed to be in these secret caves?'

'According to legend, Arthur himself and all his knights, who are sleeping until England calls on their services again.'

'More symbolism?'

She shrugged. 'There's more: the legend goes on to say that every seven years, on midsummer's eve, a giant gate opens in the side of the hill allowing entry to that place.'

Mallory surveyed the imposing hill thoughtfully. 'Looks like we're in for a night of surprises.'

For a while, the flow of blue energy faded in and out of view, but eventually Mallory found himself picking out stronger arterial routes leading towards a focal point. As he followed the more potent lines of force, he was overcome by a strange sensation of distortion. Leaves and branches moved too quickly; shadows lengthened at an alarming rate. It felt as if time was accelerating, and when he checked the arc of blue sky visible through the foliage above them, he was unnerved to see the colour shifting to magenta as clouds hurtled overhead. The sun shifted from yellow to red and rushed towards the horizon.

He gripped Sophie's arms. 'Call me jumpy, but I reckon we need to reach our destination by nightfall or something bad's going to happen.'

'Any particular reason?'

'A gut feeling.' Increasingly, he found that his instincts were rarely wrong, as though he was becoming more sensitive to subtle warning signs.

Sophie nodded and picked up her speed.

As the darkness washed in from the east, gloom rose up around the trunks of the trees and the sounds of the hillside became eerily magnified. Every windborne rustle became a predator at their backs, every footstep the thunderous beat of a buried heart.

Fifty yards ahead, the energy flows congregated just below the lip of the hill's flat summit. As night fell, they began to run. In that same instant, a whispering rose up from the trees, echoing across the deserted hillside. They couldn't make out the words, but there was something in the sound that made them feel sluggish and gloomy. They slowed to a walk, then stopped and looked around for the source.

'What is that?' Mallory asked.

'I can feel it in my head,' Sophie said. She swayed, mesmerised and suddenly overcome by melancholy.

Mallory grabbed her and forced her to look at him. 'Don't listen.' He propelled her onwards as fast as she would go, scrambling over humps, tumbling through nettles, stinging and winding themselves. The unsettling whispering continued, unmistakably growing closer.

'It's hunting us,' Sophie gasped. 'What is it?'

'Just concentrate on running.' Mallory's eyes darted around the hillside, but it was impossible to see clearly in the gloom.

They emerged from the trees and bushes on to a grassy slope where they had a clear view of a surging and spitting whirlpool of Blue Fire ahead.

'That must be the entrance,' Sophie said, gasping for breath.

The whispering was now so loud it felt as if it was filling Mallory's head and pressing in on him from all sides. With it came a black despair urging him to give up. As he struggled to fight it off, a shape loomed out of the shadows of the trees. Mallory grabbed Sophie and pushed her behind him as he drew his sword.

'What is it?' Sophie said.

Mallory couldn't answer. It looked like a walking corpse, a tall, thin man with otherworldly almond-shaped eyes whose body had been broken on a rack. The skeleton showed through at the ribs and the forearms and on the left side of its jaw. At first, Mallory thought it was brandishing a sword in each hand, but as it marched towards them, Mallory realised that the swords had actually been embedded in the thing's wrists – the weapons were now a part of it. A luminous purple mist drifted from its mouth and ears and eked out of the corners of its eyes; it was the source of the whispering that was making them feel so despairing.

'Now would be the time for a good spell,' Mallory said.

32

'You know it doesn't work like that,' Sophie replied. 'I need time, ritual space . . .'

The warrior bore down on them, weaving its rusty, bloodstained swords in an intricate attack pattern. Mallory attacked it vigorously. It responded instantly, parrying and then thrusting. Mallory jumped back athletically and avoided the dual attack as the creature's weapons cut rapidly back and forth like a bacon-slicer.

They battled for several minutes but the warrior didn't appear to tire, and Mallory began to wonder if it was actually an animated dead thing. And its strength was astonishing. The twin blades crashed down on him like pile-drivers, jolting him to the bone. Only his Knight Templar training and whatever innate power lurked in his sword kept him alive.

As he manoeuvred to avoid another attack, his foot caught in a rabbit hole and he went down hard. The warrior poised to swing a sword towards Mallory's head. In that instant, Mallory saw an opening. He managed to swing his sword in a short arc, hacking through the warrior's left ankle.

The thing continued to attack as it fell, but it had been thrown off-balance. Even so, the flat of its sword still clipped Mallory's temple, stunning him.

When he came around, Sophie was attempting to drag him up the slope. From further down the hill he could hear the sound of riders crashing through the undergrowth towards them.

Mallory lurched to his feet, his chest burning from the exertion of the fight. He tried to push Sophie towards the Blue Fire but her head was bowed, and when she looked up her eyes were crackling with sapphire energy.

'It's all right,' she said. 'This place is like a battery . . . I can draw on it . . .'

Mallory was unnerved by what he saw in her face – a primal fury about to be unleashed. Coruscating energy erupted out of her in a flash. When his vision cleared, there was a massive scorch mark across the slope and the warrior was nowhere to be seen. But from the trees the sounds of the riders drew closer, magnified as if their steeds were as big as rhinos.

'Come on,' Sophie said. 'I've only bought us a few seconds.'

As Mallory and Sophie neared the whirl of Blue Fire, they heard the riders break from the tree line. Mallory turned to see three more of the hideous undead warriors, this time riding huge beasts that resembled horses but had scaly hides and cloven hooves.

Just as Mallory was preparing to make a last stand, the ground trembled and there was a sound like an avalanche as turf and soil tore back in a shower of earth and pebbles. In the gulf that opened up before them was revealed a majestic stone arch big enough to encompass four men standing on each other's shoulders. Around it, the Blue Fire licked and sparked, but the centre of the arch was as black as space. Mallory had no time to contemplate it, for Sophie put one hand between his shoulder blades and shoved him into the gateway.

Pain made Mallory black out again as his ribs smashed against something hard. When he came around, he knew instantly that he was somewhere far removed from the slopes of Cadbury Hill. He had expected the air to be dank, but it had a sharp, fresh tang that was physically invigorating. He could smell tar-smoke from a torch more acutely than anything he had ever smelled before.

He was lying on smooth stone flags, ice-cold against his cheek. Levering himself up, his first impression was that he was sprawled in a temple, almost Egyptian in its scale and grandeur, with stone columns soaring into the shadows overhead and wall murals of breathtaking detail, the blues, golds and reds glowing in the flickering light of torches mounted at regular intervals all around. Sophie was at his side, just as mesmerised.

Incense drifted in their direction and Sophie stirred. 'Are you OK?' She helped Mallory to his feet; he winced.

'No. Couple of cracked ribs from the fight. I'll have to take it easy. Where are we?'

'I don't know. Feel up to having a look round?'

Sophie took one of the torches from the wall and led the way. The atmosphere grew more oppressive as they progressed into the heart of the temple. They couldn't shake the impression that they were being watched, that someone or something was going to come upon them suddenly from behind. There was a disturbing hallucinogenic quality to everything; the edges of their vision were distorted and fragmented; the pounding of their hearts rose up and faded, echoing both within and without.

Their path was blocked by an enormous cat, easily as big as

Sophie, with staring eyes as round and large as plates. Mallory and Sophie stopped sharply, but the cat didn't move; it simply stared at them as if it could see right into their heads.

Mallory's hand went to his sword, but Sophie stopped him. 'Wait,' she whispered.

'That is the creepiest thing I've ever seen,' Mallory said under his breath.

Beyond the cat the floor ended abruptly. Three paths moved away over the gulf, each one barely wider than a human foot.

'It's a test,' Sophie whispered. 'Whatever's in there, they're not going to let just anyone enter. We have to prove we're worthy.'

'It could be a test,' Mallory agreed, 'or it could be a booby trap to take out anyone who comes near the place. You get halfway along one of those paths and the thing crumbles under your feet. That's if we can get past McCavity there.'

'Why don't you walk up to it and see what it does?'

'Why don't *you*?' Mallory considered drawing his sword, then decided Sophie was probably right. Whatever the thing was – and it certainly was not a cat, despite its appearance – there was no point in antagonising it.

Sophie pushed past Mallory and walked tentatively towards the cat. When she got within six feet of it, its hackles rose and its mouth opened to reveal gleaming teeth. The huge eyes still didn't blink. Sophie came to a sharp halt.

Mallory walked up beside Sophie. The cat glared at him and made a deep, rumbling warning sound in its throat. 'Still sure I shouldn't use the sword?' he asked.

Sophie hushed him; he could see she was deep in thought. After a moment, she said, 'How can we prove to it that we're worthy to enter? That we're not a threat?'

Mallory considered her question, then quickly drew his sword. The cat leaned forward, spitting, those huge eyes filled with malice. Before it could leap at him, Mallory threw the sword behind him. The cat instantly calmed and returned to its original watchful position.

'I hope you're right about this,' Mallory said in a way that masked his implicit trust of her. He got down on his hands and knees and crawled towards the cat. His tension eased a little when he realised that it was not making any threatening sounds or movements; it simply stared at him with those eerie eyes.

When he reached the cat, he rolled on to his back and bared his throat. There was one brief moment of connection when Mallory saw a flickering alien intelligence in the saucer-eyes, and then the cat lunged, jaws gaping wide. Sophie screamed. Mallory screwed his eyes shut, waiting for the pain as his throat was ripped out. He felt hot breath on his skin, the prick of teeth. And then nothing.

When he opened his eyes, the cat was holding his throat in its mouth, poised gently. It could have torn him to pieces in the blink of an eye. It remained that way for a few seconds while Mallory's heart thundered, then it withdrew and turned its attention to Sophie. Mallory scrambled past it and beckoned for her to follow suit.

When Sophie was standing by him, shaking after her experience with the huge beast, he held her close for a second, and then they turned and walked to the edge of the precipice. Beyond, the abyss fell away into deep shadow far below.

'Which one?' Mallory said.

Sophie took a deep breath to calm herself. She didn't need Mallory to tell her that they would probably only have one chance. 'They all look the same,' she said.

'But there has to be one true path,' Mallory said. 'That's how this works in all the old stories. So how do we know which is the true one?'

Sophie closed her eyes while she pondered, and after a moment a smile came to her lips.

'What?' Mallory asked.

'Close your eyes.'

Mallory did as he was told. 'OK . . . now what?'

'Go calm. Feel. Really *feel* with your senses. You know which one is the right path now, don't you?'

At first, Mallory couldn't understand what she meant, but gradually the realisation crept over him. The lines of blue force that had crisscrossed the hill also ran through this place, though at that point they were invisible. But Mallory could feel them even through the soles of his boots, buzzing gently, soothing him with their caress. He stepped forward, following the faint sensation. It led directly to the right-hand path.

'So we've got to trust that the freaky Blue Fire is leading us to the right one,' he said.

'That's the point, isn't it? We're showing trust – and humility. Two qualities that mean we're worthy to find what lies ahead.'

'I'm glad one of us has got it all figured out.'

As he prepared to take the first step on the path, Sophie took his hand and squeezed. 'It's the Pendragon Spirit, Mallory. Think of what it represents.'

Her words reassured him and, tentatively, he edged out on to the precarious path. It felt like tightrope walking; he had to hold his arms out to keep his balance, not looking down, moving one foot in front of the other only when he was sure he was secure and balanced. Sophie followed in his footsteps.

When they'd gone about twenty feet, Mallory realised that the other two paths had disappeared. Theirs was the only path leading into the gloom ahead.

Mallory was soon sleeked with sweat, his concentration so intense that his head hurt. He didn't say a word to Sophie for fear of distracting her, but every time he heard her foot skid slightly on the stone, his heart beat wildly.

He didn't know how they carried on. Each step became a mountain to climb, each movement a mantra of whispered prayer. But finally they reached solid ground and collapsed on to the stone flags, hugging each other in relief.

When they had recovered, they found themselves confronted by two stone doors. An image of a dragon eating its own tail was carved in the stone lintel over the point where the doors met.

'I think this is it,' Sophie said, with barely restrained excitement. She stepped forward and cautiously placed the palm of her hand on the centre of the dragon circle.

With a fizz of blue sparks, the doors slid open with a deep rumble to reveal a row of iron railings, and within them a gate. Sophie pushed it gently. It swung open with a reverberating creak to allow them entrance to an inner sanctum. More incense smouldered in one corner and the torches on the walls burned more dimly, imbuing the chamber with a reverential air. Small stone platforms, each one big enough for a man to lie on, lined both walls, and at the far end a similar platform stood alone, raised up to waist-height. Intricate carvings of serpents lined its base.

'Oh,' Sophie said quietly.

'What is it?'

'This is where the knights should be sleeping, waiting to be awakened.' She gestured at the low stone plinths. 'And that larger one is where the king should be.'

'I thought you said that was a metaphor.'

'It is, but look, it's obvious,' Sophie replied, confused.

'Nothing is obvious.' As Mallory walked towards the stone dais at the end of the chamber, the torches in that area burned more brightly to reveal a space beyond.

'If there's no hero waiting to come back when England really needs him, what does that mean?' Sophie said, oblivious to Mallory. 'Has something happened to him? Is there no hope?'

'Look at this.' Mallory was supporting himself on the raised dais, one hand clutching his injured side. He was looking into the area beyond where a brazier burned with the cool blue flames of the earth energy. In the middle of the flames lay a stone, round and grey with no discernible markings.

'Is that why we were brought here?' Sophie said, disappointed. 'It doesn't make any sense.'

'Never judge a book by its cover. See, I have a cliché for every occasion.' Mallory steeled himself. Although he knew the blue flames didn't burn like ordinary fire, it still took a leap of faith to plunge his hand into their depths. As he leaned in, a column of blue fire surged up to the ceiling high overhead. For the briefest instant, Mallory saw a face in that blazing pillar, but it was gone before he could register its features. But it left him with one piece of knowledge: the object in the fire was called the Wish Stone. Mallory retrieved it quickly and the column of fire instantly died away.

At the same moment, the Wish Stone came to life on his open palm. Crackling blue light sprang out of it, forming an image in the air of two men crouching next to a stone tomb with a woman standing nearby. The picture, which Mallory thought resembled a hologram, hung over the stone for a few seconds and then winked out.

'What's that all about?' Mallory said.

'No idea. But it's got to be important.' There was a note of doubt in Sophie's voice.

'I think that just about defines anti-climax. Night of the living dead outside. Throat nearly ripped out in here. Almost fall to my death down the crack of doom. The prize: a fucking rock.'

'Let's get out of here,' Sophie said. 'We can sort out what this means later.'

Mallory slipped the Wish Stone into his pocket. 'I'm going to get my sword back now, and if that big mouser is sitting on it, I'm going to use this stone to—'

'All right, so you're a big man,' Sophie said. 'Let's go.'

The day after briefing Hunter and his team, the General moved along the corridors of Brasenose with a renewed vigour. Ever since the Fall, it had all been about logistics – getting the supply lines in place, ensuring that the base was secure, developing policies and plans. Finally he felt as if they were in a position to take the first steps towards a campaign that would drive out the invaders.

He marched into Kirkham's suite of laboratories and eventually found the scientist in a darkened room far away from the main area of activity, labouring over a model of a town laid out across a large map table, illuminated by a single light overhead.

'So this is where you get away from it all to play with your toys,' the General said sarcastically.

Kirkham was unruffled. 'It's a model.'

'I can see that.'

'A model of reality.'

The General masked his puzzlement in case it was construed as a mark of weakness and leaned over the table to get a better look. It was a facsimile of any small town – central shopping area, streets of suburban semis, rows of terraces, a few mansions and grand residences dotted here and there.

'I created it for my next briefing to the Joint Board. The concepts are quite difficult to communicate to . . .' He paused to find the right word.

'The uneducated? Thick soldiers?'

'No—'

'Try it on me.'

Kirkham blinked through his thick glasses, clearly uneasy about going down that route.

'Go on. Tell me about reality.'

Kirkham could see that the General had the bit between his teeth; there was no backing down. He began hesitantly. 'As I said, these are difficult concepts. Understanding the nature of reality is key to the situation we now find ourselves in. I talked earlier about branes and String Theory, and their possible relationship with parallel universes – that's one view. There are others. You'll forgive me if I begin by delving into what seems to be mysticism—'

'Just get on with it.' The General continued to be engrossed by the model town.

'Reality ... material reality, such as you see around you, is regarded as an illusion in the Hindu religion,' Kirkham began. 'They have a word for it: *maya*, the veil of illusion. Ironically, many of the ancient spiritual philosophies are actually quite close to current scientific thinking.' He peered at the General. 'Do you understand that?'

'Of course,' the General said curtly. ' "*All that we see or seem, is but a dream within a dream.*" Go on.'

Kirkham relaxed a little. 'Then let's take things a step further. A hypothesis. What we perceive as reality is, in scientific terms, a network of quantum waves which have become phase-locked and act as a single entity – in the same way that a group of photons become phase-locked in a laser.'

'Yes – random light particles frozen so that they appear to be one object. You're saying that everything we see around us is not in its natural state. It's just become locked in this form and we accept that as the norm. But it's not.'

'Exactly.' Kirkham couldn't contain his excitement at the General's receptiveness. 'Now imagine if this phase-locked system could be affected as a whole by a human mind concentrating on one small part of it, in the same way that all systems are affected by a change of one tiny aspect. That could be perceived as magic by those who do not understand the system that lies behind the illusion.'

'So you're saying that one mind could therefore alter the whole reality?'

'In this hypothesis.'

The General picked up one of the houses from a suburb. 'So where does the town fit in?'

Kirkham took the house from him and carefully replaced it. 'All that I've said so far is background. This is a model of our phase-locked reality. Consider that every house is a universe, or a dimension. Some are mundane, others . . . ornate. In some, little happens that we would consider unusual – the father comes home from his day at the factory, his dinner is on the table. In others, the family has access to technology the previous father cannot begin to comprehend from his limited life experience. We know from our intelligence there are at least two adjoining dimensions—'

'This one and the Otherworld.' The General began to see the model in a new light as the ramifications of Kirkham's hypothesis began to reveal themselves to him.

'The place the Celts called T'ir n'a n'Og, exactly,' Kirkham continued. 'The two are apparently very different places. But consider this: what if there are other dimensions just like our own, so alike that you can barely tell the difference.' He tapped a row of terraced houses. 'The only differentiating factors being a picture here, an ornament there. You could go from one to another and not realise you were in a different place.'

'Perhaps that's what happens when you die.'

'I think that would be delving too far into the realms of mysticism.' Kirkham wandered around the table, looking at the town from different angles. 'But who knows? Really, when you get to this level, who knows anything? We have our hypotheses, but no way to test them.'

The General examined some of the imposing mansions on the edge of town, one of which had the creepy appeal of the Addams Family home. Then he looked towards the edge of the table and the gloom that lay beyond, and shivered.

Kirkham, however, wasn't finished. 'What if someone decided to knock down his house and rebuild it in a different way, or add an extension, as we discussed earlier—'

'One mind concentrating on a part of the phase-locked system, thereby altering the whole of it?'

Kirkham nodded encouragingly.

'You know, sometimes I get the strangest feeling that the world wasn't meant to be the way it is,' the General mused. 'It's odd . . . unnerving. I have this idea that I was living another life, and then everything changed. Do you ever get that?'

Kirkham didn't answer.

The General's initial curiosity had been replaced by uneasiness at the overwhelming enormity of what was being shown to him. 'This wasn't the reason why I came,' he said, abruptly changing the subject. 'Have you heard anything about one of the enemy being brought in for interrogation?'

'One of the gods?'

The General nodded. 'Because if it's true, I want you involved. If you can discover their true nature, it would help us a great deal. A great deal.'

'I've not heard anything,' Kirkham said.

'Mister Reid isn't always forthcoming until he's sure he's covered his back, front and both sides. Curse of the intelligence profession. Shits, all of them.'

'I'll make some enquiries.' Kirkham pressed his glasses against the bridge of his nose, a nervous reaction.

The General turned towards the door, adding almost as an afterthought, 'If you find anything out, report directly to me. I want this matter and my request kept strictly confidential.'

'Understood. It won't go any further.'

'One last question.' The General paused on the threshold and looked back at the tiny town. 'You talk about reality being phase-locked. Is that a random occurrence? Or was it made that way?'

Kirkham stared at the General for a long moment, then said simply, 'I can't answer that.'

The General nodded thoughtfully, but as he slipped out, Kirkham glimpsed an unsettled look in the military man's eyes.

Sophie helped Mallory out into the cool night air on the slopes of Cadbury Hill, his face drawn from the pain in his ribs. He leaned over to brush the hair from her ear and whispered, 'I'm not going to be much use if those freaks are still out here. Can you do anything?'

Sophie's face was ghostly in the moonlight breaking through the clouds. 'I can try,' she whispered. 'There's a way of making us hidden in plain sight. I don't know if those things will be able to sniff us out anyway, but . . .' She shrugged. 'I just need some time to concentrate.'

The words had barely left her mouth when there was a disturbance in the trees just below the scorched grassy area her earlier spell had made. Mallory drew his sword, illuminating his face with the thin blue light emanating from the blade. But instead of one of the warriors on the bizarre horses, a man ventured out. He was wearing camouflaged combat trousers, incongruously and pointlessly matched with a red silk shirt.

'I don't know how you managed to disappear off the face of the earth, but you gave us a right old run-around,' the man said. 'Two minutes from picking you up and then – *poof!* – gone. Nice trick if you know how.'

'Who are you?' Sophie said. Mallory stepped in front of her, sword at the ready.

'The name's Hunter and I am ... well, words don't do me justice.' He approached them confidently. 'I'd put that down, mate,' he said to Mallory. 'You'll have somebody's eye out.'

'Tell you what,' Mallory said, 'take one more step and I'll have two eyes out.'

'I don't think so. All right, boys.' Hunter made a come-hither gesture and six men emerged from the trees all around.

Mallory eyed the circling men. 'Looters,' he said, though that didn't sound quite right.

'Actually, we have the stamp of officialdom and the full weight of the Government behind us.' Hunter nodded and the men drew their guns. 'There's no need for any nasty stuff. I'm sure we've all got the same interests at heart – to clear out all the monsters and freaks and get our world back. I've come with an invitation for you to help us—'

'You know who we are?' Mallory asked. Beside him, Sophie rested her chin on her chest and closed her eyes. Silently, her lips moved.

'I know you're a Brother and Sister of Dragons.'

Mallory was taken aback by Hunter's words. It was only very recently that he'd learned of his destiny. How could this stranger possibly know, too?

'Chief, she's doing something,' an acne-scarred man barked.

Sophie continued to mutter under her breath, her eyelids half-open, the whites gleaming in the dark.

'You can stop that right now,' Hunter said firmly. Mallory could see that Hunter knew exactly what Sophie was capable of doing.

Before Hunter could act, the acne-scarred man raised his gun and moved in swiftly. Mallory whirled, sword at the ready, but the pain from his ribs left him off-balance. 'Don't do anything stupid,' he snapped.

'Shut it!' the soldier shouted.

A low whispering rolled out from the undergrowth. Spooked, Hunter's team turned, guns cocked, scanning back and forth for the source.

'Come on – we need to get out of here,' Hunter said to Mallory. 'Quickly.'

'Tell him to drop his weapon.' Mallory nodded at the acne man, who had moved in even closer to Sophie. Deep in her trance, she was oblivious to what was going on around her.

'You've no need to be afraid of us,' Hunter said. 'We're on the same side—'

He fell silent as one of the riders burst from the bushes in a trail of purple mist. Gunfire erupted from all sides, but neither the rider nor its mount appeared to be harmed.

'Come on.' Her trance broken, Sophie grabbed Mallory's arm insistently.

'You called it?'

'Come on!'

Bones shattered with a sickening dry-wood sound as the reptilian horse smashed into one of the soldiers. The others continued to fire at it futilely, knowing no other way to deal with it. The horse-creature lowered its massive head, pulled its jaws wide sending saliva everywhere and then proceeded to rip and tear at the fallen man's stomach. Blood and flesh rose up in a cloud.

In the confusion, Sophie and Mallory had managed to skid a little way down the scorched grassy slope before the acne man appeared to one side, his gun aimed at Sophie.

'Stop!' he shouted.

Sophie glanced back and saw that the soldier was shaking, as if gripped by some kind of internal battle. The eerie whispering was clearly affecting him deeply: his wavering self-control was echoed, despite his training, in the gradually worsening tremor running through his arms.

Hunter came running up. 'Don't shoot, you idiot! We need them!'

The snapping and snarling rose up in a frenzy as another man fell to the horse's crushing jaws. The acne man glanced in horror at the beast and its rider, who was whirling a double-headed axe, then turned and saw Sophie pulling Mallory towards the trees. Finally succumbing to the all-pervading despair, his eyes glazed over in surrender and he fired just as Hunter slammed into him, knocking his aim awry.

The force of the bullet smashed Sophie over the edge of a hollow and she rolled into the trees, gone; no sound or movement followed.

Mallory had one second to call her name before something crashed into him and he plunged into unconsciousness.

He awoke with a sense of movement and a deafening *whup-whup-whup* sound all around. Cold wind blasted against him.

Mallory began to lever himself upright, the pain in his side now electric; he could barely breathe and was too dazed to think straight. A gun pointed into his face.

'Don't move,' one of the soldiers said gruffly, but his white face gave away his fear at what he had just witnessed.

They were on a helicopter, rising slowly. The large side door was open, revealing a square of cloudy pre-dawn sky. Hunter crouched, framed against it, peering down at the receding hillside.

'There's a group of them. What the hell are they?' he asked, concerned.

Three other soldiers sat further down the helicopter. The acne man was one of them, but he kept his head turned away from Mallory.

'Where's Sophie?' Mallory said weakly, his memory still disjointed. But when he locked eyes with Hunter, the reality hit him with force.

'I'm sorry,' Hunter said, with surprising compassion.

'She's dead?'

Hunter glared at the acne man, who refused to meet his gaze. 'He shot her. If the bullet didn't kill her straight away, she'll have lost too much blood by now for us to save her. We couldn't find her and didn't have time to search with those bastards on the loose.' He looked out into the night, avoiding Mallory's devastated gaze. 'I am sorry,' he added quietly. 'No one was supposed to get hurt.'

45

season of ice

'We are the masters at the moment, and not only at the moment, but for a very long time to come.' Lord Shawcross

The Compound lay in the lower levels of Brasenose and Lincoln Colleges, which had been linked by new tunnels hacked out within days of the Government's arrival in the city. In addition to housing Kirkham's research facility, enemies of the state were incarcerated there: trouble-makers, traitors, anyone attempting to block the slow progress of a society getting up off its knees. Yet this low-level prison was only a small part of the Compound; larger by far was the high-security section, access to which had always been beyond Hal's clearance. He'd heard rumours about who was imprisoned there, but since the Fall rumours were all anyone had and none of them could be trusted. It was a sign that events were coming to a head that he had been issued with a pass inside.

Yet Hal was too preoccupied to get excited about the General's decision to ramp up his responsibilities. The call had come fifteen minutes earlier in the thin dawn light at the end of a long day and sleepless night of tearing himself apart over his confrontation with the Caretaker. At first he had considered reporting the manifestation – what the Caretaker had told him was surely of importance – but the more he vacillated, the more he pulled away from that route. Hal comforted himself with the thought that once he had decided what it all meant he would make a full disclosure at the Cabinet office. Yet he knew, quite powerfully, that the Caretaker's message was meant for him alone, if he could ever decipher its meaning. And so he had sat quietly in his room, turning it over and over in his head. For a loyal public servant like Hal, his inaction felt like a grand betrayal and the guilt ate away at him constantly.

The guard at the main door checked Hal's pass and directed him along a maze of corridors to a section sealed off with a steel gate. The guards here were hard-faced, clearly capable of shooting him in the blink of an eye and losing no sleep over it.

In the high-security section, the doors were thicker and lacked the small shuttered window usually provided for the warders to check on the inmates. Disturbing sounds emanated from the unseen inhabitants. From one cell came a howling like a wild animal's cry, accompanied by frenzied clawing at the walls. And in another, something wet and sticky lashed back and forth.

Hal found Reid and Manning deep in conversation. Manning had a touch of glamour that belied her Home Office position, but Reid was always the perfect spy, ready to fade into the background at any moment. Beyond them, workmen were adding even greater electronic security to one of the cells. Manning and Reid stopped talking when they saw Hal.

'The General sent this urgently.' Hal handed over a sealed envelope to Reid. 'Your eyes only.'

Reid opened it and gave a brief, triumphant smile. 'We're on our way.'

Manning was distracted by the work taking place in and around the nearby cell. Hal thought he sensed a touch of uneasiness about her.

'Who's in there?' The words came out before Hal could stop them and he waited to be reprimanded for breaking the department's rule of no questions, any time.

But Manning was oblivious to protocol. She continued to stare at the cell as she gave her distracted answer: 'Prisoner Zero.' Hal was not enough of a neophyte to probe further.

'Tell the General we'll both be around for the interrogation,' Reid said to Hal. 'We'll do it in four-one-four – there's a two-way mirror.'

'Got it.'

As Hal turned to retrace his steps, a disturbance broke out just ahead. A guard staggered backwards out of an open cell door, his

SA80 spraying bullets all around. He was wearing an ABC isolation suit, a red arterial spray gushing from a ragged tear down the front of it.

Suddenly the corridor was filled with the most terrible sounds: jungle shrieks, haunted moans, insectile chittering and a low, chilling susurration. The prisoners had smelled the blood.

Hal was rooted by the sight for a second too long. Just as he was about to run back up the corridor, a small black shape bounded from the cell on to the chest of the still-twitching guard. At first, Hal thought it was a spider the size of a small dog, then some kind of lizard. Finally, he realised he was looking at an imp that would not have been out of place in a medieval wood-carving. It was the glossy black of crude oil and covered in gleaming scales. Its body had human proportions, but its head was oversized, like a baby's. A pointed tail lashed back and forth.

'Take that,' the devil said with a swipe of razor-sharp talons, 'for presumption. And that for stupidity. And this simply because it is my nature.' The talons became a blur of rending and tearing.

And then the imp stopped, sniffed the air and turned its head in an oddly mechanical way towards Hal. Hal's blood ran cold as the devil's red eyes fell on him.

'Aha!' the imp said with jubilation. It sounded like a throaty old man. 'Fresh meat.'

It leaped from the seeping corpse so fast that Hal couldn't keep it in his vision. Bouncing off the walls and ceiling, it hit Hal full force in the stomach. He fell to the floor, winded, as the imp did a little mocking dance around him. Before Hal could lever himself up, the devil jumped to squat on his chest with surprising weight.

'Now, now,' it said, with a malicious grin, 'no running before we exchange pleasantries.' It hooked one talon in the corner of Hal's mouth and pulled his lips into a grimace. The finger tasted gritty and vinegary. 'A thin covering on fragile bone,' the imp continued. 'What a strange and ineffective design.' But then it paused, puzzled, and sniffed the air over Hal's face. 'What is this?' The imp grew oddly uneasy. 'The stink of righteousness? The rank odour of life?' It pressed its face close to Hal's so that its burning red eyes filled Hal's entire vision, its spoiled-meat breath nearly making him retch. 'The Pendragon Spirit?'

Hal was too terrified to read anything in the imp's manner at that moment, but later, on reflection, he would believe that he had seen a hint of fear.

A second later, the creature was wrenched off his chest. Four guards in ABC suits lifted the imp into the air before clamping around its neck a metal collar with an attached chain. The imp let out a high-pitched, agonised scream, thrashing wildly as if the very touch of the collar burned it.

As the guards dragged the imp back to its cell, the cacophony from the other cells grew even louder, the cumulative noise now tinged with fury and hatred. Hal pressed his hands over his ears and staggered to his feet to catch his breath. The imp's cell door clanged shut, followed by several resounding thuds as the creature threw itself at the door.

The other occupants continued to rage until a strange sound reverberated from the far end of the corridor where Manning and Reid were being protected by other guards. It had the organic tone of a voice, but sounded to Hal something like a tolling bell. Immediately, whatever creatures lay behind the closed doors fell silent, and the quiet that followed was infinitely more disturbing.

Breathless and frightened, Hal stumbled out of Brasenose and into the High Street where two men were grunting and sweating as they attempted to fix the wheel of a cart. He was instantly hit by a wind sharp with the bite of winter. A flurry of snow stung his face. Puzzled, he looked up to see grey clouds now obscuring a sky that had been blue when he had entered the building. Snow in June? Even the final few things they had been counting on were fading away. Fastening his jacket, he turned into the icy gale and hurried towards Queen's College.

Just after 6 a.m., he found Samantha buried behind a mound of paperwork in her tiny office in the Ministry of Intelligence. No one kept regular hours any more. Her repeated complaints about deadlines and a possible sacking fell on deaf ears and eventually Hal convinced her to take an early breakfast.

Shivering, they made their way to one of the pubs that opened before dawn for the market workers. At that time they'd be able to find a quiet corner away from the usual gossiping cliques from the Government offices.

'I can't believe this weather.' Samantha sipped a herbal infusion, which everyone now drank instead of tea. 'Everything's gone mad.'

'Everything went mad a long time ago,' Hal replied.

Samantha caught his flat delivery and asked him what was wrong. Hal enjoyed the concern in her eyes. Cautiously, he related his meeting with the Caretaker and the mysterious transformation of Oxford.

'I will report it,' he said. 'Soon.'

Samantha wasn't listening. ' "Something is coming"?' she repeated hesitantly.

'That's what he said. But what I don't get is, why did he tell me? It was as if he thought I could do something about it.'

'Maybe you can.'

'I'm a glorified librarian, Samantha. I'm barely any use in the job I *do* do. I'm not like Hunter—'

'Stop going on about Hunter,' Samantha said sharply.

'The Caretaker was talking about the Brothers and Sisters of Dragons as if I had some way of contacting them. They need to be brought together, he said. But one of them has already fallen.'

'Brothers and Sisters of what?'

'You know – the Five who fought at the Fall.'

'Oh. Right.'

'They've been in all the recent intelligence reports. You should know that – it's your department.'

'You don't think they actually let me read the files, do you? I have to look the other way while I stick them in a drawer.'

'You've not heard Reid say anything?' Hal drank his herbal brew, but wished he'd ordered a beer; he felt the urge to get completely drunk.

'No, but then I've not been listening.' She paused, stared at him curiously. 'Do you want me to?'

'You could lose your job—'

'Do you want me to?' she repeated.

Hal took a deep breath, then jumped straight in. 'Only if you can find anything out without putting yourself at risk. I can't believe I'm asking you to do this. Hunter doesn't reckon I've broken a rule in my life—'

Samantha smacked his thigh so hard it stung, then laughed at his startled expression.

'Sorry,' he said, abashed.

'Don't make me do it again.' She finished her drink. 'I'd better get back. I'll do what I can. Just don't expect miracles.'

'I never expect those,' he said morosely. Then another thought struck him. 'There was something else. You know all those cells in the high-security wing under Brasenose?'

'Where they keep the prisoners?'

'So they say.'

'No prisoners?'

'No human ones. I think they've captured a whole load of the things that came with the Fall. And they didn't sound very happy.'

Samantha blanched. 'God, if they got out . . .'

'One of them did while I was there. Nearly killed me. But that's not the point. It spoke to me. It said it could smell the Pendragon Spirit on me – does that mean anything to you?'

Samantha shook her head blankly.

'I don't know what's going on any more,' he said. 'The only thing I can think of is King Arthur's surname in the legends.'

'King Arthur,' she mused, before adding hesitantly, 'Yesterday, Mister Reid asked me to pull some files. They all began with the codename Grail . . .' Her voice trailed off.

'Arthur Pendragon.' Hal turned the words over thoughtfully. Then: 'King Arthur . . . the Grail. It's got to be a coincidence.'

'In this day and age, you can't rule anything out, Hal,' Samantha said.

Halfway back from Somerset, Hunter had to order one of the men to render Mallory unconscious. The knight was as strong and potentially lethal as the General had intimated during the briefing. Once he'd fought his way past the pain from his broken ribs and realised that his girlfriend had been killed, he took out two men in as many seconds, one with a chop to the larynx, another with a punch that sent his victim the length of the helicopter. The blows were delivered with a cool equanimity, but Hunter could see the familiar ice in Mallory's eyes. Every raw emotion the knight felt had been bound up and battened down to fuel his single-minded response. It was a look Hunter had seen in many a soldier in difficult circumstances. There would be no dealing with Mallory now; the knight would be like a bear-trap – get too close and you'd lose a limb, maybe an eye, possibly your life. And he'd never be satiated. He wouldn't deal, wouldn't help; they might as well just lock him up until it was all over.

'Not so smart now, is he?' the acne-scarred Grieg said. Hunter could see that he was considering giving Mallory's prone form a kick.

'You won't be so smart when I give my report to the General.' Hunter stared out of the window, past the blizzard of white towards the glittering lights of Oxford in the sea of darkness below.

'I had no choice—'

'There's always a choice. One of the targets is dead. The other is next to useless now. You've ruined the mission.'

'What use is he, anyway?'

Hunter turned to him. 'If you had a brain, Grieg, you'd be halfway to being dangerous. As it is, you're just a psycho who shouldn't be let near loaded weapons. You were tooled up and ready to kill something the moment you came out of the briefing.'

'He just wanted to hit back at something, Chief.' Porter, the one Mallory had knocked down the helicopter, sat nursing an aching jaw. 'You can understand that, after all the losses we took during the Fall.'

Hunter nodded to Mallory. 'He might be the only chance we've got to hit back. At the Fall, we lost every battle we engaged in – we didn't even have the weapons to make it a competition. That means we have to be especially clever now, use whatever resources really work. Fight back with the new rules, not the ones we impose on ourselves. The attitude of this idiot here–' Hunter jerked a thumb at Grieg '–is just going to mark us up for extinction. The new dinosaurs, lumbering around till we're just fossils.'

Hunter turned back to the window. At times like this he was ready to quit. He'd never felt as if he really fitted in, couldn't remember how he had ended up in the job in the first place. All his performance reviews noted his attitude problem, inability to follow orders and blatant disregard for authority. Yet somehow he kept rising through the ranks. Before the Fall it had been bad enough, with every request for a transfer refused. Now he couldn't get out if he wanted to.

The helicopter came down in the Deer Park. Hunter climbed out beneath the thundering blades, with his men carrying Mallory on a stretcher behind. A cluster of people were silhouetted against the bright lights of Magdalen.

He motioned for the men to take Mallory straight down to a holding cell where the medics could check him over and then sauntered as nonchalantly as he could manage in the direction of the crowd. The snow was already starting to settle on the grass.

Running to meet him was Reid and two of the shifty, faceless men who populated his department. He stopped the stretcher and briefly searched Mallory before hurrying up to Hunter.

'Weapon?' he barked.

'What's this? A word-association game? If so, I'll say "penis". A big one.'

'Did he have a weapon?' There was a flush of excitement in Reid's cheeks that made him oblivious to Hunter's attempt to rile him. Hunter didn't like the look of it.

'A sword. In the chopper. There we go again with the word association. That Freud bloke really had it sorted, didn't he?'

'I'm taking it down to my department for tests, if you want to mark that in your report.'

'There's a stone in there, too. Makes pretty pictures in the air.'

Reid had dived into the chopper before Hunter had time to say anything else.

The General came up next, accompanied by a small coterie of serious-faced advisors. 'What does he want?' he asked suspiciously, peering after Reid.

'Typical spook-looting.'

The General nodded. 'Leave the chopper here. You've got forty-five minutes for debriefing and to grab a bite and then we're off again.'

'Trouble?'

'We'll see.' The General marched away into the snowstorm with his coterie hurrying behind him like a gaggle of geese. Hunter watched them go, strangely unnerved; and his instincts never let him down.

When he turned back to the helicopter, Hal was standing beside him. 'Bloody hell, will you stop creeping up on me?'

'We need to talk,' Hal said.

Hunter walked quickly, forcing Hal to skip to keep up; it was a game Hunter liked to play. 'You're like a bloody ghost. Natural stealth abilities. You should be doing this job instead of pushing paper around an in-tray or whatever it is you do to waste your time.'

'Something's up.'

'There's always something up.' Hunter noted the concerned tone in Hal's voice and relented. 'What's wrong?' It was the first time he had looked his friend full in the face and he was surprised to see the depth of the worry there. 'All right,' Hunter said. 'If you don't mind watching me shovel food into my face, you can talk while I eat.'

Hunter and Hal sat alone in a corner of a sprawling refectory once used by students. Hunter listlessly played with a plate of cold lamb and mashed potatoes while he listened to Hal relate the pieces of the information he had started to put together.

Afterwards, Hunter said, 'The mission I've just been on was to Cadbury Hill. Old stories say it was the site of Camelot. All rubbish of course, but . . .' He took a mouthful of potatoes and grimaced as he swallowed. 'They can never get the bloody lumps out. But . . . it's a hell of a coincidence,' he finished.

'What's going on?'

'I don't bloody know, mate, but I'll tell you this: that Caretaker bloke didn't choose you at random.'

Hal put his head in his hands and thought for a long moment. 'I don't want this. I went straight from university into the MoD for a quiet life – shuffle a few files, eventually carry the odd ministerial briefcase.' When he raised his head, the look Hunter had seen earlier had grown even more intense. 'You can sum up my life in two words: nothing happened. And that's just the way I like it. Safe. Secure. No risks attached. What's gone wrong?'

'You know what they say: if you're not living, you're dying. Maybe this is just what you need.'

'Like hell.' Hal thought for another moment and then said, 'What do I do? Go to the General—'

'No chance,' Hunter said vehemently. 'Never trust anyone in power. Haven't you learned anything while you've been working here? They'll either lock you up in one of their little cells while they *investigate* you – for three or four years – or they'll bang you up for being a potential traitor.'

'Well, I'm not supposed to deal with this myself, am I? I'm not you, the man who's seen every country in the world—'

'And shagged all the women and drunk all the booze.' He tapped his belly. 'Getting close to eating all the pies, too. Listen, you can do anything you want. You're in charge of your life.'

Hal shook his head. 'No.'

'Look, you're not in this alone. I'm here. We can figure this out together. When I get back from my little jaunt with the General, we'll have a chin-wag, put two and two together ... there's an answer somewhere.'

'The Caretaker said something was coming. That we'd been noticed. I'm worried something really bad is going to happen.'

'Me, too, mate.' Hunter shoved his plate away from him. 'Me, too.'

Sophie felt as if she was at the bottom of a deep, dark well. In the tiny circle of sky visible high overhead, she could just make out the morning sun behind clouds. But she couldn't feel her body at all. *Floating in the water*, she thought. She could float there for ever—

'Sister of Dragons! You must hear me!' The voice was insistent, but mellifluous and soothing.

Despite her desire to continue drifting, Sophie found herself rising up the well until she was looking into a woman's face. At first, the features appeared to run like oil; Sophie thought that she was in the presence of some famous artist whose name she couldn't quite recall, then a wise woman from a camp she had once passed through. As her perception cleared, the sense of familiarity faded. The woman was beautiful and sensitive, her dark eyes flashing in a pale face surrounded by long black hair that shone in the light of the moon.

'Who are you?' Sophie was surprised by the weakness of her voice.

'Your kind once called me Ceridwen, amongst many other names,' the woman replied. Her gaze left Sophie to dart around the dark hillside with apprehension.

Sophie wondered briefly if she was dreaming, for it appeared to be snowing. It was only when she attempted to move that she realised how numb her body had been; pain shot through her as if she had been stabbed. She looked down to see blood staining the whitening grass.

'Do not move, Sister of Dragons. Your light burns low,' Ceridwen said. 'You have little time left for the Fixed Lands unless your wound can be staunched.'

Sophie let her head flop back, her vision swimming. 'Mallory,' she whispered.

Ceridwen was doing something at her side, from where the pain emanated. On the edge of her vision, Sophie saw a soothing blue glow and the pain eased a little. 'There,' Ceridwen said, 'that will hold for a while. But you need to rest and heal.'

'I was shot—'

'Hush. We need to leave this place. Something terrible is happening. The Lament-Brood are here, only a few of them, but if they find us, they will corrupt us both. Yes, even I, even a Golden One.'

Ceridwen lifted Sophie as if she weighed nothing at all.

'Where are you taking me?' Sophie said weakly.

'Far away from this place of sorrow.' The words caught in Ceridwen's throat. 'Though in these bitter times, even the Far Lands are tainted with misery.'

Before she could utter another word, the soft, unnerving whispering of the Lament-Brood rolled across the hillside. Sophie raised her head enough to see the riders on their reptilian mounts emerging from the trees.

'What are they?' Sophie asked.

'Agents of the Void,' Ceridwen replied. 'The abyss has beckoned.'

Sophie began to slip back into the well. Ceridwen backed away from the approaching riders, but there was the sound of others approaching to close off their retreat.

'There's nowhere we can go,' Sophie muttered. 'They've got us.'

When Ceridwen didn't reply, Sophie knew she was right. The last thing she heard before she slipped into darkness was the sound of the horses' hooves thundering across the hillside towards them.

Hal walked with Hunter along the empty, ringing corridors and out to the Deer Park where the helicopter waited. Neither of them felt like speaking.

The snow gleamed crisp and even across the grass in the morning light, with only one trail of multiple footprints leading to the waiting chopper; the General and his men were already on board.

'He's keen,' Hal said.

'What the bloody hell is up with this weather?' Hunter snapped. 'I hate snow. I hate it!' He turned to Hal and his familiar rakish grin had returned. 'Keep the home fires burning. And don't talk to anybody, all right? Don't do anything dangerous like thinking for yourself. Do what I say.'

'I will.'

Nodding his goodbye, Hunter ran towards the helicopter, ducking low beneath the blades that had just started to whirr. Hal waited until it had disappeared and then turned back to Magdalen with a heavy heart.

Inside the ancient buildings it was unusually deserted. Most of the staff was in the New Library, which had been converted to an operations room for whatever the General had been planning. Hal was to report there later for a briefing.

As he made his way to his room for a rest, he heard footsteps approaching. For some reason he couldn't quite explain, Hal felt the urge to step out of view. He slipped into one of the darkened offices and waited with the door ajar.

A few seconds later, Catherine Manning marched forcefully by, the echoes of her heels clack-clacking off the walls. She was talking to herself.

'If I can get close to the PM, I think I can turn things around,' she said.

Although Hal could see no sign of a radio or mobile phone, Manning acted as if she was having a conversation with someone unseen.

'All it takes is a little—' Manning paused suddenly a few feet past the door behind which Hal was hiding and then turned to look back. Hal slipped away from the door before she saw him.

'Where?' she snapped.

Hal's blood ran cold. He backed further into the room, banging against a desk top, stifling an instinctive cry and grabbing the edge to stop the desk from grinding across the floor. Quickly, he ducked underneath it.

He was just in time, for the door swung open silently at the touch of Manning's fingertips. Hal could see her legs as she stood there silently for an unbearable few seconds. Then: 'There's no one here.'

Hal only breathed again when he heard her heels disappear up the corridor. The troubling questions came thick and fast. To whom had she been talking? How had she known that he was hiding there? Why had she mentioned the PM, who was ensconced in his war bunker at Balliol and rarely seen by anyone outside the Cabinet? It left him with the feeling that some deep, dark plot was being put in motion.

And overriding it all was the sense that Hal could no longer trust anyone.

Strong winds buffeted the helicopter from side to side as they flew over the Scottish Border counties. They'd already been forced to put down for several hours to avoid bad weather and the mood on board was strained. Snow encrusted the edges of the windows, making it difficult to see more than a few feet out, though there was nothing at all visible in the night-dark countryside below.

Hunter stared out into the snowstorm, lost in thought. The General had refused to say what they were going to see, but his demeanour suggested it was not good.

In the days since the Fall, electric lights had been missing from much of the countryside at night, so Hunter at first assumed the glimmer he saw on the horizon to be just an illusion caused by the snow. But as they moved closer, he realised it was fire, and closer still the reality became apparent: it was an enormous fire.

'That's it?' he asked.

The General came to sit next to him. 'I think so.'

'What's going on?'

'While we were plotting our strike-back, the enemy decided to move first.'

Hunter gazed at the flickering flames. The smoke billowed up into the snow-filled clouds. 'That's a town?'

'Lanark.'

'It doesn't make any sense. The gods have left us alone for so long because they *know* we're no threat to them. They can pick us off as and when they like, so why would they be launching a full-scale assault now?'

'Nevertheless, our intelligence says that's what's happening. And as you know, Hunter, in the absence of being able to do anything more effective, we have at least established a first-rate intelligence network. Probably better than the one we had before the Fall.'

'Can we get closer?'

'We'll go as close as is safe.' The General sat back. He was surprisingly at ease, and when he next spoke, Hunter understood why. 'I've spent months arguing for a chance to repel the invader. Months. Manning was too cautious. Reid was always after more intelligence; more, more, more. He'll never have enough. The others always sat on the fence because no one was big enough to take the really tough decisions, so the PM was always swayed by those two. Now the balance of power has to shift. We can't sit around and do nothing. We need to mount a robust defence and then strike back with devastating force.'

'Have we got any? I know I'm devastating in my own way, but I don't think I'd be much use against that.'

'We have things at our disposal.' The General looked away, his body language suggesting that was not an avenue that should be pursued.

Hunter ignored the signals. 'Conventional weapons? You know they've failed in the past. You tried to use a tactical nuke during the Fall, didn't you?' Hunter attempted to keep the loathing out of his voice, though he'd remonstrated loudly about the idiocy of his superiors down the pub at the time. 'As I remember from the leaked report, the bomb became wrapped in trees that appeared to have a life of their own and then somehow turned into a flock of birds.'

'Some of the backroom boys have finally managed to adapt to the new rules we find ourselves operating under,' the General replied curtly. 'Even Reid has made a few helpful suggestions in that area. Frankly, I'd attack them with a handful of magic beans if I thought it would work.'

Hunter's attention was fixed on the destruction below. The pilot took the helicopter in from one flank to fly parallel to the wall of fire, just above the level of the treetops. Every building in Lanark was aflame, a field of devastation that stretched as far as the eye could see. But that was not what left him pressing tightly against the glass for a better look.

'They're establishing a beachhead,' the General said.

The enemy moved out of the fire relentlessly, so thick on the ground that the white of the recent snowfall was almost obscured. It reminded Hunter of nothing so much as an ant hill he had disturbed as a boy.

'How many of them are there?' he said with hushed awe.

Some of the figures looked oddly human. Others were bestial, moving from upright to all fours and back again. A few resembled medieval siege machines, yet they were alive somehow, alien life forms clearly wearing their war-like purpose, every pounding of their enormous limbs like the beat of a drum. And all across the landscape a purple mist drifted, swathing the figures as they made their slow, purposeful progress across the land.

As the helicopter swooped nearer, Hunter made out a group of figures distinct from the others: four bulky shapes surrounding a tall, thin one; the only details he could pick out were random images illuminated by the lick of flame. Yet there was something about them that made him feel sick to the pit of his stomach. He felt instinctively that they were the ultimate threat.

'They're not like anything we've seen before,' Hunter said. 'What are they?'

The General's eyes gleamed with a sickening light of anticipation. 'Are you ready for a fight?' he asked.

The helicopter shook briefly in a random gust of wind. Hunter grabbed on to the straps for support, shivering as the temperature dropped another degree. The pilot moved the helicopter away from the invading force, heading back towards Oxford. The snow, which was coming thicker and faster, soon obscured all signs of the threat.

Hunter shivered again, this time not from the cold.

Winter was coming in hard.

chapter four

the final word

'The lamps are going out all over Europe; we shall not see them lit again in our lifetime.' Edward Grey, Viscount of Falloden

Lime and lavender filled the air, the scents cloying and a little sickly as if masking more disturbing odours. The overpowering aromas filled Sophie's senses before she opened her eyes, more heady than anything she had ever experienced before. When her eyelids did finally flutter open, she clamped them shut again immediately, so bright was the light. It took her a second or two to acclimatise, and slowly conscious thought returned with the vivid sensations: at first a simple awareness, then puzzlement, then concern.

Cautiously, she opened her eyes again, shielding them with her hand as she took in her surroundings. She was lying on a table of white marble. Slowly easing herself upright and swinging her legs off one side, she saw white marble everywhere in the large, columned room, so that it appeared to blaze in the sunlight that streamed through glass skylights far up in the lofty ceiling. It reminded Sophie of drawings she had seen of the homes of the gods in Greek mythology. But there was a pleasing organic aspect to the straight lines, with vines wrapping themselves around some of the columns and trees growing up through the floor to the ceiling. Songbirds fluttered back and forth amongst the highest branches. Nearby was a sparkling spring that ran into a reflecting pool with a soothing bubbling. Peace lay heavy all around.

'Welcome, Sister of Dragons.'

Sophie started at the honeyed voice. She turned to see Ceridwen looking at her with a warm smile that had been absent the first time Sophie had seen her face. And with that thought came another rush of memory: the strange, twisted warriors on their reptilian mounts rushing towards her.

'Not dead, then?' she said, not quite able to believe it herself.

'Not dead,' Ceridwen replied, faintly amused.

With her was a man in scarlet robes. The colour was shocking in the bright white of the room. Sophie experienced the same unnerving shift of perception she had felt when she had first seen Ceridwen, but after a second, the man's face settled into a form she could comprehend. He was hollow-cheeked, his nose aquiline, his eyes a piercing grey set off by the red scarf tied around his head to hold back his hair. His tall, thin frame was a stark contrast to Ceridwen's voluptuousness.

'This is Dian Cecht,' Ceridwen said. 'He has admitted you to the Court of the Final Word.'

The name felt like a cold breath on the back of Sophie's neck. 'Not in my world,' she said to herself, knowing it to be true the moment the words left her lips.

'Dian Cecht is the name by which he was known amongst the tribes of the Fixed Lands,' Ceridwen continued. 'He is a wise man, a healer, a maker of great things.'

Sophie's hand instinctively went to her side.

'Yes, Sister of Dragons, I repaired you,' Dian Cecht said.

There was something in his tone that made Sophie feel queasy, but she attempted to show gratitude. 'I could have died.' The shock brought another rush of realisation. 'You're two of the gods that came with the Fall.' Then: 'Why are you helping me?'

'You are a Sister of Dragons,' Ceridwen said with a note of puzzlement, as if that should be explanation enough. When she saw from Sophie's face that it wasn't, she added, 'Existence is at a cusp. The old ways are ending . . . our ways . . .' Dian Cecht flinched at this, but said nothing. 'Your ways are in the ascendant. Fragile Creatures are poised to rise and advance, to become something . . . greater. And the Brothers and Sisters of Dragons will have a part to play in that. You are important in so many ways,' Ceridwen added warmly. 'It is believed by the *filid* of my people that if Fragile Creatures do not reach their potential, then all of Existence may come to an end.'

'Not *all* of our kind believe that,' Dian Cecht added coldly.

Ceridwen came over and took Sophie's hand. Her fingers were cool and delicate; up close it appeared that her skin exuded a thin golden light. 'You are important, Sister of Dragons. To everything.'

Ceridwen led Sophie to another room where there was bread and fruit on crystal platters and a decanter of water. 'Eat and drink freely and without obligation. You must build your strength, for we have a long journey ahead of us.'

Ceridwen moved into an adjoining room where she fell into deep discussion with Dian Cecht. Sophie was so hungry that she didn't listen to the conversation at first, all her attention focused on the food, but eventually it intruded on her thoughts.

'Is it true?' Ceridwen was saying.

'It is. The Devourer of All Things is here. The prophecies are coming to pass in these days,' Dian Cecht replied.

'Is that the end of this song? The seasons have passed for Existence and all things under it?'

'Here in the Court of the Final Word, the very heart of Existence has been probed,' Dian Cecht said. 'Secrets and mysteries have been laid bare. Know this: nothing is ever truly destroyed, and nothing new is created. There is only change. That is the one rule above all rules.'

There was silence for a moment and then Ceridwen said quietly, 'And what of death, then?'

Dian Cecht's reply was barely audible. 'There is no death.'

'You say that, even now? The Golden Ones have always been strangers to it. But in recent times . . .' Ceridwen fell silent. 'Is there coming an end? Is there nothing we can do, or will the Devourer of All Things abide?'

Another long silence, then, 'I have already taken steps.'

And then Dian Cecht and Ceridwen must have left the annexe by another door, for after that there was only quiet.

Sophie fell into a deep sleep and dreamed of Dian Cecht, though at times it appeared to be more than a dream, as if she had half-woken and seen or spoken with him before drifting into sleep again. In his red, red robes she saw him striding across worlds, taking a scalpel to the heart of the sun; nothing could contain him. He scared Sophie deeply, for she felt he would do anything to achieve his ends, and that he knew more, much more than everyone else. Secrets and mysteries. Mysteries and secrets.

And then his face filled her entire vision and he whispered, 'The next time you see me, you shall not see me.'

It was still light when Sophie woke. She ate and drank some more, maintaining the surface calm that had served her so well throughout the many devastating upheavals since the Fall. But inside she fought desperately for equilibrium in the face of gods and legends and the suggestion that she was something greater than the scared little girl she felt like in her worst moments.

Once Sophie had recovered enough to walk, Ceridwen led her through the Court of the Final Word with a troubling degree of urgency, Dian Cecht shadowing them. For some unspoken reason, he steered them away from certain corridors that led deep into the heart of the gleaming complex, and eventually they came to a massive entrance hall constructed from more white marble. Here there were windows five storeys high, all of them glazed with glass stained in various shades of red so that the hall appeared to be running with blood.

Ceridwen turned to Dian Cecht and said, 'Are you sure you will not accompany us?'

He shook his head. 'They will not come near the Court of the Final Word. Of all the great courts, this one is immune to any attack.'

Ceridwen nodded. 'All know what lies within.'

A cold smile crept across Dian Cecht's lips and once again Sophie was afraid. 'The Court of the Final Word stands alongside Fragile Creatures,' he said to her, but his words were hesitant. 'Go in peace and go with speed. The Far Lands are no longer safe, for any of us.'

'Where are we going?' Sophie asked Ceridwen.

'To one of the last bastions of the last hope for all Existence, Sister of Dragons,' Ceridwen replied. 'A place where we can make a final stand, if needs be, or to plot with our allies a way to save everything.'

There were so many questions Sophie wanted to ask, but she could sense that it was not the time. Instead she focused on being patient until she could successfully find a way back to her own world and Mallory.

As they approached the gigantic doors, they swung open soundlessly to reveal a vista over a glorious countryside of rolling green, forests and streams, a landscape of romance and mystery that made Sophie's spine tingle. It appeared to be late September, still warm, the leaves turning gold and red and brown. In the hollows, mist was rolling.

Tethered just outside were two chestnut mares with bridles of onyx and ivory. Ceridwen motioned to Sophie to mount one and then climbed on to the other mare easily.

'Go well, Daughter of the Green,' Dian Cecht said to Ceridwen. The warmth in his voice made Sophie reappraise him. He was too complex to judge, too unpredictable.

Ceridwen smiled sadly and then spurred her mount down the path that led from the court across the countryside. Sophie followed, glad to leave the Court of the Final Word behind.

The path wound like a golden ribbon over the green, but after a short distance Ceridwen eased her horse off into the long grass. 'We shall avoid the main byways,' she said, 'and make our way through the quiet, secret places, the silent forests, the mist-filled valleys, the whispering heart of the land.' She flashed a comforting glance at Sophie. 'Those places belong to me.'

The wind traced liquid patterns in the grass as the two horses eased down the slope towards a stream that Sophie could see glinting in the light. At that moment the sun came out from behind a cloud, transforming the entire landscape into a transcendent, hazy temple. The hairs on Sophie's arms prickled as the quality of light and the subtleties of scent and temperature worked their spell on her.

'I've dreamed of this place,' Sophie said to herself, surprised at the force of the realisation. 'When I was a girl, this was always where I wanted to be.'

'The Far Lands stay in all our hearts,' Ceridwen said. 'It is the place from which we all spring and to which we all return, eternally.'

Sophie understood in that moment how she had been shaped as

a woman by the thoughts that had come to her during her childhood, the yearning for a place where nature truly lived, where mystery was a part of daily life and where there was a profound sense of meaning underpinning everything. Without truly knowing, she had been on a quest from her earliest days; and it was this land that had called to her. The swell of emotion was so shocking that she couldn't prevent a fugitive tear.

'This place is your home?' Sophie asked.

'It is our home now. The Golden Ones are a race ruled by infinite sadness. Our true homelands are lost to us; we may never return. But the Far Lands and the Fixed Lands make adequate replacements.'

'So much has changed since the Fall,' Sophie mused. Images of the dark days following the gods' return rushed through her mind: the burning cities, the failure of technology, the riots, the economic collapse, the desperation of people unable to accept the new rules reality had thrust upon them. In the end, only a few had the ability to adapt and survive, those defined by a particular worldview, perhaps; Sophie wondered if the ones who were truly at peace since the Fall were those who had been on the same inner quest as her. In the newly re-formed world, she had an abiding sense of coming home, despite all the upheaval and the suffering.

'You talked about some kind of threat?' she said eventually.

'There are threats all around us,' Ceridwen replied enigmatically. 'Threats from within. Threats from without. For my people, the greatest threat is ourselves. We are at war. The battles rage even now across the Far Lands and no Golden One is safe. Never would we have thought to see this day.' The devastation in her voice was heartbreaking.

'Why are you fighting each other?'

Ceridwen raised her sad face high so that the wind made her hair billow behind her. 'Because of you, Sister of Dragons. You and all your kind.'

'What do we have to do with it?' Sophie asked, baffled.

'Fragile Creatures are at the point of rising and advancing . . . of becoming like the Golden Ones—'

'Gods?'

'Some of my people think that is the way of Existence. We have always had a close relationship with your kind. We would shepherd you to the next stage. Others . . .' The word caught in her throat. 'There are those who think you should never be allowed to attain your potential. That you should be eradicated as a race so that the Golden Ones can never be supplanted.'

'So the fate of the human race depends on which side wins?' Ceridwen's silence was all the answer Sophie needed. A chill crept over her, for she sensed from Ceridwen's conversation with Dian Cecht that things were not going well for those who had sided with humanity. 'What about the threat from without?'

'It is also the way of Existence that our races are tested to the extreme. Crisis heaped upon crisis. And the threat from without is the greatest crisis of all.' Ceridwen's horse carefully picked its way down a tricky bit of the slope where rocks and stones protruded from the grass. At the bottom of the incline, the stream trickled soothingly. 'Something has crawled up from the very edge of Existence; it is the opposite of everything that lives – and it has noticed you Fragile Creatures. It sees your potential and it does not want you to shake off your shackles and become something greater, for to do so would make you a threat to its very reason for being.'

A dark shadow fell over them both, but when Sophie looked up, the sun still shone brightly. 'What is it?' she asked uneasily.

'It is an idea, a notion of negativity. Where we see a threat, some would see nothing at all, for it is only defined by what it is not. Darkness and despair enfold it.'

'Does it have a name?'

'Many names, but none capture its essence, for how can you describe something that is not? Legends call it the Void. Even now it exerts its subtle influence on the Fixed Lands, attempting to eradicate all Fragile Creatures like an infestation. It is greater than anything you can imagine, yet smaller; more powerful, yet in the true and blinding light of the Blue Fire, completely powerless.'

'And it was controlling those warriors who attacked us at Cadbury Hill?'

'The Void's very nature is to corrupt, to strip life and hope from a being and to control it. The act of giving up personal freedom is to surrender to Anti-Life. Even the gods are not immune.'

Sophie was lulled into a deep introspection by the motion of riding. She knew how powerful the gods were, had heard tales of them destroying entire army units with a wave of a hand. If the

Void could take control of them, what chance did Fragile Creatures stand?

'But if it's so . . . vague, how are we supposed to fight it?' Sophie asked.

'Only the Brothers and Sisters of Dragons may repel it. The Quincunx, the Five Who Are One. But therein lies the problem.'

'What do you mean?'

'The answer to that question lies ahead of us, and you will discover the truth for yourself. But for now, enough talk of dark things. Let us celebrate the life and the green that surround us.'

They moved into a thickly wooded area, the trees pressing hard along the banks of the brook, their branches crossing overhead to form a cathedral roof of leaf cover beneath which Sophie could feel the sanctity with every echoing splash of her horse's hooves. Once the reverberations died away, there remained an abiding silence too sacred to shatter.

And so they rode quietly, with Ceridwen leading the way, and after a while Sophie began to wonder if she had indeed come to heaven.

The journey along the winding course of the stream continued for more than an hour. After the initial stretch where the trees bustled tightly against the banks, the wood thinned enough to allow Sophie a brief glimpse of a green world where fantastic fungi swarmed in ochre patterns over fallen trees and tiny, gleaming purple flowers sprang up in a carpet of colour that shimmered in the filtering light.

But after a while, the mist that had occasionally drifted across their path grew more constant until a heavy greyness lay over everything, sapping echoes and distorting birdcalls. The trees presented themselves like dark spectral figures before they were swallowed up again in the passing.

Sophie shivered in the damp air and wished she had brought some warmer clothes with her. 'How much further?' she asked. She instinctively lowered her voice to a whisper that was lost in the mist.

'A while,' Ceridwen replied. 'We will follow the course of the stream through the Winding Wood to the great plain. And there, beyond it, we shall find the Court of Soul's Ease.'

'Is that like the place we've just visited?'

'Each of the twenty great courts has an atmosphere that is

peculiarly its own, but even so, nowhere else is like the Court of the Final Word.' Ceridwen's hesitant voice made Sophie think this was perhaps a good thing. 'The Court of Soul's Ease has been through a great many changes. Now, though, its destiny has been made plain.'

The low, mournful baying of a hound rose up somewhere away in the mist. The sound made Sophie shiver, but she couldn't tell if it was near or far.

'Should we be worried about that?' Sophie asked. As soon as the words had left her lips, another howl arose, and then another, until soon there were several dogs baying.

'They are the Hounds of Avalon,' Ceridwen replied. 'Also known as the Hounds of Annwn. Sometimes they join with the Wild Hunt, pursuing lost Fragile Creatures through the night. At other times, they roam between the worlds, questing for who knows what. Some say they hunt the answer to a question that could shatter Existence. But they are most active at times of greatest threat to your world, the Fixed Lands. Our stories say that at the end of all Existence, they will be all that remains, baying for what has been lost. Their howls will join together into one shattering note of despair.'

'So when the Hounds of Avalon come, that's it? Game over?' Ceridwen's story made Sophie feel sad and troubled, but eventually the howling of the dogs faded away and Sophie gradually forgot them.

Twilight began to draw in, though in the mist the only way to tell was by a subtle shifting of the quality of the grey. By this time, Sophie was chilled to the bone and felt a deep urge for a warming campfire.

'Should we make camp for the night?' she asked.

Ceridwen, who had been distracted for a while, shook her head. 'There are dangerous things loose in these parts. Better to be on horseback ready to flee than trapped on the ground and forced to fight a battle we would certainly lose.'

Sophie did not like the feeling of powerlessness that had descended on her since she had awoken in the Court of the Final Word. The realisation that she had been transported somewhere else while she hovered between life and death had been destabilising, and everything that had happened since only underlined that feeling; she was operating in an alien world where all the rules were hidden from her, surrounded by beings that had the power to eradicate her in the blink of an eye. Yet in her own world she had never felt powerless, not before the Fall, and certainly not since, when her use of the Craft had become supercharged in whatever new state now existed. Silently, she urged herself to take control.

The truth was, her use of the Craft had grown stronger by the day. Where once it had taken hours of ritualistic preparation, she could now control and direct the subtle energies of the Blue Fire with a visualisation of sigils and words of power, simple keys that operated in the secret language of the unconscious. She wanted to know what was out there that was making Ceridwen so uneasy, sure that the simple act of knowing would give her a feeling of control over her environment.

But when she muttered the word that would trigger a shift in her perception, she was surprised by the result. There was the familiar sensation of her consciousness creeping out of a door at the back of her head, the feeling of taking a step aside from her corporeal form and becoming like the mist that swathed them. But as she drifted out from the horses amongst the ghostly trees, it felt as though a drill was being driven into her skull. She knew the sensation – a warning – but this was more heightened than anything she had felt before.

As she rushed back into her body, she jolted with such a sharp intake of breath that Ceridwen looked around. 'What is wrong?' the god asked with concern.

'We have to get out of here,' Sophie replied breathlessly. 'Can't you feel it?'

'I feel ... something.' Ceridwen looked around hesitantly, then whispered, 'They are masking themselves from me. They know we are here.'

As if in answer to Ceridwen's words, all the alarm bells in Sophie's mind rang at once. The mist along the brook began to thin out enough to allow her a view deep into the woods, and then it retreated further still. It was like a thing alive, swirling around the boles, rising up and over shrubs to pause briefly on the other side as if waiting.

But then, just when it appeared it was going for good, the fog stopped for a moment, wavering as if breathing, before beginning to creep back towards Sophie and Ceridwen. This time, though, the mist was not empty.

Here and there, where it thinned and twisted around obstacles in its path, Sophie could glimpse small, dark figures. At first they kept low to the ground, using the mist as a cloak, but as they neared they stood erect.

Sophie initially thought they were children, then wondered if they were just tricks of her imagination, for she would focus on one and it would seem to fade as the mist shifted.

Something whistled past Sophie's cheek. She looked around to see a crude arrow embedded in a nearby tree.

That must have been a signal, for suddenly hundreds of little figures were swarming like insects towards the brook. They were still partially obscured by the mist, but Sophie could see enough of them to realise they were ugly, deformed little men, near-naked apart from ragged loin cloths, their skin the dirty grey colour of things that lived much of their lives underground. Their hair and beards were long, filthy and matted and they clutched primitive weapons – stone axes, lumps of wood with chips of flint embedded in them, tiny bows. The attackers were filled with a primal savagery that made Sophie think of lost tribes devolving through years of interbreeding. A smell of peat and urine rolled off them.

'Ride!' Ceridwen shouted as the little men washed out of the woods towards them.

Sophie spurred her horse, raising a cloud of spray and a clatter of hooves on the pebbled river bed. But it would be impossible to gain any real speed along the tiny, meandering watercourse and the attackers were sweeping down upon them like a deluge.

Ahead, Ceridwen's mount moved with power and grace. Sophie pressed herself down along her horse's neck, urging it on ever faster. The movement on either side seen through her peripheral vision filled her with a dread that harked back to the most ancient parts of her subconscious; the men moved too quickly, their smell too revolting and bestial.

Arrows whizzed through the air all around, but Sophie could see that was not the enemy's main thrust of attack. Sheer force of numbers was the way they would undoubtedly bring Sophie and

Ceridwen down. That thought made Sophie consider what would happen immediately after, when the razor-sharp flint knives started dipping and diving. She thought of skins and meat and the instinctive fear drove her to urge her mount on with even greater force.

An arrow slammed into her saddlebag but didn't break through to the horse's flesh. Another missed Sophie's face by a hair's breadth. By that stage, the little men were almost at the edge of the bank, and Sophie had a clear view of their feral nature.

And then she was aware of movement as some of the nearest leaped. Several missed and fell under the thundering hooves of her horse, but one timed it just right. It hit her, sinking long, broken nails into her clothes. The stink of it – sour apples and raw meat – filled Sophie's nose as it started to haul its way up her body so that it could attack her with the knife it was clutching between its broken teeth. Sophie tried to elbow it off while clinging on to the reins with one hand, but it had the agility of a monkey.

Those jagged nails clamped on to her thigh, tearing through the material of her dress, raising bubbles of blood from her pale flesh. Still weak from the gunshot wound, Sophie cried out as her flesh tore. The little man dug deep to lever itself up further.

Sophie shook herself furiously, but the man would not be dislodged. Another hand snaked up to grab the saddle. From the licks of flame that rose in its eyes, Sophie knew it now had enough of a grip to go for its knife.

Yet strangely there was no panic. An abiding calmness slowly descended on her, and when she closed her eyes briefly, the sensation was accompanied by a blue colour. Increasingly, when she used her Craft, this was how it was: as if some power was visiting her from without, not arising from within.

Through closed eyelids, she experienced a sapphire flash. Every nerve in her body felt electrified and there was a smell of burned iron in her nostrils. And when she looked around, the little men had halted their advance; a dark smudge of charred material ran down the saddle and across the material of her dress, the attacker gone, destroyed or fallen by the wayside.

With a feeling of exultation, she leaned along the horse's neck once more, the wind whipping at her hair as her steed galloped onwards. Ahead, Ceridwen glanced back at her, surprise turning to respect in her dark eyes.

The little men only fell back for a moment before the arrows started flying again, but Sophie's defence had provided enough of a breathing space for the horses to gain some yards on the attackers.

The banks of the stream grew higher as they progressed, until eventually the brook was running along the bottom of a gully. At the top of the banks, the vegetation was thick and overgrowing the edge so that it almost closed over the top; it became as dark as twilight as they rode. The obscured view meant that if the little men made it up to the top of the gully, they would have trouble timing their drop on to Sophie and Ceridwen.

The sides became even higher, the bottom broader and rockier as the stream grew in size, but Ceridwen never once slowed their pace. Finally they emerged from the gully and passed through a final stand of trees into open countryside where the mist had almost dissipated. They were on the edge of green, gently rolling downs running away from them to flat plains beyond. Here the meandering stream became a great river winding its way into the hazy distance.

From the cracking of wood and the cries of birds on the wing, it was clear that the little men had not given up the chase. Ceridwen looked back to Sophie and yelled, 'Spur your mount! Put the wind behind you!'

They rode as if they were part of a storm, adrift on a sea of green. The long grass parted before them and the mist burned away in the fading sunlight. With the thunder of hooves in her ears, Sophie allowed herself one look back and was shocked by what she saw. Swarming from the dark tree line were vast numbers of the little men, an army of them stretching out on either side as far as the eye could see. They didn't slow once, even though they could see that they would never catch up and that their tiny, lethal arrows were falling further and further behind their quarry. To Sophie, they looked like an infestation, insects disturbed from a vast nest beneath the ground, surging up in ordered chaos to attack.

Only after three miles or more did Ceridwen slow down so that Sophie could ride beside her.

'What were they?' Sophie asked breathlessly.

'My people.' Ceridwen's voice was wrapped in darkness; she did not look back.

'But they're nothing like you,' Sophie said, puzzled.

'They are diminished. They have chosen the downward path, as they did once before.'

'I don't understand. How can your people have turned into those things?'

'These are not the Fixed Lands. Here in the Far Lands, everything is fluid. The closer one gets to the core of Existence, the more mutable things are. I told you that my people are riven. Those who stand against the rising and advancing of Fragile Creatures have their true nature revealed. They become—'

'Diminished.' Sophie thought of all the tales she had heard of the little people when she was younger, the exhortation to call them 'Fair Folk' for fear they would torment any humans who did not treat them with respect.

'The Courts who have sided with them are attacking across the breadth of the Far Lands,' Ceridwen continued. 'The Golden Ones have never stood against each other before. We were one people, of one mind. Events have shown many of us that we do not deserve to stand above. We are all alike, Fragile Creatures and gods. Everything we believed in now lies shattered, and there is a sense that an ending fast approaches.'

Sophie looked back anxiously. 'Will they keep coming?'

'They will always keep coming. They will not rest until all the Golden Ones who have sided with Fragile Creatures are wiped from Existence. That is how deep the fault lines run. How can you condone the destruction of your own people and stay close to the essence of What Is?' Ceridwen shook her head, consumed by disbelief. When she turned back to Sophie, her face had hardened. 'We cannot stop,' she said. 'They will attack relentlessly, hiding beneath the dark of the moon or under the cover of clouds, to come in the night and slit our throats while we sleep. We must ride without rest. Are you ready for the challenge, Sister of Dragons?'

Though she was already exhausted and hollow with hunger, Sophie nodded. So much was at stake; she would not be the one who failed.

And so they rode, across the downs and into the night, and in the morning they swept across the plains in a light rain, their clothes plastered against their bodies. Through wooded valleys and by rocky foothills, they continued without rest until everything became like a dream to Sophie and she was convinced she was a girl once more, in bed, wishing herself to a land where anything was possible.

On the third day, a fortress city of white marble presented itself to them, gleaming in the sunrise. It rose up the foothills, so vast it seemed a hill itself, the upper reaches lost in the low clouds on the edge of the mountains behind. Sophie's breath caught at the sight of the awe-inspiring assemblage of turrets and domes, obelisks, palaces, keeps and dwellings, all surrounded by a single monolithic wall. Along the ramparts, golden flags fluttered in a light breeze; majesty and wonder lay across the entire city.

'Here it is, then,' Ceridwen said. 'The Court of Soul's Ease.'

Great gates of gold and glass soaring up for six storeys above Sophie's head swung open soundlessly as the two travellers approached. Once Ceridwen and Sophie were within the shelter of the walls, the gates closed with a musical chiming. All around, tall, thin, impossibly beautiful people went about their business, their skin touched by gold. As Ceridwen led the way up a winding sunlit street, the passers-by turned to smile, reserving much of their pleasant welcome for Sophie. Everywhere there was the peace of a lazy summer afternoon.

Ceridwen dismounted in a cobbled square beside a fountain of gold, glass and white marble, the shimmering water gushing twenty feet or more into the air. Beyond lay an opulent palace, the frontage ornately carved with beatific statues, all dominated by a stylistic sun motif high above the entrance.

As the gates had done before, the door swung open as Ceridwen and Sophie approached, and several guards rushed out. They wore armour that continued the white-and-gold theme, with the same solar motif prominent on the breastplate. Though their helmets threw most of their faces into shadow, their eyes glowed golden.

'Your brother welcomes you,' the captain of the guards said, kneeling and bowing his head. 'He requests your presence in the Great Hall to inform you of the current state of the war and to hear news of the Court of the Final Word. Will you accompany us?'

'Of course,' Ceridwen replied. 'It is a relief to be in a place of safety once more.' She breathed the air, fragrant with the scent of clematis, and said softly, 'Home.'

Sophie followed in awed silence until they arrived at an airy hall where sunlight streamed through glass skylights in the roof high overhead. A group of people had gathered in the centre near a large table on which lay what at first looked like a map, but as Sophie approached was more like a hologram, three-dimensional, moving, alive. The group talked and planned in quiet, thoughtful voices, overseen by a man who was clearly their leader.

His armour was white overlaid with the faintest gold filigree so that he glowed in the shaft of light in which he stood. At first he had his back to Sophie, but when he turned there was only a brief moment of transition before her breath was taken away by his handsome features. He looked to be in his early twenties, with dark eyes and long dark hair framing a face that was both strong and sensitive.

'Greetings,' he said to Ceridwen with a warm smile, before his eyes fell on Sophie. 'And what is this? Another Sister of Dragons? My court is truly blessed.'

'Yes, brother. This one is known as Sophie.' Ceridwen turned to Sophie and added, 'In the days of the tribes, the Fragile Creatures knew my brother as Lugh. At the second battle of Magh Tuireadh, he slew Balor, the one-eyed god of death, and saved the Fixed Lands from the rule of the dark and monstrous Fomorii.'

'Hello,' Sophie said, before mentally kicking herself for sounding so pathetic.

'I stand alongside Fragile Creatures in the coming struggle,' Lugh said. 'It was not always so, but I have reclaimed the wisdom that departed me.' He smiled at Ceridwen again. 'With no small help from my sister.'

Sophie's mind was racing. Standing amongst the gods, it felt as if she was at the heart of a massive electromagnetic field: her ears buzzed so much that it was difficult to concentrate; her skin tingled and her mouth felt as though it was filled with iron filings. But as she fought to stay on top of what was happening around her, one thing came through loud and clear.

'Did you say *another* Sister of Dragons?'

★

The suite of rooms was grand by any definition and if Sophie had not known better she would have thought it belonged to Lugh. It was high up in the palace, with a balcony providing a breathtaking vista across the great wall to the sweeping plains beyond and, further still, to snow-topped mountains lying dreamily beneath a blue sky. One room led on to another, and another, and another, all with delicate tapestries lining the walls and furs scattered across the stone floors. The furniture was designed for maximum comfort, the sumptuous cushions and hanging drapes giving it the feel of some Arabian Nights tent.

Sophie found the woman on the balcony, her eyes closed as she let the sun play on her face. In her late twenties, she wore a long gown of a rich, dark green, but her hair was tied back with an elastic band, an odd mundane detail amidst the otherworldly ambience. She glanced over when Sophie stepped out into the warm air, and her attractive features carried the mark of a strong will, but also a deep sadness that looked as though it cut to the heart of her.

'Is that how I used to look?' she mused softly to herself. 'So strong and full of power?' The woman came over and took Sophie's hand warmly. 'You don't have to tell me – you're a Sister of Dragons. Are you here to have a go at me for letting the side down?'

'I just turned up here by accident.'

'There aren't any accidents,' the woman said. 'Rule number one of the new age. I'd better introduce myself, then. Caitlin Shepherd. I used to be one of you.'

'Sophie Tallent.' Sophie went to shake Caitlin's hand, then felt an overwhelming urge to hug her, two kindred spirits in a frightening land. After a moment, Sophie pulled back and said, 'You used to be a Sister of Dragons?'

Caitlin stepped away and leaned over the marble rail to survey the swarming citadel below. 'One of the great defenders of humanity. Our last, best hope. And I threw it all away to try to save my husband and son. For nothing. They died. The Blue Fire deserted me and I think I probably doomed the human race with that same decision.'

'I don't understand.'

'I'm only really just getting my head around it myself,' Caitlin said. 'But the abridged version is this: the universe or whatever lies behind it – Existence, as the gods call it – has a lot of hidden rules and one of them is this: there need to be five Brothers and Sisters of Dragons at any one time. Numbers seem vital to the whole underlying plan. On the one hand you could see it as a spell, on the other an equation – all the principal elements have to be there to make it work.' She gave a wan smile. 'I've had a lot of time to think about this.'

'So without five, we can't—'

'Act as prophecy or legend or myth intended. We either don't have the same power, or maybe we don't have the weight . . . the *gravity* . . . to oppose what's coming. So when it all goes pear-shaped, you'll know who to blame.'

Her profound sadness was so affecting that Sophie knew she would never be able to blame Caitlin for anything. Anyone who felt so acutely could not have wilfully brought about the disaster she professed was about to happen.

Sophie insisted on hearing everything, and so they moved to the nearest chamber, where the high breezes from over the citadel gently swept in through the open balcony doors, cooling them in the heat of the day. Caitlin recounted how she had been working as a doctor in the south of England when a mysterious plague swept across Britain; Sophie had seen signs of it, but nothing on the scale Caitlin had experienced. The disease had taken Caitlin's husband and son, and Caitlin's mind had shattered under the extreme stress of the situation. Gradually, though, she had come to some kind of sense, and with a small group of friends had travelled to T'ir n'a n'Og in search of a cure, for not only was the plague mystical, but it had its origin in the Celtic Otherworld.

She had fought her way through hardship after hardship to a living structure called the House of Pain on the edge of the Far Lands where she had discovered the reason for the plague: it had been created as a weapon of the Void. But to be sure of success, the Void had to destroy the defenders of humanity, the Brothers and Sisters of Dragons, by breaking their mystical number. One would do, just one, and Caitlin was it.

The House of Pain had offered Caitlin a choice: to remain there as a queen – in effect giving up her right to be a Sister of Dragons – and in return her husband and son would live. But it had been a trick, and after giving up the Pendragon Spirit that made her a Sister of Dragons, she had realised that she couldn't have her family either.

'So, I blew it – in the worst way possible,' Caitlin concluded. 'I've doomed everybody.'

The more Sophie listened, the more she felt a bond growing with Caitlin. They were true sisters. 'Anyone would have done the same in your situation. Anyone,' Sophie insisted.

Caitlin shook her head, staring out of the window at the blue sky.

'Listen to me,' Sophie said. 'We're supposed to be defenders of humanity. To turn your back on your love for your husband and child would have been to give up on that very humanity. You couldn't win whatever you did.'

Caitlin thought about this for a moment. 'You're very wise,' she said, a little brighter. 'I wish you'd been there with me.'

'Lugh mentioned that there were other Fragile Creatures here, after he told me about you,' Sophie said, changing the subject; that detail had initially been lost in the excitement of meeting another Sister of Dragons.

'Two friends who followed me from our world to this one. They think they're my protectors.' Caitlin smiled. 'I reckon it's probably the other way around.' Caitlin described how she had made her way from the House of Pain to the Court of Soul's Ease in the company of the two young men, Thackeray and Harvey. Sophie sensed that there was a bond between Caitlin and one of them, but she didn't pursue it.

'Do you want to meet them?' Caitlin asked. 'They're probably foraging for food and beer.'

'That would be fantastic. And to be honest, so would some food and beer.' Sophie suddenly realised how hungry she really was.

Halfway to the door, Caitlin paused and looked at Sophie with a grave face. 'What are we going to do now? Just wait for the end?'

'I'm not the kind of person who does that,' Sophie said with a clear note of hope. It was enough to keep Caitlin happy, but if Sophie had been asked what possible course of action they could take, she would not have had an answer.

chapter five

learning the words of fools

'Desperate diseases require desperate remedies.' Guy Fawkes

Hal had spent the day filing reports: waste-collection targets; guidelines for the establishment of a Primary Healthcare Trust; monitoring of food production targets and the local economy; a request for extra funding from the local police. At times he could pretend to himself that the Fall had never happened and that the world of mundane things continued as it always had: people's lives ticking over, no lows, no highs, just maintenance of a steady state of production and consumption.

But occasionally some document would leap out at him to shatter the illusion. Perimeter-defence evaluation reports, for instance, itemising the steps being taken to ensure that no supernatural creature made it into the city to terrorise the population. And, of course, the ever-present energy-creation management report, detailing the current state of the local power grid. It was the single thing that underpinned the slow clawback from the Fall. In those early days when technology had failed in the face of the resurgent supernatural, they had all realised that electricity was the one thing that separated them as civilised beings from some relict man cowering in fear around a campfire. One light bulb was the difference between home comforts and the Dark Ages. So, with one eye on politics and one on survival, electricity had been the first thing the Government had restored when it transferred to Oxford after the Battle of London. The residents of the city had been almost pathetically grateful.

Prosperity certainly flowed to the power base. The Government had access to the national oil reserves stored in some top-secret reservoir in the south, plus experts in every field and a weight of employees to get the job done. Hal had heard how bad things were in other parts of the country; Oxford was a paradise in comparison. No wonder strict laws had been imposed to prevent inward migration from day one.

When the last file slid into place in the cabinet and the trolley was empty, Hal knew he should have felt a sense of achievement, but he didn't. It was a job he'd done all his life and at one time he'd felt happy and secure in its mundaneness, but it no longer seemed important. That simple thought instigated a panic response – if he didn't have his job, what did he have?

He jumped as the door swung open with a crash. Hunter darted in, wincing at his unintentionally noisy entrance, and closed the door quietly behind him.

'What's wrong?' Hal said with irritation.

Hunter stared at him. 'What's got your goat?'

'Nothing. It's just . . . you're stopping me working.'

Hunter glanced at the empty trolley. 'Sorry to break your concentration,' he said sarcastically, 'but we need to talk.'

Wrapped in thick parkas, they made their way past the porter's lodge and out into the High Street. Hunter led the way to the botanic gardens across the road where he knew they'd have privacy and took a seat next to the fountain. Snow blanketed everything and more flurries were blowing in as they sat. It was odd to see plants and trees in full summer greenery poking out of drifts. The tropical greenhouses rose above the red-brick garden wall, steaming in the cold.

Hunter pulled a bottle of Jack Daniel's out of his parka and took a long slug before offering it to Hal. 'It's June, Hal. Look at it. What's going on?'

'The end of the world,' Hal muttered, uninterested.

'You know what – I reckon it is.'

Hal gagged on the JD as he checked to see whether Hunter was joking.

'Back in the day, the Royals used to look out for portents, and if this weather isn't one, then I don't know what is.' Before Hal could sneer, Hunter told him what he'd seen on the helicopter ride to Scotland. 'We're being invaded,' he said finally, 'and I've got this gut feeling that whatever it is is worse than any of those so-called gods and devils and little fucking fairies that came with the Fall. When I saw those things in Scotland, I got a feeling, Hal.' He took the bottle back with undue haste, then held it tightly as though for comfort. 'They're here to wipe us out. Get rid of the infestation once for all. The balloon's gone up. Apocalypse. Armageddon.' He snapped his fingers. 'Poof!'

Hal thought for a moment and then said angrily, 'Look at us.'

'What?'

'Look at us! Why are we friends? Answer me that. I'm a clerk. I file files. You kill people—'

'Steady on, mate.'

'A crisis in my day is if a document on "taxation levels" accidentally finds its way into "L" instead of "T". Meanwhile, you're slitting some poor bastard's throat or shoving a screwdriver into his ear.'

'That would be an unfortunate use of work tools.'

'We've got nothing in common.' Hal shivered in a gust of icy wind and huddled down further into his parka.

'Why are we friends?' Hunter mused. 'Well—'

'Apart from the fact that no one else will put up with you.'

'Oh.' Hunter considered his response, then said, 'Well, we're friends because I know why you're talking about this instead of what we should be talking about. We're friends because in all the world you're the only one I can tell about slitting some poor bastard's throat and know you won't judge me. And we're friends because I'm the only one who will sit and listen to you drivelling on about filing Wanky Polemics under the Dewey Decimal System and Rat's Arse Rates under A to Z. You're a boring fucker, Hal, and no mistake. But I love you for it.'

Hal snatched the bottle back and drank more than he should have in a single draught. 'So it's all coming to an end,' he snapped. 'I'm inclined to say, so what?'

Hunter jumped to his feet and leaped on to the edge of the fountain, in danger of plunging backwards through the thin sheet of ice into the dark water beneath. 'Because this is the worst time for it to end. We've got a chance to make a fresh start. Put everything right. Build the kind of world we should have. We're newborns, Hal, and you don't sacrifice infants.'

'If it's as bad as you say, what can be done about it? The PM, the General—'

'You can't trust people in power.'

'How can you say that? You work for the Government. They pay your wages.'

'They pay me to do a job. And I do it. But they don't buy *me*. Those in power always think they're doing things for the *people*. They're not – they do things they think they would like done if *they* were the people. Do you get me? Old song: "The public wants what the public gets" – beats some old philosopher any day. And that's how the ones in power think.'

'What are you saying, Hunter?' Hal asked wearily.

'I'm saying, mate, that when push comes to shove, it might be up to us to do something.'

'Us?' Hal said incredulously.

'Us. You and me. Against the world.'

'Now I know you've gone mad.'

'Desperate times bring out the best in everyone, pal. And disaster is necessary if you want to be resurrected.'

'I don't want to be resurrected.'

'Everyone does. From the life they're living to the life they should be living.'

'So, what – you're saying I should learn how to use a gun so we can go out like Butch and Sundance?'

'I get to be Sundance. He was the good-looking one.'

'Stop it, Hunter.'

'We're going to do something, Hal, and you don't have a choice. I just haven't decided what yet.'

Hal tossed Hunter the bottle, then set off down the path towards the High Street without a backward glance.

'They said Nero was mad, too!' Hunter roared after him before laughing as if he'd just heard the funniest joke in the world.

Hal made his way along the High Street in the face of the gusting wind. Night was falling, earlier than he had anticipated. It would have been much more sensible to go back to his warm room, so perhaps he was as crazy as Hunter after all. The snow drifted against the shops and restaurants, still closed from the days before the Fall but close to coming back into use. Hal could see the occasional swept floor and fresh lick of paint, and sense an almost painfully building anticipation. Human nature was intrinsically optimistic; no one would imagine an even greater Fall coming so hard on the heels of the last one.

Hal picked his route randomly, letting his subconscious drag him this way and that, lost to his thoughts. His mind turned naturally to Samantha, as if she was the only thing in the world that truly mattered; he guessed in his world she probably was. Basically, he was pathetic, he decided; when it came to any kind of emotional life he was paralysed, stuttering like some monastic fool whenever he met a woman. Except this wasn't just any woman. Samantha made him feel special whenever he saw her. But why couldn't he express it to her? It was his parents' fault, obviously, or his teachers'; some trauma during his formative years. Or perhaps he really was pathetic.

The city looked magical under the coating of snow. The dreaming spires gleamed white against the night sky, the domes and ancient rooflines like frosted cakes. Hal stood at the crossroads where the High Street met St Aldate's and turned slowly in the deserted street. Surveying the city, he realised how much he loved it. It represented so much more than the agglomeration of bricks and mortar that shaped its fabric; its history made it a living thing; its dedication to centuries of learning made it something greater; and he couldn't help but think that in some way they were spoiling it, though he couldn't quite grasp how, or why.

As he shuffled around in the snow, raising little fountains of white every time he turned, movement caught his eye. *Something* was heading along Blue Boar Street. It was near to the ground – measured, tiny sparks of light floating in the gloom.

Hal hesitated. Thoughts of the strange, dangerous creatures that now existed beyond the city boundaries dampened his curiosity. But then a soft, lilting song floated out across the drifts, so light and organic it could have been a breeze itself. It was hypnotic, and before he knew what he was doing he had advanced to the end of the darkened side street.

The sight was stranger than anything he could have imagined. A column of tiny figures was making its way along the gutter – men, women and children little more than eight inches high, dressed in clothes that appeared to come from a range of different eras: medieval, Elizabethan, Georgian, some in Victorian top hats and long coats. Hal even made out miniature horses and minuscule dogs in the sombre procession. Some of the figures carried tiny lanterns aloft on crooked sticks to light their path as they walked and sang. A strange atmosphere hovered around them, like an invisible mist into which Hal had wandered. It felt as if he was in a dream, watching himself watching them.

The little man at the head of the column had a long, curly beard and eyes that gleamed all black as if cast in negative. He noticed Hal and held up a hand. The others came to a sudden halt. All eyes fell upon Hal.

'What are you doing here?' Hal said. It sounded as though his voice was coming from somewhere else.

'What are *you* doing here?' The little man's voice had a deep, echoing quality.

'I live here,' Hal replied. He realised that he felt drunk or drugged, for he was responding to something that was inherently absurd, yet it all made the clearest sense to him in a way that things only did when you were intoxicated.

'These are not the Fixed Lands,' the little man said, puzzled. 'These are the Far Lands. You are in Faerie, Son of Adam. Take care.'

'I don't think so,' Hal replied. The little man's face darkened and Hal decided it would be best to change the subject. 'Where are you going?'

'From here to there. And probably back again.'

'Your song is very . . . pleasant.'

This compliment pleased the little man immeasurably. 'We sing the Winnowing as we walk the boundaries of our dreams,' he said proudly. 'It is a song that came from the days when the worlds were new and we have learned it so deeply that it sings in our hearts, even when we sleep.'

'Why are you singing? Are you celebrating something?'

The little man grew horrified at this. 'Celebrating? Celebrating?' he roared so loudly that Hal took a step back. 'We sing to save the worlds! We sing to bind the weft! To keep all Existence from unravelling! For if we did not, who would? I ask you that, Son of Adam! Who would, in these dark and desperate times when all is falling apart?'

'Oh. I see,' Hal said, not seeing at all.

The little man leaned forward to peer at Hal curiously. 'Is it . . . ? Do my eyes deceive me? A Brother of Dragons?'

Hal grew instantly tense. 'I don't know what you mean,' he said, edging backwards.

'A Brother of Dragons!' The little man turned to his fellows and clapped his hands excitedly before returning his attention to Hal. 'Then you join us in the defence of the worlds. You stand on the edge of the Great Gulf to hold back the night.'

The words filled Hal with a terrible dread. 'I can't do any of that.'

The little man looked puzzled at first, and then increasingly disturbed. 'But you are a Brother of Dragons.'

'Stop saying that!' Hal snapped. 'I don't know what any of this means!'

With his heart thumping so hard that his pulse filled his head and drove out all thoughts, Hal ran from the side street, slipping and sliding through the snow, desperately searching for the life he knew.

The General sat in his office in Magdalen's president's lodgings surrounded by books describing military victories in minute detail, and sketches and paintings by war artists from down the years: the Crimean, the heat and dust of the South African veldt in the Boer War, the swamping mud of Flanders, the march into Berlin, the Belgrano going down, Kuwait with the burning oil fields in the background, Baghdad broken by cruise missiles. And there, at the end of the room facing his desk so that he would always see it, a painting of the Battle of London, four Fabulous Beasts circling, belching fire at a black tower while the capital burned in the background. The greatest defeat in a campaign of many defeats. A whole platoon wiped out by shape-shifting creatures in Scotland. The retreat from the Lake District. The Battle of Newcastle, during which the city was razed to the ground and the entire RAF obliterated.

And now this latest assault. He would defend his country with every whit at his disposal, but he couldn't help thinking that he would be the one in the long, unbroken line of British military leaders who would preside over the complete destruction of the island nation.

On his desk were photographs of his wife and daughter taken before the Fall. These days they barely knew him, their presences passing like ghosts at irregular meals, or during the occasional function when he never even got time to speak to them. Would his sacrifice ever be recognised?

There was a knock at the door and the Ministry of Defence ministerial advisor admitted Manning, Reid and the few other members of the Cabinet who were not dealing with the immediate crisis. The General didn't trust Manning – he had always been convinced that she didn't have the backbone to go the extra mile. Sooner or later she would let them all down, most likely at the worst possible time. Reid was a thoroughly dislikeable human being, but at least he was a perfect security officer. The other Cabinet members he could take or leave; weak men and women not up to the job, desperate to be somewhere else, knowing no one else would do the job if they departed. They gathered in the assembled chairs and waited silently.

'I wanted to give you the opportunity to see the available intelligence before we go into the full Cabinet meeting to brief the PM,' the General said. 'There is a lot to take in.'

'It's all gone pear-shaped,' the foreign secretary intoned.

The General set his jaw; there was a man without a job as a result of their inability to contact any other country since the Fall, and he was already preaching defeat.

'We have a situation,' the General corrected. 'An attack has been launched in the Scottish Borders. The enemy is establishing a beachhead, with the intention, we can only assume, of preparing for a full-scale invasion of the country.'

The ministerial advisor drew the curtains and took up a position at a digital projector. The General nodded and the screen hanging on the opposite wall came to life.

'This film was taken by a reconnaissance unit and transmitted back shortly before the men were wiped out.'

It was difficult to make out what was going on. Smoke billowed back and forth across the screen. It was night and there were trees all around. Occasional bursts of fire flashed here and there, and to all intents and purposes, the image looked like a vision of hell. Sharp blasts of static blared out intermittently, making some of the Cabinet members clutch their ears, and every now and then the picture was disrupted by jagged rips of white.

'What's up with the sound?' Reid asked.

'The digital signal is repeatedly interrupted whenever the main enemy is near,' the General replied. 'The research team suggests that their physical make-up may interfere in some way with technology.'

Every person in the room jumped as a figure lurched into view. Its shiny black skin looked like polished latex, flecked here and there with red, but as it approached the camera the skin ran away like oil to reveal a form constructed out of bone. But this was not its skeleton in any traditional sense. There were cow bones, a pig's jaw, human tibiae, fibulae and a rib cage, tiny bones that might have come from mice and birds, plus more indistinguishable items of animal and human origin, all topped by a horse's skull. It looked like a human figure built by a conceptual artist, but it moved swiftly and with a reptilian vitality, a purple light glowing in its empty eye sockets.

'Jesus Christ,' the chancellor said in a hushed, sickened tone.

The bone-creature moved like a rattlesnake to grab a soldier standing off-camera. There was a roar like rocks falling on metal and the soldier was whisked aloft as though he weighed nothing. Bony protuberances rose mysteriously from the creature's body before shooting out rapidly to impale the soldier. The screams were worse than the deafening bouts of static. The camera wavered, but the operator remained true to his mission.

Once the soldier was dead, the creature pulled his body close. It looked like a hug for a departed but respected enemy, yet within seconds it was clear what was really happening. The soldier's bones gradually burst through his skin to be absorbed into the body of the thing that had killed him, drawn, almost magnetically, into the depths of the form. What remained was tossed aside with a soft, squishing sound that the camera picked up with sickening detail.

The audience was rooted in horror. The General, who had viewed the footage twenty-seven times, searched their faces, seeing the same emotions he had felt himself with each subsequent viewing.

A hand with long, unnaturally thin fingers appeared in the middle of the screen. It was apparent to everyone that it was made of insects and other small, wriggling creatures. A honey bee crawled near the wrist. Beetles and flies, brown and amber centipedes, wasps and midges, all together in one seething morass.

The hand moved forward rapidly towards the camera lens; a jagged flash of white, then black.

Silence fell on the room for a long moment, then Manning asked, 'What kind of a defence can you mount against something like that?' Her question was followed by supportive mutterings.

'A robust defence, the best we have,' the General replied without revealing the anger he felt at her defeatism.

'What are you planning, General?' Reid was thoughtful, unruffled, his expensive pinstripe suit an echo of another time.

'We've mapped the terrain and the location of the enemy's force. They've made no attempt to hold a defensible position—'

'They don't care,' Manning interrupted.

The General ignored her. 'A direct assault could decimate them.'

'Conventional weapons?' Reid asked.

'For the time being. I've made no secret of my disdain for the so-called supernatural artefacts that you've been amassing since the Fall. If Mister Kirkham – or anyone, for that matter – can convince me firstly that they work and secondly of their reliability in a battlefield scenario, then I will obviously put them to good use. Until then, we utilise the tried-and-tested methods.'

'They didn't work at the Fall, so why should they work now?' The foreign secretary looked as if he was about to cry.

The General tried to keep his rising anger in check, but it was becoming difficult. 'It's a matter of application and strategy—'

'You tried a tactical nuke at Newcastle,' Reid noted.

The General gritted his teeth. 'As I said, *if* any of the so-called experts at our disposal can find an unorthodox weapon that works, I will use it. The onus remains, as it has done since the Fall, with the Ministry of New Technology.' *Or the Ministry of Magic as the squaddies contemptuously called it*, the General thought. It had proved a useless distraction from the outset; nobody could get any of the artefacts to work effectively, and it was unlikely they ever would. If they were still functional, there was a mechanics behind them that no one could grasp.

'What about the local population?' Manning asked. 'Do we need to arrange evacuation?'

'Intelligence suggests that the enemy has already wiped out all civilians in the immediate vicinity. There's a portion of Scotland to the north-west under the control of an organisation called Clan McTaff. They used to be a group who dressed up in medieval garb and the like for battle re-enactments of the fantasy kind.' The General shook his head wearily. 'Obviously they were extremely well equipped for life after the Fall.'

'What are you saying? That fantasy gamers shall inherit the earth?' Manning noted with sarcasm.

The General ignored her. 'They've established a small, sustainable community but they don't appear to be under any immediate threat. The enemy seems to be directing its attention towards the south—'

'Towards us,' Reid noted.

'A decapitation exercise would be standard practice,' the General said. 'Destroy the Government, all resistance falls apart.'

'You're ascribing them human motivations,' Manning said. 'How can you even begin to guess what they're planning?' Her eyes were cold, hard and distrustful.

The General remained calm. 'Leave the military planning to me, Ms Manning. You concentrate on doing whatever it is you do best.' He checked his watch. 'Now, I think the PM is waiting for my assessment. I hope I can count on your full support.'

'What else can we do?' the foreign secretary said resignedly. 'Bang the drums loudly. And off we go to war.'

Mallory's whole body ached from the wounds he had sustained on Cadbury Hill and then from his rough treatment at the hands of his captors. But he had experienced worse, particularly in the grim days during his training as a Knight Templar at Salisbury Cathedral when the Church authorities had decided he was a troublemaker who couldn't be trusted to keep the Faith. He'd survived then and he'd do so now. Life had hardened him since his younger days, the times to which his subconscious would never allow him to return. Before, the death of the woman he loved would have left him broken and pathetic; now his grief was an icy foundation deep inside him. On it he piled cold hatred and bitter thoughts of revenge, building a temple through which he would find an exit.

But even there, in his bleak cell, the miserable, haunting image wouldn't leave him alone. A burst of fire in the darkness, like the breath of a Fabulous Beast. It would break into his mind unbidden, stirring the deepest recesses of his memory where all the nasty things lay hidden. A notification of his death, now tied inextricably to the death of Sophie. Death was all around him, all the time.

The emotions around the memory had grown even more intense, as if Sophie had helped him to keep them in check, and now that she was gone the door had been thrown open wide. Sometimes he would pummel the side of his head to try to drive the desperate thoughts away, or bite his lip until the blood ran.

And sometimes in his weaker moments he felt as though he was falling apart. A hard focus on revenge for Sophie's murder was all he had to cling to.

The room was spartan: a chair, a chemical toilet, a cheap collapsible bed. He guessed it had been an office once, before the powers that be had turned it into a holding cell. There were others nearby; every morning and night he could hear his jailers moving along the corridor, silently distributing food. Yet the sounds that came from the other cells disturbed him immensely: inhuman shrieks and cries, an alien cacophony. He was in prison with beasts. Was that how his captors perceived him?

The chains on his wrists suggested so, though they'd only been put on after he'd attempted to kick the door down and then head-butted a guard. Some people had no sense of humour.

Mallory's face hardened at the sound of drawing bolts. The door swung open to reveal the man who had led the team that had captured him, the most unlikely leader of a security force that Mallory could imagine. He'd heard the guards mention his name – Hunter – but they all spoke of him with a respect bordering on fear, despite his dandyish appearance.

'Here for the torture?' Mallory said.

'We don't do torture as a rule, but keep asking – you might convince me to make an exception.' Hunter closed the door with a surreptitious glance into the corridor. 'Unofficial visit. Stand at ease.'

Mallory clanked the manacles attached to his ankles. 'Quite the comedian.'

'I like to keep the prisoners entertained. Raises morale.' Hunter spun the chair around and sat on it backwards.

'You know I'm not going to answer any questions – with or without torture.'

'Fair enough. Then you die with us.'

Mallory eyed Hunter obliquely, but couldn't read the truth – or otherwise – of the statement.

Hunter stared at his boots for a second or two, then said, 'I'm sorry about your girlfriend. I mean that. She shouldn't have died. The wanker who did it has been punished. Severely. I know that won't make it right, but I reckon that to the kind of bloke you seem to be, it will mean something.'

'And how are you getting punished? You were his leader. I thought that's where the buck's supposed to stop.' The cold anger in Mallory's voice made Hunter look up sharply.

The two of them stared at each other, measuring, judging. Mallory saw some of himself in Hunter, but that didn't lessen his feelings.

'Don't come here talking about Sophie,' Mallory said eventually. 'It'll only make me want to kill you quicker.'

'All right, I won't talk about her. But I meant what I said.'

'You know what, I'm sick of authorities messing with my life. Back in Salisbury it was the Church. Here it's little boy soldiers who still think the rule of Government means something. Have a look at the world out there: it's chaos, everywhere. You're just playing at this, pretending it's still like it was before the Fall, while reality passes you by.' Mallory felt his repressed emotions about Sophie fighting for release. He forced himself to remain calm. 'Why have you gone to all this trouble to bring me here? I'm a nobody. You're just wasting resources—'

'You're not a nobody. You're one of the most important people in Britain at the moment.'

Mallory grew still; he could see the seriousness in Hunter's eyes.

'Do you know what I mean?' Hunter pressed.

When Mallory said nothing, Hunter stood up to face Mallory on his level, cracked his knuckles, then proceeded to pace while he spoke. 'I've just come back from Scotland. We've been invaded. I don't know what they are, but they're worse than all the things that came with the Fall. A friend of mine, he was warned by some kind of Higher Power. It told him we'd been *noticed.*'

Mallory flinched. Hunter saw it from the corner of his eye and struck like a rattlesnake. 'You've heard it, too.'

Mallory considered not replying, but it was pointless. 'I met one of the gods on my travels. She said the very same words. We've been noticed. Something is rising up from the edge of the universe to destroy us.'

'Well, it's here. Or at least the advance guard are. I saw them. Things don't look too good.'

'You want the honest truth? Now that Sophie's gone I don't really care. Maybe it would be better if the whole human race was wiped out. Even after we've been taught a nasty lesson by nature, we're still venal, malicious, hypocritical, back-stabbing, selfish killers.'

'That's just me. Don't judge everybody by the same yardstick.' Hunter quickly realised that his feeble attempts at humour weren't working and changed tack. 'OK, you say that now, but I reckon that deep down you don't believe it. I'm a good judge of character, have to be in my job – life or death decisions, see? Not like meeting someone in a pub. And I say you're decent. Someone who'd do the right thing in any situation. And what proves me correct is that you're a Brother of Dragons. Whatever power put you in that exclusive club is going to go for good men and women. Not a little bit good. The best. Heroes. That's quite a pedigree, and I'd say it's a huge burden to shoulder, but you'll live up to it or you wouldn't have been chosen in the first place. See – circular logic when you say it like that.'

Mallory lay down on the bed and closed his eyes. Suddenly he felt weary. Obligation. Responsibility. That's all it had been for so long. He wanted a rest.

'Another thing,' Hunter continued. 'This thing that's *noticed* us . . . I reckon it's the reason you exist. The Brothers and Sisters of Dragons, defenders of humanity, were created to stop this thing that wants to eradicate us. Make sense?'

'Here's a little irony,' Mallory said. 'There are rules of Existence you don't even know about. Patterns. Things have to be in place for everything to work, like some big magic ritual. And for the Brothers and Sisters of Dragons to do their business, there has to be five of us. And you've killed one. So congratulations. When they take stock of who doomed the human race, your name will be at the top of the list.'

'So what are you saying? If there aren't five of you, it's all over?' Mallory could see Hunter's mind whirring. 'What about the last five? The ones who fought at the Fall?'

'You know the stories – two of them are dead—'

'But three of them are still around somewhere.'

'I don't think it works like that.' Mallory was going to say more, but he could see that Hunter was no longer listening to him. After a moment, Mallory continued, 'So all this, Sophie's death, it's all about the Brothers and Sisters of Dragons. Because you short-sighted, meat-headed, pig-ignorant politicians and soldiers think you need to control us to get us to do the job charged to us by some authority much higher than you.'

Mallory had clearly struck a nerve. 'There's been a lot of stupidity done in the name of politics. Don't expect any better of this regime,' Hunter said.

As Hunter stood up to leave, something struck Mallory forcibly. 'What's going on here?' he asked. 'This chat wasn't sanctioned, was it? If you'd been sent here by your superiors, you wouldn't have come alone. There'd at least have been someone taking notes.'

'You're not as dumb as you look.' Hunter smiled, giving nothing away, and slipped quietly out of the door.

Hunter raced through the empty halls. He found Hal drinking whisky alone in his room, staring out through the frosted panes at the snow-swept college grounds.

'Everyone's looking for you,' Hal said, his words slurred. 'The troops are shipping out tonight.'

'Never mind about that.' Hunter snatched the whisky bottle from Hal and took a long draught. 'I've got a job for you while I'm gone.'

'What? Refile your CD collection?'

'Stop feeling sorry for yourself. You're not the one going to his death.'

'Don't say that!'

Hunter was taken aback by Hal's unusual passion. 'I want you to use all the many – and I'm sure there *are* many – skills at your disposal to find out what you can about the Brothers and Sisters of Dragons—'

'What?' Hal's face looked unnaturally white in the candlelight.

'Old members, new members. There's supposed to be five of them. We've identified two. See if you can dig up any secret files—'

Hal shook his head. 'I'll never be able to do it.' It was a lie: Samantha had already offered to help.

'Don't be so defeatist. I know I love drama, but this is for real: it's life or death. I'm counting on you, Hal.' Hunter's eyes narrowed; he could see something in his friend's face. 'What is it you're not telling me?'

'Nothing.' Hal looked back out of the window.

'If you know anything about these people, now's not the time to keep it from me—'

'I don't know anything,' Hal replied firmly. 'I just don't think you're going to have much luck finding the other three. Needles in a very big haystack.'

For the first time, Hunter felt a barrier between himself and the man who had been his only real friend for the last few years. He was surprised how sad it made him feel.

'Come on, you'd better see me off,' Hunter said. 'I don't want you developing a Wilfred Owen complex later, so best get all the tears out of your system now.'

They made their way out of the college buildings in silence. The troops were preparing for dust-off in the Deer Park behind Magdalen, the stink of oil and gasoline on the night wind powerfully evocative in a way they would never have imagined a few years ago, when it was commonplace. There were twenty troop choppers lined up on the makeshift airfield, the snowy perimeter marked by flares and burning oil drums.

'Not much of an army,' Hal said.

'This is just the top brass and intelligence.' Hunter mentally checked off his ammunition and felt the weight of the pistol at his hip. 'We had troops stationed in Rochdale and Barnsley and they've already been mobilised. Should have made camp by now.'

'You think you've got enough men?' They both knew the fatality figures during the Fall and there'd been numerous problems with recruitment since.

'We have what we have. They're well armed.'

'I don't know how you can be so optimistic, Hunter.'

'Nobody ever achieved anything by aiming low.'

The General marched past with his coterie, heading towards the nearest chopper, then paused and came back to Hunter. 'We're counting on you.'

'I know.'

The General met his eyes for a moment, and Hunter was pleased at the degree of defiance the General saw there.

'What was that all about?' Hal asked when the General had disappeared into the chopper.

'I'm going to be leading a small team behind enemy lines once they start the frontal assault. Cut a few hamstrings, that kind of thing.'

'You're mad. That's suicide.'

'It's my job. I can't start moaning about it when it gets tough.' He shrugged. 'Actually, it's the job of the Brothers and Sisters of Dragons, but in their absence it looks like it comes down to me. Chief substitute for the saviours of the universe. I suppose that's something.' Hunter thought Hal was going to cry.

Before Hunter could ask what was wrong, he heard the crunch of footsteps in the snow behind him. He turned to see Samantha, buried in a massive fur-trimmed parka, her arms wrapped across her chest. She paused uncomfortably before him.

'You look even more gorgeous than usual in that,' Hunter said. It wasn't a line: the oversize parka made her features more fragile and beautiful and emphasised the intelligence in her pale eyes.

Hunter expected to feel the sharpness of her tongue, but all she said was, 'I heard what was happening.'

'You can't keep anything a secret around here.'

Samantha visibly steeled herself, then grabbed Hunter's head and planted her lips on his. They felt full and hot, and he was suddenly aware of a depth of emotion coming up through her skin like the heat from a fire. When she broke off, she stared deeply into his eyes for the briefest moment, but it was enough to underline everything he had sensed in her kiss.

'You'd better come back, Hunter.' She spun round and marched away towards the buildings.

For the first time in his life, Hunter was lost for words.

'She didn't even know I was here,' Hal said, but Hunter was distracted by the jumbled thoughts rolling through his mind as he watched Samantha's form become obscured by the swirling snow.

'Bloody hell. I think she likes me,' he said, amazed.

The choppers' engines fired up one after another, the whirling blades raising a snowstorm around them. Hunter ducked down, covering his face with one arm, and clapped Hal on the shoulder; his friend appeared dazed.

'Don't worry, mate. How can I not come back after that?' Hal stared at him, troubled and distracted. 'Don't worry, I'm not going to hug you.'

'Take care, Hunter.' Hal forced a smile, then ran for the cover of the college buildings.

Hunter hurried, keeping low, to climb into the second chopper, his heart racing. He felt strangely out of sorts, excited yet unsettled by the discovery of some so far unconsidered part of himself. As the chopper rose on the unsteady currents, he stared down at the snow-swept field, then at Magdalen as it dropped away below him and finally at the disappearing city. He could still taste her on his lips.

chapter six

the politics of war

'It can only be done by blood and iron.' Otto von Bismarck

The army had dug in along a ridge of hills south-east of Moffat in the Scottish Borders, but they were barely prepared for the near-arctic conditions. The ground was as hard as iron, frozen to a depth of at least twelve inches underfoot, and the wind that blew from the north felt harsh enough to take the skin from their faces. Overnight the temperature plummeted to minus ten, worse with the wind-chill factor.

'Bloody hell, Hunter. This is a nightmare.' Clevis stamped his feet and clapped his hands as he circled the campfire, little more than the tip of his broken nose visible in the depths of his hood.

Hunter looked out over the tent city and the constellation of campfires spread across the hillsides, each one trailing a thick line of black smoke up to the colour-leached dawn sky. 'You know what I'm thinking? This is a new Ice Age.'

'It's not bloody fair. We'd barely got over the Fall when the plague came along. And now this.' Clevis sounded petulant, but he was barely seventeen, hardly trained, emotionally immature. And Hunter had to take him on a potential suicide mission. Clevis shouldn't have been there at all, but with forces so badly depleted they had to make do in many different areas, even if that meant sending a barely trained youth on a Special Forces operation. They needed the numbers to make the plan work and Hunter just had to hope that the others would cover for the lad. Clevis really didn't know how unfair it was, but Hunter did, and that knowledge troubled him deeply. He liked Clevis; for all his faults, the boy was decent-hearted and truly believed in the cause for which he was fighting.

As Hunter surveyed the snowy wastes stretching away towards the sooty streak of black on the horizon that signified the enemy's location, he realised that Clevis was staring at him. 'I've told you not to do that.'

'Sorry.' Clevis wiped the back of his hand across his dripping nose. 'It's just, I was thinking—'

'Well, don't.'

'How many men have you killed, Captain?'

One hundred and sixty seven.

'I can't remember.'

Every face locked in place, eye colour, hair colour, method of dispatch.

'It's a dirty business, Clevis, but we do it so other people don't have to.'

He would never forget any of them.

'What's it like?' Clevis asked hesitantly. 'I mean, when you actually . . . do it?'

'Stop asking impertinent questions. We've got a job to do.' He prayed that Clevis could escape any killing. The act was like a worm in an apple, getting fatter by the day with each mouthful it devoured. Nobody was immune. Hunter consoled himself with the knowledge that Clevis would probably be dead before he had the chance to raise his weapon.

'We begin Operation Clear Skies at oh-seven-hundred hours.' The General rested his two meaty fists on the trestle table in the conference tent and surveyed Hunter's team. 'By that time, you will be deep in the heart of enemy territory. Your mission is to cause as much disruption to the enemy's lines as possible. Chaos and confusion are the order of the day. Let them know we are not weak. That we are not going to roll over and die. By the end of this day, I want them reconsidering their decision to invade.'

Hunter cast a surreptitious glance across his team. Apart from Clevis, there were four others, all hard men, all aware of what potentially lay ahead for them. Bradley was from Kent, a scar running down his left cheek like an exclamation mark, the result of an Iraqi bayonet. Next to him, Coop was slight but more focused than anyone Hunter knew; he was from Birmingham, but with strong Jamaican roots. Spencer was a hard man, and silent, Ormston a sneaky little shit who was surprisingly reliable in a crisis, both of them from some Godforsaken industrial town or other in the north. They rarely spoke about their pasts; the present, for all its misery, was clearly so much more appetising.

It was Ormston who raised his hand to speak first. 'Excuse me, sir, but do you have any idea what might be waiting for us over the hill? I heard there was a film—?'

'Very poor quality. You wouldn't learn anything from it that would help you,' the General lied. Even Hunter hadn't seen the video, but he knew exactly why it was being kept from them: no one would venture over that hill if they knew what horrors were waiting for them. But wasn't that the case in any war?

'The frontal assault will give them hell,' the General said. 'You have my word on that. We're throwing everything at them, every weapon at our disposal apart from nukes.' He hesitated; such weapons were clearly still an option for another time. 'The strategy is for massive shock, devastate their forces within the first twenty-four hours.'

Hunter fought the urge to smile. If wishes were fishes they'd need a sea of batter.

'God be with you,' the General said. 'Go into the fray with good heart. It is a just fight, for the future of our country and our people.'

The General nodded and Hunter led his men out. They made their way in silence across the camp site until Bradley stopped suddenly and exclaimed, 'Bleedin' 'ell. Look at that.'

The sky behind them was black. At first, Hunter thought it was a whirlwind of dust, but as it drew closer he could see irregular edges and rapid movement within the body of the darkness.

'Birds,' Spencer said flatly.

'Crows.' Coop looked at the approaching cloud uneasily.

'Now that ain't natural,' Bradley said in hushed tones.

The crows' actions became even more unnatural as they neared. Initially, their cawing was discordant in the early morning peace, but gradually they fell eerily silent. They descended in a wild flapping cloud over the hillside behind the camp, settling on trees, hedges, fences, filling the fields so that the snow was obscured by an oily blackness; it looked to Hunter like some horrible pollution was running down the slope towards them.

Once they had landed, the crows fell still. It looked to all the men as though the birds were watching the camp with their gleaming eyes, waiting. Hunter knew the symbolism and wasn't about to say anything, but Coop spoke up. 'They used to say that crows gathered before battles, waiting to feed on the dead, as if they knew exactly what was going to happen.'

'Yeah, but look how many of them there are!' Ormston said. 'They must be expecting a right bloody feast!' He laughed loudly at what he thought was a great joke, but he was the only one and eventually his humour drained away until there was only the soft whisper of the wind across the snow; and the men watching the crows; and the crows watching the men.

The chopper swung in low over the snowy wastes before hovering over the dust-off point. Hunter and the rest jumped the remaining six feet into the heart of the blizzard raised by the whirling blades. They were already under the cover of nearby trees as the deafening drone of the helicopter receded behind them.

Polar fatigues helped them blend in as they moved swiftly and silently along the hedge lines to a deserted farmhouse overlooking the enemy encampment. Hunter made his way quickly to a bedroom that still smelled of its former occupants and found a window that allowed him the best view with the hi-res binoculars. But he only needed his eyes to learn the true meaning of 'encampment'. The enemy filled an entire valley, lining the floor and the hillsides for a good ten miles, packed so closely that not a single square of white was visible. The scene was unspeakably eerie, for there was none of the back-and-forth movement that Hunter would have expected in a camp; the enemy stood stock-still to a man, resembling a Chinese terracotta army, all facing the direction where the Government troops were preparing for the attack. The chilling scene suggested that the enemy were machines that did not need to move or talk or eat or feel any emotion; they were simply waiting for the moment when they would be unleashed to crush anything in their path.

Clevis slipped in next to Hunter and froze the moment he looked out of the window. 'Jesus Christ. We don't stand a chance.'

Hunter used the binoculars to get a better look at the enemy. The ranks comprised many different types, many different species: tall, willowy men stood next to squat, brutish troglodytes; things with a hint of the reptilian next to others that were almost as insubstantial as ghosts. But all of them looked as if they had died and been remade: weapons had been embedded into their bodies, swords emerging from forearms, nests of spears protruding from ribcages, exposed bone visible everywhere. And there was an odd purple mist drifting from their eyes and mouths. Even more disturbingly, some of the enemy were human. They looked very much as though they might once have been the residents of the area, now transformed like all the others.

Hunter could feel Clevis shaking next to him. Without looking, Hunter said, 'On the positive side, I can only see swords and . . . pikes? A few axes, spears . . .'

'See?' Ormston brayed. '*They* don't stand a chance.'

Hunter pushed past them to carry out a weapons check and prep them for what was to come. They had small arms and SA80s, but their most effective response was the small but devastating plasma explosives they carried in their backpacks. Each one would take out fifty of the enemy at least – a drop in the ocean compared to the thousands that lined the valley, but if the explosives were used effectively they could make their mark.

Coop took out his cross and chain and kissed it before slipping it back into his parka. The rest of them looked to Hunter, still and silent with their thoughts. He checked out of the window one more time, then gave the nod.

Ground zero was hell. Shells rained in from the distant batteries with barely a second between each explosion. Thick black smoke mingled with the strange purple mist, blasting back and forth in huge, billowing clouds. The noise was as deafening as a foundry and the ground vibrated as if a permanent earthquake ripped through the strata. Body parts flew everywhere.

The detailed briefing had told Hunter and his team exactly where the shells would fall. Their safe route was prescribed through thick tree cover, but they were still close enough to the carnage to view the sea of arms, legs and heads spread out across the fields. Earplugs protected them from the worst of the noise, but it still felt as if their heads were full of a swarm of bees; Hunter gave his orders via previously arranged hand signals. Occasionally, they would lose sight of each other in the sweeping smoke, and at those times it felt as though they were already dead, walking through some eerie purgatory towards judgment.

Hunter's mind had the calm of a pool at twilight. He existed wholly in the moment, seeing, hearing, reacting, but not feeling. In that state, he gave himself up to the shadow-figure that rode the mare of his conscious mind, the true Hunter who had made him so good at being fearless, emotionless, inhuman in battle. The Hunter he hated.

The trees and the snow and the mist reminded him of the hills of Bosnia, the stink of the mass graves heavy in the air as he hunted Serb mercenaries. The thunder of the shells was Baghdad all over again, slipping in and out of the shadows of the sun-baked souk.

How had he ever got into it? He'd wanted to be a zoologist. Animals, that's what he lived for, endlessly fascinating, nature's little wonders, from the aphid to the zebra and all points in between. There wasn't a single wrong turn he could identify; it was the cumulation of a thousand tiny steps, each one insignificant in and of itself but all leading him away from the magic path into the deep, dark forest. To this place, where body parts crunched underfoot.

He led the way through the trees into a culvert under a road, then along the path of a trickling brook to a point where a sword of thick forest plunged deep into the heart of the enemy forces. With skill, they could move through the trees unseen, releasing their explosives into the midst of the opposition.

Their hot breath turned the air white as they gathered in the dense vegetation beneath the shadows of the branches. Hunter checked his watch: nearly time. The fields ran away from the forest down a slope to a road winding along the valley bottom. When the smoke and purple mist cleared in a gust of wind channelled along the cut, Hunter saw the enemy still standing, their ranks now mottled by circular blast marks. He could feel the unspoken questions radiating from the men around him: *Why don't they run? Why don't they attack? Why are they waiting to die?*

Hunter looked at his watch again and then signalled to the others. Quickly donning masks attached to portable oxygen canisters, they dropped low. Though they were beyond the estimated blast area, they still had to be cautious.

The shelling stopped. In the disturbing silence that followed, Hunter's ears still rang, but he removed his plugs to listen for the drone of the approaching jet. It was a Tornado GR4, one of the few they still had left after Newcastle. When it was overhead, Hunter shielded his eyes.

The fuel/air explosive was detonated fifty feet above the valley. Those immediately beneath the blast were vaporised instantly, others nearby seared by the tremendous heat. Hunter and his team were far enough away that the shock wave didn't burst their eardrums or rupture their lungs. The oxygen was sucked out of the air in the immediate vicinity of the explosion, which would have been devastating for human troops, but Hunter doubted its effectiveness on this enemy. He was proved right when the thermal winds cleared and he looked up. On the periphery of the blast zone, the enemy still stood, waiting, but there was now a massive hole in the heart of the force where flames raged out of control.

Clevis and Ormston high-fived before restraining themselves, but Bradley, Spencer and Coop were already coolly removing the explosives from their knapsacks. Equipped with what were essentially hi-tech catapults for launching the plasma bombs, they moved like ghosts through the trees. One after the other, they emerged to fire and then retreated back into the forest depths before they were seen.

Scores of the enemy fell with each blast. There was none of the panic and chaos that the General had hoped to engender, but at least they were cutting swathes out of the enemy lines.

The team continued with the guerrilla attacks for ten full minutes, but as the blast from one of Clevis's launches died away, Hunter saw that a change had taken place. The enemy were moving – but not slowly, not like robots coming alive in some fifties science fiction movie. In the blink of an eye, they were suddenly in rapid motion up the other side of the valley, weapons ready, but still eerily silent.

Hunter was convinced that he and his men had not been seen, but some of the enemy had now turned to the trees where they were hiding. He had the creepy feeling that the enemy didn't need to see, that they had abilities far beyond anything anyone had imagined.

'There's something back here – in the trees.' Coop's voice had the first faint tremors of uneasiness.

There was no time to respond: the enemy moved forward too quickly. Hunter faced an attacker resembling some over-muscled barbarian from a Schwarzenegger film, naked to the waist where a blood-stained animal fur hung. He wore a twin-horned Viking helmet on top of a matted mane of red hair and a long fiery beard. Half of his face was exposed skull, and more bone could be seen protruding from his meaty forearms and muscular thighs. Both hands were welded together around an enormous broadsword, bone and flesh merging directly into the metal. Purple mist streamed from his eyes and mouth, as if a fire raged within him.

The closer the barbarian got, the more Hunter felt despair welling up inside him. He realised instinctively that it was another weapon, subtly inflicting psychological damage. And it was effective: he had to fight hard to stop himself giving in to its damp pull.

Hunter switched to his SA8o. The bullets cut a swathe across the attacker's torso, but didn't slow him for even an instant. The barbarian's shadow engulfed him, and then the broadsword came crashing down. Hunter had a second to grip the gun with both hands and hold it ahead of him to block the sword. He knew it was futile, but although the gun shattered, it did just enough to deflect the sword from splitting his skull in two.

Instead, the blade ripped flesh as it slid down his arm before slamming against his shoulder blade. Hunter was driven to his knees in pain, but he used it to focus his mind. As the barbarian came at him again, Hunter ripped open his knapsack, pulled out one of his few remaining explosives and hurled it. It was stupid to release it so close to him, but it was a last resort.

The explosive hit the barbarian in the middle of his stomach and he dissolved in a mist of meat and bone. Hunter was thrown backwards ten feet, and when he clawed his way back to vertical his head was ringing. He muttered, 'Take that, you bastard.'

There was no time to glean even a glimmer of satisfaction. Ranks of purple-misted enemy moved towards the forest, bristling with weapons and filled with a mute, mechanistic savagery. But as Hunter ran back into the cover of the trees, he saw a sight that hit hard. On the tree line, Bradley stopped firing his SA80 and let the weapon fall slowly to his side. In his face was a dismal acceptance of the worst that life had to offer. Hunter knew he had succumbed to the waves of despair that washed off the enemy. A tremble ran through Bradley; the gun fell from his hand.

Hunter yelled a warning, but Bradley was transfixed by a tall, thin figure, almost majestic with its golden skin and long hair blowing in the breeze. The god languorously raised a hand with an arrow protruding from the wrist bone, and then drove it into Bradley's throat.

Hunter was horrified to see that Bradley even bared his throat slightly for the killing blow. Blood spouted from the wound and bubbled from Bradley's mouth as he choked and bucked and went down on his knees. The enemy withdrew the arrow with a ripping sound, then grabbed Bradley's head and twisted sharply.

Still holding Bradley's sagging head, his killer leaned forward, mouth wide, and exhaled forcefully. Purple mist rushed out of him and with a life of its own flowed into Bradley, into his eyes, his ears, his nostrils, his mouth. Within a second, Bradley began to mutate. Bones shattered and twisted, breaking through his flesh. Though dead, Bradley reached out one twitching hand to grasp his SA80. When his fingers closed around the handle, his skin and bone flowed like oil, merging with the weapon.

Seconds after he had died, Bradley was standing next to the god that had killed him, moving with the same mechanical tread into the forest to search for his former comrades.

Hunter searched through the trees for the others, cursing to himself. How could you hope to defeat a force that could turn even your own fallen to their ends? The more they killed, the stronger they got; they didn't feel, they didn't think; their only purpose was to destroy.

Hunter needed to get this information back to the General, but as he sprinted through the trees, Ormston staggered into his path. The transformation that had overcome him was unnerving: his face was drained of all blood, and his constant shivering revealed a man terrified of his own shadow. 'They've got Clevis,' he said with a voice like a bird in flight.

All Hunter's training told him he should not be distracted from getting the vital intelligence back to his commanding officer, but he couldn't get Clevis's frightened face out of his mind; the boy still had an innocence that Hunter barely remembered, but knew was worth saving.

'Show me,' he said.

Ormston looked sickened at the prospect. Instead, he pointed back through the trees and then zigzagged away frantically. Hunter knew Ormston wouldn't get far in his state of panic.

Behind him, the enemy crashed through the thick vegetation at the forest's edge. Drawing a knife from his boot, Hunter moved stealthily away from them in the direction Ormston had indicated. He soon spotted movement deep in the shadows amongst the pines. With his breath clouding in the freezing air, he hid behind a tree to steady himself before proceeding on his belly through a thick carpet of fern. Some kind of strange structure stood nearby.

Raising himself up slightly to get a better look, Hunter saw something that looked like a doorway constructed out of meat, yet it seemed to have grown out of the spongy vegetable matter of the forest floor. When he looked through it, he was shocked to see stars gleaming in alien constellations, planets circling seething suns that had never been glimpsed by human eyes.

He recoiled sharply. It felt as though something was looking back at him, peeling his flesh and bone aside to get deep into the core of his mind. The sensation made his skin crawl. Looking around, he saw other similar gates situated randomly at other points in the immediate vicinity.

A cry rang out – he recognised the voice as Clevis's. Hunter moved as quickly as he could without revealing himself and came upon a scene that was even more shocking than anything he had yet seen.

A thing completely constructed out of bone was clutching Spencer, who flailed wildly. His skeleton was being drawn out of him, easing through skin and muscle as if they had the substance of water. A pile of shapeless black skin lay nearby, which Hunter took to be the remains of Coop, and within a few seconds Spencer's pink skin landed next to it with a sickening plop.

With a disgusting flourish, the bone-thing absorbed Spencer's red-stained skeleton into its own mass. When it had finished,

Hunter could see Spencer's vacant orbits staring hollowly out of the centre of the monster's chest.

The bone-thing, which was larger and more terrifying than any of the enemy Hunter had witnessed so far, was not alone in the gloom of the forest. Other equally imposing figures stalked around the area in ritualistic patterns, as though they were drawing invisible lines on the ground. Hunter saw something that was alive with forest birds, their flapping, twitching bodies forming a kind of skin. Another figure was made out of snakes, frogs, newts and other lizards and amphibians, green and slick, catching the light as it moved. The third had larger woodland animals wrapped into its frame, rabbits, foxes, mice, squirrels wriggling as if they were trying to break free from an invisible cage. And it was this one that dragged Clevis behind it as though he was a spoiled child refusing to go to school.

Hunter had a split second to weigh the situation. He was smart enough to know that any attempt to save Clevis was hopeless, yet even so he leaped towards the animal-thing with a wish and prayer. His only hope was that the fury of his attack would allow Clevis to break free and that in the confusion they could both escape into the undergrowth. But when he plunged his blade into the depths of the snapping, snarling mass of fur to no effect, he knew the game was up.

The animal-thing turned towards him and stared with eyes made up of the multiple orbs of the creatures it possessed, and then reached mouse-fingers for Hunter's face.

'Hunter!' Clevis cried tearfully. 'Get me out of here!'

Hunter wrenched his knife free and staggered backwards. A buzzing arose behind him.

The animal-thing saw Hunter's interest in Clevis and dragged the youth forward. There was no sadistic glee or malice; it acted with the neutrality of someone brushing away a minor distraction, dragging Clevis in tight against its chest where the fox and badger heads snapped and tore at his flesh. Clevis's cries were muffled by the fur, but Hunter could see his eyes swivel towards him, pleading.

Hunter attempted another attack, but the buzzing was all around him now, and before he could move he felt a seething at his neck that grew tighter and held him fast. He could only watch as Clevis's features were torn apart, his lifeless body leaving a red smear as it slid down the animal-thing's torso to the ground.

Choking, Hunter was lifted effortlessly off the ground and turned around. The source of the buzzing was now apparent. The thing that held him was made of insects, in the same way that the others had used other kinds of natural matter to give them corporeal form. The insect-thing withdrew its grip, but Hunter was still magically suspended in the air.

It stood before him, eight feet tall at least. As it surveyed him, once again there was no recognisable emotion, not even curiosity. Hunter had trouble focusing on the creature, for its body was such a writhing mass of insects that its outline appeared permanently blurred through movement: bees, flies, wasps, gnats, beetles, roaches, all these and more crawled and wriggled, burrowing or attempting to take flight without ever being able to leave the creature's gravity.

Hunter stared into its insectile eyes and got the same feeling he had experienced staring through the meat-doorway: an alien intelligence travelling back along his line of vision to examine his own mind forensically.

The insect-thing held out one hand, palm upwards, and a swarm of insects rose off it, sweeping towards Hunter. He closed his eyes, turned his head away, but they enveloped his head, forcing their way into his nostrils and through his clenched lips. The buzzing filled him, followed by the sickening sensation of crawling creatures working their way into his nasal passages.

He fought the urge to choke and vomit, and then suddenly all sensation was lost. His consciousness was circumscribed by the insectile buzzing, inside him, outside, everywhere.

And then he wasn't there at all.

Insects crawled around the edges of his vision, but he knew that it was not his eyes but his mind that was examining the fractured hallucinatory images he could see. It took a second or two for him to realise that the creature was attempting some form of communication, but it was so inhuman that there was no frame of reference. The images shattered, twisted out of shape, moved from incomprehensible alien forms to pictures he could almost recognise. It felt as if he was tuning across the wavelengths to find a channel he could understand.

The process came to a halt with an image of a wasp as big as a bus nestled in a strange, irregular landscape that appeared to be made out of the same kind of meat as the doorways. It buzzed up and down the scale, insistently, distractedly, but the meaning was lost to him.

Yet some form of comprehension began to grow deep in his subconscious. A power as big as the universe had become aware of humanity. Its nature, if that was the right word, was to oppose life, not only in its form, but also in its essence: what it meant in terms of positivity, advancement, connectivity, hope, goodness – all the things that on his better days Hunter dreamed life really was about.

This power, this Anti-Life, was a gulf of nothingness that went on for ever, yet could be constrained on the head of a pin. Trying to comprehend what it really was made Hunter feel sick. He forced his thoughts to move on, but before he left the subject he realised its motivation: the eradication of everything it was not. The Anti-Life could not rest until humanity was gone or circumscribed. A name came and went, not from the thing itself, but from somewhere without: the Void.

And so it had come to Earth, acting through agents and generals and outriders who prepared the way for its ultimate ascension. Again, Hunter discovered names that existed somewhere, but did not come from the Void itself. The zombie-things that leaked purple mist were called the Lament-Brood.

The five creatures he had come across in the forest were the Void's generals, leading the charge against humanity. They had no form in and of themselves; they were *ideas*, nothing more, clothing themselves in the matter of the physical world, negativity given shape and identity. The Lord of Bones, the Lord of Birds, the Lord of Lizards, the Lord of Flesh. And above them all, the force that would see humanity wiped away – the King of Insects.

Hunter was not a religious man, but childhood images of Satan haunted him; here, he felt, was true evil: dispassionate, relentless, capable of causing death on a grand scale, without any meaning at all. A quote came to him from a Sunday School class: Revelation 19:19 – 'Then I saw the beast and the kings of the earth and their armies gathered together to make war against the rider on the horse and his army.'

The giant wasp's message was clear: there was no hope, it really was all over and the world was about to be remade in the image of Anti-Life. Hunter tried to imagine what that would be like, but all he kept coming back to were those self-same childhood lessons, with their talk of hell and burning souls.

The wasp was so huge that it could not take flight and so it pulled itself forward obscenely on its spindly legs, until its head filled Hunter's vision and he could see himself reflected a thousand times in its multifaceted eyes. The wasp opened its maw wide, trailing strands of sticky acids, and lunged. The stinking, wet dark closed about Hunter hard and he was sucked in and down.

And then he was hovering in the air once more before the King of Insects, wasps and flies crawling all over his skin, across his eyes and lips, skittering legs and wings setting his nerve endings afire as revulsion filled him. It felt as if his time had come and he was pleased at how calm he felt. Those who kill for a living think about death a great deal. He had once seen a man plead, sobbing, offering to give up his girlfriend in his place, even though he knew it would do no good. Hunter had always hoped he would be brave enough to go with dignity.

But instead of delivering the killing blow, the King of Insects twisted its outstretched hand and then snapped it shut. Hunter felt a squirming in his belly, rising up his spine, growing faster until it reached the back of his head, and then he shot out of himself as if strapped to a rocket.

Hovering somehow amongst the tree branches, he looked down to see his body still hanging in the air before the King of Insects. A second later, an irresistible urge drove him up through the trees and into the grey sky. Hunter felt simultaneously detached and queasy, as though he was in a dream on the verge of turning into a nightmare. Far below in the blasted valley, hundreds of scattered enemy corpses formed fractal patterns in the thick snow. Gliding forward over the next ridge, he caught the familiar wisps of purple mist drifting in the wind. It had just started to snow again, adding to the otherworldly ambience.

But when he had a clear view of the white landscape, raw emotions broke through his detachment. It was carnage, worse than any battlefield he had ever seen. The Lament-Brood were a purple-edged wave swamping the feeble ranks of the army. Guns cut them apart, but it took at least fifty rounds, and as quickly as one fell, six others took their place. The enemy were brutally efficient. Rusted swords cleaved heads, hacked off arms, left trails of steaming entrails in the churned, red snow. Spears rammed through flimsy skin and muscle, arrows plunged into eye sockets. The despair the Lament-Brood engendered was a weapon in itself, and many soldiers simply laid down their arms to have their bones snapped and life extinguished by dead but powerful hands.

It was a rout beyond any defeat the army could have envisioned. As fast as men fell, they were brought back to unnatural life to swell the ranks of the enemy, going on to kill their friends and colleagues with vigour. Explosions roared flames and gouts of smoke high into the air as ammunition was detonated and batteries overrun. Fire raged in several of the tanks in the front line. There were no tactics, no weapons that would make any difference. It was only a matter of time.

And just as that thought entered Hunter's head, choppers carrying the General and other COs rose up behind the lines. A retreat had been ordered, but it was too disorganised to be effective. Men tried to pull back, but the Lament-Brood kept coming, picking them off as they fled.

It's all over, Hunter thought, dimly grateful for the remaining detachment that still swathed him.

One final shell was loosed into the sky before the enemy swamped the lines. It rushed towards Hunter, passed through him and came down beyond the ridge. When the explosion resonated all around, he suddenly felt as if a rope at his waist had been tied to a speeding car. Yanked backwards, he flew over the valley and down towards the forest, now blazing from the strike which had impacted right at the point where his body had been suspended.

chapter seven

night falls in the dreaming city

'*Heaven cannot brook two suns, nor Earth two masters.*'
Alexander the Great

There are times when the world feels like an irritating distraction, even when buildings are collapsing, blood is flowing and people are crying about the end of the world. Some things are more important. Hal understood that clearly as he made his way along the corridors of Queen's College. All he could think about was the kiss Samantha had shared with Hunter, how it had been a whole conversation in a single moment, a complex communion of secret yearnings, confused romance, hope, worry, sexual attraction.

It had made him realise that those who live their lives in their heads, as he did, made it easy to deceive themselves. The imagination is a trickster, he thought, tempting with illusions to drag you off the path so he can laugh uproariously at your rude awakening.

In his mind, Samantha had always been the one who would save him from his mundane existence. And now there was no hope of that ever happening. Lost in his dreams he might have been, but he was a pragmatist when faced with harsh reality. He felt colder than the unnatural winter outside, as though every thought he had was laced with frost. So cold that he felt he would turn to ice, then slowly melt away when the thaw came.

Reid's department filled a vast complex of rooms, all sealed, all silent; a place of unspeakable secrets that gave no hint of their existence; of quiet suggestions that turned the mind to horror; of the brush of fingertips at midnight.

Hal was met by an underling at the entrance to the sanctum sanctorum and led into an area he had never visited before and had never thought he would. He was finally shown into a room with a security system that exceeded anything Hal had seen throughout the extremely secure offices of Government. Reid waited within, talking in hushed tones to Dennis Kirkham. With a troubled expression, the chief scientist examined a sword suspended in a holding frame.

'Ah, here he is,' Reid exclaimed when he saw Hal. 'Will you excuse us, Mister Kirkham? Business.'

Kirkham disappeared in the silent manner that always character-ised his comings and goings, and Reid came over to Hal with a faint swagger. To Hal, Reid always appeared to be on stage pretending to be some spy he had seen in a sixties movie; he had charisma, and cool, and a touch of arrogance, but it felt as if it was all hanging loosely over someone else entirely.

'Look at this,' Reid said, indicating the sword. 'We retrieved it from the fellow brought back from Cadbury Hill.'

'The Brother of Dragons?'

'That's the chap. Doesn't look much like a champion of the human race, I must say, but that's by the by. I believe, and certainly he believes, that this is one of the three great swords of legend—'

'Sir?'

'We're frantically playing catch-up here, Mister . . . ?' Reid fumbled for Hal's name without any sign of embarrassment, even though he spoke to Hal several times a week.

'Campbell,' Hal said.

Reid nodded, but didn't deign to use Hal's name. 'The rules have changed, as we all know,' the spy continued. 'We can no longer sneer at the supernatural, or magic. Those words simply define something we can't quite understand at this moment in time. We know that myth and legend, what we thought were simply fairy stories, contain secrets coded into them. Truths. Many of them, pieced together, provide a secret history of what was going on behind the scenes of our illusion of a rational world. Do you understand what I'm saying?'

Hal nodded.

'The difficulty is deciding what is true and important to us, and what is merely embellishment to make them good stories that will carry those truths through word of mouth over generations. A lot of it is symbolism, one element representing another . . .' Reid waved his hand with irritation. 'Not my department. We have people who deal with that kind of thing. But what I can understand is that it's a code, and we're in the process of cracking it.'

He returned to the sword. 'One of the great British legends is of three powerful swords. Weapons, fantastic, earth-shattering weapons. One is called Caledfwlch, or by another name, Excalibur, with which I'm sure you're familiar. Another was believed to be consumed by, or filled with, fire, with an implication that its power was corrupted in some way. And this is the third. Our Brother of Dragons was told it's called Llyrwyn, but that isn't any name I've come across before. And he also appears to be completely unaware of its capabilities. If we can find out how to access that power, imagine what we could do. We certainly wouldn't be on the back foot any longer.' Reid's eyes gleamed.

For the first time, Hal looked around the room properly. Rack upon rack of cases were lined up like a futuristic library. But they did not hold books. There were more weapons – axes, a bow and arrows that appeared to be made of gold, a spear – and artefacts that ranged from the mundane to the bizarre: odd lumps of rock, jewels that glowed eerily, a crystal ball in which fleeting images came and went, a carpet, a mirror with a carved frame of tormented figures, amulets of all shapes and sizes, caskets and boxes, some plain, some encrusted with more colourful jewels, the skull of some beast with horns, a stuffed figure of a tiny man with wings; and those were only the items in Hal's immediate line of vision.

Reid nodded when he saw Hal's expression. 'We've amassed quite a collection, haven't we? My men have been very busy since we received the first hints that the Fall was taking place. You remember what it was like – the failing technology, the seemingly ridiculous rumours of fantastic creatures, then the deaths . . .' He shook his head in faux-sadness. 'I'm not one to blow my own trumpet, but I put this entire project in motion right then. Don't deny the evidence of your eyes, I told my superiors. Adapt or die. Sadly, they died. But I moved quickly, sending out agents to seize whatever might help us when the time came to fight back. And it is a remarkable achievement. Some of these objects . . . well, they'd take your breath away if you saw what they could do. Some we will never take out of their security cases. Too dangerous even to touch. We're working on the others . . . close to a breakthrough in some areas,' he said proudly.

Hal's attention was drawn to a lantern, like an old miner's lamp, sitting on the top of one display case. A blue flame flickered inside, veering strangely at a sharp angle in one direction. 'What's that?' Hal asked.

Reid examined it, puzzled. 'I've never seen that before. And what's it doing out of its case? Don't worry, I'll get Kirkham to secure it.'

Reid was dismissive, but there was something about the lantern that resonated with Hal. Even as Reid led him away to a case on the far side of the room, Hal couldn't help but look back. The lantern made his skin tingle, and he felt as if there were feathery fingers probing gently into his mind.

'You're probably wondering why I brought you down here,' Reid said as he came to a halt before a case that contained an eight-pointed silver star next to a stone – Hal assumed it must be the Wish Stone that the Brother of Dragons had retrieved from Cadbury Hill. Reid slipped on a pair of plastic evidence gloves and went for the Wish Stone before diverting to the star. He plucked it out and handed it to Hal. 'This is an unusual item. What do you think of it?'

Hal was surprised that Reid was canvassing his opinion on anything. He held the star up to the light, which revealed an almost invisible gold filigree covering the star with strange symbols and runes. The object felt oddly warm to his touch, and while his eyes told him that it was an eight-pointed star, his hand suggested a different shape.

'No idea,' Hal said. 'Some kind of talisman? Where did you find it?'

'A site in Cornwall. We've puzzled over it for a while. But that's a conversation for another day. This is what I wanted to show you.' Reid put the star back in its case and picked up the Wish Stone. 'Another artefact this Brother of Dragons was carrying when we found him. He's refused to answer any of our questions about where he got it, or what it's for, which suggests it has some importance, but we believe he recovered it from Cadbury Hill. It may even have been his reason for being there. Here – hold it.'

The moment the Wish Stone came into contact with Hal's skin, crackling blue light surged out to trace a picture in the air of two men next to a tomb, overlooked by a woman. Hal dropped the stone and Reid caught it with a deft movement. 'Careful!'

'Sorry. It shocked me. How does it work? What was that scene?' Hal felt as if he had seen it somewhere before.

'We have no idea what it represents or what it means, whether it's something we should be studying or just a distraction.'

'Why are you showing it to me?'

'We need you to find out what it is. Do some research – you're good at that, I'm told.' Reid's attention was already wandering; he clearly didn't care whether Hal found out what the stone was for or not.

'Do you want me to report directly back to you?'

'Yes, of course.' Reid walked away, stripping the gloves from his hands with a loud snap. He turned, raising his finger for emphasis. 'Don't say anything about this to anyone else. Do you understand?'

Hal nodded, confused by the mixed signals he was receiving. But the image from the stone was already tugging at his subconscious. He felt instinctively that this was important.

The air had the summer twilight smell of a hot day cooling, of rolling grassland and wild flowers and the tangy musk of distant forests. Sophie stood on the high balcony with Caitlin at her side, looking towards the west. The reddening sun, bisected by the dark horizon, lay against a sky of shimmering gold and flaming orange. Far below them, the Court of Soul's Ease was quietening as the residents hurried to their homes after a day of business in the bustling, otherworldly city. Yet the evening was not entirely peaceful, for a drone of activity came from beyond the sturdy walls.

Sophie wrinkled her nose. 'Can you smell that?' In one hand she gripped a spear she had drawn from the armoury, the tip gleaming silver, the shaft hard wood branded with mystical symbols; it never missed, she was told.

'Smoke. The fires are starting.' Caitlin's weapon of choice was a longbow and arrows.

The moment the words had left her mouth, bursts of red and yellow flared up in the pooling shadows beyond the walls, illuminating what at first sight looked like a mass of swarming ants surrounding the entire city. As the firelight flickered and the shadows washed back and forth across the teeming multitude, it became clear that it was an army of the little men who had attacked Sophie and Ceridwen on their journey to the court.

'I came here for safety while I looked for an opportunity to get back home,' Sophie said bitterly. 'Now I'm stuck here under siege. Mallory probably thinks I'm dead. Goddess knows what else is happening in our world.'

'I think being in the wrong place at the wrong time goes with the territory,' Caitlin said quietly.

Sophie cast a secretive glance at her. In the four days since she had arrived in the Court of Soul's Ease, she had got to know Caitlin very well. A deep sadness filled her, but most of the time she managed to mask it behind smiles. Sophie could easily imagine Caitlin as a GP back in the real world. She cared deeply about everyone, enough to swallow what must have been a toxic amount of grief to ensure that she didn't make anyone else suffer along with her. That thoughtfulness alone would have been enough to win over Sophie, but Caitlin also had an admirably quiet strength and resilience. Sophie thought that the two of them would probably become friends, given time.

Yet one great barrier lay between them. Sophie was a Sister of Dragons, and Caitlin was not, not any more. It tormented Caitlin in many ways, layering more misery on top of her mourning: she feared that the whole of humanity would pay the price for what she saw as her weakness of character. And the loss of that inestimable quality that set them apart as Sisters of Dragons was as devastating as if she had lost the use of her legs. Probably more so, for Caitlin had confided in her the previous night that it was as if she had been given a glimpse of heaven, only to have it snatched away for evermore. It wasn't just the strength and healing ability that she missed, but the sense of being connected to the entire universe; she was bereft in more ways than one.

'Don't jump – we need you.'

The brash Birmingham accent had become familiar to Sophie over the past four days. Harvey stood in the middle of Caitlin's quarters, a working-class youth as out of his depth as anyone could possibly get, yet who still acted as if he was heading down to his local. Sophie liked him immensely. Beside him was his friend, Thackeray, a deep thinker who liked to pretend he was a doomed romantic. They had both found themselves accidentally caught up in the events that had brought Caitlin to T'ir n'a n'Og, but for their part had stuck by Caitlin resolutely, giving her the strength to keep going. Thackeray was easy to read; every aspect of him suggested that he was deeply in love with Caitlin, and Sophie had the feeling that Caitlin returned the affection on some level, though it was never discussed.

Harvey shifted uncomfortably when Sophie and Caitlin came in from the balcony. 'You two freak me out,' he said bluntly. 'It was bad enough when she was going all Wonder Woman on us.' He nodded to Caitlin. 'Now there's you as well. Where's it going to end?'

'He loves it really,' Thackeray said. 'He's got this fantasy about amazons—'

'Oi!' Harvey punched Thackeray hard on the shoulder. 'That was the beer talking. Anyway, you shouldn't be repeating what I tell you in confidence.'

'We found a pub. The Sun. Big surprise in a city ruled by a sun god,' Thackeray said.

'They give us free beer,' Harvey said excitedly. '*All given freely and without obligation.*'

'The way we figured it,' Mallory said, 'we could either hang around here, getting under your feet and offering less than useful opinions on how the siege could be broken—'

'Or we could get pissed,' Harvey finished.

'Not really a contest, was it?' Caitlin said. 'As long as you're enjoying yourselves.'

'Before you go castigating us, we've got a message,' Thackeray said. 'There's a big war conference wrapping up down in the main hall. And they want to see you two.'

'Finally,' Sophie said. 'They're going to break the siege so that we can get out of here and back home.'

Thackeray shook his head. 'I think they're just going to sit back and wait.'

★

'Maybe whatever it is that makes us Sisters of Dragons attracts bad things like this,' Sophie said to Caitlin as they marched into the great hall.

Lugh was waiting for them, his solar armour burnished red in the light of the setting sun that streamed through the floor-to-ceiling windows. Behind him, Ceridwen waited with a serious expression.

'It is the Pendragon Spirit that shapes your days and nights, guides you to be where you should, where you are needed. It is the power that binds everything together,' Lugh said.

'What did your war conference decide?' Caitlin asked impatiently.

'The hidden passage out of the Court of Soul's Ease is still blocked by . . . the enemy.' Lugh still had difficulty considering his own people a threat. 'The only way out is through the gates.'

'So you're going to attack them head on?' Sophie said.

'We fear a slaughter,' Ceridwen said. 'Many of my people would be destroyed. That is not our way.'

'It's the only way,' Caitlin said. 'It's a waste of time trying to talk peace when the other side is determined to wipe you off the face of the land. And you know they won't settle for anything less.'

Her words clearly rang true with both Lugh and Ceridwen, but the weight of their traditions and culture kept them ambivalent.

'The battle will come when it will. We know that. We have always known it, but have been unable to face up to what was coming.' Lugh's handsome face was filled with a deep melancholy. 'I regret that you have been caught up in our familial strife, Sister of Dragons.' Lugh addressed Sophie directly; Caitlin flinched. 'You should not be here. You are needed elsewhere.'

Sophie noticed a concern in their body language that she had missed before. 'What's wrong?'

'The final days have come. The Fixed Lands are being consumed by the Void, whose true name is the Devourer of All Things. The Far Lands will follow, and all the lands beyond,' Lugh said.

'Then it's started,' Caitlin whispered.

'What has?' Sophie looked from Caitlin to the gods and back.

Seeing Sophie's mounting concern, Ceridwen stepped forward. 'The arrival of the Devourer of All Things has always been foretold by my people. It was one of the stories we brought with us when we

121

left the four great cities of our glorious homeland to become wanderers, cut off from the source. "The Devourer of All Things shall come and consume the light." That story is the sadness at the end of our own tale of dissolution.'

'You knew about this?' Sophie asked Caitlin.

'I knew that the Void had sent outriders to prepare the way, but it could have taken weeks or millennia to turn up.'

'What are we talking about here? Some kind of monster?' Sophie asked.

'The Devourer of All Things is the underside of Existence, bound to it even while constantly opposing it,' Lugh answered. He held out his arms to indicate the wider world. 'Existence is everything. All time, all space, all lands. What, then, is the Devourer of All Things, which is the dark reflection of Existence? A monster? No. It is immeasurable, incomprehensible. It is everything, too.'

Sophie and Caitlin stood quietly for a moment while they attempted to understand what Lugh was telling them. Finally Sophie said incredulously, 'If it's what you say it is, why aren't you doing something? What's the point in being wrapped up in this civil war if everything is coming to an end?'

Lugh smiled, a father explaining the ways of the world to a child. 'How can you fight everything?'

'There are two conflicting stories the *filid* sing on the nights when we reflect on our beginnings,' Ceridwen said. 'One is that all we see and feel is the construction of a just and right Existence, and that we are all part of that. The other is that all we see and feel is flawed and corrupted, a prison created by a dark force to separate us from the true glory of Existence. The Court of the Final Word has long sought the truth, and evidence exists supporting both stories. But consider this: what if both are true? What if Existence has two faces, continually turning, and when one looks upon us, the other is alerted and attempts to seize control?'

'So you're just going to sit back and let it happen?' Sophie said.

'The only way to stop the Devourer of All Things would be to use the Extinction Shears,' Lugh said, 'and none know where they now lie—'

'I don't care about any of this,' Caitlin said furiously. 'If you're saying that the world's under some kind of threat, we need to be there, doing what we can.'

'I understand your desire,' Ceridwen said, 'for this is the reason the Brothers and Sisters of Dragons exist—'

'Is that what this is all about?' Sophie interrupted. She grabbed Caitlin's arm. 'We've got to get back. They need us.'

'They need *you*,' Caitlin replied. 'I'm the one who spoiled it all, remember? If there aren't five of us, we're weakened.'

'We will do what we can, Sister of Dragons, but there is no path back to the Fixed Lands from the Court of Soul's Ease,' Lugh said. 'The war council will continue its debate, and I will make your case for decisive action. But in the meantime there is nothing we can do.'

Outside the great hall, Caitlin grabbed Sophie by the shoulders and said passionately, 'I want the Pendragon Spirit back. I'll do anything.'

'Nobody can bring it back – it's a gift. You know that,' Sophie said sympathetically.

'We can petition Higher Powers. It must come from something, right? These gods, they keep talking about Existence as though it's alive. We could ask it. You use the Craft. You could try.'

'I wouldn't even know how to start. It's too big, Caitlin. Trying to make that kind of contact would be beyond any mere human.'

'There are people here who could help.' Caitlin's face was filled with desperation. 'Will you at least try?'

Sophie couldn't refuse her. 'All right, I'll do what I can. But there could be risks. There's always a price to pay, and the more you're after, the bigger the price.'

'I'll do anything,' Caitlin said. 'I'll pay any price.'

Sophie hoped those words wouldn't come back to haunt Caitlin.

During her stay in the Court of Soul's Ease, Caitlin had kept her ears open to the whispers that washed back and forth through the city like a tide. She had learned of the many wonders that existed there, some obvious, some hidden behind the scenes, suggested but never discussed. One such was the Tower of the Four Winds.

Night had fallen by the time they located the mysterious tower in the section of the court that resembled the Moorish quarter of a

Spanish city: white stone, minarets, ornate awnings and fragrant smoke blowing in the warm breeze. It lay high up the hillside, and when Sophie turned to look back over the court spread out below her, the sight took her breath away. Tiny white lights had sprung up everywhere, like fireflies in the dark; there were candles in windows and lanterns hanging over shops along the streets, tiny suns holding back the night. It was magical. If the circumstances had been different, Sophie knew she could have whiled away many days in a place of so many wonders, large and small.

The tower stood in a walled garden filled with palms and orange trees and small, spiky shrubs. A white-stone path wound through the vegetation. More lanterns hung from the trees, attracting moths in clouds. The gate was unlocked.

Caitlin caught Sophie's arm. 'Let's go carefully.'

'Why? Guard dogs?'

'I've heard some strange things. The one who lives here might be dangerous. There are stories about him . . .' She caught herself. 'Let's just be careful.'

'Do you want me to go first?'

'I'm not a complete invalid,' Caitlin snapped, instantly regretting her tone. 'I'm sorry. All this . . . I'm on edge.'

'Don't worry.' Sophie smiled, but she was growing increasingly concerned about Caitlin's desire to make amends for her perceived mistakes.

The tower was constructed from ivory, glass and gold, each element merging into the other with a delicate architectural sensibility that instilled a quiet wonder. The path led to a mahogany door covered with iron studs. A bell-pull hung beside it. Caitlin hesitated and then grabbed the pull to announce their presence.

For a long minute there was no reply. Then, gradually, a rhythmic hissing rose up from the vegetation on either side of the path. As Sophie and Caitlin waited with thumping hearts, snakes slithered on to the path and headed towards them. The serpents glowed so brightly that the women couldn't be sure if they really existed or if they were constructed of green and red light.

Sophie removed her spear from the harness on her back, though she wasn't at all sure it would have much effect on the snakes if it came to it.

The snakes moved quickly along the path and then split into two groups, curving around on either side of Caitlin and Sophie. They continued up the sheer, slick walls of the tower and came together over the top of the door, where they began to crawl into each other's mouths. The serpents merged, becoming larger, until finally one huge snake undulated down to bring its eyes on a level with Caitlin and Sophie's. They glittered red with a disturbing intelligence.

'Speak your business,' the snake said with a soft sibilance.

'A Sister of Dragons and a Fragile Creature are seeking the wisdom of Math,' Caitlin said.

There was a brief pause before the serpent replied, 'That name has not been heard since the days of the tribes.'

'But it still holds, does it not?' Caitlin persisted. 'Math, great magician, brother of the goddess Don. He was a friend to Fragile Creatures in times past.'

'There are no times past,' the snake hissed. Another pause. Then: 'Enter, and prove yourself worthy to stand before the Seer of the Seven Worlds.'

With a fizz, the snake dissolved into tiny balls of light that drifted away on the breeze. A second later, the studded door swung open, releasing a heady aroma of incense.

'I don't like the sound of that,' Sophie whispered.

'Nor me. When they're not being pompous, these gods are more than a little sneaky.'

Caitlin stepped over the threshold and made her way to a staircase that wound upwards around the inside of the walls. It was lit intermittently by tiny lanterns, but there were still many troubling pools of shadows. The silence that filled the tower was not peaceful; it felt as if some loud bell was just about to toll.

Caitlin and Sophie moved hesitantly up the stairs, each trailing a hand along the cool wall for support. When they had reached what they guessed was the halfway mark, the atmosphere became oppressive.

'Can you feel it?' Sophie asked. 'Something's coming.'

A sound like the wind through leaves echoed softly at first from further up the tower, drawing closer. Caitlin and Sophie waited with mounting apprehension, until the first signs of something approaching were indicated by undulating shadows cast by the flickering lanterns.

'More snakes,' Caitlin said. 'Lots of them.'

As they rounded the next bend in the stairway, Caitlin and Sophie saw that these weren't the light-snakes they had encountered at the foot of the tower, but hard-scaled, sharp-fanged serpents that were undoubtedly real. Yet they had an otherworldly ambience that made them even more menacing. Several were as broad as Sophie's body, their tails lost in the dim recesses of the upper tower, but the majority ranged from the width of an arm to barely larger than a finger, shimmering greens and scarlets and golds, with strange black patterns along their skin that resembled runes. There were so many snakes that they filled the stairway up to Sophie's waist, a slow-moving tidal wave that would easily engulf the two women.

Sophie grabbed Caitlin's arm. 'Come on. We have to go down.'

'We can't,' Caitlin said desperately. 'This is our one chance. If we go down, he'll never let us back up again.' She turned to Sophie, her face hard and determined. 'You go. You don't have to do this.'

'You're insane! Look at them.'

The nearest snake had the hood of a cobra, but strange alien growths like mushrooms lined its back. It reared up to bare its fangs, venom sizzling where it splashed on the steps.

'You'll never survive one bite,' Sophie pressed.

Caitlin surveyed the mass of writhing bodies, almost close enough to touch now. Then she said firmly, 'It's a test. Math wants to see if we're up to the *honour* of meeting him.'

'Yes, dead or alive, it would seem.'

The nearest snake moved within striking range. Caitlin made her decision and then lay flat on the stairs.

'What are you doing?' Sophie said incredulously.

'He said we had to prove we're worthy. He wants us on our bellies, supplicating.'

'You're mad.' Sophie looked from Caitlin to the snakes and then back down the stairs. Then she recalled what she and Mallory had had to go through in the temple beneath Cadbury Hill and knew that Caitlin was right. Cursing under her breath, she threw herself down. 'If I survive I'm never going to forgive you for this.' She closed her eyes and pressed her face hard into the cold ivory of the steps.

The serpents reached her a second later, a writhing mass pressing down so hard that Sophie felt she might suffocate. The sensation of constant movement above her made the bile rise in her throat. Their skin was dry against her face, forcing their way through her hair, wriggling past her cheeks, under her nose, forcing her lips apart with their tiny bodies, pressing against her eyes.

A minute later she was drowning beneath a sea of serpents, her face crushed into the hard steps, blood on her lips, in her mouth. In a desperate attempt to distract herself from the horror of what was happening, she grunted rhythms in her throat, made up tunes in her head, anything that might take her mind away.

And then the claustrophobia set in and she began to choke, but the weight above her was so great that she couldn't have lifted herself up from the steps if she tried. Panic rammed rational thoughts aside and she knew, in that instant, how easy it would be to go insane.

The snakes continued to come for what felt like hours, until Sophie couldn't believe there were so many snakes in all the worlds. Just when she thought her last breath was about to give out, the mass above her grew lighter, and then quickly receded.

Finally, she was on her knees, choking and spitting, unable to believe that she hadn't received one bite. Caitlin was beside her in the same state, yet strangely smiling. She grabbed Sophie's arm and indicated down the stairs in the direction the serpents had gone. Sophie looked around, but there were no snakes to be seen anywhere.

'You're not telling me that was all in my mind,' Sophie choked.

'It was real all right,' Caitlin said. 'And we survived.'

After a moment gathering themselves, they started back up the winding stairway. The aroma of incense grew stronger, and eventually the stairway opened out into a room that covered the whole floor at the very top of the tower. Four windows at the cardinal points looked out over the glittering lights of the dreaming city. In front of each sat a creature that resembled an animal, but had the same otherworldly quality as the snakes – a gleam of intelligence in the eye, or an odd movement of the mouth as if it was muttering to itself, or an unusual size.

There was an enormous boar, fat and bristling, its piggy eyes green and furious; a hawk that was almost as big as Sophie; a salmon, again as big as a person, sitting in a large wooden chair, its tail flapping against the wooden floorboards; and a bear, watching them contemptuously. All were fastened in place by an iron chain attached to a ring bolted to the floor. The four beasts radiated an air of menace that made Sophie and Caitlin wary of venturing too close.

Purple drapes covered with gold and silver magical symbols lined the walls between each window, and the floorboards were marked with similar magical symbols. A brazier gave off the heavy incense, while other mystical objects stood around. Several lanterns burning with a dull red light hung on chains from the ceiling; a brass telescope, maps and charts lay on a table, flanked by books and flasks of philtres.

And in the centre of the room, nearly seven feet tall, stood Math. Long black robes covered his entire body and on his head, protruding from a four-holed cowl, was a brass mask with a different face in each of the holes: a boar, a falcon, a salmon and a bear.

'You survived the test,' he said from the mask of the boar, with a voice that was strangely gruff. 'I would have expected no less from a Sister of Dragons. But from a Fragile Creature?' He tilted the mask towards Caitlin. It would have been easy to wilt under the cold eyes just visible behind it, but Caitlin held her head proudly.

'We have come to ask a favour of you,' Caitlin said.

'A boon?' Math was clearly intrigued by this. 'For you – the Fragile Creature?'

'For my friend,' Sophie interjected, 'who was once a Sister of Dragons, too.'

'Ah.' The brass mask nodded and Sophie was disturbed to see the real boar at its window nodding in time. Math's hands protruded from the voluminous sleeves as he brought his fingertips together; they were brown and scabrous, as if they had been severely burned. 'And what would this boon be?'

'I wish . . .' Caitlin took a breath before steeling herself to continue. 'I wish to have the Pendragon Spirit within me once again.'

Math grew rigid. With a soft whisper, the mask rotated so that the salmon's features faced them. When he spoke, his voice had changed, too, and was now soft and liquid, somehow. 'You ask me to make you a Sister of Dragons again? Impossible! That is a gift that can only come from Existence.'

'You have to!' Caitlin's voice cracked.

The eerie mask turned again until the face of the bear appeared. 'You dare raise your voice to me!' Math roared. Caitlin took a step back. Behind Math, the bear was straining at his chain, eager to break free to tear Caitlin to pieces.

Caitlin, though, was undeterred. She looked to Sophie with tears in her eyes. 'Please.'

'We're sorry if we've offended you,' Sophie said. 'My friend didn't mean it. She came here because she heard you were the greatest magician in the Court of Soul's Ease, and if you can't help her, no one else can.'

There was a long period of silence that ended with the appearance of the falcon's face. 'I can petition Existence on your behalf. But there are dangers, even for one such as me. I will demand a fine price to take such a step.' There was a subtle slyness to his words.

'Anything,' Caitlin said before Sophie could stop her.

If she could penetrate the mask, Sophie knew she would see Math smiling. He turned his head in her direction. 'I ask for very little,' he said, 'but it is this: a simple memory from a Sister of Dragons. A precious memory, a rare and unique thing. But it will not be missed.'

Caitlin could now see the danger, but it was too late. 'I'm the one who should be—' she began, but Math waved her silent with a burned hand.

He pointed a long, scarred finger at Sophie and said, 'You must agree. One simple memory.'

'What does it mean if I give it to you?' Sophie asked.

'It will be gone from you for ever, nevermore to be recalled. But what is a memory? An ephemeral thing.'

Sophie's heart was pounding. 'Which memory?' Sophie asked hesitantly.

'The memory of your first meeting with the one you love.'

'Oh, no,' Caitlin moaned.

Sophie felt sick. The image of Mallory sitting with her in a camp in Salisbury flashed through her mind, the smells, the sounds, his expression, the way she had felt disoriented and happy and sexy, realising the near-instant attraction. All that, gone for good; it would be like losing a physical part of her. But then she looked at Caitlin and saw her desolation, and thought of what good they both could do; of the chance they had to save the human race. She didn't really have a choice.

'All right,' she said. She was aware of another secret smile beneath the mask, and then Math reached out his fingers and brushed her forehead. It felt like a steel hook was squirming in her brain. As he pulled back his fingers, there was a flash of intense pain and she screamed. A blue spark followed his fingers. Math guided it to the table where he uncorked a flask. He directed the spark inside before re-corking it hastily.

'Sophie, thank you,' Caitlin said. Her face was filled with guilt, but beneath it lay a desperate hope.

Sophie didn't hear. She was trying to recall her first meeting with Mallory, but there was a horrible black hole in her mind that refused to budge however much she poked and prodded it. And she realised with a note of panic that she no longer knew why she loved Mallory, just that she did; it felt like coming into a movie twenty minutes after the start.

Math made them gather near to him within a protective circle. Candles guttered on the circumference in front of each of the windows. The animals all strained at their chains. Slowly, and with a voice that didn't appear to come from any of the faces, Math began a chant in a language Sophie and Caitlin didn't recognise. It hurt their ears when they attempted to focus on any of the words. The god continued for five minutes, his voice rising and falling but growing continually louder. By the end he was shouting so loudly that Sophie and Caitlin covered their ears. A great wind blew into the room, snuffing out the candles' flames one by one. Each of the beasts began to make a terrible howling sound that could not have come from any animal. The noise rose up to the roof until it seemed to have a life of its own and rushed around the room with the wind. The beasts tore at their chains and threw themselves back and forth in a furious desire to break free.

Math stopped his chanting and pointed out of the western window. 'Look!' he roared above the cacophony.

Sophie and Caitlin both turned and, a second later, not knowing what they had seen, they plunged into unconsciousness.

When they awoke, an uncommon stillness lay across the room. The four beasts cowered against the windows and Math was slumped in a chair at the table as if he had no strength left within him.

'It is as I said: the Pendragon Spirit cannot be brought into this Fragile Creature,' he said flatly through the falcon mask.

'That's it?' Caitlin said. 'Then this was all for nothing?'

'No.' Math levered himself to his feet, his power slowly returning. 'There is still hope for you. You are a child of Existence, and like all of your kind you have the potential to be greater. The Pendragon Spirit shall come to you again.'

Sophie thought Caitlin might faint at this news. 'When?' she said desperately. 'Soon?'

'When you have proved yourself ready,' Math replied.

Caitlin thought about this for a second, then turned to Sophie. 'I have to do what I can to prove I'm worthy. Don't stop me doing this, all right?'

Not knowing what Caitlin was planning, Sophie agreed, but had a suspicion that she was not going to like it.

'I know it's possible for the gods to become a part of Fragile Creatures,' Caitlin began. 'You can enter us. Possess us.'

'Some can,' Math said.

'I know this,' Caitlin said. 'And I know which one I want inside me. I have a bond with her. I know her power and I can use it in what we've got coming.' She took a deep breath and then said, 'I want you to contact the Morrigan, and I want you to make her become part of me.'

'You're crazy!' Sophie said. 'You can't seriously be asking for that.'

'I can, and I am,' Caitlin said defiantly.

'Don't you understand? She's the goddess of death, war, bloodshed—'

'And sex, creativity, new life,' Caitlin countered impatiently.

'You won't be able to control her – she'll control you. She's the most unpredictable, the most dangerous . . . I'm very skilled in the Craft, but even I'm careful about calling on the Morrigan.'

'Trust me, Sophie, we've got a bond, her and me. I've been to hell and back in my life. I know exactly what the Morrigan is about, believe me. This is my only chance to do something that might help. As some weak, Fragile Creature, I'm worthless—'

'Not true.'

'It is in the context of what's coming up. You know that's right. You know it. You're going to need all the help you can get.'

Sophie relented a little. 'I still think it's a mistake.'

'You'll change your mind. We're going to make a good team – a witch and a warrior.' Caitlin turned to Math. 'Can you do it?'

'The Dark Sister might choose a host who has the Pendragon Spirit inside her. But why should she bond with a Fragile Creature?' At its window, the boar snorted and stamped its hooves impatiently.

'Tell her there'll be blood and death on an epic scale. There'll be a war to end all wars, and I'll be in the thick of it.'

Math raised one twisted hand to the mouth of his boar mask in silent consideration and then turned to his table. He selected two phials, one filled with red dust, the other with a granular black powder. He took a pinch of each and flung them on to the brazier.

The stench of the smoke made Sophie grip her nose in disgust; it smelled of charnel houses, of bonfires after the battle, of iron and bone. Math turned to the west once again and uttered a word of power that left Sophie staggering. An instant later, an unearthly silence fell on the tower, dead air, no echoes even when she dragged her boot over the floorboards.

An overpowering sense that something was coming gripped Sophie, but this was not the anticipation she had felt when Math had called for the Pendragon Spirit. This time she felt dread, every fibre urging her to flee.

A cloud, blacker even than the night sky, was visible through the western window. It surged towards the tower with a rising sound like thunder, swept around it, then rushed in through all four windows at once with a deafening, wild movement. Crows, hundreds, thousands of them. Sophie threw herself backwards, almost falling down the stairs. The crows filled the room in a dense wall of black, flapping wings.

From the floor, her hands covering her head, Sophie caught occasional glimpses of Caitlin. It looked as if the birds were attacking her, pecking at her eyes, her face, trying to batter their way into her stomach. Sophie called out to her, but her voice was nothing beside the tumult.

After barely more than a minute, the crows departed. As she pulled herself to her feet, Sophie expected to see Caitlin's ragged corpse lying broken on the floor. Instead, her friend stood erect and unharmed, radiating a fierce beauty and a dark power that made her almost impossible to look upon. On her shoulder sat the biggest crow Sophie had ever seen, its black, beady gaze heavy upon her.

'Are you . . . are you OK?' Sophie ventured.

Caitlin answered with a cold glint in her eyes and an even colder smile.

Night had transformed Oxford into a magical city as Hal made his way into the centre. Candlelight flickered in many windows and the street lamps made the snow glitter on the roads and rooftops, occasionally illuminating stray snowflakes drifting down.

One hour ago, he had met with Samantha. Hal had kept a brave face while she handed over notes on the Brothers and Sisters of Dragons that she had copied from Reid's files. They spoke of links to the Arthurian myths and to a greater mystery that intrigued Hal immensely.

Samantha had risked everything to get the information and Hal knew she had expected a greater show of gratitude from him. But if he had released even a hint of emotion, everything inside him would have come out in a deluge that he would have regretted for the rest of his life. Instead, he had simply promised to hand the notes over to Hunter as soon as he returned, and then took his leave.

He couldn't go back to a room that now felt so small and cold, so he had decided to walk off his sadness, and now he was glad he had. There was something magical in every aspect of the city, and he felt as if he had been allowed a glimpse of the secret spark at the heart of the mundane.

He kicked up flurries of snow as he walked, wishing Hunter was there to experience it with him. He couldn't blame Hunter for Samantha's action; they were the two most important people in his life and if he was completely objective they probably deserved each other. Hal missed his friend; for all his licentiousness, there was a poetry to Hunter that Hal admired because he knew he lacked it himself. He had the sneaking feeling that Hunter always saw the secret spark, while Hal only ever saw the mundane.

He was worried for Hunter's safety. There had been no official news from the front line, but rumours had started to circulate that things had gone badly. There were always rumours running wild in the incestuous Government community, and most of them usually turned out to be false, but this one gelled with expectation. Some said that the General and the top brass had flown back from the front early and were now sequestered in the War Room ensconced in the bowels of Magdalen's New Library. Others said that the General had already shot himself with a silver bullet and the enemy was only ten miles from the city limits. There was talk of mass casualties, of a fifth column within the city itself, even that the enemy's commander had already agreed terms with the Government and was preparing to take over.

His thoughts were disrupted by a sparkling trail that gleamed across the sky from one row of rooftops to another. It looked at first like a jet's vapour trail, and as he watched the sparkles broke up and drifted away. A second or two later, another trail appeared further down the street, and at the head of it was a glowing golden light, moving slowly. It turned sharply and moved towards Hal, yet Hal felt no fear, only an incipient wonder.

As it neared, Hal was amazed to see a figure about the size of a ten-year-old boy at the centre of the golden light, flying gracefully. The boy swooped down and circled Hal at a distance of a few feet, examining him curiously. He wore what appeared to be a baggy golden romper suit, gloves and boots that looked to be as soft as socks with long toes that flapped as he flew. Over his head was a mask that looked like a nightcap that had been pulled down too far, with eye-holes cut into it.

'Well I never,' the boy said in amazement. 'A Brother of Dragons.' Then: 'Please. You must help me.'

'Who are you?' Hal was amazed that he had reached such a state that nothing surprised him any more.

'I have many names, like all who live in the Land of Always Summer, and, as you are no doubt aware, my Name of Names must never be revealed. But you may call me Petronus.' He bobbed on the currents, growing more anxious. 'Come.' He gestured for Hal to follow. 'Help me.'

Hal didn't sense any threat from the strange boy and so reluctantly followed him into a tiny alley between two shops. At the far end was a tiny golden glow in the snow.

'Help her. Please,' Petronus said desperately.

The fading light was coming from a tiny winged woman. Her eyes were closed and her breathing shallow.

'A Fragile Creature attacked her,' Petronus said desperately. 'Fired its weapon at her as she flew on the night winds.'

One of the guards, Hal guessed; they always had been trigger-happy. 'What can I do?'

'You are a Brother of Dragons,' Petronus said.

Hal was on the brink of brushing the boy away, but the tiny woman's fragile state called out to him. Hesitantly, he scooped her up to try to warm her in his hands. As he did so, a blue spark burst from him and crackled into the frail body. Instantly, the golden light began to grow stronger.

'You have saved her!' Petronus sounded on the brink of tears.

The woman recovered quickly, and soon she was standing on Hal's palm, blowing him a kiss. Then she waved a cautionary finger at Petronus, and with a twirl shot up into the sky, trailing stardust behind her.

Hal was at first struck dumb by what had happened, but then he quickly grew irritated. 'Look, what are you?' he said.

'How rude!' Petronus swooped high into the air before drifting back down from side to side like a leaf falling from a tree.

'I'm sorry,' Hal said, stamping his feet to keep warm. The memory of the blue spark troubled him greatly. 'But why are you here?'

'Why? Why not? This is my home!'

'Oxford?'

'No, silly! I live beyond the furthest star, on the other side of the mirror, in the misty vale where the golden apples grow. If you want to be poetic.'

Hal considered this comment for a moment, sieving through the little he had gleaned of mythology. 'The Otherworld?' he asked eventually.

'That is another name for it, as is T'ir n'a n'Og. There are names and names and names, and when you are as old as I am you'll realise that names are meaningless, for they never really capture what a thing is.'

'But this isn't Otherworld,' Hal protested. 'This is . . . the world.'

Petronus laughed. 'How ridiculous! I am here, so it must be the Land of Always Summer.'

Hal looked around. 'But it's winter.'

'Then that proves the matter, for the Otherworld is a land of contradictions.' Petronus spotted the tiny woman's glimmer of golden light high over the rooftops. 'My friend! I must go!'

'Wait! How do you know I'm a Brother of Dragons?' Hal asked.

'So many questions! How does anyone know? It's as plain as the nose on your face. You're a blazing Blue Fire, like a little star come down to earth.' Petronus pulled up his mask to reveal slanted eyes filled with the wildness of nature, and pointed pixie ears. He gave Hal a wink, pulled down the mask and then soared high into the sky and was gone.

Though he felt as if he was walking through a dream, Hal's mind was racing. What Petronus had said about being in Otherworld gelled with what he had been told by the little people he had heard singing the other night. What could it possibly mean?

It wasn't the only matter preying on his mind. Every time he heard someone or something call him a Brother of Dragons, it filled him with an unaccountable panic. Those words hinted at a future where he would have to give up the quiet, thoughtful life he had made for himself. It was a future where chaos ruled and anything could happen, where there were no certainties, no breakfast at seven-thirty, no lunch at one, no dinner at seven, no Sundays off, or sitting back with a good book as twilight fell. The name spoke of sacrifice and bloodshed and death and upheaval and all manner of unpleasantness, of the kind of life in which Hunter would probably revel, and which consequently was anathema to Hal. If it was true that he had somehow been selected by a Higher Power to be a defender of humanity, then that Higher Power had certainly got it wrong, for he had nothing whatsoever to offer.

Lost to his thoughts, Hal wandered down a side street off St Aldate's to cut through to one of his regular haunts. It was a familiar route, but this time he was confronted by a pub he had never seen before. It looked oddly quaint and historical in a slightly unrealistic way, as though it had been prepared for a film set.

Through bottle-glass windows filtered the ruddy glow of a fire and the gleam of lanterns, with a great many deep shadows in the areas between them. The warped glass did not allow a clear view inside, though there were clearly many drinkers within. Their hubbub leaked out through the ancient, scarred oak door. The second storey overhung the first in a Tudor style, complete with the requisite black beams and white paint, and from it hung a sign that said 'The Hunter's Moon', with a picture of a full moon partially obscured by cloud and what appeared to be a man with a wolf's head.

It looked surprisingly inviting, and so Hal ventured in without a second thought. It was only when the door had banged to behind him that he realised his mistake. The occupants of the pub were a strange, otherworldly group. There was a man as thin as a needle, nearly seven feet tall, wearing a stovepipe hat that made him even taller, his fingers so long and thin that they looked as if they were made of stretched toffee; a woman with long blonde hair that moved with a life of its own – she had a seductive look about her, but mad, dangerous eyes; a giant of a man wearing furs and a battered wide-brimmed hat, a string of conies around his neck and a blunderbuss hanging from his belt; another woman as bent, twisted and wrinkled as a crone from a fairy story, black shawl and white cap, a black cat perched on her shoulder, her cackle like the rattle of stones on a coffin; and more, all odd and out of place. Further towards the back, the revellers were even more bizarre; Hal glimpsed horns and scales and forked tails.

'Bless my soul, it's a Brother of Dragons!' the tall, thin man said.

Before Hal could back out, he was grabbed by numerous hands and dragged to the bar where the landlord loomed, overweight and black-bearded, his arms as thick as telegraph poles, both of them covered with tattoos of disturbing symbols.

'Pour the lad a drink, Drogoff!' someone called. Another agreed raucously, and the landlord reluctantly served up a tankard of foaming ale that was almost as big as Hal's head.

'Ooo, it ain't often we get someone like a Brother of Dragons in here,' the crone cackled. 'We's honoured.'

'What is this place?' Despite the dreamlike sensation that gripped him, Hal was beginning to feel the first pangs of incipient panic.

The big bear of a man with the blunderbuss levered himself out of his chair and loomed over Hal. 'Why, it's The Hunter's Moon, good brother. Best inn in all of the Far Lands.'

'I don't know what's real or not any more,' Hal said. His route to the door was blocked by more strange characters crowding around to see the new arrival. They were curious, but there was also unmistakable good will towards him, which made Hal feel a little more at ease.

'The only real stuff's in 'ere,' the crone said, tapping the side of her head. 'We make the rest of it 'ow we want it to be. Everybody knows that.' With shaking hands, she grabbed a tiny goblet from the bar and knocked the contents back with gusto.

'Steady on, Mother,' the man in the stovepipe said. 'The poor lad's a bit disoriented. You know how it is when they first venture into the Far Lands. Give him room to breathe.'

The woman with the snaking hair glided forward, her hypnotic eyes burning into Hal. 'Even Jack, Giant Killer, was adrift in his first days in Faerie,' she said sibilantly. She moved a rotating finger slowly towards Hal's temple, until the blunderbuss man gripped her wrist tightly. The woman hissed at him like a serpent, then pushed her way to the back of the bar.

'Have to watch yourself round here, good brother. You're not at home any more. There are many dangers, if you don't know what you're doing.' The blunderbuss man clapped Hal heartily on the back. 'Come on, drink up!' he roared. 'Join in the fun! I'm Bearskin. The fellow in the hat is Shadow John and this is Mother Mary.'

'I don't understand what's going on,' Hal said. 'I was walking through my home town, and then somehow I ended up here.'

'That happens sometimes,' Shadow John said, resting his long-fingered hands on a silver-topped cane. 'There are thin places between the Fixed Lands and Faerie. Sometimes Fragile Creatures can just fall through, without even making the transition—'

'Not just Fragile Creatures.' A new person had appeared on the fringes of the group who resembled nothing so much as a medieval woodcut of the devil, complete with red-tinted skin, horns, a goatee beard, furry animal legs and cloven hooves. 'One day I dropped right out of the Far Lands. I had to walk halfway across the Fixed Lands before I found my way back. It was a close call, I tell you. They can be a savage lot when their ire is raised. Followed my footprints up hill and down dale, they did, before I managed to slip back.'

Bearskin thrust the tankard into Hal's hand and encouraged him to drink with the exhortation, 'All given freely and without obligation.' Everyone laughed raucously, though Hal didn't get the joke.

The beer was the best he had ever tasted, with a vast complexity of subtle flavours and delicate aromas, but after less than a quarter of the tankard he was already feeling heady. Yet while his conscious mind flirted with drunkenness, it unleashed his subconscious to work overtime making connections that began to unveil a hidden picture. Hal decided that here was an opportunity he should seize to glean as much information as he could. So much time and energy had been expended by several ministries in the search for the nature of the Otherworld and what had happened in the days before and after the Fall, and they had found next to nothing. All the knowledge Hal gathered would be vital in the war effort; and perhaps, Hal thought, it would move him a few rungs further up the ladder; he had languished at his current level for far too long.

'So,' he began, 'your world exists alongside my own – the Fixed Lands, is that right? Side by side?'

'Beside it, behind it and right in amongst it,' Mother Mary said. 'Didn't you listen to any of the old stories when yer were a kid? We was always there, amongst you, sometimes seen, more often than not, not.'

'You've always exerted an influence?' Hal said.

'There were some who felt the need to shape and guide,' Shadow John said.

'And some who just liked mischief and menace,' Bearskin added. 'But make no mistake, we've always been around. Played a bigger part in your affairs than you could guess.'

'Invisible,' Hal mused, 'but always there.' That thought set an alarm bell ringing in Hal's mind, but the reason why remained irritatingly elusive.

For the next hour, Hal asked many questions, about Otherworld, the Caretaker, the invasion, and while he received some answers of note, many were couched in riddles that left his head aching. Then, as he sipped on his beer, a twinkle of light passed quickly behind the bar. Hal glimpsed Drogoff the barman stooping low, his face puzzled, but after a moment he gave a resounding cheer.

'What is it now?' the Devil said with irritation.

'A hero!' Drogoff said with arms raised. 'Our young friend is a hero!'

'We know that,' Shadow John said superciliously.

While Hal buried his face in his tankard, Drogoff proceeded to tell the entire bar how Hal had saved the tiny flying woman. Suddenly the attention Hal received was even more glowing.

'I always knew them Brothers and Sisters of Dragons wos a good lot,' Mother Mary said drunkenly. She dabbed at one eye. 'To save one of us . . . and a miserable lot we are . . . that's just . . .' She couldn't find the words and so downed another drink.

'I didn't really do anything,' Hal protested.

'The mark of a true hero!' Bearskin proclaimed. 'More beer, Drogoff! And don't put any water in this one!'

The rest of the evening passed in a haze of beer, fragrant pipe smoke and stories that made Hal's head spin. Some were so unbelievable that Hal wondered if the pub's strange inhabitants were playing games with him. The feeling of being in the middle of a dream grew more potent the longer he was there, and Hal felt uneasily that the longer he stayed the more dreamlike it would become, until he didn't want to leave. It was compounded when he attempted to check the lateness of the hour, for however much he screwed up his eyes, he could not make out the time on his watch. He put it down to the drink, but the matter niggled away at him.

'I think it's time to go,' he said as he drained the last of his fourth tankard of beer.

A disappointed outcry rose up from the increasingly large group that had gathered around him during the course of the discussions.

'But you haven't yet told us any tales of the Brothers and Sisters of Dragons,' Bearskin protested. 'We never tire of those.'

'About how the Giant Killer set up your Brotherhood in the days of the tribes,' someone called out.

'The one about the tomb in the Forest of the Night. "*A kiss shall awaken him.*" I remember that part,' said another.

'I'm sorry,' Hal replied, 'but I don't know any of those.'

'You don't know?' said Shadow John incredulously. 'But it's who you are!'

The feeling that he was betraying some great heritage made Hal even keener to go. 'I'm sorry. Perhaps another time. It's getting late.'

'The hour is always late,' Mother Mary said with a cackle.

Drogoff leaned across the bar. 'Stay the night, young lad. We've got rooms free. A quiet one, if you like, or one where we can send all the pleasures you would ever need.' He nodded towards three incredibly beautiful women leaning against a post in the middle of the pub, sipping drinks the colour of absinthe from long glasses. They looked quite normal until one raised a hand to wave to Drogoff and Hal saw a third eye embedded in the palm. It winked at him.

'Some other time,' he said with a shudder.

Shadow John slipped a friendly arm around Hal's shoulders. 'We've enjoyed your company, young lad. And for your act of great compassion you may call on us any time.'

'True, too true,' Bearskin said. 'Call on any of us who drink here in The Hunter's Moon. Right, lads and lassies?' Loud agreement echoed around the pub. Bearskin grinned, showing two rows of pointed teeth stained with blood. 'Call on us if you need any help, any time. We're always ready to help out a friend.'

'And friends like us you cain't do without!' Mother Mary's shrieking laugh ended in a series of hacking, phlegmy coughs.

'How do I call on you?' Hal asked.

Bearskin and Shadow John shared a secret smile, before Bearskin dipped into one of his voluminous pockets and pulled out a shiny red gem that glowed with an inner light. 'This is a Bloodeye,' he said. 'Stick it in your pocket. You'll forget it's there until you need it. Then hold it and say "Far and away and here" and whichever of us you need will be just around the corner.'

' "Far and away and here"?' Hal checked to see if Bearskin was joking, but he seemed quite serious.

'Aye. It's as good as any.'

Hal said his goodbyes and slipped out into the night. It was even colder than it had been earlier, and the chill was exacerbated by the beer. Overhead, Petronus's glittery trail darted back and forth. Hal pulled his coat around him and trudged in the direction of his quarters, surprised that he felt more alive than he had done in

finding arcadia

'Is man an ape or an angel? Now I am on the side of the angels.'
Benjamin Disraeli

Moments of ice, moments of heat.

Fate has a strange way of intruding into lives. It's possible on occasion to trace back the compounded good fortune of a well-lived life to one event that, if whipped away, would have changed everything that came after to such a degree that the life would not have been even half as well lived; perhaps it would have been quite miserable. The whole edifice of wellbeing built on one random incident. Hunter found the capriciousness shudder-inducing. Walk a little slower, indulge yourself with a more lingering glance at something that has caught your eye, and everything could be different; everything could be bad. The only way it became bearable was if you believed that the universe inherently looked after the living creatures that inhabited it, and that the mechanics of the system would always pull towards the best possible outcome. Hunter liked to think that was true; he had enough evidence from many of the lives around him to consider it to be so. But he was never sure.

Case in point: seven years earlier, a late screening of *It's A Wonderful Life* at the National Film Theatre on the South Bank in London. Hunter had come out of a long meeting at the MI6 offices at Vauxhall profoundly depressed. For the first time, it had felt as if his life was slipping into shadow. There had been the incident in Bosnia, one terrible act committed for the greater good; and then the briefing – at which, he recalled, Reid had been a very junior but highly ambitious attendee. The list of potential hotspots was followed by details of Hunter's next three missions; no feeling human being should have been asked to undertake them, but Hunter had accepted them without batting an eye. It was simply the path he was on.

And so he had wandered, lost in thought. He could have gone into the nearest pub to drown himself in Jack Daniel's, and then on to the brothel in Battersea, which had been his intention. But something made him pause outside the NFT, with its poster of Jimmy Stewart and Donna Reed. A moment later he had bought a ticket and was fumbling in the dark to find a seat.

The film had washed over him, his thoughts too bleak to take it in. But on the way out, he had been following a young man with a large briefcase that had burst open, spilling files all over the foyer. As Hunter helped collect them up, his barbed small talk and louche attitude had been deflected by the young man's intense nature. Hunter had felt some inexplicable but profound connection with the dark, troubled depths in the stranger's eyes and when he discovered that they both shared a Government background, Hunter had persuaded the man to go for a drink. As was Hunter's style, one drink had become many and by the time Hunter had left his acquaintance on the doorstep, vomiting, the basis of a friendship had been formed.

The young man, Hal, had been Hunter's turning point towards a life well lived. It would be too glib to say that Hal had reset Hunter's priorities, but certainly in Hal Hunter saw some kind of redemption. When the Fall came, Hal had been ahead of the game, reading the signs, briefing Hunter on the re-emergence of the supernatural while others in the Government had laughed and protested that it was some sort of disinformation campaign to camouflage a terrorist attack. And when the Battle of London had finally burst with devastating ferocity, it was Hal who had convinced Hunter to leave the city to the warring gods and monsters, and to the monstrous beasts that had destroyed whole sections of it with the fiery blasts of their breath. Most of their colleagues had died in the atrocity that had befallen Parliament and

Whitehall. And as he had stood on Hampstead Heath looking over the raging fires and plumes of black smoke, Hunter had clapped an arm around Hal's shoulders and proclaimed that he owed his life to Hal; jokingly, of course, but he had meant it all the same.

They were like two very different halves of the same person, each with their own individual quirks and characteristics, which, when brought together, made a much better whole. They both knew it, and they both knew they were lucky to have found a deep and abiding friendship in the small details of their lives, because it was quite obvious they couldn't exist without each other.

Heat, flaring intensely, giving way to excruciating pain. Hunter's thoughts jolted out of their deep introspection into a monochrome world. White snowflakes drifting dreamily down against blackness. White snow all around, black patches obscuring it here and there: heads, legs, arms and blasted tree branches, chunks of rock and earth. His thoughts swirled, desperate to get back to the cocoon of memory.

Someone was tugging at him.

'Come. You cannot stay here.' The voice was like shattering glass.

'Where . . . where am I?' Hunter was surprised to hear how weak and sluggish his voice sounded, as if he was coming out of a three-day bender.

'Come.'

Pain lanced through every part of Hunter's body as he was lifted effortlessly. It cleared his mind enough for him to realise that he was shaking with cold and shock; he blacked out instantly.

Samantha was kissing him passionately, and he was feeling emotions that had not been stirred for many a year. He'd always liked Samantha, but he would never have guessed she would ever trigger those kinds of feelings. He wanted to kiss her again and again, but the sensation was drifting away to be replaced by more white, everywhere white . . .

Hunter emerged into the harshness of the world, still so cold that he could barely feel his body. He was in a sheltered spot that protected him on three sides from the harshest blasts of the gale. Before him, snow-blanketed hillsides rolled away into valleys. More snow was falling.

The battle. The ghost-flight. The shell falling. Memories and all their accompanying sensations rushed back with such force that he jolted against the rocky outcropping that surrounded him. Once again he felt that instant of horrific realisation rip through him when he had appeared back in his body just as the explosion threw him through the air. How had he survived? Hunter quickly checked his limbs – all present and intact, a miracle in itself – but his fatigues were shredded and covered with an inordinate amount of dried blood.

'The Pendragon Spirit is already healing you.'

Hunter started at the same breaking-glass tones he thought had previously come to him in a dream. The voice emanated from the direction of a deep snowdrift. Slowly his hand searched for his gun; it wasn't there, nor was his knife. Two red circles appeared in the snow. They disappeared, returned, and Hunter realised with shock that he was looking into a pair of eyes.

What he had taken to be a snowdrift rose up to reveal itself as a strange creature with a crab-shaped head atop the body of a man. It was clad in tattered rags that blew back and forth like the trailing appendages of a jellyfish. Both the physical form and the clothes were so white that they merged perfectly with the surrounding snow.

Hunter bunched his fists, though he didn't have the energy to fight.

'I am a friend,' the creature said.

Hunter weighed this, decided it was probably true. 'You're the one who dragged me off the battlefield.'

'I was walking the hillsides in my search when I saw you blazing like a blue star. But your fire was dying.'

'I was freezing to death.'

'Yes. This world has grown very cold, and your injuries were grave.'

'Hunter checked his limbs again, puzzled. 'Just scratches.'

'Now. But not earlier. I brought you to shelter so that the Pendragon Spirit would have time to heal you.'

'Right. I grew myself some new limbs. I always knew that skill would come in handy one day.' Hunter's mind was already racing ahead: he had to get back to debrief. All the information he had garnered about the enemy would be vital. 'What are you?' he asked obliquely.

'I am Moyaanisqui, sometimes called the White Walker. I search for the Cailleach Bheur. She has unleashed the Fimbulwinter in anticipation of the End-Times. She is near. Have you seen her?'

'I have no idea what you're talking about. Thanks for saving me and all, and not that I'm ungrateful, but I need to get out of here.' Hunter could feel his strength returning with each passing moment; it felt like a trickle of electricity bringing life to his limbs and his thought processes. There was something so clearly unnatural about the sensation that he paused to reflect once more on what had happened. 'What did you just say . . . the Pendragon Spirit?'

'The Blue Fire. It burns within you.'

Hunter examined his hands. A scratch he had seen moments before had now disappeared. 'What's happened to me?'

'I met one of your kind in recent times,' the White Walker said, 'in the Far Lands. But she had ice inside her, where in you the fire burns clearly.'

'What do you mean, "one of my kind"? A human? The Far Lands . . . is that . . . the Otherworld?' His mind raced even faster.

'Yes, a Fragile Creature. She was the first of your kind I had met. But she was not like the others with her. She was special – like you.'

In the deep caverns of Hunter's subconscious, something stirred. The information the White Walker was imparting was something he already knew instinctively, although he had no idea how.

'Since my encounter with her, I have learned more of your kind,' the White Walker continued. 'Brothers and Sisters of Dragons. You are one of the Five.'

Blue sparks flared in Hunter's mind, and for a second he thought he might black out again. *Impossible*, he thought. *Coincidence*, and a score more denials, but he knew it was true. Suddenly the world looked a different place, his whole life turned on its head. He needed time to think about what it all meant. Glancing rapidly around, he searched the bleak hillsides. All roads had been obscured; there was no sign of life.

'Can you help me to get out of here?' he asked.

'I need to find the Cailleach Bheur,' the White Walker said hesitantly.

Hunter struggled to pull himself up the rocks to his feet. He wouldn't be able to get far in his current condition.

The White Walker reached forward with fingers that resembled hoar-frosted icicles and grabbed Hunter's hand. The touch was so cold that Hunter felt it sink deep into his bones. 'Come, then,' the White Walker said. 'I will take you, for how could I refuse such a source of wonder?'

Hunter found himself lifted effortlessly on to the White Walker's back. Flickers of frost crusted Hunter's eyelashes. The cold infused every part of his body until it seemed as though the whole world had turned white.

The White Walker set off down the slope with a fast, loping gait. The Scottish countryside fell by in a blur. Hunter clung on as tightly as he could with fingers he couldn't feel, yet inside, mysteriously, his soul had started to soar.

They hadn't gone far when Hunter saw a figure standing on a hilltop nearby. It was indistinct at first, but gradually Hunter made out an old woman with wild hair, like a black crow hunched over against the wind. Clinging on to a tall staff for support, lightning danced around her so that it seemed as if she was at the heart of a storm.

'That is the Cailleach Bheur, known by some as the Blue Hag,' the White Walker called above the wind. 'The one I seek. I will return to beg her to stop the Fimbulwinter.'

In that instant, the cryptic comments the White Walker had made earlier fell into place. 'She's causing this weather,' Hunter noted aloud. 'And it's not going to stop, is it?'

'Not until all the worlds are white, and the only ones left are the Cailleach Bheur and me. As Existence falls into the dark, the winter shall go on for ever.'

Hunter closed his eyes against the knives of the wind and clung on tightly, urging the miles to fall away quickly. Events were turning bad faster than anyone had realised.

'It *was* here,' Hal stressed when he saw the condescendingly weary expression on Manning's face. She wore a long fur coat with a muffler and a tall fur hat, like some Russian aristocrat out of *Doctor*

Zhivago. Hal had watched her warily since the night he had seen her talking to an invisible companion, but since then she had exhibited no other unusual behaviour. In the background, four bag carriers and advisors in suits shifted uncomfortably in the biting cold.

'Mister Kirkham?' Reid stamped his feet as he indicated the bare brick wall on the side street where Hal had said The Hunter's Moon had been situated. Reid, at least, had taken Hal seriously. When Hal had turned up at his office at 9.00 a.m., he had quickly arranged for a visit to the site.

Kirkham examined the wall carefully. He had an ultrasound probe, a Geiger counter and an EMF monitor, which he proceeded to set up in the thick snow that had been falling all morning. 'I have to say, in all our research we've never come across any buildings translocating, or the appearance of any clear portals to the Otherworld through which a mortal could travel,' he said.

'Doesn't mean it can't happen,' Reid said. 'Bloody hell, in this world right now, anything can happen.' He clapped hands clad in expensive leather gloves. 'When is this weather going to turn? I swear it's even colder than yesterday.'

'One degree lower, according to the latest figures,' Kirkham muttered as he examined a swinging needle on a display.

'We can't stay here too long,' Manning said, checking her watch. 'You haven't forgotten the emergency Cabinet session?'

'How could I?' Reid snapped. 'But after what happened up north, any information we find here could be even more essential.'

Hal sensed a tension between Reid and Manning that had escalated since the last time he had seen the two of them together. Since he had joined the civil service, Hal had been aware of politicians jockeying for power and influence, something that had, if anything, grown more intense since the Fall. But there was an added dimension to Reid and Manning's rivalry that he couldn't fathom.

'I can't find anything,' Kirkham said. 'We could always put this position under surveillance in case it reappears.'

'Or in case this young man gets drunk again and hallucinates another experience,' Manning added tartly. She turned on her heels and marched back in the direction of the main thoroughfare, with the four assistants slipping and sliding to keep up.

While Kirkham packed up his equipment, Reid said quietly to Hal, 'Ignore her. Probably her period. Look, I think this is vitally important information and I think you should take it to the highest level.'

'Me?'

'The PM needs to know about this and it should come from the horse's mouth, not be buried in the middle of some report that he only has ten seconds to read. Or from some lackey he probably doesn't trust anyway. This could be a turning point.'

Hal was taken aback. The chain of command had always kept him well away from any minister not directly involved in his particular sphere, and certainly never allowed him near the PM. But Reid appeared sincere; whatever had happened in Scotland clearly had everyone rattled.

'How do I go about getting an appointment?' Hal said.

'Leave that to me. I'll find a slot in his diary. Difficult at the moment with the war on, of course, but the sooner we can get you in there, the better.' As Kirkham finished packing up, Reid leaned in to Hal and said, even more quietly, 'Just keep this to yourself. Everyone's plotting at the moment and I don't know who I can trust.' He searched Hal's face. 'I think I can trust you. Is that right?'

'Of course,' Hal replied.

Reid nodded curtly, then strode away before Kirkham noticed his interaction with Hal. Hal was concerned by the spy's parting words. Why didn't Reid know who to trust? Surely everyone was pulling together with the crisis looming. As Hal trudged back towards Magdalen, he had an uneasy sensation of movement behind the scenes, and threads being drawn closer together.

Hal found Samantha on his office doorstep, her face unnaturally pale. 'Can I come in?' she asked with urgency.

'Sorry about the mess,' Hal began, motioning to the desk where piles of files had been stacked two feet high. He had never been so behind with his work before.

'Have you heard the news?' she said breathlessly. 'Ninety per cent of our force was wiped out in Scotland.'

'Hunter?'

Samantha chewed her lip. 'He's listed amongst the missing.'

Hal felt sick, but he put on a brave face. 'You know what

Hunter's like. Hit him in the face with a hammer and he'll keep coming back for more. Anyone who can survive the free-drink weekend at Mrs Damask's isn't going to fold up at the first opportunity.'

When Hal saw that nothing he could say would ease Samantha's worries, he said, 'Do you want a coffee? I've got some stashed away for special occasions.'

'That's like gold dust,' Samantha said. 'And isn't it on the protected substances list? You're supposed to hand in any supplies.'

'So some minister can have it for their personal stash?' Hal caught himself. 'Listen to me, I sound like Hunter.'

From the back of his top drawer, Hal pulled out a tiny jar wrapped in masking tape so that the contents couldn't be seen. He shook out a few precious brown grains into a couple of mugs, topped them up with water from the kettle suspended over the fire and handed one steaming mug to Samantha.

'Thanks,' she said. 'I'm glad you're here, Hal. You've been a real friend to me. It's hard to find anyone in this place I can really talk to.'

Friend. The compliment stung as much as if she'd slapped him.

'You know, I never thought you really cared for him,' Hal said.

'Neither did I. Until I realised I did, about five minutes before he flew off. He's a loudmouth, a bighead, a slut who's probably crawling with God knows how many sexual diseases and a drunk. There's absolutely no reason why I should like him.'

Hal laughed quietly. 'I know exactly what you mean. We have nothing in common at all. Whenever I go out drinking with him, I'm unconscious halfway through the night, without fail. He always gets me home, though.'

'But there's something about him. I just can't put my finger on it.'

'He's a good man, once you get past the front. He's got morals, ethics . . . hard to believe when you consider what he does. I think he hates himself a bit, which is sad. He's complicated. There are two Hunters – one you see and one you only catch glimpses of.'

'Do you know what made me think he might be all right?' Samantha warmed her hands on the coffee mug. 'That you're his friend, and I think you'd only be friends with someone who was . . . worthy.'

'That's a funny word.' Hal stared deep into her eyes, which were green like a cat's, immeasurably deep.

'He's lucky he's got you in his corner.'

'You'll make a good couple,' Hal said and meant it.

Samantha luxuriated in the taste of her coffee. Then she said, 'Do you know what one of the PAs said to me the other day? With all the strange stuff in the world today, all the magic and the gods and the wonders, we're now living in a world where wishes could come true. So tell me, Hal, if you could wish for anything, what would it be?'

He thought for a moment and then replied, 'Nothing. I've got everything I need.'

'You know, I think I believe you. You're so calm, so centred.'

'And you'd wish for Hunter to be back here, right now.'

'I think I probably would. I want a chance to see if it could work, you know?' She took a deep breath, and to Hal it sounded immeasurably sad. 'Though I might also wish for some music. I miss the radio . . . new songs . . . old songs.'

'All right,' Hal said, 'the best old song: "Wichita Lineman". Glen Campbell. No argument. Do you know it?'

Samantha wrinkled her nose. 'Sounds like something my mum would like.'

'There's a line in it that goes: "And I need you more than want you, and I want you for all time." I don't think there's a better way of describing love, anywhere.'

She giggled. 'You're such an old romantic.'

'Yes,' he said with a smile. 'I am.'

In his cell, Mallory brooded and planned and waited for his moment. He still couldn't bring himself to think of Sophie's name or what had happened to her. Every thought he had was channelled towards his escape. He'd tested his manacles and they were as effective as they should be in a high-security wing. The guards always came around in twos with his food, one training an SA80 on him. But Mallory knew he had two things to his advantage: since Sophie's death he really didn't care if he lived or died; and he knew his abilities – and in particular the abilities of the Pendragon Spirit – better than his captors did.

The training he had undergone at Salisbury Cathedral to become a Knight Templar had also pushed him to the upper limits of physical and mental fitness. Focusing the mind, preparing for extreme hardship, were now embedded in his system. He had hated his time in the brutal regime, but it had taught him to be a survivor. All told, he was ready.

And so, when the guards came with his lunch, Mallory gathered himself. 'Bring it over here,' he said, nodding to the tray with the plate of what appeared to be vegetable stew on it.

'Get lost.' The guard with the gun waved the barrel at him.

Mallory knew the guards hated him. They didn't know why they did, but the fact that he was imprisoned along with all the other dangerous freaks in the high-security wing damned him by association. 'I've had enough of all this – the way you treat me. I deserve better.'

'Boo hoo,' the one with the tray mocked.

Mallory took a step forward.

'Oi!' The one with the gun grew tense, thrusting the weapon more menacingly. 'Back.'

'No,' Mallory said. 'I've reached my limit. I'm not going to rot in this hole. I'd rather die.' Mallory continued to walk towards them.

The guards backed away, a sliver of panic driving the contempt out of their eyes. The one with the tray put it down and thumbed his radio. 'Section fourteen to base. Incident at B-twenty-nine. Prisoner unruly. Send back-up.'

'It won't do any good,' Mallory said. 'I can kill with my bare hands. I've been trained.'

'Back off!' the one with the gun shouted. 'I will fire.'

'Better do it,' Mallory said, 'because you're going to be dead in five seconds.' Mallory rushed the guard without another warning.

Acting on instinct, the guard fired a short burst. The rounds tore through Mallory, flinging him back against the wall hard. Slipping down to the floor in shock, he watched his blood puddling around him. There was pain, and then numbness as the dark crept up on him.

The last thing he heard was one of the guards saying, 'You fucking idiot! You've killed him!'

After Samantha had cheered up a little she returned to her office, leaving Hal steeling himself to venture out into the cold. He fought his way through drifts that built up as quickly as the street workers cleared the snow away, and eventually reached the Bodleian Library. Its vast resource of books amassed over four centuries was one of the main reasons that Oxford had been chosen for the new seat of Government. After the destruction of central London and the waste laid to much of the country's infrastructure, the fragility of humanity, its knowledge and traditions was belatedly acknowledged. The Bodleian contained everything of value that the human race had ever achieved, condensed into racks and shelves, the Holy Grail of civilisation. It was going to be protected at all costs.

Hal went to the Old Library and entered the Lower Reading Room. He expected several hours of shivering at a table while the librarian brought the necessary tomes to him, but it was as warm as a hothouse inside.

'Best place to be,' the chief librarian said from his seat behind the main enquiry desk. 'We've got protected status, so we can have as much fuel as we want for the heating system.' He appeared oblivious to everything else that was going on beyond his cloistered world. He had a mound of snowy white hair and thick glasses that made his eyes appear unfeasibly large. Despite the heat, he wore a heavy jumper with brash, multicoloured hoops.

Hal took a seat in the general reference and enquiry area where he could occasionally steal glimpses at the snow drifting down outside. It also allowed easy access to the lower reserve to pick up the books dropped off by the librarian. He was in for the long haul. He had a vague idea of what he was looking for, but it would take him a while to pinpoint it exactly. Hal was now sure that the strange blue hologram-image that emerged from the Wish Stone reflected a painting. That much had emerged from the depths of Hal's memory, but which painting and what it might mean eluded him completely.

He spent the next two hours wading randomly through art books before admitting to himself that he wasn't getting anywhere. His methodical mind was exasperated by his methods, but his basic information was too limited to begin any structured search. The computer system was up and running, one of the first non-

Government systems to have been restored after the Fall, but even a scan of the OLIS online catalogue didn't give him any guidance.

As he sat and stared out of the window for inspiration, his fingers found a strange object in his pocket. He pulled it out and was surprised to see the Bloodeye that Bearskin had given him in The Hunter's Moon the previous evening. As Bearskin had told him, Hal hadn't remembered he had it, or he would undoubtedly have shown it to Reid.

He thought for a moment and then held the jewel in the palm of his hand and whispered, 'Far and away and here.' Hal didn't know what he'd been expecting – some flash of light or burst of coloured smoke, perhaps – but there was nothing. Irritated that he had allowed himself to be made a fool of, he slipped the stone back into his pocket.

Yet a few seconds later there was an overpowering smell of wet fur. Hal looked around to see if a dog had found its way into the library and was greeted by a low, rasping laugh that sounded very much like an old man's, unsettling with a hint of malignancy. Goose pimples rose up on Hal's arms.

Hal looked around again, and then almost fell backwards off his chair in shock when his gaze returned to his desk, which had been empty a split second earlier. A tiny, misshapen man now sat there, rolling his eyes at Hal. Naked, his wrinkled, leathery skin was grey-green, his ears pointed, his teeth an unnerving row of needles, and his fingers ended in broken but lethal-looking talons.

'Cat got your tongue?' the little man said nastily.

'You're here because . . . I called you?' Hal said hesitantly.

'We all answer the Bloodeye. A friend in need is always to be answered. Though I've never seen a friend like you.' He bared his teeth at Hal.

'What's your name?'

'I have many names. Some I'll answer to, and some I won't, and one is secret, never to be told. But you can call me Maucus.'

'Will you answer to that one?'

'We'll see, won't we?'

Hal was unnerved by the little man's attitude and wondered if he might be better off, and safer, if he sent Maucus away.

The little man appeared to read Hal's mind, for he said, 'You have nothing to fear when the Bloodeye has called. But do not come across me at other times, for then I may not be so generous.'

Feeling a little more confident, Hal asked, 'What are you?'

'My kind live in the book stores and libraries. We drink the smell of paper and eat the joy of people who find a piece of information or a story they desire. Sometimes we'll hide books, usually at the point when the one wanting them is reaching the end of a long, laborious search. Just for fun. We're always there, but your kind never sees us, hiding on top of the stacks or behind the shelves. You think we're rats or mice, or birds on the roof.'

'I want—'

'No!' Maucus jumped forward so threateningly that Hal rocked back on his chair. 'Don't tell me! Words that aren't written down could be lies. They disappear. People forget what they said.'

'How can I tell you, then?'

'Give me your hand.'

Hal hesitated, then extended his right hand, palm upwards. Maucus gripped it with a strength belied by his size; Hal tried to wrench it back, but couldn't. Maucus bared one of his talons and slashed a thin red line across Hal's hand.

As Hal cried out in pain, the little man smiled sadistically, then bent forward and lapped Hal's blood. Hal was sickened by the sight, but it only lasted a second before Maucus bounded off into the shadowy depths of the library.

A few minutes later, he returned with a book, which he dropped on the desk. It fell open at a picture of the same scene projected by the Wish Stone.

It was a romantic painting of three men dressed in what looked like togas crouched around a stone tomb. A woman in luscious orange and blue robes looked on. The men were pointing at an inscription on the tomb: *Et in Arcadia Ego*. The scene was set in some idyllic rural setting, on a hillside, with trees against gold-tinted clouds passing across a brilliant blue sky. The light suggested twilight, or perhaps dawn.

Hal read the inscription underneath: *Les Bergers d'Arcadie – The Shepherds of Arcadia* by Nicolas Poussin, Musée du Louvre, Paris.

Hal knew his Latin – the inscription translated literally as 'And in Arcadia I' or 'I am in Arcadia, too' – but Hal had no idea what it meant. More puzzling was why a seventeenth-century painting should be revealed by a magic stone that must have been hundreds if not thousands of years older, if it truly had been buried under Cadbury Hill.

Clearly the picture must be very significant indeed for a unique and powerful object like the Wish Stone to have preserved its image, but its meaning escaped him. As Hal examined the painting more closely, he noticed that something wasn't quite right. 'The picture is back to front,' he mused. 'Or the image is. The stone shows the woman on the left. The painting has her on the right. And everything else is reversed, as well. The image doesn't show the whole of the painting, either – it's cropped very closely around the characters.'

'Ah, but there's the mystery,' Maucus said. 'Do I have to do everything for you?'

'Yes, please,' Hal said tartly, emboldened.

Maucus glowered coldly and Hal wondered if he had gone too far. But then the little man disappeared into the library once more, returning a few minutes later with a book about Shugborough Hall, a stately home in Staffordshire on the estate of the Royal photographer, Lord Lichfield. Once again, the book fell open at the correct page, only this time it revealed a photo of the reversed Wish Stone image of the shepherds. But this was no painting. The photograph showed a carved stone relief known as The Shepherd's Monument that stood in the Hall's nine-hundred-acre grounds.

Hal read that the monument and a mysterious inscription carved beneath it – O.U.O.S.V.A.V.V., and underneath a 'D' and an 'M' – had been a mystery for more than 250 years. Charles Darwin had been observed mulling over its meaning, and Josiah Wedgwood had spent many hours trying to crack the code. Some believed that it held the secret of the whereabouts of the Holy Grail, others that it was a memorial to a lost love of Thomas Anson, who had created the estate in the eighteenth century.

'There *is* a mystery here,' Maucus said, once again as if he could read Hal's mind. 'But is it buried deep or does it lie on the surface where only one with the right vision may see it?'

Hal felt a surge of excitement at the puzzle that had been presented to him. Here was a conundrum in which he could immerse himself; more, he was sure it was something where he could finally make a valuable contribution. The hint of long-buried secrets made him feverish. Hidden knowledge, dark wisdom – the mystery hinted at both. 'I need more information,' he said.

'Enough!' Maucus spat. 'If it's slaves you need, then look amongst your own kind. Do not insult me by demanding too much. Rather, give thanks for the aid I have offered.'

'I do thank you,' Hal said, wary that Maucus was on the brink of attacking. 'Very much. But where do I go from here?'

'Tread your own path, coz. You have had enough from me.'

Maucus disappeared so quickly it was as if the little man had decided he would simply no longer be seen. Yet his odour remained for a long while after, and Hal had the uneasy feeling that his former helper was still watching from some hidden vantage point, weighing up whether or not he should teach Hal a very unpleasant lesson.

It worried Hal sufficiently that he packed up his books and dropped them off at the enquiry desk, answering the librarian's questions about his progress with a blank smile before hurrying out into the bitter day.

The mood after the Cabinet meeting was desolate. The General attempted to hold his head high as he marched out of the darkened room towards the Ministry of Defence offices, but once inside he was crushed by the absolute devastation of his plans. There was nothing good to report; there was no hope that he could see. He'd attempted to put an optimistic spin on the debriefing, but everyone had seen through it. The PM had asked about the deployment of battlefield nukes, and the fact that even the leader was considering such extreme action on British soil showed that they were approaching the last act.

'General?'

He turned to see Manning, who, for once, had not said a single word during the meeting. 'Catherine.'

'I notice you left a few details out of your report. How long before the enemy reach Oxford?'

'I omitted that strand because to consider it would be an admission of failure. We will stop the enemy long before they reach Oxford.'

Manning's dismissive shrug made the General burn inside, but he maintained his surface calm.

'Battlefield nuclear weapons? How many are you planning to use?' she asked. 'How many have we stockpiled? You suggested that there appears to be a near-endless supply of the enemy . . . all flooding over from the Otherworld, I presume. Logically—'

'I don't concern myself with theoretical arguments. There are several tactical options we haven't begun to try.'

'How long, General?'

The General cursed under his breath, realising why he disliked the woman so much. 'We can't estimate anything at the moment. The enemy's advance has come to a halt just south of Berwick. We don't know how long they're going to stay there, or why.'

'But you have an idea.'

The General chose his words carefully. 'Intelligence suggests that the enemy is eliminating any potential opposition.'

'So they're eradicating the population as they advance, pausing, cleansing an area, moving on. Berwick has fallen?'

The General nodded.

'We can't rely on conventional means, General. We have to put our faith in other measures.'

'No option has been ruled out, Catherine.'

The General was distracted by a young assistant from his offices who was trailing snow behind him as he ran towards them. 'General, sir,' the young man said breathlessly as he skidded to a halt. 'There's been a survivor, sir. From the rout, in Scotland. He's on his way in by chopper now.'

The General turned back to Manning. 'I have to go.'

'Consider what I said, General.'

But the General was already doing his best to forget her, and all politicians, as he followed the assistant back to the Ministry of Defence offices. All he needed was one break, a single flaw in the enemy's defence, and he would strike back with maximum force. If the survivor had any new intelligence, he would seize it forcefully and then he would show Manning and all the others exactly what he stood for.

Hunter was in much better shape by the time the chopper touched down in the Deer Park. His amazement at the healing ability of the Pendragon Spirit had been superseded by a long period of intense reflection on what it meant for him to have been chosen to receive such a power. In one instant he had been forced to look at himself and his place in the world in a different light. No longer could he pretend that he was just a foot soldier drifting from mission to mission. He now had a purpose, and an obligation, if only he could decide what they were.

The General met him as he climbed down from the chopper. 'I should have known you'd be back.'

'Yes, sir, and thank you for your good wishes.' The General allowed Hunter some latitude as he always did, but Hunter knew he couldn't push his superior too far this time.

'I hope you've come back with some useful information,' the General said.

'I believe so, sir.'

'We'll head straight to debriefing. Your men?'

'All dead.' Hunter's stomach twisted at the loss of those under his command. The hardest to accept was Clevis; his uncomprehending face at the moment of his death was burned into Hunter's mind.

'You look remarkably hale and hearty. Not even a scratch?'

'I have very thick skin.'

By the time they reached the debriefing room where most of the top brass had already congregated, Hunter had decided what information he was going to reveal and what he was going to hold back. He described in unflinching detail how the enemy took over the fallen and added them to its ranks, and he watched as faces grew steely when he described the King of Insects and the four Lords leading the attack. His account of what was really causing the arctic weather only added to the dark mood in the room. But there was some talk of a potential ally when he told how the White Walker had helped him to the nearest outpost, where he had rested while he made radio contact and waited to be picked up.

But of the Pendragon Spirit and his role as Brother of Dragons, he said not a word.

After the General had given Hunter a day's leave to recuperate, Hunter slipped quickly away and sought out Hal, who seemed to have transformed his office into an art gallery. Hunter cast his eye over the large and small copies of the same painting and said, 'It's a bit late in the day to pretend you have some culture.'

160

Hal smiled warmly. 'I was starting to get worried.'

'I thought I'd trained you better than that.'

Hal suddenly came alive in a manner Hunter hadn't seen before. 'I've got something to tell you,' he said, motioning to the pictures pinned all over the walls. 'I'm investigating an artefact that Brother of Dragons brought back from Cadbury Hill.'

Hunter perked up at this. 'Go on.'

'It links to this painting, and then to a monument at some stately home called Shugborough Hall. I don't know what it all means yet, but I'm sure it's important.' He paused, unable to restrain a grin. 'More than important.'

'Right.' Hunter thought intensely for a moment. 'You've got to keep me up to speed about that. But don't tell anyone else before you tell me.'

'Why?'

'We've discussed this. I know best,' Hunter replied. Hal shook his head wearily. 'That Brother of Dragons . . . Mallory. He's still around? They've not carted him off to some arse-end of the country for interrogation?'

'He was shot.'

Hunter grew grave. 'Dead?'

'They thought so, at first. Last I heard he was in surgery in the high-security section. They're fighting to save his life.'

'Bloody hell. They couldn't even take him out of security when he's at death's door. They must be scared of him.'

'What's all this about?' Hal said with exasperation. 'Did you bang your head while you were out playing soldiers?'

'I've got something to tell you. But you have to swear you won't tell anyone.'

'Of course. Nothing would induce me to pass on the contents of your sleazy mind.'

'I'm serious. OK, you might not believe this . . . in fact, I can guarantee you won't. I'm a Brother of Dragons.'

The blood drained from Hal's face so rapidly that Hunter was concerned for his friend's health. 'It's not the end of the world, mate. You'd better sit down. The way I see it, it's a good thing.'

Hal listened while Hunter related all he had learned from the White Walker. 'So I've got this . . . power in me called the Pendragon Spirit,' he said finally. 'If you could have seen how I healed. Bloody hell, I looked like I'd been tossed around an abattoir after the battle. Now I'm back to my fantastically attractive former self.'

'What else does it do?'

Hunter was concerned at the intensity he saw in Hal; his friend looked as if he was close to desperation. 'I haven't worked that out yet, but I reckon there's some kind of bond between the Five. I know I felt something when I met Mallory, like we had a lot in common, as if I'd known him for years. I need to talk to him again. Decide what to do.'

'You're not going to report this?'

'What, and have them lock me up like him? No chance. The bottom line is, everybody reckons the Brothers and Sisters of Dragons are the last hope we've got for surviving this nightmare. And having seen what happened in Scotland, I haven't got any faith in the conventional force's ability to hold the line. I have to do something.'

'What can you possibly do? Whatever this Pendragon Spirit is, it doesn't make you some kind of superhero. You go up against the enemy and you'll be dead in a minute.' Hal's voice was filled with tension.

'I don't know what I can do, but I do know I've got a responsibility to do *something*.' Hunter watched Hal's face fall and added, 'Don't worry, I'm not going to go on some suicide mission. I need to find the rest of the Five—'

'But one of them's already dead. You know that.'

'Yeah, but I've got a plan.' Hunter gave a theatrical smile, but when Hal didn't respond Hunter said, 'What's wrong?'

Hal thought for a moment, then said, 'I'm scared.'

'Don't be. I'm going to do my damnedest to find a way out of this. And now I feel as if I've got some kind of chance. There's a reason I am what I am. If it was all hopeless, there wouldn't be Brothers and Sisters of Dragons, would there?'

Before Hal could answer, Samantha burst in. 'I heard you were back.' Her smile said more than her words.

There was an awkward moment between the two of them. Hal pretended to shuffle through some papers on his desk until Hunter said, 'So . . . do you fancy a quick one?'

Hunter saw Hal flinch at the inappropriateness of the comment, while the warmth drained quickly from Samantha's face. 'You really are a disgusting pig. I just came to welcome you back and now that I've done it, I'm going.'

Even after Samantha had departed, her frostiness still hung in the air. Hal said with exasperation, 'Why do you do that?'

'Do what?'

'You know, Hunter. Act like a moron.'

'It's my nature.' Hunter was not oblivious to the offence he had caused; in fact, he had chosen his words carefully, playing a part that would not raise any suspicion. It also had the effect of keeping Samantha at arm's length; Hunter knew very clearly what was to come, and suspected the eventual outcome, and it seemed uncommonly cruel to let Samantha think he might be coming back to her. No fairy-tale romance for him.

'Things are going to change very quickly and I need you to watch my back,' Hunter said.

'Change, how? I don't like change.'

'I know. Every file in its place. But if we don't shake things up quickly there's not going to be any files left to file.'

'All right,' Hal said hesitantly. 'What do you want me to do?'

'I might have to go AWOL for a while—'

'You're mad! They'll have you shot!'

'Only if they catch me. I want you to keep your ear to the ground. If they start getting a lead on me while I'm away, do whatever you can to muddy the tracks. I know it's dangerous—'

'Of course I'll do it. You shouldn't have to ask. But where are you going?'

'I don't know yet. I don't know if I stand a chance of finding what I'm looking for – better men than me have failed. I might be going on a fool's errand. But I have to try. It feels like . . . duty.'

Hal dipped into a drawer and pulled out the file of notes Samantha had passed on to him.

'What's that?' Hunter asked.

'Everything we know about the Brothers and Sisters of Dragons. Might be some use. You'd better thank Samantha for it the next time you see her. She did the dangerous work.'

Hunter felt a critical mass building. Soon events would be running away from him and he would have to use everything in his power to keep up. He worried about compromising Hal's position

– the Government would not flinch from taking harsh action if it saw disloyalty or treason. But he was convinced that Hal had the strength of character to see it through, even though he knew his friend didn't recognise that strength in himself.

Hunter and Hal shuffled around each other awkwardly before Hunter clapped his friend on the shoulder. The gesture didn't begin to match their strength of feeling, but they knew each other well enough to comprehend all that was unspoken.

'Look after yourself,' Hunter said. And then he slipped out of the door, and with a wink he was gone.

Mallory came to consciousness in the room set aside as an intensive care unit. He was numb from the drugs and strung out from the pain of his wounds and the operation, but still the haunting death image played with his mind. *Fire in the dark.* It might have been the drugs, or his nearness to death, but now he knew what it was: a gunshot to the head. Suicide. But if he'd killed himself, how could he still be there?

With an effort, he thought through this cloying barrier to the surprising realisation that his plan had worked. Deep inside him, the Pendragon Spirit was doing its work, knitting flesh, repairing organs.

When he had forced the guards to shoot him, Mallory hadn't known if his injuries would be beyond his healing ability. He had long been aware that minor cuts and bruises faded fast, that he fought off colds and viruses easily, that exhaustion came much later than it would to anyone else. But could major organ damage be repaired, and could it happen quickly enough for him to see his plan through?

As he sat up, pulling off wires to the monitors and removing a drip, he was forced to acknowledge how bad he felt. But he still had more strength than he should have in the circumstances. Though the next few hours would probably be agony – with the prospect of causing himself even more serious harm – he felt he probably had enough strength to see it through.

His vision washed back and forth drunkenly. Shakily, he lowered his legs to the floor, convinced they'd buckle under him. After a few seconds' rest he managed to stand up, but then some stitches pulled on his abdomen and warm blood seeped into the bandages bound tightly around his middle.

Yet the more he moved, the more strength flowed into his limbs, as if the act of fighting made the Pendragon Spirit come alive. With an effort of will, Mallory forced his pain into the background and proceeded slowly to the door.

The corridor was empty, but Mallory knew it wouldn't be long before he encountered some resistance. His footsteps echoed softly along the starkly lit passage, but as he rounded a bend he noticed something curious: the lights had grown dimmer. With a shiver, he realised that the temperature had also dropped several degrees and that he could now see his breath.

He advanced uneasily, for there was no obvious explanation for the changes. Peering around the next corner, Mallory saw a lone guard standing outside a door white with hoarfrost. It was from here that the cold was emanating and in the vicinity of the door there was a deep, suffocating gloom. The guard wore arctic fatigues, thick gloves and boots, a parka with the hood up and a scarf wrapped across his mouth. From the measured rise and fall of his chest, Mallory could tell he was either asleep or close to it.

Mallory weighed his options. It was a long way back to attempt to find another route out, but the chances of any path being free of resistance was slim. Yet he knew he still wasn't up to any hand-to-hand fighting, even if he could get close enough to commence it.

Before he could make his decision, he was grabbed from behind and pulled back up the corridor, a hand clamped across his mouth to prevent him from making any noise. Then Hunter stood before him, one finger pressed to his lips.

Mallory couldn't understand why Hunter hadn't raised the alarm, but he didn't have the strength to resist. Hunter pulled him through an open door and into a darkened, empty cell.

'What do you think you're doing?' Hunter said in an attempt at mockery, though he was clearly impressed. 'You're dead on your feet and you're about to take on the British Army.'

'Come closer. I'll show you what dead means.'

'Big talk. But now that we've got the macho posturing out of the way, we need to discuss something of importance.'

'I don't want to talk to you.'

'You'll talk to me because you and I are cut from the same cloth.'

Mallory instantly saw in Hunter's eyes the unimpeachable truth of that statement. That single moment of contact between the two men ran so deep that it changed both of them for ever. 'What do you mean?'

'I'm a Brother of Dragons.'

'No.' Mallory knew his denial was a lie the instant the word left his lips; a veil had been lifted and he could suddenly see Hunter as he truly was. It was all there – Mallory could almost feel the Pendragon Spirit radiating out of Hunter, like a dull heat.

'Sorry,' Hunter said. 'Looks like they let anybody in the club.'

After his exertions, Mallory suddenly felt profoundly weak and had to lower himself into a chair.

'I know it sounds like a coincidence—'

'There aren't any coincidences.' Mallory took a deep breath to steady himself. 'The Pendragon Spirit, the Blue Fire – call it what you will – it runs through everything. It's the structure behind the surface of the universe. It *arranges* things.'

'So it made sure I was in the right place at the right time. Or wrong time, depending on which way you look at it.'

'And it brought us together. It puts the pieces on the board, but it doesn't play the game. That's down to us.' Mallory cursed under his breath. 'I can't believe it's you.'

'I know there's a certain irony—'

'It's more than that! You killed one of us! Not directly, but you brought it about. And now I can't even get my revenge by killing you.' Mallory caught himself. 'There's no point talking about that now.' His shivering helped him change the subject. 'What's up with that room with all the frost on the door?'

'It's one of the prisoners they've brought in recently. Some say it's one of the gods – one of the Tuatha Dé Danann. I can't see that myself. They couldn't even hold you. How can they keep a god prisoner?' Hunter noticed the bloody bandages around Mallory's midriff. 'You're bleeding.'

'I'll heal. I just need some time to rest.'

'Are you up to getting out of here?'

'That was the general plan.'

'I've got another one.'

Mallory looked at Hunter, intrigued despite himself.

'Since you've been in here, we've been invaded. The Brothers and Sisters of Dragons are the last chance we have of stopping the complete destruction of life on this planet. But from what I hear, it's going to take five of us, or the magic . . . the power doesn't work.'

'That's the rumour.'

'We're one down already,' Hunter continued, 'and we don't know who the other two are.'

'Carry on. You're not making me depressed at all.'

Hunter paced the room while he talked. Despite himself, Mallory was developing a grudging admiration for his new associate. Hunter continued, 'But we're not the first Five.'

'The way I understand it,' Mallory said, 'throughout history, for God knows how many centuries, there's always been Five. When one lot completes whatever mission they've been chosen for, the power moves on to the next Five.'

Hunter turned sharply; he'd reached the crux of his plan. 'But does the power leave them completely when it moves on? Or do the old Five just go into retirement?'

'I've no idea. What are you getting at?'

'There were five Brothers and Sisters of Dragons who fought at the Fall. Everyone knows the story – they've become part of modern mythology. They're the reason the Government expended so much energy looking for you.'

Mallory made a dismissive gesture. 'So? Two of them died. Jack Churchill, the leader, and Ryan Veitch, the one who's supposed to have betrayed them. At least, that's how the stories go. These days you can't tell what's truth and what's been made up.'

Hunter smiled like a cat. 'Two of them are dead. Three are still alive. And we're going to find them.'

chapter nine

four journeys

'*We hear war called murder. It is not: it is suicide.*'
Ramsay MacDonald

Sophie watched Caitlin stride out along the battlements in the pre-dawn dark, thunder and lightning given flesh. Though the gods lined the ramparts, golden-skinned and beautiful, tall and powerful, Caitlin was above them, god and mortal combined, greater than the sum of the parts. As she passed, a ripple ran through the gods in their shining armour: eyes turned her way, body language shifted, whispers passed from mouths to ears.

'How long is this going to last?' Thackeray's eyes were deep pools of concern.

'Until she gets back what she feels she's lost,' Sophie said.

'Then let's hope she gets it back quickly.'

Harvey hovered uncomfortably behind his friend. 'She scares me. When you look in her face, it's like she could do anything. But there's something about her that's a bit horny, too.' Thackeray glared at Harvey, who shifted awkwardly. 'Sorry. Just stating a fact.'

'Do you think she's done the right thing?' Thackeray asked Sophie.

Sophie could see that he felt he was losing the woman he loved, at a time when she hadn't even decided if she loved him back. What could she say? No – this is the worst decision she's ever made? The Morrigan will eat her up and spit her out? Nothing human can hope to contain the Morrigan's ravenous desires and epic emotions?

'Caitlin's strong. If anybody can do this, she can,' she said, and it was true. Sophie wondered if she could match Caitlin's drive to sacrifice anything for the common good. She thought of Mallory – could she sacrifice him? But whenever his face came up in her mind now, it was misty, and a weight of uncertainty hung around it. The price she had paid to Math was proving bigger with each passing day. She missed Mallory deeply, and loved him immensely, but increasingly it felt as if she was experiencing those emotions second-hand.

As Caitlin returned from her walk along the battlements, it felt as though an enormous battery was drawing near to them, so charged was the air in her presence. She was now dressed in the colours of her mistress: a scarlet silk shirt was a blaze of bloody colour against the black of her trousers and boots, the leather weapons belts that crossed over her chest and hung at her hips, the black leather gauntlets; her hair hung loose and that, too, appeared to have turned almost black. But it was her eyes that struck everyone the most: they now appeared to be almost all pupil, as if two black holes led into the depths of her head.

'They're going to attack later. No mistake.' It was Caitlin's voice, but it was laced with a frostiness that made them all shiver.

Sophie peered over the battlements into the sea of shadows that washed away across the plain from the walls. In it, numerous bonfires burned as far as the eye could see; it gave the illusion of stars blazing in the inky night sky.

'How many of them are there?' Harvey asked fearfully.

'So many that we're never going to get out of here again,' Thackeray replied with a quiet desolation.

Sophie had seen the extent of the army the previous evening, just before the sun had set: thousands of little people, dark and hairy like rats, swarming over one another in anticipation of the feast ahead. It was impossible to believe they had once been like the stately gods of the Court of Soul's Ease, before their base desires had devolved them.

Amongst them were huge weapons, many of which Sophie didn't recognise; others resembled medieval siege machines, though on a grander scale. They had been brought from their own former courts, or looted from the courts that had fallen before them.

'This is all so pointless,' Sophie said with frustration. 'They're fighting over the evolution of humanity. Meanwhile, we're getting wiped out by something they could help us defeat.'

'This is *our* destiny.' Lugh had walked up silently behind them. 'We must decide the future of our own kind before we turn to yours.'

Thackeray leaned on the ramparts to peer at the massed ranks. 'I think it's already been decided, don't you?'

'You're still sure they're going to attack today?' Sophie asked Lugh.

'They have the weapons they need. They have the forces. There is no reason for them to wait any longer. And if the Court of Soul's Ease falls, our remaining allies will swiftly follow – perhaps even the Court of the Final Word.'

Sophie conjured up an image of Dian Cecht in his scarlet robes and his mysterious words to her in a dream: *The next time you see me, you shall not see me.* 'Why didn't Dian Cecht come here?' she asked. 'Surely it's safer.'

'As always, he has his own business to unfold. Great things take place in the Court of the Final Word, greater than you or I could ever imagine. And it is said that Dian Cecht now undertakes the greatest work of all.'

Sophie was impressed by Lugh's nobility in the face of what many in the court secretly considered an impending disaster. She turned back to the enemy and listened to the slow beat of drums that had risen up in their midst. 'You have the resources to repel them?'

'We have a formidable armoury. And we have her.' Lugh nodded towards Caitlin before walking away to inspect his troops.

Thackeray approached Caitlin hesitantly. 'How are you?' he asked, as though talking to a stranger.

'I am the Nightmare,' Caitlin replied dreamily, looking past him towards the star-sprinkled sky. 'She is the rider . . . I am the horse . . . and we bring with us the dark.' A jolt ran through her and she turned to Sophie, Thackeray and Harvey. 'You don't have to worry about me. I'm still the person you know. But now I feel as if I've got electricity ripping through my veins. I can see further than I ever could before, in the tiniest detail. I think I could run for ever without taking a break. It's like being some kind of superhuman.'

There was a gleam in Caitlin's eyes that made Sophie uneasy. 'There's got to be some other way back to our own world, aside from getting involved in this fight,' she said.

'If there is, I don't know it,' Caitlin said. 'There are only certain places where it's easy to cross over, and there's no such place in this court. Fighting our way out is the best chance we have.'

Thackeray gave voice to the fatalism they all felt. 'Fighting our way past that lot? That's no chance at all.'

Caitlin was dismissive of his tone. 'We have to do what we can.' She returned to the battlements in a manner that suggested they were all irrelevant.

'I tell you, she's going to go psycho,' Harvey said. 'She'll turn on us next.'

'She won't,' Thackeray said defiantly.

Sophie wasn't so sure; everything she had heard about the Morrigan warned that the goddess was unpredictable, her rhythms chaotic, her agenda her own.

'Can't you do something?' Thackeray said to her desperately. 'Get us out of this madhouse? You've got all these wacky powers. The shit's going to hit the fan later and I'd rather not be around when it does.' He paused, then added, 'And I don't want Caitlin here, either.'

'I don't know what I can do. This is a different landscape, with different rules.' Thackeray looked at her with such fierce hope in his eyes that she couldn't turn away. 'I'll find something,' she said, moving away quickly before they saw her confident smile fade.

The winding streets were ablaze with lanterns and candles in the early-morning darkness as Sophie hurried over the cobbles, asking every passer-by if they had seen Ceridwen. Eventually she was directed to a large white building resembling a mosque, with minarets and slit windows. Inside, lilting music played quietly. In stark contrast to the mood at the walls, the serenity inside was so potent that Sophie calmed quickly.

A hallway led into a maze of rooms, all of them filled with vegetation – tall, sharp-leafed plants in huge round pots, others in beds set into the floor itself. Clematis and ivy entwined around pillars, hanging like cobwebs overhead. A path wound amongst the plants, with a Celtic spiral pattern in mosaic swirling along its centre.

Sophie followed it until she came to a vast hall filled with oaks that had pushed up through the stone flags to fill the roof space with their canopy. Everywhere, paper lanterns hung from the branches so that it appeared as if the upper reaches were alive with fireflies. With the music and the incense and the lights, there was an atmosphere of subtle magics; Sophie felt at home.

Somewhere nearby, a mellifluous voice was singing.

'Ceridwen?' Sophie called out.

The singing stopped. 'Above your head, good sister.'

Sophie looked up to see Ceridwen reclining on a platform in the branches with lanterns hung all around its edge so that she was bathed in light. Ceridwen motioned for Sophie to climb a rope ladder to join her. The platform was covered with sumptuous cushions on which Ceridwen lay, occasionally sucking on a bubbling hookah.

'Has the battle started, Sister of Dragons?' Ceridwen asked lazily.

'Not yet, but they'll be at it soon. Shouldn't you be there?'

'There is nothing I can do. My world is green and living, not dead and blood-stained. That place belongs to your new companion, my dark sister.' She was plainly concerned about Caitlin's bond with the Morrigan.

Sophie sat on one of the cushions as the dreamy atmosphere closed around her. 'You've helped me a great deal so far, but I need your help again.'

Ceridwen nodded slowly, her eyes huge and dark.

'We have to find a way back to our world. We're needed there.'

'You know there are no doorways to the Fixed Lands in the Court of Soul's Ease, sister.'

'I know. But is there another way? Is there anything I can do?'

As Ceridwen silently read Sophie's face, Sophie knew there was something. She waited patiently while Ceridwen sucked on the hookah again. Finally the goddess said, 'You have great power, Sister of Dragons, and even you do not know the extent of it. You can manipulate the spirit-energy as well as your predecessor, though you have yet to learn to control it. Use your Craft. Let the Blue Fire burn through you, and it may yet show you a way home.'

'How do I do that?'

'Ritual, sister. Unleash the serpent-energy, let it rise up through you. You know how.' And Sophie did, and she knew what a terrible thing she would have to do to achieve it. 'There is a place between the Far Lands and the Fixed Lands,' Ceridwen continued, 'a Watchtower from which all of Existence can be viewed, all can be reached. It was a haven for some of my kind in times past, a place where we could not be seen by hungry eyes. Let the Blue Fire light your path to the Watchtower and then seek your way home. But there will be dangers. Other things have taken refuge in the Watchtower in these troubled times, and they may resent your presence.'

'Thank you,' Sophie said.

She made her way to the rope ladder, but as she put her foot on the first rung, Ceridwen said, 'You must beware, sister. Not all dangers will come from expected quarters.'

As Sophie climbed down into the shadows, she knew exactly what Ceridwen's warning meant, and she feared what was to come.

'I think you've got a suicidal streak.' Hunter led the way down a darkened corridor in the heart of Queen's College. They'd made their way there after slipping out of the Brasenose/Lincoln underground complex. Behind him, Mallory paused regularly to gather his strength. 'After escaping a high-security cell, most people would have been jumping the last train to Freeville.'

'I'm not most people.' Mallory was wearing a thick parka with the hood pulled up to obscure his identity; Hunter had lifted it from a cloakroom. One of the guards would be going home cold.

'It's a sword. They went out with chastity belts and pigs' bladders covered with bells.'

'It's not just any sword.'

'What – it's got a built-in iPod?'

Mallory steadied himself against the wall. 'Don't you ever shut up?'

'Wit and conversation are forgotten arts in this modern world. Anyway, don't be such an ungrateful bastard. I'm getting you out of here. Your *master plan* had so many flaws it must've taken you –

what? – four minutes to put it together. Left to your own devices, you'd have been back in your cell before the painkillers wore off.'

'You think.'

'Crawling on your hands and knees in deep snow leaving a trail of blood through the centre of Oxford is a bit of a giveaway.'

Hunter paused outside a nondescript door. He'd already conned his way past three sets of guards. That would virtually guarantee a treason charge once his crimes had been revealed in the morning light, but his next act would be the final straw. Moving to a security panel, he tapped in the numerical sequence he'd memorised the one time he'd accompanied Reid to the store, when the spy had very rudely ordered him to wait outside. This was a good way to get his own back for such gross disrespect.

'Thirteen-thirteen,' he said. 'The number of betrayal twice over. If Reid had a touch of art in his soul he'd appreciate the irony.'

The door slid open and they slipped inside. Rows of glass cases gleamed in the light. 'What is this place?' Mallory asked weakly.

'The Museum of the Damned. Every magical artefact and weapon we've managed to steal, loot or stumble across since the Fall.'

'Reckon we could find something else of use in here?'

'Not worth the risk,' Hunter said. 'Half these things would turn you into stone or make you sprout an ass's head before you had a chance to work out what they were for.'

'There it is.' Mallory came alive when he saw the sword in its new case three aisles down. He hurried towards it with what Hunter considered the eagerness of a junkie.

'It really is special?'

'You don't know the half of it.' Mallory smiled with a mixture of relief and desire. 'Myth says there are three swords of power, three weapons that could shatter the world. And this is one of them.'

'You didn't get it in a Christmas cracker, then?'

'It was a gift . . . from the gods. In Otherworld.'

Hunter stiffened. 'You've been there?'

Mallory nodded without taking his eyes off the sword.

'What's it like?' Hunter said hopefully. 'I've read the briefing papers. Some stories say it's like heaven . . . others reckon it's more like a land of dreams.'

'It's whatever you make it,' Mallory replied. He crooked his elbow and shattered the glass with one blow. Once the sword was in his hand, blue light limned its blade.

'All right,' Hunter said. 'Let's get out of here.' Now that the mission was entering its final and most serious stage, Hunter became workmanlike and focused.

They hurried back up the aisle and then came to a sudden halt. Near the door stood an old-fashioned lantern, a blue flame quivering behind its glass. It hadn't been there when they'd entered.

Hunter's gaze flickered rapidly around the room. 'I wonder who left that there.' His words were clearly meant as a warning for any intruder.

The mystery deepened after they had searched the room and discovered that they were definitely alone.

'Do you think it's meant for us?' Mallory said as they stood over the lantern. 'I've had some experience of this supernatural shit and nothing ever happens without a reason.'

Hunter was entranced by the blue flame, which was bent at an angle as if continually blown by a draught. Steeling himself, he waved his fingers over the lantern's handle, then snatched it up. The flame continued to bend; it was not due to a draught.

'Weird,' he said.

'Let's take it with us. At worst, a lantern on a dark night will come in handy.'

Mallory hid the sword and the lantern in the depths of his parka and then they made their way out into the silent city. At one point, Mallory almost stumbled and fell, and Hunter gave him an arm to support him. It had stopped snowing, but the last fall was still thick on the ground; it was beginning to surpass the abilities of the street workers to clear it.

'How are we going to get out of this city?' Mallory said. 'Anything that hasn't got tracks will be snowed in.'

'Horses,' Hunter said. 'There's a Government stable at Nuffield College. They use them for expeditions into the countryside around the city. Saves fuel.'

Mallory grumbled. 'What a way to go – frozen in the saddle.'

'We can pick up some winter gear and supplies from the quartermaster near the stables. It's not going to be a fun jaunt.' For the first time, Hunter couldn't hide his deep concern beneath a glib manner. 'Are you going to be all right?'

'Just get me out of the city. Once we've found a place to make camp, get some sleep, food, I'll pull myself together.' Mallory came to a halt, the pain making him look much older than he was. 'Look, thanks for getting me out. I appreciate it. But I don't think I'm ever going to be able to forgive you for Sophie. Every time I look at you, I just think of how she . . .' The words stifled in his throat.

'I don't expect you to like me,' Hunter said, 'just to do whatever it is you're supposed to do.'

Mallory nodded once, tersely. He could live with that arrangement.

They reached the stables within the hour, shivering intensely from the harsh wind that swept down New Road. The night watchman was a youth of about seventeen who appeared to know who Hunter was and acted with due deference. Two horses were brought quickly, saddled and ready to go. Hunter left Mallory to rest and returned fifteen minutes later with two bags filled with supplies, warm clothes, tents, cooking equipment and anything else they might need on their long journeys.

In the bitter night air, Hunter helped Mallory on to his mount. Mallory's face was as white as the snow that was once again falling, and Hunter was afraid his comrade would be dead before the day was out if he didn't get rest, Pendragon Spirit or not. The going was hard for the horses until they reached the roads outside the built-up area beyond North Hinksey where the wind had made the snow drift to the sides, allowing a clearer path.

Once they had put a few miles between them and the city, Hunter led the horses into the centre of some dense woodland where they would not be seen. He pitched a tent, collected as much dry-ish wood as he could find to build a roaring campfire and then cooked some food while Mallory lay wrapped in his thermal sleeping bag.

Yet as they ate their food, Hunter was surprised to see how quickly Mallory was recovering; a faint flush had returned to his cheeks and he had more energy to talk.

'I think you've pretty effectively burned all your bridges,' Mallory said as he cleaned the last of the soup from his bowl.

'It's a fair guess that I won't be going back to my day job. No great loss.'

'This business has a habit of taking over your life. When I found out I was a Brother of Dragons I was trying to set myself up for a life just looking after number one. Suddenly I was lumbered with obligation, duty and all those things.'

'Complaining?'

Mallory considered this for a moment. 'No. Having a purpose is like . . . going on holiday. A break from worrying about what you're going to do with your life. Have you left anyone behind? A wife? Girlfriend?'

'Many, many girlfriends. So many women, so little time. I'm pretty rootless.' He thought about Samantha and her kiss, and how he had briefly felt a real connection with her. 'The world's falling apart. Getting involved would only complicate matters. And with what we're going into, it wouldn't be very good for the woman, would it?'

'Maybe when it's all over.'

They exchanged a long glance, silently recognising the truth and the lie.

'So where are we going?' Mallory said, changing tack.

'Government intelligence says that one of the three survivors has set up camp in Glastonbury. Got some kind of college for magicians going on, or something. The name we've got is Shavi – don't know if that's first or last.'

'That's not far from my old stomping ground. All right if I give that a try?'

'Sure,' Hunter said, 'but it's not an easy ride. No one we've sent down there has returned.'

'He killed them? I thought he was supposed to be a champion of humanity.'

'I don't know any more than that. We were on the brink of sending a full force in there to haul him out when this whole thing blew up.' Hunter paused, considering his words. 'Suddenly things look a whole lot different from this side of the fence.'

'That happens. Sounds like the Government hasn't changed – still fucking with people's lives. What have they done with the other two – locked them up in Dartmoor?'

'We haven't been able to track them down. From what we hear, they're travelling together. One of them is called Ruth Gallagher—'

Mallory nodded. 'She's the big witch-queen. Trained Sophie.' Mallory felt a twinge of desperate emotion, battened it down.

'The more you look, the more you see these strands tying everything together. It could get a little unsettling if you let it.'

'The other?' Mallory asked.

'Some woman called Laura DuSantiago. Don't know anything about her.'

'So if you have no idea where they are, how are you going to find them?'

Hunter leaned out of the tent mouth to throw another log on the fire. It sizzled and spat as the frost-rimed wood hit the heat. 'I think I'm getting the hang of this. Whatever made us Brothers of Dragons brings us together to do a job. So I'm just going to let it.'

Mallory held out his hands, inviting the warmth of the fire to ease the bitterness from his bones. 'You're just going to sit here until they turn up?'

'I'm going to ride and see where I find myself.'

'Very Zen. Or stupidly optimistic. One of the two.' Mallory leaned back into the tent and pulled out the lantern. 'You'd better take this, then. You're going to need something to light your way on those dark, lonely nights.'

Hunter took the lantern and fastened it to his bag. 'I'll treat it as a good-luck charm. Until it turns into some monster in the middle of the night and slits my throat.'

'When we get back, where do we meet up?'

Hunter thought for a moment, then said, 'There's a brothel on Saint Michael's Street in town. Ask for Mrs Damask. Anyone will direct you.'

'You're sure it's wise to come back to Oxford?'

'The way I see it, we're all being drawn there. We need to regroup there in case anyone else turns up.'

'Start at first light?'

'If you're up to it.'

Mallory smiled as he unzipped his parka and tugged free the bandages wrapped around his midriff. The wound beneath had almost healed.

★

Hal had stoked the fire in his office every fifteen minutes, but it had little effect on the biting cold that insinuated its way through the very walls. He'd bundled himself up in his overcoat and wore a pair of fingerless gloves while he worked, occasionally taking a swig of some bitter alcoholic concoction that the main gate security guard had brewed up in one of the secret stills that now proliferated across the city. The only relief from the bitter temperatures was losing himself in his project, as he now grandly called it.

He'd worked feverishly, oblivious to all sense of time, until the chime of the clock told him it was getting on for dawn. His room was a claustrophobic space crammed with paintings and books and mysteries, illuminated by the flickering light of several candles. In search of clues, Hal had immersed himself in anything he could find on the Poussin painting and its symbolism, and on the Shugborough Hall monument. Instinctively, he was somehow convinced that his investigations would lead to a devastating revelation that would change the course of the war. Everything pointed to the vital significance of the Wish Stone – the way it had been hidden, the way it had been found, the coded message designed to deter the unworthy. If he was right, he had finally found his role.

Hal couldn't decide if it was a by-product of his obsessive investigation, or even a sign of encroaching madness brought on by a world where anything was possible, but he was starting to see hidden connections slowly developing into a sense of some arcane master plan. The more he delved, the more connections he saw, so that at times he looked up from his books unable to tell what was real and what was a product of his overworked imagination.

So engrossed was he that he didn't hear the knock on his door. He only jolted out of concentration when a figure loomed over him. It was Samantha.

'I saw your light through the window. What are you doing working at this hour?' she asked, concerned.

'Important business for Mister Reid.' Hal considered how much he should tell her for fear of putting her in danger, then added, 'I think it might lead to something that could change the course of the war.'

'Really?' The admiration in her eyes excited him; he wanted more of it. 'Can you talk about it?' she asked animatedly.

Relenting, Hal explained about the stone recovered from Cadbury Hill and the mysterious message it contained. 'Why this painting, or its reverse image at Shugborough? Why was it thought important enough to preserve at Cadbury? How could it be linked to a picture painted hundreds of years later?'

'But what makes you think it has any relevance at all?' Samantha settled into a sagging armchair near the fire and poured herself a glass of the moonshine.

'Two people – two very important people in the crisis we're seeing now – were drawn to Cadbury, to find this. Those two people were supposed to be part of the last defence of humanity, against whatever it is that's attacking us now. And I think they were led to find this because the picture is a code that reveals something they could use in the fight, perhaps some kind of weapon.'

'That's amazing. Mister Reid must think a lot of you to give you a project as important as this.'

'He trusts me. I get the feeling that . . . well, that doesn't matter. Anyway, I'm starting to piece it together.'

'How far have you got?' Samantha asked, excitement and a moonshine buzz bringing colour to her cheeks. 'Is there anything I can do to help?'

Hal was thrilled by the prospect of the two of them working closely. 'Can you spare the time? You're normally up to your neck in work.'

'I've been twiddling my thumbs ever since the war started. What I do isn't a priority any more.'

'Well, if you're sure . . .' Hal couldn't contain a smile any longer. 'OK. We're a team. Let me tell you what I've found out so far.' He stood up to point to a print of *The Shepherds of Arcadia*, with the shepherds and the stately woman gathered around the tomb with its intriguing inscription. 'There's been a lot of debate about the meaning of this ever since Poussin first painted it.'

Samantha stood and leaned towards the print, to examine it more closely. 'What's Arcadia?'

'It comes from a long tradition of pastoral poetry going back to the Greeks. Basically, the poems brought to life an imaginary place – a kingdom of Utopia. Scholars spent a long time searching for the origin of the phrase "*Et in Arcadia Ego*", but there's no classical source.'

'So Poussin made it up?'

Hal nodded. 'Which makes me think that phrase is the key. One translation suggests it means "And in Arcadia I Exist", with the scholars believing that "I" is death. Hence, even in Utopia, there's death.'

'That's a little morbid.' Samantha returned to her seat, warming her hands by the fire.

'But you'll notice that the shepherds and the woman don't seem too concerned about this. In fact, if you look closely, they seem to be pondering the meaning of the inscription. Yet strangely, Poussin painted another painting, very similar and also on the Death in Arcadia theme, a few years earlier. In that version, the shepherds and the woman are visibly shocked to discover the message. There's also a skull on top of the tomb. It's much more sombre.'

'So he changed his mind. Suddenly death wasn't so scary.'

Hal smiled. 'My conclusion exactly. But why? And this is where it gets stranger. "*Et in Arcadia Ego*" is an anagram of the Latin phrase "*I Tego Arcana Dei*", which means "Begone! I conceal the secrets of God".'

Hal saw the light of inspiration rise up in Samantha's face in the same way he had felt it when he first made the connection.

'The secrets of God,' she whispered. 'So the tomb could hide this weapon or whatever it is? Would it be that literal? Somewhere there's a tomb with a weapon in it?'

'I don't know. Trying to piece these things together is a nightmare because you can't work out what's fact and what's your imagination joining non-existent dots. For instance, there's a popular myth linking Poussin's painting to the Knights Templar, and Mallory, the man who found the Wish Stone, was trained at Salisbury to be a member of the new Knights Templar order that the Church, or what's left of it, is establishing.'

'This all sounds like some bizarre conspiracy theory.'

'I know. And it gets worse. The image released by the Stone is a near-reversal of the painting, and on the estate at Shugborough Hall in Staffordshire there's a stone carving in the gardens of *The Shepherds of Arcadia* with the same back-to-front positioning of the figures.'

'I visited there when I was a girl,' Samantha said. 'It was lovely, very peaceful.'

181

'Shugborough's history has lots of odd little sidelines which may or may not be relevant.' Hal took a sip of the moonshine as he sought out one particular book. He spoke as he flicked through the pages to get the names and dates he needed. 'The grounds were laid out in seventeen forty-eight to forty-nine by Thomas Wright, a self-taught mathematician with an interest in the esoteric. He used to tour Britain drawing what he called "druidic" remains, and in seventeen fifty he published a book called *An Original Theory of the Universe*. It was the first book to explain the Milky Way as our view through a galaxy. But Wright also had very strong views about the existence of an infinite number of universes, or dimensions, or whatever you want to call them, all radiating out from a divine centre. There was a revival of druidism at the time, and this was one of the ideas that came out of that.'

'How does that fit in?'

'I'm not sure, except coincidences are cropping up all over the place and I'm not sure any more that they are coincidences. One of those defenders of humanity I spoke about has set up a college at Glastonbury to teach druidic knowledge. And Wright was brought to Shugborough by two men, Roger Gale and the Earl of Pembroke, who had both worked with the famous antiquarian William Stukeley, surveying Stonehenge and Avebury.'

'So we're talking about old mysteries, other dimensions, Utopia . . .' Samantha came to stand next to Hal, leaning over him so closely that he could smell the scent of her skin. It was almost overpowering.

Struggling to concentrate, he continued, 'The owner of Shugborough, Thomas Anson, was also interested in these old mysteries. Anson commissioned the Shepherds' Monument in seventeen forty-eight, at the same time as he had his dining room built. And that room featured Isis and Serapis, who are Alexandrian mystery-cult deities. Anson was a curious character. He was a member of the Royal Society and supported the most advanced scientific thinkers, including Erasmus Darwin and Josiah Wedgwood, but he was also a member of the Divan Club, one of the lesser Hellfire Clubs founded by Sir Francis Dashwood, who revelled in immorality. And where does that leave us? Lots of facts . . . and little else, just the hint of something waiting to be found.'

Samantha mulled this over for a moment and then said, 'I think we need to go to Shugborough, don't you?'

'You and me?'

'Who else? Mister Reid will want you to investigate it fully. You can ask for me to come along to help you with your research. There won't be a problem. Unless you don't want me to come?'

'No, I do, very much,' Hal said hastily. 'But it's dangerous out there. We don't know how far the enemy have advanced—'

'Stop making excuses and start making plans!' Samantha gave him a wink and a smile that was unknowingly sexy before she slipped out of the door. Suddenly Hal was left with the feeling that everything was going right.

It was still half an hour until dawn as Sophie raced from Ceridwen's temple back to the walls, but long before she reached them she knew the attack was imminent. Huge braziers of oil burst into flame like miniature suns along the great expanse of the ramparts, and a resounding cry rang up from the guards whose armour now gleamed golden in the firelight.

Sophie was breathless by the time she reached the top of the winding stone steps where the warm wind buffeted her after its journey across the vast plain. Thackeray came over anxiously.

'I thought you were going to miss the action,' he said edgily. He kept glancing back towards the vertiginous drop to the ground far below.

'What's happening?'

'They're massing at the foot of the walls.'

'What do they hope to do?' Sophie asked. 'They'll never be able to use ladders to climb this high. I thought they'd be relying on those weird machines to pound us into dust.'

'I'm not so sure.'

Thackeray took her to the wall. Sophie felt dizzy when she looked straight down, but the discomfort was quickly subsumed by a creeping uneasiness when she saw the little men swarming like ants against the monolithic stone blocks at the base of the walls.

At that moment, Lugh made his way on to a raised stone platform that jutted out from the battlements over the city. It was dominated by a flagpole made of silver from which Lugh's solar standard fluttered. Along the ramparts, the gods fell silent. As one, they turned to face Lugh, a majestic figure, tall and proud and strong.

'These are dark times.' His voice rang out like a clarion over the Court of Soul's Ease. 'Brother against brother. The Golden Ones riven. Who would ever have thought such a day would come? Since the days of our great wandering from the four shining cities of our eternal home, we have been as one, united by a single belief, bound to the heart of Existence.

'But all has changed. We, here, in the Court of Soul's Ease, still maintain that single belief. It is others who have strayed from the path of faith, who have turned against everything that binds us. All we hold close to our hearts is now at risk, for if our brothers find victory in the coming battle, they will be on another path. No longer Golden Ones, for we are what we believe. Therefore, do not think that you fight against your brother. Do not waste your heart in anguish at this crime against Existence. Rather, believe that you fight for the essence of who we are. You fight for our long traditions and belief. You fight for what has gone . . . and for what is yet to come.'

Lugh lifted his helmet and placed it firmly on his head. A resounding roar rang across the rooftops of the court as the defending forces raised their weapons high. Defiant and proud, Lugh pushed his way into the heart of the throng and moved to a central position, ready to fight shoulder to shoulder with his troops.

'You can see why the Celts were so in awe of these gods when they first ventured into our world,' Sophie said to Thackeray.

She looked round for Caitlin and found her standing precariously on a gargoyle jutting out from the battlements, oblivious to the gulf beneath her or the winds that pulled her this way and that. The power of the Morrigan shone out of her like a black light, passionate, resolute, brutal. The warriors in her vicinity gave her a wide berth, casting quick glances in her direction, then looking away in case she saw them.

Sophie turned and grabbed Thackeray, who was also staring at Caitlin anxiously. 'Time's running out,' she said. 'I need you to help me.'

'What can I do?'

'This isn't our fight. We have to get back home where we're needed—'

'Look over here!' Sophie was interrupted by Harvey, who was clinging to the ramparts as he peered over the side. Sophie and Thackeray rushed to his side and looked down queasily from the heights into the sea of shadows at the bottom. There was movement in the centre of the dark.

'What's going on?' Thackeray squinted, trying to pierce the gloom.

'Look! Look!' Harvey said, stabbing his finger frantically at something only he could see.

But as Sophie and Thackeray stared, their eyes gradually became accustomed to the gloom, and then their hearts began to beat faster.

'They don't need ladders,' Sophie said. 'They don't need anything.'

'Jesus Christ.' Thackeray's voice had fallen to a whisper. 'They're going to swarm over us like insects.'

The little men were climbing up the walls along the whole length of the monolithic barrier. Their relentless progress was conducted with an obscene scurrying motion that made them resemble spiders, arms and legs outstretched on either side of them, heads close to the wall, eyes never deviating from their target. Sophie couldn't tell whether their fingers and toes were finding minute cracks and crevices or if they were sticking to the stone through magical means or some innate ability that came with their devolved state. Hundreds of them were moving upwards, rapidly becoming thousands. There was something about the upward swarming of the black specks that made Sophie's stomach churn.

'We should fight,' Thackeray said, distracted by the sight.

'What? Are you mad?' Harvey shouted, his Birmingham accent growing thicker with his anxiety. 'What can we do against that?'

Thackeray looked from Harvey to Sophie. 'The gods are helping us out – we're the reason they're in this mess. The least we can do is lend a hand to stop them being overrun. I mean, how hard can it be? We just drop things on them to knock them off the wall.'

'Look how many there are!' Harvey protested. 'Everything inside the city will be outside, and they'll still be climbing up!'

In Thackeray's face, Sophie saw the decency and bravery that had been hidden from her before. He was a normal person trying to do the right thing in a nightmarish situation. The least she could do was help.

'You two run off, find whatever weapons you can,' she said. 'I'm going to stay here and do my bit.'

'You're going to get all witchy?' Harvey said suspiciously.

'Just go.'

As they headed off, Sophie bowed her head and attempted to find the calm place inside her. Her Craft worked best in peaceful, quiet locations where she could use ritual to focus her mind. But she'd had remarkable success on the frantic chase from the Court of the Final Word; she was hoping it was just a matter of willpower.

She heard the clank of swords against stone as the defenders rested their weapons; the murmur of their voices; the wind keening over the rooftops; Lugh, far along the battlements, barking orders. Eyes shut, concentrating hard, all the distractions began to fade until she was left in the quiet dark of her head. Her ritual had been practised a hundred times or more. She muttered her trigger-word and the dark changed to a sunlit grove not far from her parents' home where she had first felt the call of the Craft and the world from which it spun. Amongst the oaks and ash was a pool in which a fish swam lazily, its silvered scales glinting in the beams of sunlight breaking through the canopy.

Sophie leaned over the pool and said, 'I call on you, Brother Salmon. Help your friend.'

The salmon rolled its eyes towards her and replied, 'What would you have me do?'

Sophie emerged from her trance with a start, the words of her request ringing in her head. Already storm clouds were gathering. From deep in the night, a great wind rose up.

Sophie felt as if nails were being driven into her skull. When she looked around, she saw Caitlin staring at her from her perch on top of the gargoyle, a smile of dark pleasure on her lips.

Below, the little men still scurried up the wall. They were now close enough that she could see their mean, beady eyes. The one at the head of the swarm suddenly fell backwards with a shriek, an arrow protruding from between his eyes. Caitlin had hit him perfectly, in the dark, with an accuracy surpassing most human ability. So fast that her arms were a blur, she released four more arrows, all hitting their targets exactly. Sophie was sickened by the gleeful bloodlust she saw in Caitlin's face; for the first time since Sophie had known her, she seemed truly alive.

The wind rushed across the plain like a living creature, plucking several of the little men from the wall and flinging them far out into the night. Sophie could control its direction and force – just – but each burst of mental energy took its toll on her. She focused. A lightning bolt crashed down. Stones exploded from the wall and more of the enemy fell back, smoking, their eyes liquid, their insides cooked.

Sophie kept up the assault from the elements for as long as she could, but eventually she fell back, her head swimming, so exhausted she could no longer stand. She had personally destroyed more than a hundred of the swarming attackers, but for every one she slew, ten more took their place. The leading edge of the swarm was close to the summit now, their harsh grunts echoing all around.

'You did great.' Thackeray was suddenly next to her, helping her back from the edge. 'You need to rest now, get away from here.'

'No,' she said in a small, breathless voice. 'Once I get my strength back—'

'Just lie here,' he said, leaving her at the top of the stone steps where she could get a good view of the battle, 'but after they start to break through the ranks, do your best to get down and away.' He paused. 'What did you want earlier?'

'Later,' she said weakly.

Thackeray ran back to the ramparts where Harvey waited with a sickened expression. They were both armed with enormous swords that made them look like boys in comparison.

Weak, barely able to prop herself up, Sophie drifted in and out of consciousness so that the unfolding battle had all the reality of a bad dream. The little men swarmed over the ramparts, small and brown and vicious, tearing with their little knives, striking with broken nails and sharp teeth. The gods, tall and stately, responded just as savagely, though their brutality was masked behind the measured sophistication of their balletic strokes and skilful attacks. Bodies were cleaved in half by the gods' swords, heads split in two. But though the knives and teeth of the little men had but small effect on the heavily armoured gods, it was clear they would eventually overwhelm the defence by sheer force of numbers. Sophie faded in and out, but still they came, clambering over the bodies of the fallen, attacking relentlessly, seemingly with no thought for their own safety.

But then there was a flurry of activity and the tide appeared to turn. A terrifying demon swept along the battlements, hacking and slashing in a blur of sword and knife, carnage in human form. It was Caitlin, and she was laughing and shrieking with the ecstasy of the moment, no longer human.

In her daze, Sophie thought she saw Caitlin rise up into the sky, grow larger, become the destroyer of everything; her sword came down on the city and a sea of blood rose up and washed everything away.

And then there was only darkness for ever more.

chapter ten

avalon dawn

'Vox populi, vox dei.' Alcuin

('The voice of the people is the voice of God.')

Light filtered through stained glass, flooding the whole hall with a demonic red, framed at the edges by blue and green. As Sophie gradually came back to consciousness, she had the odd feeling that she was surfacing from a dream into a dream. Colours too florid, distant sounds given uncertain solidity by odd echoes.

She had never been in the room before, but it had the ambience of a church. The stained-glass windows ranged from floor to ceiling along the vast eastern walls, presenting pictures of gods in battle and victory, and it was clearly the first rays of dawn that were turning them to fire. The floor was grey stone flags on which wooden benches stood, oriented towards a lectern, while the ceiling was cathedral-high and vaulted.

Sophie was propped up on the rear bench, flanked by Thackeray and Harvey. Lugh was at the lectern and had clearly just given a speech of some kind, for the gods who filled the remaining benches were taking their leave. Sophie had the feeling that these were the senior members of the court, for Ceridwen was there, and Math; she didn't recognise any of the others, but they wore their gravitas like a cloak.

'We were starting to get worried about you,' Harvey said with some affection. Sophie had been convinced for a while now that he was starting to develop a crush on her.

'I blacked out,' Sophie muttered, 'after calling up the wind and the lightning. Much good *that* did.'

'Oh, it helped,' Thackeray said. 'But not as much as that did.' He nodded towards the figure striding towards them.

'We drove them back,' Caitlin said, her eyes gleaming. 'But they'll return, and soon.'

'We'll never be able to fight them off,' Thackeray said. 'We surprised them this time. They never expected us to have a secret weapon that was such a killing machine.'

'Even you won't be able to kill all of them,' Harvey said to Caitlin, but he wouldn't meet her eyes.

Lugh marched up and addressed Sophie. 'His words are true.'

'I didn't hear your speech. What did you tell everyone?' Sophie said.

A deep sadness lay just below the surface of Lugh's composed expression. 'The enemy is too numerous. We cannot defeat them.'

'What are you saying?' she asked. 'That you're going to surrender?'

Defiance flared in Lugh's eyes. 'In all our long history, the Golden Ones have never admitted defeat. We are trapped here, unable to strike back effectively. We must escape, regroup, find another haven where we can plot our next attack.'

'How are you going to get out of here? The only exit is through the gate, straight into the enemy's hands.'

'I have charged my brothers and sisters with finding a solution.'

'But what if they can't come up with anything?'

'Then we stand, and fight, and greet Existence with the sun in our faces and pride in our hearts.'

The small group fell silent as Lugh marched away. The air of impending doom in the room was palpable.

Sophie said quietly, 'Whatever it takes, we're getting out of here.'

The road west from Oxford was hard going. Mallory reasoned that the main thoroughfares would be easier to travel, but heavy snow had still built up, so deep in places that even the horse found it difficult to pick a path through. Some days he barely covered two miles. He took the A40, skirting Witney, and then when he reached

Northleach turned south down the arrow-straight route of the old Fosse Way towards Cirencester. One advantage of such a route was plenty of abandoned buildings where he could seek shelter if the blizzards became too intense, and many occupied ones where he could try to beg a few moments' warmth by a fire or a bed for the night.

But many people were suspicious of him. With the collapse of the rule of law across most of the country, there were too many rogues at large. Others refused him any food, fearing that the bizarre summer-winter would devastate the already fragile food supply; most crops would already have died, and what they had stored needed to be conserved. After the tenth shotgun pushed into his face, he decided to shun human contact altogether.

With each passing mile, Mallory had grown stronger, the pain of his wounds becoming a distant memory. But the bitter cold assailed him, and at times he wondered if he would be able to continue. Every morning he woke with a deep ache gnawing at his bones that not even the campfire outside the tent could dispel. And then there was the long day in the saddle, riding into the harsh wind, the frost building up on his chest and on the beard he had decided to grow to protect the skin from being flayed from his face. In his thermal sleeping bag at night, he dreamed of warmth, but thought he would never feel it again.

Increasingly, the harshness of the outside world drove him deep inside his own head, where memories, dreams and emotions stewed and mingled so that sometimes he found himself unable to tell what was real and what was fantasy.

But always he returned to the single image of a gunshot in the dark that was imprinted on his deep subconscious. The revelation that had come as he lay drugged and in pain had been too raw to contemplate immediately, but now it had taken on a terrible gravity that dragged him back to it constantly. Perhaps it had been a suicide attempt from which he had recovered? But if that was the case, why did he have no memory of any hospitalisation – or had that, too, been locked away from his conscious mind? No, he was sure it represented his death, but the questions that came with that recognition threatened to drive him mad.

If only Sophie had been there, she would have helped him to find a solution; she would have soothed him.

But then, as he concentrated on the blast . . . the fire . . . then darkness, a rush of other memories broke through, like ice shattering on a pond. Another life, setting up a club, music, criminal figures propelling him to a choice no one should have to make; and then some unspeakable act which he still couldn't face that drove him to suicide. It shocked him out of his drifting state so sharply that he almost fell from the horse and had to pull back on the reins to bring it under control.

The rush of memory brought deep depression along with the shock. Since Sophie's death, the world had already become senseless. But now that his own inner world was equally un-tethered, he felt as if he was going mad.

Gasping for breath, he didn't see the figure that appeared suddenly in front of him until his mount shied away.

'There's a monster!' It was a man of about eighty wrapped in several heavy jumpers and wearing a pair of ancient paint-spattered trousers. An old-fashioned hearing aid was visible in one ear and a pair of silver-rimmed glasses held together with a plaster was jammed on the bridge of his nose. Anxiety made him throw his arms up and down as if he was exercising.

Mallory brought the horse under control and barked, 'What the hell are you doing, you idiot?'

'There's a monster!'

'I heard you the first time. What are you talking about and what's it got to do with me?'

The old man managed to calm himself enough to get his words out. 'Over that way.' He flapped his arm towards the east. 'It's got my granddaughter. And you . . . you've got a sword. You can fight it. Are you a knight? From Salisbury? We've had a few of 'em round here. They help out, when they're not Bible-bashing . . .' His words disappeared in another bout of panic.

Mallory couldn't afford to break his journey, but the old man was so desperate that he was on the verge of tears. 'How far?' he asked with irritation.

'Two miles—'

'Two miles! That's about a day's travelling in this weather!'

'No, no, the road isn't bad. The trees overhang, so it's kept the snow off,' he protested. 'Please . . . my granddaughter . . .'

He wrung his hands and, for the first time, Mallory could see that he was on the point of collapse; he must have walked the distance searching for help. Could Mallory ignore his plea, possibly sacrifice a woman to one of the nightmares that had stalked the land since the Fall? 'Come on,' he said wearily, holding out a hand to help the man on to the back of his horse. 'Jesus, you're lucky I'm such a soft touch.'

As they made their way along the lane, Mallory was relieved to find that the old man had not been lying. The snow lay thinly, marred only by the old man's footprints.

'What's your name?' Mallory asked.

'Stanley Hahn.'

Mallory could feel the old man shaking from the cold as he clung on. 'You'd better tell me what happened.'

'My son and daughter-in-law died in the Fall,' Stanley said in a fragile voice. 'My granddaughter, Jenny, got us set up in Barnsley House just over the way. But last night there were strange lights in the gardens and then a fire . . . a big, big fire. We thought a plane had crashed. Jenny said she was going to investigate. I told her not to, but she never listens to me any more.' He sobbed silently for a moment; when he managed to calm himself, he continued, 'When she didn't come back after half an hour, I went to see where she'd gone. There was a terrible snowstorm blowing. I could barely walk into it. And then . . . and then . . .'

'You found her.'

'The monster had her! It was all wrapped around her and they were both on fire. But Jenny wasn't burning. I don't understand it. I don't—'

'All right, calm down. She's still with it?'

'I ran back to the house to find a shotgun, but I was afraid of hitting Jenny. I went back this morning and she was still there . . . still standing with it . . . I didn't know what to do. You'll help me, won't you? You'll help?'

Mallory sighed, but it was answer enough for the old man, who proceeded to sob quietly with relief.

After a journey of fifteen minutes or so, the road brought them up to what looked like an enormous mansion, three hundred years old at least, built of Cotswold stone with large windows and tall chimneys, and set in formal gardens.

'Is that it? Bloody hell, you've been living in a right old pile,' Mallory said. 'What's this place again?'

'Barnsley House. It's famous. It used to have gardens that people came from all over the world to see. Bit overgrown now. Then it was turned into this plush hotel, but it was empty after the Fall so we moved in. Thought it would be safer here.'

'The place is so big, if anybody came looking for you, it'd take them a month to find you inside.'

'They're in the pool garden. Will you go? I'm afraid.'

Twilight was already drawing in and Mallory considered leaving any confrontation to the morning, but he knew that the old man wouldn't let him. 'You get in the house. I'll see what I can do.'

'Thank you, thank you,' the old man sobbed with pitiful gratitude.

Mallory lowered him to the ground, then turned his mount in the direction Stanley had indicated. An abiding stillness lay heavily on the thick snow. Yet as he surveyed the lengthening shadows of the black and white world, he felt an odd tingling deep inside him as though some invisible energy was radiating out from a source just ahead.

He rode on a little further and then dismounted. When he drew his sword, the blue light that always limned the blade was brighter than he had ever seen it. Cautiously, he made his way across the overgrown but still ordered gardens. He kept low, but it was impossible to progress quietly on the frosted snow.

Finally, he glimpsed a frozen pool through an entrance in a winding hedge. Blue light shimmered on the ice and surrounding snow and there was a tang of burned iron in the air. His heart beating insistently, he followed the light to its source.

The sight that greeted him was stunning; slowly, the sword drifted to his side. Blue Fire blazed without heat or sound, and at its heart, coiled around itself in a vast area of crushed trees, shrubs and hedges, was a Fabulous Beast more glorious than any Mallory had ever seen. In Salisbury, he had experienced them up close as they soared on the winds, leathery wings beating, metallic scales glinting red, gold and green as the furious flames belched from their mouths. But this one appeared to be made of the sapphire flames that raged around it; at times, Mallory could see through the scales to the vascular system beneath, and beyond, into its organs.

It was completely blue, and its eyes, as they probed him, were the deepest blue, too.

Standing motionless amongst the flames yet untouched by them was a slim, attractive woman in her thirties, her face the colour of alabaster and just as unmoving, made even paler by the long black hair that framed it. But it was her eyes that held Mallory. Unblinking, they were the mirror of the Fabulous Beast's, as blue as the sky on a summer day.

The Fabulous Beast's tail coiled tighter around her legs, as if it knew Mallory was about to drag her free; the tip of the tail tapped at her shin, like a cat's.

Mallory was not afraid. The Fabulous Beast's flaming breath could turn whole cities into an inferno; they were unpredictable, chaotic, terrifying in appearance. Yet Mallory was convinced that they were inherently a force for good, tied in some way to the spirit-energy that coursed through the earth itself.

As the blue light on his blade gleamed brighter still, Mallory realised that his sword was calling out to the Fabulous Beast, which in turn was calling out to the sword, and through it, to Mallory himself.

'I suppose this is what being a Brother of Dragons means,' he said.

'It is the First.' The voice echoed so loudly all around that Mallory took a step back; it was deep, masculine, but with a hint of sibilance. More disturbingly, Jenny's lips had formed the words, but the voice was certainly not hers.

'Jenny?' Mallory didn't expect a response and shifted his attention to the Fabulous Beast. 'This is the First? The original? The father – or mother – of them all?' But as he said the words, Mallory realised it was more than that.

'The First has been waiting for you, Brother of Dragons.'

'Waiting? Even I didn't know I was going to be here.'

'The First knew.' The odd dislocation of voice and Jenny's moving mouth continued to unnerve Mallory.

'Why is it after me?'

'You are bound into the great events that are unfolding. These days of crisis are only the beginning of a great upheaval that will decide the path of humanity for all time to come. Here, now, is the axis around which everything turns. Foretold since the dawn of your race, everything that has happened has been in preparation for this. Every moment of suffering that has shaped and guided your kind. Every joy, every sorrow, every victory, every defeat. There has been meaning in even the smallest thing, even a leaf falling from a tree, but your people have never had the perspective that would allow them to understand.'

'OK . . . destiny . . . fate – I can understand that,' Mallory said cautiously. 'Big things are happening and I've got a part in them. I knew that already. So, again, why me, why here, why now?'

'The truth and the fire, Mallory. The truth and the fire.'

The tone of the words made his blood run cold. Something skittered in the back of his head; dark thoughts emerged at the tug of the Fabulous Beast's blazing stare.

'Five new Brothers and Sisters of Dragons have been chosen for these crucial times. The King and the Queen are true to the patterns of old. The remaining three were selected for chaos and confusion. The Devourer of All Things, known in these times as the Void, cannot easily read them or predict their actions, and the Devourer of All Things sees all, knows all.'

Mallory understood: 'Their unpredictability means they can blindside the Void.'

'That is why they were created. But one has already fallen, though she fights to return to the field.'

'Who are they?' Mallory didn't want to ask the question, but like a moth drawn to a flame he couldn't resist.

'The Broken Woman. The Shadow Mage. And the Dead Man.'

The rushing cold washed through Mallory and he thought for a second that he might faint. His heart was pounding; panic fastened a strap across his chest. 'No. I don't want to hear any more.' He stepped back another pace.

'You will only reach your potential through full self-knowledge, Mallory. This is the reason you are here, now. The First is the key and you are the lock.'

'Don't,' Mallory said. He was shaking. The squirming at the back of his head had grown unbearable. He clutched at his temples with his free hand; it felt as if his skull was about to crack open.

'The sword you carry is more than a sword. It is a part of Existence, as are its two brothers. But it has been disguised to hide it from the Devourer of All Things. Now is the time to return it to power, Mallory, and by doing so unlock your mind.'

Against the palm of Mallory's hand, the sword throbbed in response to the beast.

'Come. Plunge your sword into the purifying flame and cleanse yourself in the process.'

'No,' Mallory said. 'I can't do it.'

'You fear the death you have experienced, Mallory, and the events leading up to that death, for your true self knows them well. But understand this: you have been reborn. There is always hope. It is not visible in the small things, but when you soar high, you can see it clearly, Mallory. In you, in your very being, is this lesson.'

Emotion surged up in Mallory. He remembered his parents, his childhood, the feeling that he had let them down. He recalled his first meeting with Sophie, in the pub in Salisbury, and later at the travellers' camp, where he had come to realise that he wanted her and needed her. The feeling that she was the key to his redemption. And then her death, and the grief burrowing its way into his soul, and the knowledge that by losing her he had lost his only chance of salvation. A hot tear blazed down his frozen face. He hesitated, then thought: what did it matter? What did anything matter? He strode forward and plunged the sword deep into the blue flames.

The fire rushed up the blade as if it was kindling, and then up his arms and into him, burning through his mind, his soul, until everything was blue. He didn't know how long he remained in that state, but the next time he came to consciousness, he was staggering around in the snow, with the sword still blazing blue in his hand. He felt as if he'd had a massive shot of adrenalin.

In his head, it felt as if a stopper had been pulled from the bottom of an enormous vat. Thoughts and feelings surged through him, three hundred movies playing at the same time, all speeded up to a blur. He knew instantly who he was and who he had been, what terrible act he had committed and how he had atoned for it. He saw himself pull the trigger, the blaze of fire across his head, and his death.

But then, miraculously, he was alive again, driving a stolen car to Salisbury shortly after the Fall, and he knew he wasn't of this world at all. The point of his death had been an instant of transition. Somewhere there was another world, a little like the one he was in, with people who loved and hated and who were forced to do unspeakable things. But he had the feeling that it was a greyer world, without wonder, where meaning was not so clear and where the joys of life had been diffused. A world where the Fall had never happened.

It was the reason why he was so unpredictable, why the Devourer of All Things would not be able to see him clearly. He didn't fit properly into the landscape of this world, like an old bottle washed up on a beach. Whatever was watching skittered over the anomaly to preserve the purity of the holistic view.

'There are worlds upon worlds upon worlds, Mallory. All connected, all joined to the source.' For the first time there was a faint smile on Jenny's lips. Mallory shivered; he had the feeling that something beyond her, beyond even the Fabulous Beast, was speaking to him through them both. 'Your world no longer exists, in the way that this world exists,' she continued. 'Existence has shifted. A new structure has been raised around you.'

Mallory felt whole for the first time; and more, he realised what it meant to feel whole. Along with it came a deep sense of purpose. 'I'm not going to fail,' he said. The sword felt like a bomb on the brink of exploding, and whatever energy it contained surged into him and back, combining, infusing.

'You are the Knight, Mallory,' Jenny said. 'You carry in your heart the standard of Existence.'

'You've done your duty now,' Mallory said to her, 'and I thank you for that. You can come back to your grandfather now.'

Her sapphire eyes blazed brightly, and Mallory already knew the response before the words appeared. 'I cannot, for I am now with the First. I am its conduit in this world. There must be many sacrifices to achieve the shining future.'

'You're going to stay here?'

'I will be there at the end, for better or worse. Even if the Hounds of Avalon cry to the moon. Go now, Mallory, Brother of Dragons. The world waits for you.'

Mallory turned and left them, but even when he had reached the shadow of the house in the gathering gloom, he could still feel their presence, warm at his back.

He found the old man cowering in the lounge next to a dead fire. Mallory did his best to explain what had happened, but the old man's sobs were still hard to bear. Afterwards, when Stanley sat in a plush armchair staring blankly into the corner, Mallory remade the fire and cooked them both a small dinner. He knew it would be hard for Stanley to survive on his own, especially if the bleak winter continued. Mallory encouraged him to find others in the area, but the old man simply shook his head silently.

The next morning, which was bright and clear but at least a degree colder, Mallory set off for Cirencester with renewed vigour. The cold no longer bothered him as much. Whatever else had happened when he plunged his sword into the Blue Fire, it had given a boost to the Pendragon Spirit. He felt he could do anything, win any fight. He stopped at the nearest inhabited house and convinced the residents to seek out Stanley and offer what help they could, but he could see the growing fear in their faces. The winter that had corrupted the land was driving its ice deep into their hearts. Everyone was starting to believe that the end really was approaching.

The next three days passed without incident and on the fourth, when Glastonbury was within reach, Mallory noticed a change. The day appeared slightly warmer, the wind not so bitter; the snow that had been falling faded away to reveal a clear blue sky. At first he wondered if it might be his imagination, but the closer he got to the town, the more the temperature increased. The hard-packed snow grew thinner, turned to slush, melted away completely. The icicles on the houses and the fences disappeared in the warmth of the sun. The leaves on the trees, the shrubs and flowers and vegetation that had shrivelled in a cold they had never expected to endure gave way to verdant life, the perfume of honeysuckle, the colours of hedgerow flowers. Birds called and there were cattle and sheep in the fields. Residents greeted Mallory with a cheery wave as he rode by. And finally it became too hot to wear his cloak. He stripped it off and turned his face to the sun, surprised at how quickly he had forgotten the sensation of its warmth on his skin, realising how much he had missed it.

By the time he reached the town it was summer again, and all was right with the world.

'You'll never get in there.' The farmer eyed Mallory wryly as he leaned on a gate, gently swinging the hammer he had been using to fix the adjoining fence.

'What have they got – guards? Dogs?'

'Flying pigs for all I know, lad.' The farmer shielded his eyes from the sun. 'We get one or two of you a week. Riding in from God knows where, or on foot, all thinking they can turn their lives around. I 'spect the word's all over the country now about what we've got down here.'

'And what have you got?'

The farmer tapped his nose.

'You don't mind having the college in town?'

'Nooo. They look after all us locals. Keep us in food – crops have never been so good since they came down, and the beasts have never given so much milk. They know a thing or two, and no mistake. And they keep us safe.'

'So, what? They've got guards? Some kind of militia?'

'They don't need guns.' He nodded at Mallory's sword protruding from its scabbard. 'Or pig-stickers like that. There's more than one way to skin a cat.'

Mallory could see that he wasn't going to get anything useful out of the farmer, so he nodded politely and urged his horse on. It wasn't a surprise – he'd got the same response from everyone he'd encountered as he neared the town boundary.

As Mallory drew closer to his destination, he was surprised to see that a massive flood had cut off the centre of the town and the Tor from the surrounding countryside. At first he presumed it had been caused by run-off from the melting snows on the periphery of the warm zone. But as he skirted the deep water and marshland seeking a path through, he realised it had turned Glastonbury into a naturally protected island.

He was forced to approach from the south where there was a thin defensive bank that formed a land bridge to the edge of Wearyall Hill. As he drew closer, he saw that the entrance to the bridge was marked by an arch of thick, entwining blackthorn. And hanging from it was a severed human head. It was a lurid green-black from the early stages of decomposition, but strangely untouched by birds and insects.

As Mallory guided his horse to pass under the arch, the head's eyelids snapped open and Mallory jolted back in his saddle, his sword drawn in an instant

'Who goes?' The rotten lips parted to reveal black teeth. The eyes rolled as if unused to seeing and eventually focused on Mallory. The deep horror embedded in them only enhanced the chilling image.

'I want to visit the college.'

The head made a low, rattling exhalation. 'Only those who have been invited may enter. Turn back or face the consequences.'

'I'll try my luck.' Mallory guided his horse forward until the head emitted a high-pitched scream that brought him to a sharp stop.

'Know then my story! In life I was sent to capture the leaders of this college, and in this act I killed one who had come here to learn. Now my punishment is to hang here for evermore as a warning to all others who trespass. Of those who have ignored me, none have returned this way.'

'Sorry, pal. I don't have a choice.'

'Then cross the Perilous Bridge, traveller. And pray to whatever god you recognise.'

The stink of the rotting head floated into Mallory's nostrils as he passed beneath it. The second his horse put one hoof on the slim land bridge, the head began to scream again. Mallory kept moving, but the head continued to wail like a siren, warning of the intruder's impending approach.

The water on either side was like glass, giving the impression of another world existing just a stone's throw away. At times, Mallory was almost overcome by the illusion that he could dive in and swim to the green island he saw there. The image was broken only by the occasional chimney protruding from the sunken houses beneath.

On the other side of the bridge he picked up the road again and rounded Wearyall Hill. A cathedral-like mood of tranquillity lay over the town as he rode into the centre. In a world of constant upheaval, that in itself was unnerving. Something special hung in the air, a subtle power filling his lungs, calming him; he felt at home.

The centre of town looked as if it had been unaffected by the Fall, though there was a definite absence of people and all the premises appeared deserted. But as he rode forward, he was confronted by a wall of trees across the street – oak, hawthorn, rowan – so dense that he would not be able to ride through. Their trunks broke through the tarmac, soaring up tall and proud and looking decades old. Mallory dismounted and tethered his horse before inspecting the barrier more closely.

There was a tiny path leading through the trees along which he could just about squeeze, but he would have difficulty defending himself if he was attacked – which, he guessed, was the whole point. No other entrance was visible, so, reluctantly, he pushed between two trunks and began to edge sideways along the route.

He estimated that the stand of trees was only twenty yards across at best, but it was impossible to see the other side and the path didn't take a direct route. Perfumed flowers of a kind he didn't recognise hung down from the branches and every now and then there were other strange blooms on either side, like rare orchids, gleaming black with the texture of skin, or others, like lilies, with a cloying aroma.

After ten minutes, Mallory began to wonder why he wasn't coming out of the other side. Fifteen minutes on, he had begun to accept that he was in some kind of maze, though he couldn't begin to guess how it could continue for such a distance. He decided to turn back to see if he had missed a branching path. He walked for half an hour and when he found no other path and had not reached his starting point, he realised that he was caught in some obscure trap.

For the next hour he pressed on in one direction. He was convinced that he never passed the same point twice and by that stage he realised there had to be some magic at play. Perhaps the other intruders who had attempted to break into the college were still wandering along the path somewhere ahead of him, or had died of starvation and fallen into the vegetation by the wayside.

It was futile to keep walking. Mallory leaned against the trunk of a tree to think logically. But after a few moments of racking his brains, he realised he was having trouble ordering his thoughts. Cotton wool packed his skull and honey trickled down his spine; if he closed his eyes, he could probably sleep for a long, long time.

If he had continued along the path for a little while longer he would probably have been lost, but there was still a small part of his mind sending warning signals. One of them drove him to draw his sword. The blue flames erupted around the blade and the air was suddenly singed with the aroma of burned iron. The smell cut through the claustrophobic scent of the flowers and the rush of energy gave him a jolt. In that instant, Mallory realised what was happening.

Quickly, he tied his handkerchief across his face, unsure whether it would do the job. With what little energy he had left, he leaped up to slash at the hanging flowers and any others he could reach on either side of the path.

He moved quickly, pressing the handkerchief to his nose and mouth with one hand, and after a while of hacking and chopping, the confusion in his head began to lift. Either the invisible pollen, or the scents themselves, were some kind of narcotic that had subtly tied his thoughts in knots.

Not long after, the path fell back into sharp relief and the dreaminess receded. Within minutes, he caught a glimpse of buildings on the other side. When the exit became visible, he broke into a run.

He was only feet away from breaking out into the open when a vine-like plant with long thorns swung across the path with a life of its own. Mallory ducked, but one of the thorns ripped open the flesh on his cheek. It felt as if acid was burning its way into his system. His legs grew sluggish, refused to obey his mind, until he was staggering around like a drunk. Within seconds, he collapsed. Paralysis flooded through him. He was aware of other vegetation moving around him, grass and tendrils wrapping around his legs and arms, enswathing him in green like a mummy. Darkness began to close around his vision and he knew that if the paralysis reached his heart, he would die. Slowly, he was being tugged into the undergrowth where he would never be found.

Filled with excitement, Hal waited for nearly three hours before he could finally see Reid. The chief spy had been in conference from long before breakfast with a succession of ministers, military advisors and nondescript people Hal had never seen before.

When he was finally ushered into Reid's darkened office, Hal could see the toll the current crisis was taking on the man. His face was drawn and tired, and it looked as if he hadn't received any good news in a long time.

But he seemed to brighten a little when he saw Hal and offered him a cup of real tea. Hal took it gratefully before pouring out all he had learned about the Poussin painting and the mysterious monument at Shugborough Hall.

'All I need is your blessing to go to Shugborough,' Hal concluded, 'and the resources to do so. I know it's dangerous—'

'It is dangerous,' Reid stressed. 'The enemy is advancing very rapidly. They're already crossing Yorkshire and Lancashire. It won't be long before they reach Staffordshire.'

The news was a harsh blow to Hal. He'd always believed that the Government would come up with something to stop the enemy in its tracks and had never given the possibility of failure a second thought. 'We haven't got a response?'

'No effective one. We've tried . . .' Reid dismissed the thought with an irritable wave of his hand.

'I'm sorry,' Hal said contritely. 'I know you can't talk about it.'

'It's not that. I think the time has come for radical action. Others don't agree. But that was always anticipated.' He took a long sip of his tea, lost to his thoughts for a moment, and then added, 'I trust your judgment, Mister Campbell. If you feel this is important for the war effort, then do it. Just make sure you're in and out as quickly as possible. I can provide you with a helicopter – there's no point taking any road vehicles out in this weather.'

'I'd like to take an assistant. To help with any local research.'

Reid shrugged, uninterested. The phone rang and Reid snatched it up, his mood brightening as he listened. When he replaced the receiver, he said, 'Good news. The PM has agreed to see you for ten minutes.'

'What? When?'

'Now.'

Hal grew anxious. 'I haven't prepared—'

'Doesn't matter. Just speak from your heart. With everything that's going down at the moment, you probably won't get another opportunity. And I believe this to be very important. The PM needs to hear it.'

'OK,' Hal said hesitantly. 'Now? Really?'

'Now.' Reid stood up and waited for Hal to rise before hurrying him to Balliol where the PM's private offices were situated; normally, no one with Hal's low-level clearance ever got anywhere near them.

Once they were outside the prime minister's door, Reid clapped Hal on the back and whispered, 'You'll be fine.' He swung the door open, but Hal knew he wouldn't be able to speak for a few seconds, for his heart was wedged firmly in his throat.

Mallory woke on a rough wooden pallet, his head thick and his limbs heavy. The aroma of wood smoke filled the air. When he finally accepted that he had survived his ordeal, he managed to lever himself up on his elbows to look around. He was in a roundhouse like ones he had seen as a child in history books about the Celtic era. A small fire crackled in the centre of the room, the smoke winding its way up through the hole in the centre of the turf roof. His bed was positioned so that he could see straight out through the open door across the lush Somerset countryside. The sun was rising, framed perfectly between the door jambs, golden and large and misty.

'You're bloody lucky.'

Mallory strained around to see who had spoken. A man leaned on a gnarled wooden staff, watching Mallory with a suspicious expression. Mallory guessed he was well into his sixties, but he was so fit and lithe that it was difficult to tell his true age. He could just as easily have been a hundred. His skin was browned from days in the sun, but his long grey hair was matted with dirt and grease and hung lank around his shoulders. He wore a dirty cheesecloth shirt, open at the front, shapeless, filthy trousers and a pair of well-worn sandals. He looked like someone who had spent his life at the music festival they used to hold annually just outside the town.

'If someone hadn't seen you getting wrapped in the defences you'd have been gone for good,' the old man continued.

'Who are you?' Mallory said. He was already surreptitiously searching for his weapon. His scabbard was empty.

The old man realised what he was doing and gave a brief, hard smile. 'Where did you get the sword?'

'None of your business.' Mallory swung his legs on to the floor, his head spinning.

The old man brandished his staff. 'See this? I've split more heads open with it than you've had hot dinners. You couldn't beat me even if you were fit, and look at you now. Better answer my questions before you're out cold again.'

'I'm not answering any questions,' Mallory said defiantly.

The old man moved his bony, angular body like a ballet dancer, swinging the staff in a blur. The tip thudded against Mallory's windpipe before he had even seen it coming.

'All right,' Mallory choked.

'The sword. That's one of the three great swords. Too powerful a thing for a weedy little weak-arsed runt like you. Who did you steal if off?'

'I didn't steal it. It was given to me.'

The old man eased the pressure of the staff a little and eyed Mallory curiously. 'Who gave it to you?'

'A woman called Rhiannon.' Mallory saw the flicker of recognition in the old man's face and added, 'In the Court of Peaceful Days.'

'You've been to T'ir n'a n'Og?'

Mallory nodded and the old man lowered the staff and paced away. 'They'll let any bugger in these days,' he muttered, opening a box in one corner. The familiar blue light of the sword illuminated his face. 'You'd better take it, then. But don't think it'll give you an advantage.'

Mallory's legs still felt weak, but when he plucked the sword from the box the familiar energy surged into his limbs.

'You're a Brother of Dragons?' the old man asked.

'Yes. The name's Mallory.'

The old man snorted. 'Sounds like a girl's name to me.' He leaned on his staff once more and surveyed Mallory's face. 'I'm the Bone Inspector. I run this here college.'

'I've travelled a long way to get here,' Mallory said. 'I'm looking for someone who used to be a Brother of Dragons . . . someone who fought in the Fall.'

'Then you've found him.'

Mallory turned to see a tall, slim young man with Asian features standing in the doorway. Long black hair framed a handsome face with perfect bone structure, and his natural beauty was accentuated by the black clothes he wore. 'My name is Shavi,' he said.

chapter eleven

the other side of life

'My country is the world and my religion is to do good.'
Thomas Paine

Mallory emerged from the roundhouse into the beauty of a Glastonbury dawn. The air was fresh and sharp, a pearly mist drifting ethereally in the hollows, shimmering in the golden sunlight. The only sound was the birdsong rising up from the green landscape spreading out on all sides far below.

The roundhouse was set on the side of the Tor, just beneath the level of the terraces that formed a processional pathway to the top. Mallory observed that the college covered a vast area, from the roundhouse down the hillside, across the streets of formerly residential houses and into the grounds of the abbey. It encompassed the Chalice Well, nestling on the slopes at the foot of the Tor. The new college buildings were plain, built in a Celtic roundhouse style, and were dotted throughout the area. Nature was being allowed to reclaim parts of the old town, with new trees sprouting here and there, ivy and climbing plants swarming over brick and concrete. It was a place that looked at peace with itself.

'Breathe deeply,' Shavi said softly. 'Let the tension ease from your body. Here you can be yourself. Here you can be everything you ever wanted to be.'

His words brought an unexpected juddering sigh from Mallory; he had the sudden feeling that he wanted to stay there and turn his back on the harsh daily battles of life.

'This is a mystical place,' Shavi continued, 'and now the true power in the land is being allowed to rise up. We have returned it to its old use, as a college for learning and study of the mysteries of Existence. Here the important things are life and love, faith and hope.'

'And don't you forget it,' the Bone Inspector said gruffly.

Mallory could feel the magic in the very air as Shavi and the Bone Inspector led him to a small campfire where they would watch the dawn turn into day. Down at the foot of the hill, Mallory could see people emerging to greet the morning. 'You've taken a lot of people under your wing.'

'Many feel the call to come, in their blood, in their dreams.' Shavi looked beatific with his eyes closed as he felt the warmth of the sun on his face. 'Nearly two thousand years ago there was a great race of wise men who knew the secrets of the stars and the trees and the land. They were almost eradicated by the Romans during the invasion.'

'Druids,' Mallory said.

'Their true name was the Culture. But they never died out. To avoid persecution they slipped into the background, hiding in plain sight in the old communities, dispensing their wisdom where they could, ensuring that all the knowledge they had gained was passed down the generations.' Shavi nodded to his grim-faced companion. 'The Bone Inspector was the last of them.'

'In this world,' the Bone Inspector said obliquely.

'But here we are building the Culture up again, training a new generation with the knowledge of millennia past and sending them out into a newly made world. Everything has been done over so that we can make a fresh start.' He smiled at Mallory. 'And this time we intend to get it right.'

'You chose a good place. Better than Wolverhampton.'

'Symbolism,' the Bone Inspector grunted. 'The Culture had their best college here. But it's also the place where the land's power is focused.'

'The Isle of Avalon,' Shavi said. 'In the Dark Ages, Glastonbury was as you see it now, an island in the waters and marshland of the Somerset Levels. Avalon was the Celtic heaven, the Otherworld, Land of Always Summer, the mystical land of the dead where the fabled apple trees grew.' He made an expansive gesture to indicate the apple trees that were now growing all over the area. 'Glaston-bury was considered to be the entrance to the Otherworld, a place that straddles the borders between this world and the next.'

'And is it?' Mallory asked.

'Oh, yes.' Shavi's smile was enigmatic. 'This is the place where legend said Arthur's body was sent after his final battle. And all places linked with Arthurian legend are tied to the Otherworld, focal points of the Blue Fire, which is the epitome of the power of transformation. But you would know all about that.'

'Bits and pieces. No one gave me a manual when I got the job,' Mallory said.

'That's for a good reason – so that you grow into it,' the Bone Inspector said. 'The only knowledge worth having is the stuff you learn yourself.'

Beaming, Shavi clapped Mallory on the back in a surprising show of bonhomie. 'It is so good to meet another Brother of Dragons.'

'How did you cope when you first found out? Because I'm worried we're making a bit of a mess of it. Letting the side down.'

Shavi glanced at the Bone Inspector, who burst into deep laughter, clapping his thigh as if Mallory had said the funniest thing in the world. 'You should have seen the last lot in the early days,' he said as he caught his breath. 'About as pathetic a bunch as you would find anywhere.'

'We came together just as the Fall was starting to happen,' Shavi said. 'At that time, no one really knew what was going on. Technology was failing; magic was springing up all over. Fabulous Beasts were flying over the land, but no one would believe in them unless they'd nearly been burned to a crisp. And then the gods came back, the Golden Ones the Celts called the Tuatha Dé Danann when they were first in this world. They wanted control over everything.'

'Except their natural enemies had different ideas,' the Bone Inspector said, 'and the Fomorii were the nastiest bastards you've ever clapped eyes on. Ugly as sin, shape-shifting, meaner even than me. With that lot going at it hammer and tongs, the Brothers and Sisters of Dragons had to hit the ground running.'

'We all had our special abilities, which we had to hone,' Shavi continued. 'I was the spiritual one, the seer. Ruth Gallagher mastered the Craft to become quite formidable—'

'I know about her,' Mallory said. 'She became the big witch-queen. Trained up my girlfriend.' Mallory was overcome with a deep sadness. Sophie would have loved it there in Glastonbury, with its peace and abiding spirituality. He had thought his grief would diminish, even if only a little, with each passing day; instead it was growing stronger and more difficult to contain.

'There was Laura DuSantiago, who gained great powers over natural things. And Ryan Veitch, who became a fearsome warrior.' Shavi's face darkened. 'Ryan died in the Battle of London. He was manipulated to betray us.'

'And the fifth? He was the leader, wasn't he?'

'Jack Churchill, though we knew him as Church.' Shavi grew sad. 'A good man. A great man. The Blue Fire burned in him the strongest. He filled the symbolic role of King. He died in the final battle, too, though we never found his body. And Ruth, who loved him dearly, was broken-hearted. She put on a brave face and attempted to get on with her life, but the last time I saw her she still looked as if she'd had a part of her cut out.'

'You've made yourselves quite a reputation,' Mallory said. 'The word's gone around about the Famous Five Who Saved the World.'

'We were just normal people, trying to do the best we could.'

'Try telling that to everyone out there. These days you're on a par with the gods. Everyone keeps talking about how you're going to come back, save the world again.'

'That's your job now,' the Bone Inspector said.

Mallory ignored him. His attention was fixed on Shavi. On the surface he appeared to be a calm, simple man, but beneath that façade lay complexity, Mallory was certain. If Shavi had once been a 'normal man', Mallory didn't believe that was the case any more. He had grown into the role thrust upon him, and even sitting there on the hillside enjoying the dawn he exuded a great strength and charisma that made him a natural leader.

'There's even a movement out there that's elevated Ryan Veitch to some kind of Anti-Christ,' Mallory said. 'The Great Betrayer, who's going to come back and put the world to rights. Or wrongs. Everything gets twisted in the telling. Your story keeps doing the rounds, with little bits added here and there. You're all mythical now.'

'Poor Ryan is not coming back,' Shavi said. 'He was misunderstood, troubled, but not really bad. He simply could not overcome his failings. He was buried on a hillside in North London.'

'Better not spread that around or they'll be digging up his body for the resurrection.' Mallory could see that Shavi was enjoying the peace he had found. After so much sacrifice, how could Mallory ask him for more?

'I still can't understand what happened.' The Bone Inspector shook his head, perplexed. 'We all thought Jack Churchill was destined for big things – someone who'd lead us on to the next level. There were prophecies, stories passed down from the earliest days of the Culture. I was sure they referred to him.'

'He had great power inside him, certainly,' Shavi said. 'He wasn't allowed to reach his potential – he could have changed the world.' Mallory could see that the death of Jack Churchill still affected Shavi deeply.

Shavi broke the conversation by asking Mallory to come for breakfast with them. They wandered down the Tor in the warming sun, with Shavi greeting everyone he encountered by name. Mallory saw respect in all the faces, and in some, something approaching reverence.

They ate porridge sweetened with honey in a large roundhouse at the foot of the Tor. It was a communal dining area, and throughout the course of their meal men wandered in and out to grab a bite. All kinds had made their way to the college, from teenage boys to grizzled, white-haired men in their seventies and eighties. Some resembled old hippies, with faded clothes and sandals, while others had the clean-cut elegance of barristers or the tattooed swarthiness of motor mechanics.

'No women?' Mallory said. His memories of the disturbingly testosterone-heavy regime of the Salisbury Knights Templar were still raw.

'The sexes have different strengths,' Shavi said. 'Women are better practitioners of the Craft, at manipulating its subtle energies, its raw emotional power. Ruth Gallagher endeavoured to spread the word to women across the country. The Culture's power has always been shaped by male energies. But we would never turn a woman away if she felt the call, and I'm sure Ruth would not turn her back on a man.'

'It's not a monastery,' the Bone Inspector said. 'No bromide in the tea, no rules about stamping on sex, or stopping people drinking or doing whatever they want to do to get out of it. Besides,' he added with a gap-toothed grin, 'they'll be out in the world soon enough when the teaching's done, and then they can get to know all the women they want.'

After they had finished their meal, they made their way into the grounds of the abbey where the main teaching was carried out. Many had already made an early start. A group of young men sprawled on the grass before an elderly tutor, charts of the night sky spread all around. Near the main teaching roundhouse, a group session of t'ai chi was being conducted.

'I adopted a very idiosyncratic curriculum,' Shavi said with a smile as they stood to watch the graceful movements. 'It seemed to me that we had an opportunity to enhance the long traditions of the Culture with the best of Eastern philosophy and belief systems, thereby creating a profound new wisdom for this dawning new age.'

'About that new age dawning—' Mallory began.

But Shavi silenced him with a hand; he did not wish to be rushed. 'I know some of the reasons why you have come,' he said. 'But let's not discuss them here, where we might be overheard.'

Shavi led the way to a much smaller roundhouse in a secluded spot in a distant corner of the abbey grounds. Inside, the only light came from a small fire that, from the mound of ash and charcoal, appeared to have been kept burning for a long time. The Bone Inspector shut the door and barred it.

'This is the only building with locks in the college,' Shavi said. 'It is also protected magically from external attack, or from any party viewing from a distance. There are many powers who do not want to see this college thrive. We are always on our guard.'

They sat around the fire, the flickering flames casting their faces a dull red against the shifting shadows. 'There's trouble,' the Bone Inspector said, 'or you wouldn't be here.'

'Trouble?' Mallory said. 'That's one way of describing it. It's called the Void. What is it? No idea. The best description I've got is that it's the opposite of life and it's here to wipe out everything on earth. Apparently we're some kind of infestation with ideas above our place. Though I have to admit, there are times when I agree with that estimation.'

'We are aware of this great darkness,' Shavi said gravely, 'and we have known of its approach. I am ashamed to say I am responsible.'

'What do you mean?' Mallory asked, startled. The atmosphere in the roundhouse appeared to be growing more oppressive.

'During the Fall, one of the rules of Existence was broken. I was the reason and the cause. I should take the blame.' Shavi closed his eyes, remembering. 'I died during the struggle.'

Mallory felt a frisson at the connection. 'You look pretty good for a dead man,' he said wryly.

'I remember a place of mists and desolation, of a graveyard that went on for ever.' Shavi shivered. 'But I was needed. Five Brothers and Sisters of Dragons were necessary for the struggle. Barriers were overthrown and I was brought back to life. But there was a price to pay. There is always a price to pay. Before I departed the Grey Lands, I was told these words. I have never forgotten them. *In times to come, you will discover that you cannot evade your punishment, and it will be inflicted not only upon you, but upon your world.*' Shavi swallowed, his throat dry. 'That voice . . . that voice hidden in shadows . . . So terrible. *Beyond the edge of Existence, the Void is stirring.* My actions . . . the breaking of the rule of life and death . . . brought us to its attention.'

'*You have been noticed.*' Mallory repeated the words he had heard from one of the gods.

'Yes. Because of me. And I have carried this burden with me since the Fall,' Shavi said desolately, 'dreading the day when I would hear that the Void had arrived, selfishly hoping it would not be in my lifetime. And now that day has come.'

The Bone Inspector read Mallory's face. 'You're surprised we know what's happening?'

'You've got a little paradise going here, cut off from the rest of the world. You haven't even got the bad weather.'

'Doesn't mean we're ignorant of everything that's happening elsewhere. We're not thick – knowing things is part of what we do here,' the Bone Inspector said.

'The wintry weather you talk about was what first alerted us,' Shavi said. 'It is the Fimbulwinter, as foretold in Norse mythology.

The first sign of the end of the world – Ragnarök. Three successive winters without any intervening summers, and during this time war will follow war and brother will kill brother.'

'Sounds like situation normal,' Mallory said.

'Everything that has happened in recent times has been leading towards this, and all of it was foretold in the ancient stories,' Shavi explained. 'The Fall, the first change of the season leading towards the end. Autumn, if you will. And now the Fimbulwinter – *The Great Winter* – the herald of the Void's arrival. The Fimbulwinter has been released by the Blue Hag – the Cailleach Bheur – as the world winds down.'

'How come you haven't got the snows here?'

'We have been using subtle magics to hold back the relentless flow of events so that the Brothers and Sisters of Dragons can fight. The power in the land is most potent here. Glastonbury is a node in the Fiery Network. The earth energy can hold back the winter, at least for a while.'

'So, the way I understand it,' Mallory said, 'the Brothers and Sisters of Dragons are the only ones who can hope to oppose the Void. But I can't even begin to see how that could be possible. I had enough trouble with a handful of Government thugs.'

'There are greater powers at work, and you can tap into them,' the Bone Inspector said forcefully. 'You might even say you represent them. Don't ever forget that.'

'But five's the magic number, right?' Mallory said. 'And there aren't five of us. Two are missing – we've got no idea who they are. There's a psycho-soldier, goes by the name of Hunter, who's off walking the land like Kwai Chang Caine. There's me. And then there's my girlfriend, Sophie Tallent.' Mallory steeled himself, but he still felt queasy saying the words. 'And she's dead.'

Shavi and the Bone Inspector flinched as one.

'So we're not even halfway to making a fist of it. Things don't look good. Hunter and I decided that the best chance we had was to seek out some of the old Brothers and Sisters of Dragons to make up the full complement.'

'It doesn't work like that,' the Bone Inspector snapped.

'The Pendragon Spirit is strong in those who are currently chosen,' Shavi said, 'but much weaker in those who have completed the task for which they were selected. I still feel it in me, but these days it is like a single flame whereas during the Fall it was like a raging fire.'

Mallory prodded at the ashes with a stick. 'I can't say as I'm surprised. We always expected a catch. So that's it? It's over?'

'There's always hope,' the Bone Inspector said so fiercely that Mallory thought the old man was going to lean across the fire and hit him. 'That's what you lot are all about.'

'My friend is right,' Shavi said. 'You have travelled far to ask for my aid and I will answer the call, for how could I not in this time of greatest need? It will be an honour to stand shoulder to shoulder with a Brother of Dragons once more. And even if I can be of little use, I will strive to do my best, as our kind always do.'

Mallory was impressed, and a little chastened, by the levels of decency he saw in the young man sitting opposite him.

'I'll come, too,' the Bone Inspector said.

'No. You must stay here.' Shavi was firm. 'If it is possible that we can find some kind of victory, it is unlikely that I will return. That is not fatalism. It is simply probable. You will be needed here to continue our work, for the new age that we have won.'

'And if I do go with you I'll be next to bloody useless. That's what you're saying, isn't it?' the Bone Inspector said gruffly.

Shavi laughed, and it was an infectious sound that made Mallory laugh, too, despite the darkness of their conversation. As they made their way back across the abbey grounds, Mallory was glad he would have Shavi fighting with him, even if, as he guessed, they would have no chance of winning.

Night had fallen by the time Hal and Samantha's helicopter whipped across the snow-blanketed Staffordshire countryside towards Shugborough Hall. It felt as if the days were rapidly growing shorter, until soon there would be nothing but constant night.

'I still can't believe you got the opportunity to meet the PM,' Samantha said, huddled in the depths of her parka as she watched the white world speed by below. 'He's been locked away since all this blew up.'

'He's under a lot of pressure. I get the impression he's being pulled from pillar to post. Everyone in the Cabinet, every advisor, seems to have an opinion on what to do. Everywhere you go you can hear them arguing amongst themselves, over dinner, in the bars, in the corridors. I wouldn't fancy being the PM right now.'

'But he listened to you, didn't he?' Samantha said warmly.

'He listened. I don't know if he took anything in, though – he was so distracted.' Hal recalled the PM's face the minute he had stepped into his room, so grey and drawn that he was almost unrecognisable. There was a report on his desk to which his eyes kept drifting, and as they moved towards it, Hal could see a deep dread in them, like a dark pit. Hal didn't know what the report said, but he knew what the PM thought it meant: no hope.

Yet strangely that had only enthused Hal all the more. The PM may not really have paid heed to what Hal had said, but Hal was convinced he was on the right path. It was only logical to him that a conventional response would never work against such an unconventional threat; the only way to oppose it was to utilise something as strange and illogical and potentially devastating as the threat itself. Quite clearly that meant something supernatural. Reid had the right idea with his treasure trove of mysterious artefacts, but nothing in there was big enough. It needed the Brothers and Sisters of Dragons and whatever grand design they tapped into.

And after so long feeling weak and ineffectual, Hal felt as if he was finally living up to whatever was expected of him in his role as a Brother of Dragons. He might not be wielding a sword like Mallory or staring death in the face like Hunter, but he was using his own particular strengths: his logical mind, his attention to detail, his forensic approach to problems. It sounded almost laughable to consider those abilities on a par with martial skills, but he was sure he would now be able to uncover the great secret that was hinted at by the Wish Stone, the thing that would finally give them the upper hand. Then he would be a hero, and what a great feeling that would be after being a faceless toiler all his life.

It made it easier to cope with the guilt he felt at running away from his obligation as a Brother of Dragons during the preceding days, at not telling his best friend, and at failing to offer support and solidarity when Hunter was setting off to fight the unknown. Basically, he'd been a coward. But not any more.

'We're nearly there.' The pilot turned towards them, his voice muffled through the scarf he wore in the chilly cab. 'You still want me to set you down on the village green outside the estate? It's a long walk.'

Hal nodded. He knew it would be a hard hike to their destination through the snow, but he didn't want to draw attention to what they were doing by bringing the chopper in too close to the hall. He had a growing sense of paranoia that the enemy knew what he was doing and would attempt to stop him.

The pilot brought the chopper down on the common at Milford, the tiny village next to the Shugborough estate, now buried somewhere beneath the thick snow. Hal and Samantha jumped out and hurried away as the chopper rose quickly into the sky. That part of the Staffordshire countryside had been designated a potential danger zone because of its proximity to the wild expanse of Cannock Chase, which had become home to so many inexplicable creatures and events since the Fall. Hal checked his watch: they had an hour and a half before the pilot returned.

It was a clear night, sharp as a wolf's tooth, with the stars glittering overhead and the moon bright. The crunch of their feet in the snow was the only sound. When they reached the trees bordering the estate, Hal looked back to see their line of footprints scarring the pristine white cover. The whole countryside was at peace, still and sleepy as a Christmas card. There was an affecting beauty to it; so much of humanity's mark had been obscured and what did remain – the few houses, a lone road sign – nestled in the snow as if gradually becoming part of the natural world.

Stone gates marked the entrance to a long lane with trees on either side forming a thick cover overhead. Even with the moonlight reflected from the snow, it was unsettlingly dark. Anything could be watching their passage, waiting for the right moment to strike, and they wouldn't know until it was upon them. Samantha felt it, too, for they both stopped on the threshold. Hal felt her fumbling for his hand, which she gave a quick squeeze.

'Still glad you came?' He couldn't help whispering.

'Of course. I just didn't think we'd be coming at night . . . or that it would be so isolated.'

'You can wait at one of the houses in the village, if you like.'

'No,' she said adamantly. 'Let's do it.' She stepped on to the lane before him.

Their progress along the road was slow. It wound around the

edge of a steep bank so that soon the sight of the gate was lost, yet it was still impossible to see how much further they had to go. Both of them jumped at the slightest noise in the sound-deadened world. Just branches creaking under the weight of the snow, foxes and badgers foraging for food, Hal told himself. But he wasn't so sure. There was a strange, oppressive atmosphere that grew stronger the further they progressed along the lane. It felt very much as though they were moving away from the world they knew into one where some dark power waited for them.

Samantha stayed so close to Hal that their shoulders were touching most of the time. Hal regretted bringing her along; not that she couldn't look after herself – she would probably be more effective in a fight than he would – but because he couldn't imagine her being in any danger, and he would never forgive himself if anything happened to her.

The atmosphere was so tense that most of his energy was taken up searching the trees and listening for fugitive echoes, other feet breaking the snow behind or in front. Sometimes he was sure he heard them; other times he convinced himself it was just his imagination.

Finally the lane broke through the trees and deposited them on an area of flat, open countryside. Shugborough Hall was visible in the distance against the skyline, a large, brooding presence.

With the threatening atmosphere of the lane behind them, their mood lightened. Samantha even laughed in a release of tension, then apologised in case Hal thought she was going mad.

As they trudged across the white plain, Samantha said, 'Have you any idea what's happened to Hunter?'

Hal had considered that question long and hard and guessed that Hunter was embroiled in heroism somewhere, fighting the good fight. 'No idea,' he replied blithely. 'You know Hunter. He's a law to himself.'

'That's the problem. They're talking about treason this time. Some are saying he's deserted.'

'Do you believe that?'

'No. Of course not. He'd be the last man out. What about all those rumours that he freed the prisoner and they took off together?'

Hal guessed this was probably true. Hunter wouldn't have told

Hal his plans so that he would be able to stand up to questioning, but it was logical that he'd seek the support of another Brother of Dragons. 'Why would he do that?'

'Oh, I have no idea,' Samantha said with frustration. 'I can't understand him at all.'

They fell silent as the hall loomed up before them. The mansion house looked empty, the façade gleaming as white as the snow all around, the ten-columned portico hinting at the mysteries of ancient Greece. Two wings spread out on either side, giving the building an impressive bulk. It looked out across the sweeping fields, grand yet stern and brooding.

'Do you know where we've got to go?' Samantha whispered.

Hal had researched the hall and its history in such detail that he could find his way around the rambling old pile blindfolded. The quickest way to the Shepherds' Monument was to head to the formal gardens on the far side. But that would entail walking past the front of the mansion house with its windows like dead eyes, and that spooked him for some reason he couldn't explain.

'We go this way.' He indicated the outline of the nearest path that wound through shrubs past the side of the building. 'It's called the Lady Walk, takes you through to the gardens at the back. If we follow it around, it'll bring us to the Shepherds' Monument.'

They moved through another area of thick trees where the feeling of being watched returned in force, but then the path led them back into the open along the banks of the River Sow, its waters slow-moving and black. On the other bank, the floodplain stretched out towards Milford, the snow unmarked.

'Nobody around,' Hal said to reassure them both.

Another feeling descended on them as they left the cover of the trees and moved along the river bank, not oppressive or threatening this time, but still potent. It felt as though they had pushed through a veil into another room where the mood was alive with numerous possibilities.

'Can you feel it?' Samantha said, her voice hushed but intrigued. 'It feels as if something's about to happen.'

The sensation was so strong that Hal looked around to see if they had moved through some kind of physical barrier. To their right, they were presented with a vast area of formal lawns with stone steps leading the eye to the magnificent rear aspect of the mansion house. In the foreground was an ornate pond with a fountain in the form of a cherub and a swan.

A ruined monument rose up on the riverbank on their left, but as they passed it, Samantha grabbed Hal's arm tightly and grew rigid as she looked up at a statue of a druid mounted on the top.

'It moved,' she said. 'I'm sure it did.'

Hal watched the statue for a long moment. Something about the face unsettled him. 'We're just getting jumpy,' he said.

'You're right – I'm sorry.' But Samantha couldn't help glancing back several times as they continued on their way.

The crunch of their footsteps echoed loudly over the still gardens as the path wound back towards the house once more, passing into another heavily wooded area. A strange building shaped like a Chinese pagoda appeared out of the gloom to their left.

'What is it with all these odd monuments and buildings?' Samantha said. 'I've been to one or two of these old houses, but none of them had things like this.'

'That one's called the Chinese House,' Hal said. 'In the mid-eighteenth century, two brothers from the Anson family who owned the hall restyled the house and gardens. Thomas Anson had travelled pretty extensively – maybe he brought back designs he particularly liked. There's a Doric temple in the ancient Greek style further on. He was a member of the Society of Dilettanti, who were basically a bunch of connoisseurs of history and architecture who went all around the eastern Med collecting knowledge and artefacts and generally showing off their good taste . . .' The word died in his throat.

'What is it?' Samantha asked.

'I don't know,' he began hesitantly. 'Maybe that society was only interested in art and culture. Or perhaps they were searching for something.'

'Something linked to the mystery of the Shepherds' Monument?'

More connections clicked into place in Hal's mind. He began to glimpse a grand scheme reaching back through history. 'A lot of the societies back then were interested in esoteric knowledge but hid it behind a façade of mundaneness. Secret knowledge shouldn't be for the masses, that was the general belief. Painters, musicians, writers – they'd often use codes, sacred geometry, all sorts of things to bury secrets in their works so that only the initiated would find them.'

'You've done a lot of research,' Samantha said, impressed.

Hal stared at the Chinese House. 'Symbolism,' he mused to himself before turning to Samantha excitedly. 'Things that look normal and meaningless on the surface, but which have hidden meaning underneath. Secret symbols.' In his rush of thoughts he was starting to gabble and he could see from Samantha's face that he wasn't making sense. 'The Shepherds' Monument clearly means something beyond what it appears to be on the surface – a garden ornament. What if all the things in this garden are part of the wider secret? All linked. All meaning something when they're placed in context.' Suddenly excited, he grabbed Samantha's hand and pulled her along the path.

Finally they came upon the Shepherds' Monument, just off the path to their right, set in an avenue of shrubs with a wall of trees behind it. Hal felt a shock run up his spine when he saw it: everything about its position in the landscape suggested that it was important.

'The atmosphere is even more electric here,' Samantha said quietly. 'There has to be something in this.'

'Did you ever doubt me?' Hal walked slowly down the short avenue; the crunching echo of his footsteps now sounded strange, distorted.

When he finally stood before the monument, none of the pictures he had seen in the books had prepared him for its scale: he was dwarfed by its size. The reversed image from Poussin's painting was only one small, though central, part of the whole monument. It was framed by two giant stone columns topped by a megalithic block, with another ornamental block on top. On the large stone that straddled the columns, two faces had been carved, one smiling, one sad, like the Greek masks for tragedy and comedy. The size and shape of the framing monument reminded Hal of nothing less than one of Stonehenge's trilithons.

Underpinning the whole monument was the mysterious inscription: O.U.O.S.V.A.V.V. with a 'D' and an 'M' carved partly beneath the line. Another clue left by the Society of Dilettanti, perhaps, its meaning now lost to time. Cautiously, Hal reached forward and scraped his fingers across the rough stone surface of the Poussin relief, picking out the legend '*Et in Arcadia Ego*' carved on the tomb.

But as he removed his hand, a large blue spark jumped out from his fingertips and crackled into the monument. Hal jumped back in shock.

'What was that?' Samantha gasped.

Before Hal could answer, flickers of blue energy appeared on the relief, sizzling around the outline of the tomb before moving down the monument. Though the ground was thick with snow, Hal could see the sapphire electricity sparking beneath the surface as it surged away from the monument in straight lines.

'What are you looking at?'

Hal turned to Samantha, who was staring at him, puzzled. 'The electricity, or whatever it is.' He pointed to the lines of force moving out across the gardens.

Samantha followed the line of his finger, but shook her head. 'I can't see anything.'

'You can't?' Hal was baffled. The blue light now burned brightly through the snow, the lines reaching out across the landscape far into the distance, interconnecting – a network of fire. The brilliant blue energy was the same as that which formed the image locked into the Wish Stone. Hal could feel it resonating inside him, filling him with a tremendous exhilaration. He felt as if he could do anything, that he was linked to everything. Was this part of what it meant to be a Brother of Dragons? Was that why Samantha was blind to the power?

There was a sudden rush in his heart and the blue light exploded upwards from the ground, soaring into the sky to form a cathedral-like structure high over the Shepherds' Monument. Hal was stunned by the wonder of what was happening around him.

He turned back to the Shepherds' Monument and was shocked to see that it was transforming. The blue light had made the stone relief translucent and now the image had turned the right way around. As Hal watched, the stonework began to fold out like two shutters.

'It's like a window,' Samantha said, entranced.

'You can see that?'

'Of course I can.'

Hal's heart thumped even harder when he realised that what he

222

was seeing through the gap where the relief had been was not the trees behind the monument, but another landscape entirely. Hal made out rolling grassland, and in the distance a thick forest before a row of breathtaking mountains. In that place, the sun was just rising, casting the land in a magical light, picking out the mist in the hollows, illuminating the dawn clouds. The ethereal quality was palpable and sparked in Hal a deep yearning.

'Where is that?' The awe in Samantha's voice told Hal that she felt it, too.

'Otherworld,' he said softly. 'T'ir n'a n'Og. The Land of Always Summer.'

Across the magical landscape, Hal could just make out tracings of the blue energy that was spreading out across the countryside behind him. It was in everything, linking this world and the Otherworld, and the instant that thought entered his head, more pieces of the mystery fell into place.

'Arcadia is the Otherworld,' he said. 'Poussin is pointing us towards something in the Otherworld. The image here is reversed because T'ir n'a n'Og is the flipside of our world. It's telling us to view it from the other side!'

A surge like a strong wind came through the window from Otherworld; it felt like a bubble expanding as it passed through Hal and continued outwards, and when he looked around he was shocked once again. The gardens had been transformed, the snow gone, the quality of light that of dawn on a summer's day.

'That's why this place is so important!' Hal said jubilantly. 'For some reason, this is one of the special spots where our world and the Otherworld intersect. That's what you could feel earlier . . . the echo of it. But feel it now!'

'I can!' Samantha exclaimed. 'It's so different . . . I feel as if I'm drunk!'

'That's just the start of the mystery, though,' Hal said. 'There's more. We've just got to keep pushing.'

Suddenly there was movement in the bushes nearby. Hal whirled just in time to catch a glimpse of a small man with the legs of a goat. The figure was naked to the waist, and small horns protruded from his forehead. He winked at Hal as he danced off, clutching a set of pan pipes. More activity was apparent all around the garden, drawing Hal and Samantha away from the monument. None of it was threatening. A magical air hung over the whole landscape, and Hal found himself grinning for no apparent reason. Samantha caught his hand and they ran to investigate, laughing, as the jaunty music of the pan pipes floated across the balmy garden. Bats flitted in and out of the trees, joined here and there by what Hal at first took to be fireflies until he realised they were tiny people with gossamer wings, glowing with an inner light.

'This must be what it's like over there,' Hal said ecstatically. Then another thought struck him: 'We could use this place to cross over!'

They followed the path around in a state of wonder. Inside the Chinese House, coloured shadows moved across the walls. It looked to Hal like dragons winding sinuously across a landscape; there was fire and light and a tremendous sense of wellbeing.

At the ruined monument by the river, the statue of the druid was now gone, replaced by the faun, who perched on the highest point playing his pipes. Hal wondered if the druid was the faun, locked in stone, waiting to be released by the power from T'ir n'a n'Og. Nearby, the fountain that had earlier been dead and dismal in the snow was now gushing, but instead of water Blue Fire flowed from the swan's mouth, joining the network of interconnecting lines that spread out over the landscape.

'This is amazing!' Samantha said in awe. 'This is what it could be like always! Can you feel it, Hal? It's like . . . healing. Like I'm getting a shot of something that's making me fit enough to do anything.'

'I like that,' he replied. '*This is what it could always be like.*'

They spent the next half-hour wandering the garden in a state of awe, engulfed by sights and sounds and sensations that were so powerful it felt like a drug trip. There was magic in everything. The little creatures, the nature sprites, the tree spirits were everywhere, as if every living thing and every object had a shadow life, hidden away until a switch was thrown that allowed the true self to come out into the open. The power was so evident, so great, that Hal was convinced the war could be won if only humanity could tap into what had been released into the garden.

That was part of the secret of the Shepherds' Monument, he was sure, and it was linked in some way to the part yet undiscovered. It was a double mystery: the reversal of the Poussin painting on the relief was the clue. Two sides, both inextricably bound together. They had broken the symbolic code of one side, the mystery of the reversed painting, which was tied into the anagram of the legend – *I Tego Arcana Dei – Begone! I conceal the secrets of God*. Now they knew what the secret of God was: the Blue Fire, hidden in force in the Otherworld.

But the flipside of the mystery, the true side, still escaped him. *Et in Arcadia Ego – And in Arcadia I Exist?* If the 'Ego' wasn't Death – and he was sure it wasn't – then who was it?

Hal's thoughts were disturbed by a sudden change in the ambience of the summery garden. A note of tension intruded on the calm, like jagged violins in a pastoral musical passage. Samantha felt it, too, for she looked around uncomfortably.

The music of the pan pipes faded, and when Hal glanced at the ruin he saw that the faun was gone and the little flying people were rapidly disappearing into the trees. A stillness descended.

'I think we should get out of here right now,' Hal said.

But as they hurried along the path, a shadowy figure emerged from the thick vegetation ahead of them. It was huge, its outline moving as if seen through a heat haze. As it stepped forward, Hal was appalled to see that it was made up of the writhing bodies of animals – badgers and foxes, rabbits and mice – all melded together to give the thing shape, yet each creature still alive in some way: jaws snapped, eyes revolved.

Crying out in horror, Samantha threw herself backwards on to the ground. Hal hauled her back to her feet and turned the other way, but from the direction of the Chinese House another figure was drawing closer, this one constructed entirely out of birds.

'What are they?' Samantha said, her horror a keen edge in her voice.

The clearest escape route was along the broad walk across the ornamental lawns leading to the mansion house. Hal propelled Samantha in that direction. As they ran past the fountain, Hal saw that the expression on the statue of the cherub clutching the swan had now transformed into one of abject terror.

Leaping up the rows of steps, they reached the garden doors. Through the glass, the interior was in darkness and empty. Hal yanked at the handles and the doors swung open with surprising ease.

'Why do you want to go in there?' Samantha said, frantically looking around to see where their pursuers were. Both obscene creatures were rapidly drawing closer, but their forms clearly precluded them from running or from any particular agility.

'We can go straight through the hall and out of the front door. Quickest way back to the lane.'

Inside, the house still revelled in its grandeur. Classical works of art hung on the walls, antique furniture lined the corridors, covered with vases and objets d'art gathering dust, all untouched by looters who would only have been interested in food and weapons.

'What *are* those things?' Samantha gasped, her eyes inexorably drawn to the monstrous creatures.

'The enemy's lieutenants. Hunter called them the Lord of Flesh and the Lord of Birds in his report,' Hal replied.

'The enemy shouldn't have reached here yet.'

Samantha was right, but Hal didn't want to frighten her by replying: none of the zombie-like troops were crossing the adjoining land; the Lords were alone, which suggested to Hal that they were there for a purpose – and the purpose was him. Was it because they somehow knew he was a Brother of Dragons and they were determined to eradicate the main line of defence? Was that possible? If so, he was in more danger than he'd ever anticipated.

Hal noticed something else that was just as disturbing. The lines of Blue Fire burning along the ground warped wherever they came into contact with the approaching enemy, like opposing polarities of a magnet. In the distance, the lines had already disappeared and the snowy night landscape had returned to normal, as if the energy had been cancelled out somehow.

'Don't worry. We'll be out of here in no time,' Hal said. But as they skidded across the polished floor to the front of the house, Hal realised the lie in his words. Two more lieutenants were approaching – the Lord of Lizards, green and scaly against the snowy background, and the Lord of Bones, a rictus grin adding a macabre touch to its hideous appearance.

'Oh.' Samantha's voice was small and fragile, but devastating to Hal with its awareness of the grim reality they both faced.

'Don't worry,' he said desperately. 'Don't worry.'

With Samantha clutching his hand, he raced down a dark corridor off the hall and turned into the library. Ancient books untouched in decades lined the walls beneath an ornate plasterwork ceiling. The windows, though, were barred and Hal quickly pulled Samantha out of the room and back to the hall. The Lord of Flesh was on the veranda at the garden doors and the Lord of Bones was ascending the steps at the front.

'OK, OK. I know what I'm doing,' Hal said, as much to reassure himself as Samantha. All the windows on the ground floor would be barred, but not necessarily the ones upstairs. But he was gambling with their lives: if he was wrong, they would be trapped on the first floor until the four Lords came for them.

He had no other choice. He dragged Samantha towards the main hall staircase and they took the steps two at a time.

'I'm sorry I got you into this,' Hal said when they reached the first floor. 'I shouldn't have brought you.'

'I decided to come,' Samantha said. 'And don't give up yet.' Despite her bravado, though, she couldn't disguise the tremor of fear in her voice.

They ran into a room off the upstairs hall and Hal managed to wrench a window open. A blast of freezing air rushed in, followed by a loud crashing as the doors downstairs were rent apart. They stepped out on to the roof of the columned porch, beyond which was a long drop to the hard forecourt below. Hal headed to his left where there was a short jump to another flat area of roof on the wing, but Samantha held back.

'I can't do it,' she said. 'I'm no good with heights.'

'You're no good with getting torn apart by monsters, either,' Hal urged. 'You've got to, Samantha. Hold my hand – we'll do it together.'

Reluctantly, Samantha took his hand. Hal was surprised she'd obeyed him. Her limbs were taut and Hal was afraid she'd freeze up at the jump and drag them both over the edge. At the last moment he gave her a hard yank that propelled her into the air. They sprawled together on the flat roof, winded.

In a second, Hal was up, his heart thundering so loudly that it almost drowned out the noise of terrible damage being done that was emanating from the mansion house. From the flat roof they could climb on to a pitched roof at the end of the wing. It was slick with snow and ice and after only a few feet Hal found himself slithering with increasing speed towards the drop. Samantha screamed. Hal spread his hands out in a bid to create some traction and grabbed the edge of a broken tile that cut deeply into his fingers. The pain as the blood bubbled out helped him to clear the fear from his mind. Cautiously, he spread-eagled his body and edged along the roof, stopping every time he felt himself begin to slip. Above him, Samantha followed suit.

It seemed to take an age to reach the end of the roof. His muscles burning, Hal located a drainpipe and with some difficulty slithered down it. When he reached the bottom he looked up; Samantha was hesitating.

'Hal, I don't think I can . . .' she began.

'You made the jump, you can do this,' Hal hissed.

'I can't.' She looked around nervously as the noise from the house grew even more intense; it sounded as if the place was being wrecked.

'You have to.' Hal thought for a moment, then said, 'What would Hunter say if he saw you dithering up there? He wouldn't let you live it down.'

Samantha teetered on the brink before determination crept into her face. Hesitantly, she lowered herself on to the drainpipe and began to climb down. Hal's relief was short-lived: halfway down the drainpipe she began to lose her grip, and a second later she was falling. Hal threw himself forward just in time. The impact knocked him to the ground and stunned him for a second. But then Samantha was helping him to his feet and thanking him profusely between sobs.

The wide-open plain stretched away from the house to the trees and the lane leading out of the estate. The thick snow would make it hard going, but Hal guessed they would probably be able to move faster than their pursuers.

'Let me go on ahead to check there's nothing waiting for us. Then get set to run,' Hal whispered. Before Samantha could reply, he was running low across the thick snow. He reached a fence at the side of a now-buried road and scanned in all directions, but saw nothing. Large snowflakes began to drift down: a new storm was on its way.

Just as Hal had decided that the way was clear, Samantha cried out. Scrambling back towards the house, he found her kicking and screaming in the grip of the Lord of Birds, who had just emerged from around the side of the mansion house. Thoughts burst through Hal's confusion and desperation: why hadn't he checked that they were all inside the building? And what was he going to do now?

The Lord of Birds effortlessly pulled Samantha in closer. She shrieked in pain as pecking beaks erupted from the confusion of the Lord's form to tear her flesh. Blood splattered on the virginal snow beneath where she struggled.

It was that final sight that cleared Hal's mind to a dull white noise. Acting purely on instinct, he threw himself against the Lord's bulk in an attempt to unbalance it. The sensation of the feathers and beaks roiling against him was sickening, but he managed to grab hold of Samantha's wrist and pull her hand free of the Lord's grip.

A second later, Samantha dropped to the snow, and it was only when the Lord of Birds grabbed him with its feathery hands that Hal realised that Samantha was superfluous: Hal had been the real target.

Hal craned his neck around as the Lord of Birds pulled him in. Samantha was sprawled in the snow, dazed and trying to catch her breath. 'Run!' he yelled. 'Get back to the village! Don't wait for me!' Samantha began to argue, but Hal yelled so furiously that she jumped to her feet and set off across the snow as fast as she could go.

Pain burst all over Hal's body as the birds pecked at him with a terrifying savagery. As the Lord wrapped its arms around Hal, its aim became apparent: Hal would be pulled into the seething morass and consumed.

Blood splashed into his eyes from the beak of a ferocious thrush that was tearing at his cheek. His midriff was growing wet and warm, now numb from repeated attacks. He attempted to get some leverage so that he could prise himself free, but the Lord of Birds was too strong and its form too shifting for Hal to get a foothold. There was nothing he could do.

As he forced his head back to protect his eyes, a single thought came into his head like a clarion call. With difficulty, he wriggled one bloody hand through flapping wings and into his pocket. The Bloodeye met his fingers like an old friend, all the hidden memories of its usefulness revealed once more.

The words came to him like a dream: 'Far and away and here,' almost lost beneath the wild bird calls and frantic flapping.

Hal didn't know what happened next. He found himself flying through the air, knocked free from the grip of the Lord of Birds by a tremendous impact that stunned him. As he lay in the freezing snow, head spinning, the smell of wet fur filled his nostrils. The deafening roar of a tremendous beast echoed all around.

From the corner of his eye, Hal saw a frenzied shape attack the Lord of Birds. Feathers flew everywhere; dismembered bird heads plopped into the snow, beady eyes still rolling. Shocked alert, Hal drove himself backwards with his heels until he was far enough away to see properly what was occurring.

The Lord of Birds was being torn apart by an oversized man. Hal got glimpses through the wall of feathers – furs, a wide-brimmed hat, a string of dead conies swinging wildly – and realised it was Bearskin, the sharp-toothed drinker from the mysterious inn who had given Hal the Bloodeye.

Hal got to his feet, but he was transfixed by the inhuman fury of the attack. The Lord of Birds was being driven back, falling apart, becoming less human in form with each passing moment. But when Bearskin glanced back in Hal's direction, Hal immediately saw why: his rescuer's face was partially transformed; fur sprouted from the cheeks and forehead, the nose and mouth protruding in the first stage of a snout, the eyes big and black, his hands now covered with fur and tipped with long, jagged talons.

Hal was horrified by the ferocity he saw there, and he feared that once Bearskin had disposed of the Lord of Birds, the shape-shifter would turn on him.

'Leave!' Bearskin roared at him, the word barely distinguishable from the incoherent snarl of an animal. Hal could see from Bearskin's eyes that he also thought he might not be able to control himself.

Hal scrambled to his feet and ran just as the other Lords began to emerge from the front of the mansion house. Foaming at the mouth, Bearskin descended on the Lord of Birds in a renewed frenzy of tearing and rending. By the time Hal had reached the line of Samantha's footprints there remained only a wide arc of twitching bodies and torn wings and a faint purple mist where the Lord of Birds had stood, slowly breaking up in the snowy wind.

Bearskin turned on the other Lords, but it was clear that he wouldn't stand a chance against the three of them. Instead, he awkwardly manoeuvred the blunderbuss that hung at his side and fired a tremendous volley that rang off the hall's white walls. Hal didn't wait to see if it had any impact on the fast-approaching Lords.

Though the thick snow made his leg muscles burn, Hal ran without stopping until he reached the halfway point between the house and the place where the lane entered the trees. He allowed himself one brief glance back: something that looked like a large brown bear was moving away on all fours at great speed.

Already the memory of the Bloodeye had faded from Hal's mind, but the Lords would haunt him for ever, and the knowledge that they were hunting for him filled him with dread. Yet he had learned an important part of the mystery that he was sure was key to the survival of humanity and he was increasingly optimistic that the final pieces would soon fall into place.

Ahead of him, Samantha was just making her way into the trees. And there was his other great hope: he'd saved her life, and if he could help save the day, then perhaps she would finally see him as more than a good friend. Her love was worth fighting for more than anything else.

chapter twelve

the heart in winter

'Beware, for the time may be short.' Winston Churchill

Needles of ice blasted into the parts of Hunter's face that he hadn't been able to cover as he led his horse blindly into the blizzard. It had been blowing with fierce intensity for several hours and he desperately needed to find shelter, but it was night and no lights glimmered anywhere. He could no longer feel his feet or hands, despite the heavy boots and thick gloves. His mount's large body mass coped with the cold better than he did, but there was a limit to how much it could endure. Hunter had only made it this far with the help of the horse's strength; on foot he wouldn't stand a chance. His lifeless, frozen body would be covered by snow within the hour, never to be found again.

In his left hand, he held the lantern up high, but the illumination barely spread more than three feet ahead. He was using it more in the hope that someone would see it and welcome him out of the storm than to light his way, but he knew that was a dim prospect.

He was regretting his decision to let events lead him to his destination. There, so close to death, it felt childish and nonsensical, not the positive affirmation he had entertained when he had first embarked on his path. His choice was going to end up killing him.

From North Hinksey he'd taken the A34 and then the A423, moving north before getting lost in the snow. He had been hoping to reach Banbury and some shelter where he could rest a while, but there was little chance of that now.

Just visible in the field next to the road was an old barn. Snow heaped against its walls and lay heavy on the roof, but the door was accessible. It looked poor shelter, but it was all he had, and after several minutes of clearing snow with frozen hands he could open the door wide enough to gain access for himself and his horse.

Inside, it was as barely adequate as he had imagined. Cold wind blew through broken planks around the door, but there were numerous bales of hay that he could position to create a smaller shelter within the larger structure. His horse perked up slightly at being out of the freezing night, so Hunter left it alone long enough to break up some old, discarded furniture for a fire. The barn was large and draughty enough for the smoke to escape and soon Hunter was sitting next to the blaze, pondering his bleak immediate future. It wasn't long before the warmth and the weariness took their toll.

Not long after he had slipped into an exhausted sleep, he woke with a sudden start, calling out his father's name. Instantly, he realised he wasn't alone.

A hulking figure sat on the other side of the fire, its face obscured by the drifting smoke. Hunter's hand quickly went to his gun, but the figure didn't appear concerned. It was difficult to assess the man's height in a sitting position, but Hunter guessed he must have been well over seven feet tall. The smoke cleared a little to reveal long black hair and a black beard and eyes just as dark, though burning intensely.

'Stay your hand, Brother of Dragons,' the giant said in a deep, resonant voice.

Hunter's fingers hovered over the weapon for a moment longer, then retreated. 'Who are you? The Tooth Fairy?'

'I am called the Caretaker.'

Hunter recalled the encounter with this being that Hal had related to him just before his life had taken a turn into the twilight zone.

The Caretaker pointed ominously to the lantern; its flame flared as his finger came close. 'I am the lamplighter. Even when darkness falls, I am there to ensure that a single flame still burns.'

Hunter lounged against a hay bale and rubbed the sleep from his eyes. 'Mallory thought I was crazy just wandering around, waiting for something to happen. Well, I bet he's the one frozen up to his neck in a ditch somewhere. So you're one of the gods, right? One of the Tuatha Dé Danann?'

The Caretaker gave a faint, enigmatic smile. 'There are Higher Powers. There is always something higher. The Goddess has returned, reunited with her male reflection.' He watched Hunter's face intently. 'I am an intermediary. A guide—'

'Yes, I get it. A Caretaker. You put the chairs away after the party.'

Hunter expected a negative response, but the Caretaker simply nodded. 'I do. And I put them out before the party begins. It is my job to ensure that the master plan progresses smoothly. A higher plan so vast and timeless that it is beyond your comprehension. You can barely see even a part of it from your narrow perspective, Fragile Creature. Yet you, and your brothers and sisters, have a large part to play.'

'You see, there's one thing you're not getting. I'm not a reliable person. I like to drink. I like to have sex, preferably with as many women as possible. I like to raise hell. Not so hot on doing the right thing. Moral compass – needle all over the place.'

Hunter shifted as the Caretaker stared right into him. For a second, he had the impression that he was a small boy again, standing before his father; the image was so potent that Hunter could almost smell the starch of his father's dress uniform.

'You in a position to tell me exactly what's going on?' Hunter asked.

The Caretaker explained carefully about the Void, its nature and what it was planning, making it plain to Hunter that only the Brothers and Sisters of Dragons could oppose it. 'The lantern is called the Wayfinder,' the Caretaker continued. Hunter glanced at the blue flame as events began to fall into place; he had been meant to find it, of course – it was important. 'It is my lantern,' the Caretaker continued, 'and it is a part of Existence – not a lantern at all, but that is how you see it.'

'That flame,' Hunter began, 'blue . . .'

The Caretaker nodded. 'It is a link with the Pendragon Spirit. The power in the Wayfinder is a part of you, Brother of Dragons.

The flame points the way. Follow it and it will lead you to the person you seek.'

'That's handy. It would have been nice to know that before I started going around in circles in a blizzard, freezing my arse off.'

'Existence helps when you truly need it, Brother of Dragons. For the most part you must rely on your own strengths.'

'I get it – free will.' Hunter thought about this for a moment. 'OK. I like that. So now I've got a direction. How am I going to get where I'm going through this snow with a nag that's almost dead on its feet? You don't have a magic snowplough tucked away somewhere, do you?'

'The blizzard will break tomorrow. You will have a brief period for travel before the next storm sets in. There is food for you and your horse in a farm further along the road. The occupants died when their fuel ran out.'

Hunter felt strangely calmed by the giant's presence. 'All you need to tell me now is that everything is going to work out fine.'

The Caretaker shook his head slowly.

'What's the point in having a master plan if it doesn't all pan out nicely?'

'If everything occurred as it was meant to occur, there would be no need for you, would there, Brother of Dragons? There would be no need for Fragile Creatures, or gods, or . . . anything. This would just be a picture, never changing. There must be a chance for success or failure.'

'Why?'

The Caretaker gave his enigmatic smile once again. 'Existence has put its faith in you, Brother of Dragons.' He stood up, drawing himself to his full height, and his shadow fell across Hunter. 'Your light burns brightly in the dark. Existence has chosen well.'

He stepped away from the fire towards the door, but then a cloud of smoke obscured him, and when it cleared, he had gone. Hunter stared into the fire for a while, ruminating over what he had been told, and then he shrugged, lay down and went straight to sleep.

'What do you think is happening back in our world?' Thackeray sat in the vast blood-red hall of the Court of Soul's Ease, listening to the sounds of conflict coming from the walls.

Sophie stood nearby. She was trying to prepare herself for what she was about to do, but it was difficult to concentrate with the bizarre acoustics of the hall, where even the quietest whisper reverberated loudly. 'Time runs differently here. In our world, a second could have passed. Or years . . . maybe even decades.'

'That's why you're so keen to get back?'

Sophie sighed. 'It's hard to tell whether all this is futile. Perhaps the worst has already happened back home. There might not even be a world to return to.'

They fell silent, allowing the clatter of swords and axes to take over. The battle sounds were punctuated by dull, vibrating eruptions as projectiles crashed against the walls, launched from one of the many mysterious siege machines the enemy had in their employ. It was only a matter of time before the court fell. The small, swarthy men scaled the walls like spiders in wave after wave. The Tuatha Dé Danann, led by Lugh but invigorated by Caitlin's ferocity, drove them back time and again, but sheer force of numbers meant that the defenders would inevitably be over-whelmed sooner or later.

Sophie had to make her move before it was too late, but Caitlin was the dangerous x-factor. If she discovered what Sophie was planning, the outcome would likely be bloody.

'How are you coping with Caitlin?' Sophie asked hesitantly.

Thackeray rubbed at the tension in his neck; he was a man out of his depth. 'I'm not coping. She looks like Caitlin, she talks like her, but when I stare into her eyes, I can't tell whether she wants to have sex or slit my throat.'

'I know it's none of my business, but I can't work out your relationship.'

'It's complicated.' Thackeray was going to leave it there, but the emotional pressure was too much. 'I met her just after her husband and son died. I fell in love with her straight away, the minute I saw her – I know it sounds pathetic, but it's true. She's got this amazing quality, something special buried really deep. It got me in an instant and I couldn't let go if I tried. I think she loves me, too . . . or at least likes me a lot, and I know this is pathetic, too, but I'd even settle for that.' He sighed. 'But it's still too soon after her tragedy. All the grief and guilt are still swirling around. I understand that. Maybe someday.'

'That's what I thought you'd say.' Sophie had grown more and more impressed with Thackeray, not because he was romantic and sensitive, but because he had enough steel in him to admit it.

'How about you?' Thackeray said. 'Boyfriend back home?'

'Yes. He's a Brother of Dragons, too.'

'At least you've got some common ground, then,' he said ruefully. 'Sometimes you lot seem like you come from another planet. You're missing him?'

'More than you know. Nothing's going to stop me from getting back to him.' Sophie flinched as the missing portion of her emotional memory made all her recollections of Mallory dissipate like mist in the sun.

They were interrupted by the thunder of the enormous oaken doors being flung open. Caitlin marched in clutching two axes, with Harvey hurrying close behind, almost bent double under the weight of a variety of weapons.

'We need axes. Lots of axes,' Caitlin announced.

'She's going to be the death of me.' Harvey dumped the weapons on the floor with a clatter. 'Here – take your pick.'

'Arrows aren't effective when they're coming up the walls,' Caitlin said. 'And we probably haven't got enough anyway, even with the fletchers working overtime. But axes . . .' She wielded an axe in each hand. 'We can just decapitate them as they come over the top. The falling bodies will dislodge others. Two axes to each man doubles the kill.'

'Tiring, though,' Sophie observed.

'We do what we have to,' Caitlin said coldly. 'I'm going back to the ramparts. Coming?'

'We'll follow on.' Sophie subtly motioned to Thackeray to stay behind and hoped Caitlin hadn't seen it.

Caitlin ordered Harvey to pick up a selection of the weapons and follow her. He meekly obliged.

Once they had departed, Thackeray said curiously, 'What are you planning?'

'There's a way out of here. A way back home.'

Thackeray was stunned silent for a second, then said, non-plussed, 'Why didn't you tell the others?'

'Because it's not as simple as it sounds. I've been weighing it up ever since I found out about it. I still don't think it's necessarily the right way to go forward, but we don't have a choice any more.'

'It's dangerous?'

'Yes. Morally, emotionally, probably physically if Caitlin finds out.' Sophie steeled herself; she couldn't back out now. 'There's a place called the Watchtower, a physical building in some kind of space between the worlds. It's possible to reach it from anywhere, and access anywhere from it, as long as you have the right key.'

'And you have the right key?'

'And the right keyhole,' she said with dark humour. 'I can use my Craft to open a way to the Watchtower. Everything I learned back home works so much more effectively in T'ir n'a n'Og. I can be powerful here, Thackeray, really powerful, given the right impetus.'

'You're scaring me now.' Thackeray's troubled, dark eyes searched her face.

'Then I'd better get to the point. Imagine the Craft as a bullet. I'm the gun. But you need some kind of focused energy to send the bullet shooting out of the barrel. For small things, you can often do it with the mind – say, with words that set free subconscious energy. Ritual works better. But the best is sex. The energy freed during sex is like rocket fuel, to mix my metaphors.'

'You need to have sex?'

'With you.'

Thackeray's expression was almost comical. 'No, no,' he protested, holding up his hands subconsciously as a barrier. 'I mean, it's not that you're not an attractive woman. You are. Of course you are. But . . . it's Caitlin . . .'

'I know.'

'I love her.'

'I know.'

'Harvey would do it in a flash.'

Sophie shook her head. 'It's not just about having sex, Thackeray. It has to be with the right person . . . the right battery. Bluntly, Harvey isn't the one. You've got a lot of sexual energy ready to be released.'

'I don't know if I should be flattered or embarrassed.' He jumped to his feet and ranged around the room anxiously. 'There's got to be another way.'

'There isn't. That's what I've been considering long and hard. Don't you think I would have done this the minute I found out about it if it was that easy? You've got to do this, Thackeray. Not just for us here, but for all the people back home.'

Thackeray ran his hands through his hair in impotent silence.

'I'll tell you something, Thackeray: I've never had to go to the lengths of invoking the survival of the human race to persuade a man to have sex with me before.'

'I'm sorry.' A flicker of fear crossed his face. 'If Caitlin loves me, and if she finds out . . . if the Morrigan finds out—'

'Then we have to make sure she doesn't find out. Let's get this done, the sooner the better, while she's out on the ramparts slaughtering thousands.'

As if punctuating Sophie's words, another projectile crashed against the walls, shaking the court to its very foundations.

'Come closer.' Sophie held out her arms; Thackeray twitched like a nervous schoolboy.

It had taken almost an hour to get the preparations just right. They had moved to the privacy of the bedroom chamber in the large suite that had been set aside for Sophie after her arrival in the Court of Soul's Ease. The furniture had been moved to one side and a sacred space inscribed on the floor with red dye and candles. She'd had to guess at the cardinal points for her special sigils – compasses didn't always make a great deal of sense in that place. Incense drifted teasingly through the air, and she'd forced Thackeray to have two stiff shots of the dark, potent spirit that many of the court's residents consumed at the end of their meals. Despite being a little tipsy, he was still on edge, and that made Sophie even more anxious.

'I don't know if I can go through with this,' he said.

'This isn't helping the mood, Thackeray.'

'I'm sorry.'

Sophie turned and lit some dried herbs in a small brazier.

'Double, double, toil and trouble?'

'Just get your clothes off, Thackeray.'

She heard him mutter, 'Something wicked this way comes,' and then she turned and grabbed him and started to pull his clothes from him. She stripped off herself, quickly, and then used her hands and her mouth to get him erect.

'I don't know if I can keep it up,' he muttered.

'Don't worry, I'll help. Just close your eyes and think whatever you need to.'

She lay down in the circle and opened her legs, pulling him into her. As he began to move backwards and forwards, eyes clamped shut, a surge of emotion hit her and she had to blink away the tears. She had thought it would be easy, pure mechanics, but all she could think of was Mallory, and that she was betraying him, and that she missed him so much.

She must have grown tense, for he whispered, 'Are you OK?'

'I'm fine. Keep going.' Her emotions were too raw and the only way she could continue was to focus in that gap where her meeting with Mallory had once been; she found it ironic how something so painful now had a use. Without that loss, she might have had to give up.

They continued until they grew hot and sweaty and arousal took over from the regular flow of thoughts. In her mind, Sophie shaped the energy and infused a word of power. She managed to hold on to her orgasm so that they climaxed at the same time, and then she said the word of power with force.

The flash she experienced may have been in the room or in her own head, but when she looked around there was a doorway shimmering in one wall, like oil on water, and on the other side she could see a long corridor lit by flickering torches.

'Come on,' she whispered. 'Let's get the others.'

Thackeray withdrew and they both dressed quickly. But then Sophie noticed something strange: the bedroom door was slightly ajar. And she was sure she had closed it tightly after they had first entered.

'How long will the portal stay open?' Lugh stood in the centre of the bed chamber, surveying the entry to the Watchtower. Ceridwen stood behind him. Thackeray and Harvey waited in one corner while Caitlin remained a dark, brooding presence nearby. There was no sign that she had any suspicions about what had happened.

'It won't stay open for ever,' Sophie replied. 'It should remain long enough for you to carry out some kind of evacuation.'

Lugh was troubled. 'But will every member of this vast court be able to pass through before it closes? I fear for the safety of any left behind.'

'There will be a slaughter,' Ceridwen said bluntly.

'We could do with your help back in the Fixed Lands,' Sophie said. 'But you have to do what you have to do. We need to go.'

Lugh nodded curtly and stepped back. Ceridwen gave Sophie a brief hug. 'If we can, we shall join you shortly, Sister of Dragons.'

Sophie turned to Caitlin. 'Ready?'

'Let's do it.' Caitlin gripped one axe tightly and adjusted the other strapped to her back. Sophie nodded to Thackeray and Harvey to follow, and then led the way into the unknown.

The General steeled himself before he entered Kirkham's private lab. He thought that over the years he had learned to be immune to bad news, but the latest report had shaken him to the core. The estimates of the size of the enemy army were such that he had berated the messenger for typing too many digits. But there had been no mistake. The enemy had moved slowly south and west, converting the population to their cause; and *converting* was the ultimate euphemism for what they actually did. Hundreds of thousands had been slaughtered and remade in the image of the Lament-Brood, all of them now marching to the beat of war. And Birmingham was next.

He barged into the lab without knocking. The model town lay gathering dust to one side while Kirkham examined a purple gem illuminated by a powerful spotlight.

'What have you got for me?' the General barked so sharply that Kirkham almost swept the jewel on to the floor.

'I'm working on—'

'Nothing. That's the answer, isn't it?' The General had told himself he wouldn't lose his temper, but the blood was thundering in his head. 'Months spent tinkering away down here, the hope of the nation invested in you . . . and you've got nothing to show for it!'

The General turned to the model of the town and thrust it off the table. It shattered noisily in a heap on the floor.

'I need results!' the General raged. 'I need you to get one of those . . . one of those . . . bloody magic wands working! Anything!'

Kirkham blinked at him from behind his glasses. 'There's nothing that's reliable, General,' he said calmly. 'Certainly nothing that would deal with the magnitude of this problem. I thought the nuclear deterrent was—'

'We've tried nukes, blast it!' The General sucked in a deep breath, searching for his dignity. 'We dropped one over Tamworth. Never exploded. The pilot said it looked as if it disappeared into some kind of black hole. We've sent in troops on skirmishes, quick in, quick out, aiming for minimal casualties. They couldn't get out quickly enough. More fuel/air explosives. Anthrax from Porton Down. Nerve agents.' As the rage rushed out of him, he sagged, looking ten years older in an instant. 'We have to face the fact that conventional weapons are not going to work. From now on, we're down to wishing.'

'I'm sorry I don't have more helpful news, General. The things I'm dealing with are beyond scientific understanding, certainly at current knowledge levels.'

'We lost our only hope when Hunter went mad and smuggled that Brother of Dragons out,' the General said. 'If I find him, I'll shoot him myself. I should have done it a long time ago.'

'Even if we had access to the Brother of Dragons, I don't think we would have had time to make any breakthrough in finding a way across the dimensional barriers.' Kirkham began to pick up pieces of the broken model and replace them on the table. 'But the enemy is not the Tuatha Dé Danann. This enemy may not even have come from the Otherworld.'

'So, what? We're now easy pickings for any Higher Power anywhere across the universe?'

'Multiverse,' Kirkham corrected, pedantically.

'You really are our last hope, Kirkham.' The General walked towards the door, not knowing where he was going next or what he was going to do. 'Desperate times require desperate measures, and these are the most desperate of times. Do whatever you can. Don't worry about protocol. Don't worry about chain of command. Just pull something out of the bag.'

After the General had left, Kirkham waited until the sound of his footsteps had faded away and then picked up the phone. 'It's Dennis Kirkham,' he said quietly. 'I'm with you.'

★

True to the Caretaker's word, the bad weather held off long enough for Hunter to make good progress. With his horse and himself fed at the next farm, he followed the Wayfinder's blue flame north-east from Banbury, along the A361 to Daventry where he helped starving residents fight against a local landowner who had taken ninety per cent of the food that had been stored. Hunter killed four heavily armed thugs and then threw the greedy landowner to the mob, departing amidst cheers and the formation of a new legend; he wasn't surprised to realise that he liked the adoration.

From Daventry, he cut cross-country to Market Harborough where he stocked up on supplies and then continued across the Leicestershire countryside. It was hard going in the frozen landscape; away from the shelter of trees, the hungry wind flayed his skin and cut through even the thickest clothes. It was even worse when he passed Stamford and moved into the Lincolnshire flatlands, where there was little cover and the land resembled the Antarctic wastes. He found the A15, an old Roman road, which was marginally easier to travel than the country lanes, and headed north.

Despite the hardship, he never entertained the slightest notion that he might fail; it was all down to will, the desire to win, the hunger for survival, and he had demonstrated throughout his life that he was more than blessed with those qualities.

Finally, on a blue-skied, sunny morning when the snow glared so brightly it hurt his eyes, he arrived in Lincoln.

The city was dwarfed by the imposing Cathedral Church of St Mary, perched atop a two-hundred-foot-high limestone plateau overlooking the River Witham, its Gothic architecture given a magical appearance by the snow.

Hunter ventured past the city limits with a degree of apprehension. Since the Fall, much of the country had been gripped by lawlessness; murder was commonplace in populated areas, and Hunter guessed things would be even worse in the grip of an ice age that threatened most of the population with starvation.

Yet he was surprised to find a well-fed, generally content population. Fruit trees sprouted from the pavements, heavy with apples despite the weather. The buildings in some areas had been demolished and given over to fields where potato plants, carrot tops and broccoli forced their way through the snow. Their survival made no sense.

As he neared the cathedral, he reined in his horse to talk to a trader manning a creaking stall laden with a variety of fruits and vegetables, some of it exotic and not seen in Britain since all contact with the outside world had ceased at the Fall.

When asked about the abundance of produce, the trader responded, 'Every visitor to Lincoln has the same question. All I can say is that we're especially blessed.' He grinned. 'We've got our very own Green Angel.'

Hunter couldn't decide whether the trader had been unbalanced by too long on a diet of swedes or if he was honestly hinting at some kind of divine intervention. It was impossible to tell in a time when madness and miracles abounded in equal measure. He urged his horse forward, following the flame.

Not far on, Hunter encountered a large group of people gathered in a square, many of them wearing the black T-shirts with the red 'V' that signified followers of Ryan Veitch. Hunter had seen the mounting intelligence gathered on the group as their numbers increased, but he'd always dismissed it as just one of the many cults that had sprung up amongst people desperate for a god, any god, to drag them out of their suffering. Yet now that he had discovered his own link to the Pendragon Spirit, the matter took on a new resonance. What would it take to drive a Brother of Dragons to betray the very principle of life?

On a platform of pallets at the centre of the crowd, a speaker preached with fire and brimstone that kept the like-minds of the crowd rapt. He had a shaven head and the unflinching eyes of someone for whom brutality was a way of life. 'The day is drawing closer when He shall be returned to us!' he roared in a cod-religious tone. 'We can all see the signs – the world is ending. Only He can save us! And only we can bring him back! The mass ritual will be held shortly when we'll pray for Him to walk once more upon the Earth! In this day and age, prayer has power! The gods listen! If we concentrate . . . if we believe . . . we can change anything! The dead can live again!'

Hunter shrugged; maybe the preacher was right – it was difficult to be sure about anything any more.

★

The lantern led Hunter to the cobbled street rising steeply up to the cathedral. On either side was a profusion of medieval houses that had once been antique shops and had now returned to their original use. They were all ablaze with colour: red, pink and yellow roses swarmed around doors, clematis was still in flower, tulips and daffodils and pinks and geraniums sprouted from boxes on the pavement. Yet all around it was bitterly cold.

The steep cobbled street was treacherous with snow and ice, so Hunter dismounted and led his horse. By the time the street reached the shadow of the cathedral, dark, heavy clouds had swept across the blue sky and snow was starting to fall again.

The lantern pointed towards the main door of the cathedral, which was locked. Hunter tethered his mount and wandered the vast perimeter of the building searching for a way in, but all the entrances were barred. An unusual atmosphere emanated from the stone, not reverence or transcendence like he had felt at many other cathedrals, but a brooding sadness that began to affect him deeply. The building was strange in other ways, too: like the houses that lined the old pilgrims' route to the door, the cathedral had more than its fair share of verdant growth – ivy crawling over the windows, Russian vine spreading over stonework, the leaves turning red as though it was autumn. In Lincoln, all seasons were unfolding simultaneously.

He returned to the main door and rapped loudly. As he listened to the echoes, a disturbing sensation tickled his lower leg. He was shocked to see ivy wrapped around his ankle and crawling slowly upwards before his eyes.

Jumping backwards, he wrenched the ivy out of the ground, but it still continued to grow up towards his thigh. He tore it away with frozen fingers and hurled the remnants against the wall.

Quiet, cynical laughter echoed around the cathedral precinct. Hunter looked around for the source, but there was only stillness over the snow.

'She won't let you inside.'

A woman in a green cloak emerged from the side of one of the buildings adjoining the cathedral, her hood pulled forward so that her face was hidden by shadows.

'You want to be careful creeping up on me. I've killed people for less,' Hunter said.

'Oooh,' she replied with childish sarcasm. 'Big man, big threat.' The woman threw back her hood to reveal messy white-blonde hair above a face that had a faint greenish tint to the skin, but which didn't hamper her flinty beauty. The hardness made her appear aloof and a little arrogant, but she had a wry smile that suggested she was entertained by Hunter's appearance.

'The Green Angel,' Hunter guessed.

'Love you, too.'

'You did that trick with the ivy?'

'I can't reveal my secrets.' She teased him in a manner that some would find irritating. 'You're not a local. Come for some free fruit and veg? The store's down in town.'

'You did all that with the plants, too. I'm impressed. Green fingers.'

'Green everything.' She came over, now more intrigued than entertained. 'You're not here for food. Who are you?'

'I can't reveal my secrets.'

The woman circled him slowly, looking him up and down. 'Lean. Mean. Packing some weapons, if I'm not mistaken by the bulges under your cloak. Or are you just pleased to see me?'

'You're very sparky. Give it a bit of time and you might be able to develop it into a personality.'

The woman suddenly noticed a flare of blue illumination inside Hunter's cloak as it blew aside in the wind. She yanked at the hem to pull the cloak open, revealing the Wayfinder where it had been hanging out of sight in Hunter's hand. Her demeanour changed instantly.

'Where did you get that?'

'A giant gave it to me,' Hunter said wryly, but his mind was already turning at her recognition. 'It's called the Wayfinder.'

'I know what it's called,' she snapped. In that moment, the defences of her face were stripped away to reveal a flow of honest emotion: memories of good times, memories of sadness, hardship and suffering. It ended with a faint, contented smile as though she had just recognised an old friend.

'I think,' Hunter said, 'I'm looking for you.'

She blinked away a furtive tear. 'Come far?'

'From the ends of the Earth.' That's what it felt like to him. Now

246

that his own defences had broken down he felt a deep affinity with the odd woman, and he could see in her eyes that she felt it, too.

She put her arms around him warmly and held him in silence for a moment. When she broke away, she said, 'I'm not usually one for hugging. So don't tell anyone about that, all right?'

'Sister of Dragons.' He nodded slowly; he could see it now.

'And you're one of the new ones. The pale copies.'

'I like to think you were the prototypes and we're the definitive article.' He held out a hand. 'Hunter.'

'Is that a name or some sexual role-play thing?' The woman held his hand for a long second.

'Are you always like this?'

'I wouldn't be so lovable any other way. Laura DuSantiago.'

He looked up at the towering cathedral. 'And this is where you hang out? Nice. Bet it's a nightmare to clean.'

'Now there's a thing. Wait till you see the inside. If she ever lets us in,' she added tartly.

'"She" being . . . ?'

'Ruth Gallagher. Uber-Witch of the whole fucking multiverse. And doesn't she just know it.'

She shook her head with irritation and motioned for Hunter to follow her. This time the main door swung open easily.

'Looks like she's out of her sulk,' Laura said. 'But you still won't be able to see her yet – she'll be off brooding somewhere. Better come in and take the weight off for a while.'

Hunter followed Laura into the cathedral and was even more surprised than she had indicated he would be. The interior was a bizarre mix of tropical greenhouse and ice cave. Strange gargantuan ice formations almost obscured the lofty roof and curved across the nave, which entered into a series of tunnels through the permafrost. Yet tropical trees thrust up from the frozen floor, breaking through the stone to press against the ice, and creepers and vines hung down from above. It made the inside of the cathedral claustrophobic and disturbingly otherworldly.

'So you can control nature? Make things grow, even where they shouldn't?' Hunter asked.

'One of the pluses of being a plant.'

'What?'

'Long story. Basically, I'm an avatar of the Green, gifted – or

247

cursed – by Cernunnos. You heard of him? He's one of the Tuatha Dé Danann, a nature god, basically, or *the* nature god. Anyway, I'm his chosen one, and he's given me lots of cool powers to use as I see fit. Course, I get the chlorophyll skin, but these days there aren't many beauty parades.'

Laura led Hunter through the maze of ice tunnels to a room where a brazier glowed with hot coals. He warmed his hands over it eagerly. 'There's bread and fruit over there.' She motioned to a cupboard in one corner before lounging on a hard wooden bench. 'Now you'd better tell me why you're here.'

Hunter told her everything, from the impending end of the world at the hands of the Void, to the attack on his troops by the Lament-Brood and their lethal generals, and the fragmented state of the current quincunx of Brothers and Sisters of Dragons. Laura listened intently, chipping in with sarcastic comments or wry asides, but beneath the patina of levity, Hunter could tell that she understood what was at stake and recognised her responsibility.

'We need your help,' he said finally, 'to make up the numbers, in the hope that it might make up for one of us being dead. But we need your experience, too. To be honest, none of us knows what the hell we're doing with this Pendragon Spirit thing.'

Hunter was taken aback by Laura's laughter. 'This is the best! You're coming to us for help and advice? Listen, we were the biggest collection of fuck-ups you could ever imagine. Church – Jack Churchill – he was up to his neck in grief over the death of his girlfriend. Unhealthy? You bet. Ryan Veitch was a crook who'd killed a man, who turned out to be a relative of the Uber-Witch, but Ruth had got her own problems, one of which was a poker up her arse. Shavi, our seer, now he was cool. Not what you'd call wholly *present*, if you get what I mean, but a nice guy. And me? I was perfect, but you've got to have one or the whole thing falls apart.'

Laura was a woman who liked to play games, to distort for effect and for her own aims, and Hunter knew he couldn't trust everything she said. Their conversation was a dance, defining boundaries, deciding status; he was impressed.

'Two questions. First: if you were all so useless, how, out of all the possible candidates in the human race, did you get selected for the Pendragon Spirit?'

'Maybe you get selected at random.'

'Secondly, the Fall. Overnight, the Otherworld pumped out gods, devils, monsters, every supernatural creature that ever existed in any fairy tale anywhere. All the conventional responses failed. But you five stopped us from being wiped out. If you were so useless, how did that happen?'

'We were just lucky.' She smiled tightly, giving nothing away.

'Go on,' he pressed.

She shrugged, pretending it was old news, but the memory was carved in the tense muscles of her face. Whatever had happened to her during the Fall had shaped her character, eradicating the woman she had been before, replacing her with someone forged in the cauldron of strife.

'How long have you got?' As a faraway look appeared in her eyes, some of the hardness dropped from her face. 'We made lots of mistakes, but somehow . . . somehow everything turned out all right in the end.' She caught herself. 'All right for the human race, that is. Not so great for us.'

'You're talking about Jack Churchill and Ryan Veitch dying.'

'It's more complicated than that. Things never happen in isolation. You deal with the repercussions for ever. Anyway, you can talk to Ruth about that later. You want to hear tales of swashbuckling adventure, five people beating the odds to come up with the goods for humanity? Yeah, I can do that. It was all about the Pendragon Spirit, all those myths about King Arthur that Church was always banging on about. I don't really care about how it's all linked together. The bottom line is, despite all the failures and the mistakes, everything came together right when it needed to. Just like it was planned. And you're right, it was a big win. At the Battle of London . . .' She closed her eyes in recall. 'The city, burning . . . things swarming all over it that would give anybody nightmares . . .' She drifted for a moment.

'How did Jack and Ryan die?' he probed gently.

'We were steered to a tower that had risen up on the banks of the Thames. There was something inside . . .' An expression of distaste sprang to her face. 'A power . . . evil, yeah, definitely evil. If we hadn't stopped it, that would have been it, game over.'

'Did it have anything to do with the Void?'

'I don't know. There's nothing to say it did . . . but maybe all these things are linked together, you know? Everything that wants to stop us getting a foothold on the ladder. I used to think good and evil were ideas for kids. Too simple. Fairy-tale stuff. But now . . . on the big scale, the universal scale, I think good and evil are what it's all about. A constant war from the beginning of time to the end. And we're just little troops, cannon fodder, there to make sure things don't go belly-up for our side.'

Hunter moved closer to the brazier. He felt as if he couldn't get enough warmth.

'We confronted this thing at the top of the tower,' Laura said. 'We'd got the right tools, magic shit, a sword, a spear . . . Church was about to deliver the killing blow. Then Ryan stepped in.'

'Why did he do it?'

'He didn't mean to,' Laura said wearily. She'd obviously spent long hours turning the tragedy over in her head. 'Ryan was just that little bit weaker than the rest of us. He was manipulated, by the gods, the evil things. All those so-called Higher Powers just manipulate us all the time. And Ryan paid the price. There was a fight. He died. Church managed to kill the thing that had been waiting for us, but Ryan had thrown everything off-balance. Some kind of hole opened up in the air . . . like a hole into space. The thing went into it with its last dying gasp, and Church got sucked in after it. So we won and we lost. Story over.'

'You've been through the mill—'

'I don't want your sympathy.'

'And you're not going to get it. You had a job to do and you did it. There's always a price to pay in situations like that . . . like this. No point crying over it. So after that you came here?'

'Not at first.' Laura rubbed her fingers together and a rose grew magically out of the floor, its bud bursting, blossoming into black petals. She stared at it thoughtfully. 'Ruth wanted to pass on all her witchy skills, so we travelled the country for a while with her doing her Hogwarts bit to a load of wannabes. But her heart wasn't in it. When we reached this place she decided she wasn't going any farther.'

'And you stuck with her.'

'Somebody had to. She didn't have anybody else.' She snapped her fingers and the black rose shrivelled and died.

Hunter cracked his knuckles, then put his feet up on a small table; he'd found out all he needed to know for now. 'Must be boring here for you.'

'I'm not getting any, if that's what you mean.' She gave him a challenging smile.

'Fancy some?'

Laura thought for a moment, then shrugged. 'Why not?'

The sex was the first physical contact either of them had enjoyed for a while, and was passionate and unguarded. Hunter discovered that Laura smelled of lime and roses, but afterwards she told him that she could manipulate her scent at will. 'That's probably my greatest power,' she added, 'now that we live in a world without deodorant.'

When they were both dressed again, Laura reluctantly agreed to take Hunter to see Ruth, who Laura said would be 'brooding in her batcave'. They moved through the fantastic ice tunnels and chambers, a crystal world within the very heart of the cathedral, their breath trailing behind them in clouds.

Finally they came to a cavern so large that it dwarfed all the others. It was a work of art, with icicles hanging ten feet or more from the ceiling and reflecting surfaces designed to catch and distribute the light of many candles. At the far side was a throne made entirely from ice and sitting in it was the saddest woman Hunter had ever seen.

She was swathed in black fur, her fragile features as pale as hoarfrost. Her hair was long, dark brown and curly, and black rings beneath her eyes emphasised the painful grief in her face. Those eyes, too, were dark, filled with a surfeit of shattered emotion. A black and white woman in a frozen world.

'There she is, the Witch-Queen of the world,' Laura said quietly to Hunter. 'We've got a guest,' she added loudly. 'Get out the best china.'

Ruth had been lost to her thoughts and unaware they had entered. Her eyes flickered to Hunter, then moved away.

'I'll leave you to it,' Laura whispered in his ear before departing.

Hunter marched up to the throne. 'Are you expecting me to kneel and kiss your ring?'

'Who are you?' Ruth said coldly.

'My name's Hunter. I'm a Brother of Dragons. And I still haven't quite come to terms with that as an introduction.'

'You never will. What do you want?'

Hunter was surprised by her brusque, uninterested nature after Laura's curiosity. 'I've come a long way to see you, and Laura. You're needed, both of you.'

'I've done my bit.' Ruth's gaze was as cold as her demeanour.

'Actually, I don't think you get to resign. The way I see it, it's a job for life.'

'The Pendragon Spirit isn't as strong in me as it used to be.'

'Still there, though. A little, right?'

'I'll ask again, what do you want?'

'There's a crisis . . . actually, that's too mild a word for it.' He held out his right hand. 'You have God here, not representing any particular religion, but some higher force that stands for life—'

'Existence.'

'All right, if you want to call it that.' He held out his left hand. 'And here you have the opposite of Existence, and all that stands for. The opposite of life, an absence of being, negativity. Not death – worse . . . not existing . . .' He floundered, not sure he was making sense even to himself. He extended his left hand. 'That's what's here, now, and pretty soon none of us will be existing unless we do something. You might say, "We're only human – what can we do against something like that?" and to be honest I don't have an answer for you. But I do know that the Brothers and Sisters of Dragons were created to oppose this. We're the champions of life . . . of Existence. Maybe there's something we don't know that we can do, all working together. Maybe we can't do anything. But we have to try.'

'The magic number is five,' she said icily. 'Don't you know that? The old Five is broken. You need a new Five.'

Hunter could see that he wasn't persuading her and renewed his argument. 'I know that. One of the new Five is dead. Two haven't been found yet. That makes three vacancies. The two of us left could either hold up our hands and say we've failed . . . and that word just doesn't do it justice, since this failure means the end of all human existence. Who could cope with that? So we could say we've failed . . . or we could seek out substitutes, who might not be able to do anything. Or who might make all the difference in the world. My partner has gone to get Shavi. I'm here for you and Laura. So, will you come back? Not for me, but for everybody. For Existence.'

There was a long period of silence when the only sound was the howling wind beyond the cathedral walls. Then Ruth leaned forward and turned the full force of those dark, devastated eyes on Hunter. 'Let me tell you something. I loved Jack Churchill. More than I love myself. He was everything to me, and when he died it felt as if everything inside me shattered into a million pieces. Nothing, trust me, *nothing* comes even close to the pain I feel inside, and I've been through a lot of suffering in my short, unhappy life. Church had everything going for him. He was filled with the Blue Fire. All the prophecies spoke about how important he was to the future. He was going to lead us into some golden age. And still he died. You want to know what it means to be a Brother of Dragons? That's what it means: hope, strife, failure. Not even the best can win. You just hold the line.'

'I can live with that—'

She silenced him with a raised hand. 'They tell you grief fades with time. What I feel for Church won't fade. It's beyond grief. The price I personally paid for our success during the Fall was too high. Far too high. So don't come asking me to do it all again. I don't care any more . . . about anything. I'm just going to sit here, while the world freezes around me, and wait for it all to fade away to nothing.'

The desolation in her words was almost too painful to hear. Hunter could see that what she had been through had fractured her, but he couldn't afford to back down. 'Please . . . what's at stake—'

'I know what's at stake,' she said, 'and I don't care. You're wasting your breath.'

'If you don't come, that's it. Our last hope gone. You're the one consigning us all to the end.'

She held up one hand, palm outwards, and a freezing wind hit Hunter; he could feel ice forming across his face and body. With an effort, he tried to resist it, but whatever she was doing, she simply turned it up a notch until he realised that she would quite happily see him freeze to death. In the end, there was nothing he could do but leave.

Outside the cavern, Laura was waiting. 'Don't think badly of her.'

'How can I not?' Hunter snapped. 'She's killed everyone.'

'She might not be able to make a difference anyway.' Laura touched his face, soothing the anger and disbelief out of him. 'She loved Church, and she couldn't cope with losing him. Emotions rule us, Hunter; there's nothing we can do about it. That's the way we were made, and we were made that way for a reason.'

'Well, if that's true, I can't see it.' He sucked in a deep breath, still coming to terms with the fact that he'd failed. 'I'd better get back.'

'I'm coming with you.'

That surprised him; what little he knew of her had suggested that she would be the selfish, indifferent one. 'What's the point? You'll just be coming back to die.'

'We've got to try, haven't we?' She grinned defiantly. 'That's the job. Come on, I need to find a horse.' She turned and headed off back through the tunnels as if there was still hope.

chapter thirteen

the hour is getting late

'*Vae, puto deus fio.*' Vespasian

('Oh dear, I must be turning into a god.')

In the reverent depths of the Bodleian Library, Hal pored over a mountain of dusty volumes, but his mind was elsewhere. While reading the same page over and over again, he was back in the helicopter on the return journey from Shugborough Hall, adrenalin racing through his system, his heart pounding fit to burst, and the snowy countryside sweeping past beneath in a magical procession. And Samantha was pressed tight against him, her head on his shoulder, her arm entwined around his, and she was whispering the words he would never forget.

'You saved my life, Hal. I don't know what I'd ever do without you.'

And then there had been the kiss. On his cheek, admittedly, but it had not been chaste, he was sure; certainly not overtly sexual, either, but filled with a deep affection.

The scene played over and over in his mind. The seeds were so small, he didn't dare give them too much credence, but a tiny part of him refused to let go: there was hope; she wasn't completely devoted to Hunter; when the crunch came, she'd prefer Hal's decency over Hunter's louche amorality.

He was so lost to his ever-entwining mind games that he almost missed the item for which he had been searching. Just as he was about to turn the page of the two-hundred-year-old book he had been sifting through, his subconscious flagged up a tiny reproduction of *The Shepherds of Arcadia*. Hal read the accompanying information once, then again, this time taking it in, and finally a third time with avid concentration.

'Samantha!' he called out. 'I've found something!'

Samantha ran over from another table where she had been hidden from his view behind a wall of books.

She hung over his left shoulder and peered at the text. Hal could feel the warmth of her skin, smell her perfume, but he forced himself to concentrate.

'Listen to this,' he said, and began to read from the book. ' "The phrase *Et in Arcadia Ego* cannot be traced to any classical source. When asked of its origins, Nicolas Poussin maintained a puzzling silence. Yet on several occasions he told of a strange meeting. It occurred in sixteen thirty-seven, shortly before Poussin began work on his famous painting *Les Bergers d'Arcadie*, when, according to the artist, a young man with blue skin mysteriously appeared in his studio and entreated him to paint his first work on the subject. The angelic messenger's details were specific, and included the curious phrase, but Poussin was induced to take the secret of his painting to his grave. Poussin always grew pale when questioned about this night-time visitor. But whatever was said to him in the privacy of his studio on that occasion encouraged him to begin work on his painting the next morning, in a feverish state according to his closest friends." '

Hal stared at the page for a moment, then looked into Samantha's face, so close to his own. 'I don't know about "angelic messenger" or "blue skin", but that certainly sounds like a visitor from the Otherworld.'

'But why would someone from the Otherworld visit Nicolas Poussin in Rome and force him to paint *The Shepherds of Arcadia*?'

'Because,' Hal said, 'they wanted to preserve a clue that could be discovered hundreds of years later. Maybe they knew Poussin was going to be a great artist and that all his works would be well known down the years.'

'But why all those centuries back?'

Hal thought about that for a moment. 'Perhaps the strange visitor didn't set off all that time ago.'

'What do you mean?'

'All the legends say that time is odd in T'ir n'a n'Og. It doesn't move in straight lines. Maybe there's no such thing as time there at all.'

'You're making my head hurt.'

'Maybe the gods can access any point in time they want from the Otherworld. And maybe they picked Poussin because . . .' He paused, reordered his thoughts. 'OK, how about this? What if Thomas Anson had a similar meeting with, say, a blue-skinned man who encouraged him to commission *The Shepherds of Arcadia* in reverse for the Shepherds' Monument at Shugborough?'

'We don't know that.'

Hal shrugged and pressed on. 'And what if these gods were influencing our world all the time, but they passed into legend as angels?' he said excitedly. 'Or demons. Didn't William Blake supposedly see some hideous figure before he painted *Ghost of a Flea*?'

'I have no idea,' Samantha said with some amusement.

'Yes, yes, you're right, I'm off on a tangent. But don't you see? We're getting somewhere. Poussin painted *The Shepherds of Arcadia* because of divine intervention. It's important enough that the Tuatha Dé Danann or some other Higher Power wanted it preserved. It's got something to do with T'ir n'a n'Og. A tomb . . . a death . . . a secret in death . . . ? If it was painted over here, it was a clue we were meant to find.' His train of thoughts was rushing wildly on.

' "We" as in you and me?'

'We humans. We . . .' He paused. 'Maybe it was left for the Brothers and Sisters of Dragons.' His heart started to pound. Was it some supernatural connection meant for him alone?

'Couldn't they have left the message in a more obvious way?' Samantha asked. 'If it was meant for the Brothers and Sisters of Dragons, why would it be in a Poussin painting and a monument at Shugborough, not whatever it is the Dragon Brothers do on their day off?'

'Because . . .' Another shiver. 'Perhaps they knew that one of the Brothers of Dragons would come across this.'

'But they haven't, have they? We have. I mean, I know one of them found the original stone, but he didn't crack the clues.'

Hal disappeared in a mist of intense concentration before he said, 'They buried it deeply because it's such an important – perhaps powerful – thing that's been hidden that they couldn't risk anyone else finding it.'

'So it is something that could help us in the war.'

'Yes,' said Hal, dazed. 'I really think it is.'

The War Room was dominated by a large electronic map of the UK. Vast swathes of the North Country were coloured red, ending at a line bisecting the country from west to east and centring on Birmingham. Along one wall, three female operatives were in constant radio contact with numerous field agents supplying intelligence back from as close to the front line as they could get. The General, who had not slept for nearly forty-eight hours, regularly checked the updates, but spent most of the time inspecting maps and making calculations.

'You're in a bad mood.'

The General looked up to find Reid standing next to him. 'How do you slip in and out like that? It's bloody unnerving.'

Reid smiled without humour. 'I have to say, things aren't looking good.'

'And you ask why I'm in a bad mood?'

'The question was really just a way into finding out how the meeting went with the PM.' Surreptitiously, Reid began to shuffle through the maps on the table until the General dragged them away from him and pulled Reid away to one side where they couldn't be overheard.

'I think he's bloody losing it,' the General growled quietly.

'Oh?'

'Look at the map. We've got five days before the enemy reaches us, maybe less. They've stopped annihilating the general population and are marching straight for us here. Their army now stands at somewhere around two million. They don't eat, sleep, rest. The only way to stop them is to blow them into tiny little pieces, and even then they're not dead. What's left twitches and crawls under its own steam. I've seen the footage. It's sickening.'

'Ah. So the PM didn't go for your nuclear option.'

'No, he didn't.'

'A series of nukes secretly buried in their path, to be detonated when the army is over them. Might take out, what, even a million of them? And irradiate half of England. I wonder why the PM wasn't interested?'

The General glared; Reid would not have been so disrespectful a few weeks earlier. His bleeper went off, and when he checked the message he flung the device across the room in a fury.

'Temper, temper,' Reid cooed.

'How can you be such a cold fish? Everything's falling apart here because nobody has the backbone to make the tough decisions. Barring Kirkham coming up with something, the hidden nukes are the only chance we have. Yes, there would be some collateral damage, and I wouldn't fancy taking a holiday in the Midlands for a while, but we have no other option.'

Reid turned towards the map, tracing an imaginary blast zone in the air in his line of vision. 'What did the PM say?'

'He vacillated. "Yes, it may be our only option." But this, maybe that ... "Let me think about it." Blah, blah, bloody blah. Somebody's put another plan to him.'

'Are you sure?'

'He dropped a few clues. Is it you?' the General asked bluntly.

'Not me.'

'I bet it's that bitch Manning. I have no idea what it could possibly be. We have no other weapons—'

'Well ...' Reid interjected with a sly smile. 'Things are always darkest before the dawn, General. Remember that.'

'You can be a slimy little shit, Reid, but if you've got something going on that you can pull out of the hat, I'll kiss you.'

'Steady on, old chap.' Reid tapped his nose. 'We're working on something.'

'Well, work quicker. We've hardly got any time left.' The General cracked his knuckles. 'There's something no one's grasping. This power we're all supposed to be so afraid of isn't anywhere to be seen.'

Reid nodded; old news.

'Why isn't the Void here yet? Missed the train? Where is it going to turn up? At what point? Its army is winning the fight. Its generals are marching on the field. But still no sign of the real enemy. You've not sighted anything?'

'We've got agents all over the damn place looking for the first sign of arrival. Nothing so far. Maybe it won't turn up until long after we're all gone.'

'We need to find it the minute it gets here, stop it instantly in its tracks.'

'You think that's possible?'

It was the General's turn to smile slyly. 'If it's as powerful as it's supposed to be, why does it need an army to prepare the way? Perhaps because it's not so powerful after all. So, if we take out the army, it might not appear. Or maybe we can take it out the moment it arrives. Get your intelligence working on that, Reid.'

Reid considered the General's words thoughtfully. 'Good point. Why isn't it here? Yes, thank you, General. I think I'll do that.'

The General looked around furtively, then whispered, 'I don't know if the PM is the right person to be leading our defence. We need strong decisions, not weak-kneed umming and ahhing.'

'What are you suggesting?'

'Nothing just yet. But if we needed to replace him, would you be prepared to tell him to step down?'

Reid shook his head. 'There's nobody else in the Cabinet I'd like to see in the top job. Unless you're putting yourself forward as a candidate?'

'If I did, it would just be as an interim measure to see this crisis through. We need to get a grip, Reid. Five days tops and it's all over. I'm going to need to issue the order on the nukes within twenty-four hours.'

'Don't do anything hasty, General. You might regret it.'

'None of us is going to live to regret anything, Reid, if we don't stop this. Don't forget that.' The General's cold stare condemned Reid in an instant and then he walked away with the air of a man who had reached his limit.

In the depths of the Ashmolean Museum where the most powerful Government computers were housed, Kirkham watched the screen as the modelling wound towards its conclusion. Manning tapped her red nails on the desk top with irritation.

'I find it very hard to concentrate while you're doing that,' Kirkham said with controlled exasperation.

'And I find it very hard to wait while you continually come up with nothing.'

'You know it's not that simple,' Kirkham protested. 'This would have been nigh-on impossible even before the Fall when we had endless resources and unlimited time—'

'No more excuses!' she snapped. 'Before the Fall, you wouldn't have had a whole range of supernatural artefacts, energy sources and a whole new way of thinking to draw on. So stop whining.'

'What you're asking for is an understanding of the underpinning of reality, but even to begin to explain the concepts in layman's language is—' he began, but Manning cut him dead again.

'I don't want the mechanics, Kirkham.' She prowled around the desk like a big cat, claws barely sheathed. 'We know now that there are different levels of reality. Different dimensions. This is not theory any more. We know that there is a certain fluidity to these other dimensions—'

'Dimensions isn't really the right word—'

'Shut up. We know that so-called magic – or the "new science" as you like to call it – can affect reality, too. So, is what I am suggesting possible?'

'We're talking about non-limited consciousness causing an effect at the quantum level. If reality is phase-locked like the light in a laser, then consciousness can—'

'Is what I am suggesting possible?'

'Yes, it is possible.'

Without another word, Manning turned on her heels to snatch up her furs and then she was gone. Kirkham breathed deeply. For a second, he thought he had seen something else standing where Manning was, something in her and around her, gone in the blink of an eye. He rubbed his tired eyes and returned to the flickering light of the computer screen.

Sophie experienced a sensation of floating in water and a second later she was standing on the flagged floor of the Watchtower corridor. The chilly air smelled of damp stone and her footsteps echoed loudly off the rough-hewn walls.

'That was weird.' Harvey steadied himself beneath a hissing torch.

Caitlin appeared at Sophie's side, clutching her axes, her gaze flitting back and forth as she searched for danger. 'Are you anticipating trouble?'

Sophie still found it unnerving to hear Caitlin's voice emanating from a body that resembled Caitlin but was clearly not her. The muscles of her face were tauter, her brow regularly knitted, her eyes piercing and unblinking; subtle changes that altered not just her demeanour, but who she was.

'No idea. The Watchtower was always a waystation between T'ir n'a n'Og and our world, but that doesn't mean it's deserted.'

'Then we had better proceed with caution.'

'How do we get back home from here?' Harvey asked.

'You can get to all times and places through the doors that line the corridors,' Sophie said. 'Somewhere there's a door leading back to where we want to go.'

'We could be looking for ever!' Harvey whined.

'Look at this.' Thackeray was standing at a window. The others fell silent as they gathered round. The view filled them with a deep dread: there was emptiness, emptier even than deep space, a spiritual emptiness, but here and there fires occasionally burst and faded like stars with their lifetimes diminished to fractions of a second. 'Where are we?' Thackeray said quietly.

'Let's worry about where we're going,' Sophie said firmly, leading the way down the corridor.

It twisted and turned in a manner that made no architectural sense. Each section they came upon as they rounded a bend looked exactly the same as all the others through which they had already passed. Doors, oaken and studded with black iron, broke the monotony of the walls at regular intervals. The majority were locked, but the first one Sophie discovered to be unlocked released a blast of freezing air into the corridor. They looked out over a frozen hilltop where a gnarled figure stood, a crone dressed in rags, clutching a wooden staff, her hair wild in the wind. Icy blue light washed off her. Every now and then she would lift up her staff and shake it as if angry at the gods, and another fall of snow would come from the slate-grey sky.

Another door opened on to a scene of Caitlin, covered from head to toe with clay, beside an open hole in the ground. It was night, and raining, and she had her head back as if she was howling, her face transformed into some animalistic expression. They only had a moment to glimpse the scene before Caitlin grasped the door and pulled it shut so fast that she almost knocked Sophie to the floor.

Other doors showed scenes from their past lives, and one or two appeared to reveal future events, though they were bland and uninsightful: Harvey and Thackeray talking in a small room; Sophie standing next to an Asian man in a snowy street.

But then they came upon something that disturbed them immensely. When Thackeray threw open the next door, it revealed nothing at all, no scene, just a black void that appeared to go on for ever. The second and third doors revealed the same vista.

'OK,' Thackeray said. 'If we can only open doors that show aspects of our lives, past or future, what does it mean when the doors show nothing at all?'

'You know what?' Harvey said as they all silently mulled over the question. 'Who cares? There's nothing we can do about it. Let's just get home.'

They trudged on disconsolately with Sophie keeping a close eye on Caitlin. Every now and then, Sophie had heard her quietly answering questions no one had asked, and as they walked she was growing even moodier and more introverted, ignoring any advances from the others.

After the monotony of the long corridors, they were surprised when they found a flight of stairs breaking off to one side. Harvey eagerly led the way, skipping up the steps two at a time. He soon disappeared from view, then called back excitedly for them to join him.

The others found him lounging on a heap of sumptuous cushions in a large chamber with intricately illustrated tapestries lining three of the walls and floor-to-ceiling windows with leaded diamond panes on the other.

'What's the point in windows if you've got nothing to look out on?' Thackeray asked, tired and irritated. He collapsed on to the cushions next to Harvey.

Sophie ignored them and looked around with interest. She was struck by several unusual items in the room, but the most prominent was a three-legged piece of furniture with a dome on top, constructed from gold and silver and covered with finely detailed workings.

Thackeray saw her approach the piece and warned, 'I wouldn't go touching anything in this place.'

Sophie ignored him. Increasingly she was learning to trust her instincts and now she could feel a subtle vibration at the base of her skull, like the buzz of power lines only more pleasant. It emanated from the object.

Caitlin moved to explore an archway leading to more stairs while Sophie investigated the item. From the corner of her eye, Sophie saw Caitlin cast one dark, cold stare her way before she disappeared into the shadows.

The dome was warm to the touch. Sophie couldn't help but trace her fingers over the fine filigree. As she did so, the dome began to throb. She stepped back as it opened with a mechanical whir.

'I told you not to touch it,' Thackeray said, jumping to his feet.

Harvey rolled off the cushions and hovered near the door to the stairs. 'Leave it alone!' he said, but Sophie was entranced. The dome revealed an electric-blue ball of energy hovering in the air, orbiting slowly.

'I don't think it's dangerous,' Sophie said. She reached out and touched the surface of the globe. It shimmered as it sang to her with a soothing tone. As the notes died away, the ball changed colour slightly, becoming greener until it revealed a face distorted as though seen through a crystal ball. As Sophie peered closer, she realised the face was that of a Green Man, like the ones she had seen in medieval churches, with features constructed from interlocking vegetation. The eyes, deep and intelligent, blinked. Sophie jumped back in shock.

'Who calls?' The voice resonated clearly around the room, sounding like the wind rushing through the forest at night.

'I . . . I . . .' Sophie burbled. 'I'm sorry. I didn't mean to disturb you—'

'A Sister of Dragons?' The Green Man's eyes narrowed as though he was peering back at her through a crystal ball. He appeared to see her confusion. 'You have called to me. You know me, little one?'

'I couldn't forget you,' Sophie replied. His names rattled through her head: Cernunnos, Lord of the Green, Master of the Wild Hunt, and more, all inscribed in the heart of man.

'You are in the Watchtower?' the god said. 'Then you have

activated the Emptoreptic, known also as the Eye of Distant Dreams. It was left in the Watchtower so that in the darkest days the Golden Ones and all associated with them could be contacted, wherever they might be.'

Sophie assimilated the information quickly and instantly said, 'We need your help. The Void is coming.'

'I am aware of the Devourer of All Things, Sister of Dragons. I do what I can to help all Fragile Creatures.'

'Will you fight beside us?'

'Is that your wish?'

'Yes . . . yes – and any others of your kind, too. Anyone. Any help. We need all the help we can get.'

'Then the Wild Hunt will ride for you and your kind. And the call will go out to my own brothers and sisters. This day we make a pact.'

'Thank you,' Sophie said. 'Thank you so much.'

The Green Man faded from view, the blue globe descended and with another mechanical whirr the dome closed.

'I don't believe it. You called in the cavalry?' Thackeray was standing beside her.

'I think I have,' Sophie replied.

'This Green Man,' Thackeray continued, 'I know all the myths and legends and everything, but . . . he's a big deal, right?'

'The biggest,' Sophie said. 'Of all the gods we've encountered, he's one of the most powerful. Where's Caitlin? We need to tell her.'

Harvey nodded to the stairs behind him. 'She's up there. You want me to get her?'

'We'll all go.' Sophie was barely able to contain her excitement. Perhaps with the Green Man on their side, they might actually stand a chance.

She pushed her way past Harvey and bounded up the steps. They spiralled upwards in such a way that Sophie realised they must be approaching the top of the Watchtower. Sophie called Caitlin's name as she ran, but there was no response. Had they been stupid to let Caitlin wander off on her own?

Finally, the last flight of stairs appeared. At the top, the sucking blackness of the gulf was framed in a doorway. A figure was silhouetted against it briefly as one of the explosions flared silently in the infinite distance. Sophie called Caitlin's name again; there was still no answer. Was it Caitlin, or someone who had struck her down?

Sophie turned back to Thackeray and Harvey. 'Wait here,' she said quietly.

'What's wrong?' Thackeray asked.

'I don't know. Probably nothing. But if there is, it's better if only one of us is up there.'

Cautiously, Sophie progressed up the final few steps. A balcony ran around the perimeter of the tower's summit. It was barely two feet wide and the stone balustrade was worryingly low. Below, the full extent of the Watchtower was revealed, an Everest of stone, vast and monolithic, with carved gargoyles and faces, statues and designs, black, sloping roofs of wings, smaller turrets and towers, the ground floor lost far below in the dark shadows; all of it floating in the gulf.

Vertigo gripped her and she pressed her back against the stone. Dragging her gaze away from the dizzying view, Sophie looked both ways along the deserted balcony. Deciding against calling Caitlin's name again, she edged around the wall.

The atmosphere of that strange place dampened sound so that it felt as though her ears were filled with cotton wool. The effect threw her natural instinctive abilities awry and so she was taken by surprise when the blow came from behind her, crashing against the base of her skull.

Sophie rolled away from the wall to the edge of the balcony, stars flashing before her eyes. When her vision finally cleared, she was bent backwards over the balustrade with Caitlin looming over her, one hand gripping Sophie's throat, the other holding an axe high. Caitlin's face was transformed by dark fury, more Morrigan than Caitlin, her strength and determination inhuman.

'What . . . what are you doing?' Sophie choked.

'I saw,' Caitlin snarled, in an echoing voice that no longer sounded like Caitlin's. 'You and him, together. Behind my back. You can't be trusted. You're the enemy.'

'No.' Sophie squirmed, but couldn't break Caitlin's iron grip. 'You've got it wrong.'

Sophie saw the frenzy in Caitlin's face, her arm muscles growing tense, the axe suddenly coming down hard towards her head; no room to escape the killing blow.

Sophie clamped her eyes shut. But instead of the impact of the axe on her skull, she felt Caitlin's hand wrenched free of her throat. Choking, she threw herself forward to see Thackeray and Harvey wrestling Caitlin away.

'Get back!' Sophie yelled to them. 'She's lost it!'

A black cloud was growing around Caitlin, gaining solidity like bubbles forming on crude oil. The bubbles took shape, grew wings, became crows that suddenly burst free from her orbit, scores of them swirling all around Caitlin, assailing Thackeray and Harvey with beak and talon and beating wing. Thackeray and Harvey thrashed them away, but were driven back towards the door to the stairs.

Sophie drew her spear from the harness suspending it across her back. She held it two-handed, balanced on the balls of her feet, knowing she was no match for Caitlin in terms of physical strength.

The crows surrounded Caitlin like a thunderstorm. She was preparing to attack.

'I had to do it to open the door to this place, Caitlin,' Sophie yelled. 'I wasn't betraying you. It wasn't personal.'

Caitlin's movement was so swift and ferocious that Sophie barely saw her. She had an impression of a black wind rushing at her, the whirling axe blade a gleam of silver within it.

Sophie parried the blow through a mixture of blind luck and instinct, but the shocking vibrations from the incredible force of the attack almost knocked her unconscious. Her spear went flying from her hands and Sophie, dazed, spun off-balance. Slamming against the balustrade, she went over, unable to stop herself.

There was a brief feeling of falling before she reacted. She grabbed on to a carving protruding from the side of the tower, the shock almost wrenching her arm from its socket. She flung her other arm around it before she slipped off, but she wasn't strong enough to cling on for long. Her feet kicked over the abyss, her muscles already aching from the strain of hanging, her stomach sick from the shock of fall and impact.

Caitlin loomed over the balustrade, surrounded by the thunderous murder of crows. Yet there was a subtle change in her face, a shadow of humanity. 'I . . . I can't stop her.' Caitlin's voice had returned to a human timbre, but it was weak, barely audible. 'It's as if I've got two people in my head and neither of us can think straight. This . . . it isn't meant to be. It's driving us both mad.'

'Fight it,' Sophie gasped. She managed to swing her feet around to catch a foothold on another carving.

'If I still had the Pendragon Spirit, I could balance her out, but . . .' Caitlin's voice faded away.

Sophie saw Caitlin's face darken and knew that her moment of respite was over. Climbing back up wasn't an option. Fighting the vertigo that spun her head, she focused as hard as she could on the stone of the tower wall to block out the drop, and then searched out more foot- and handholds. The mass of carvings gave her plenty of options, but already she was shaking from the strain of keeping her muscles tense.

She swung to one side with her right foot, tested her weight on the new foothold and then followed with her right hand. She vacated the carving just as Caitlin's axe raised a shower of dust as it crashed against where she had been clinging.

Sophie moved as quickly as she could while maintaining her safety to get out of the reach of Caitlin's weapon. But in doing so, she allowed herself a glance down: it was like standing on a ledge at the summit of the Empire State Building. Her head spun so wildly that she almost fell away from the wall.

She screwed her eyes shut and rammed her body hard against the stone while she reclaimed her equilibrium. When she looked around again, Thackeray and Harvey were hanging out of a window below and to her right, urging her silently towards them.

With the last of her strength, she made it as close to the window as she could, but for the final two feet there were no more carvings to support her.

'Jump,' Thackeray hissed. 'We'll pull you in.'

'I can't,' Sophie said. 'I don't know if I've got it in me.'

'It's either that or fall.'

Sophie knew he was right. With her eyes shut, she jumped, convinced she was plummeting to her doom, and then she felt herself being manhandled roughly through the window. All three of them fell on to the stairs and rolled down, cracking heads and shins on cold, hard stone before they could stop their descent.

From above came the sound of flapping wings approaching fast.

Sophie was the first to her feet, and dragged the others after her. They careered down the stairs on the verge of falling out of control, skidding into the room with the Emptoreptic and then on, down the next flight of stairs.

The sound of the birds never relented and as they emerged back into the corridor, they knew that if they slowed they would be dead.

'Caitlin's gone. That thing's taken over.' A desperate sadness filled Thackeray's voice.

'There's still hope,' Sophie said. 'But we need to save ourselves before we can think about helping Caitlin.'

'Which way?' Harvey yelled in a panic.

Sophie randomly picked a direction and they set off as fast as they could. Whenever they felt they could spare a second, they randomly tried one of the doors en route, but on each occasion they lost valuable time that they knew they would not be able to make up. The Morrigan would never give up, and soon they would tire, and then she would catch them.

'This is ridiculous,' Thackeray wheezed. 'We could run around here for ever and not find the door. It's statistically impossible.'

Sophie wrenched open a door. 'I think it's this one,' she said.

Thackeray didn't have time to query her before she had propelled both him and Harvey through. She dived in after them, slamming the door behind them. They skidded down a snowy slope and came to a stop beside a fence next to a road sign, obscured by ice and frozen snow.

'It's winter?' Harvey said.

'Must be,' Thackeray said. They were all racked with shivers in the biting temperatures.

'We need to get to shelter before we freeze to death,' Sophie said with chattering teeth.

'How do you know this is the right place?' Thackeray asked.

'All the other scenes had an odd artificial quality, as if the backgrounds were films projected on to the walls of the room,' Sophie said. 'This one looked real.'

'It doesn't make sense. It's too much of a coincidence.' He looked at Sophie suspiciously, as if she was about to turn into a monster like Caitlin.

'Two things,' she said. 'One, I felt it in my gut, and I think it was the Pendragon Spirit telling me that this was the right door. Two, there are no coincidences. I think we were meant to find the way out, like we were *meant* to do lots of other things.'

'That's kind of creepy,' Harvey said.

'Let's move,' Sophie said. 'Caitlin will be through soon.'

'You really think so?' Thackeray said. Sadness flashed across his face, but Sophie was impressed to see him constrain it.

'She's a killing machine with the powers of a god. No compassion, no empathy. She's not going to stop until I'm dead,' Sophie said bitterly. 'And you know what the worst thing is? I helped to make her this way . . . and I gave up an utterly valuable, unique thing to do it. And now I'm going to die as well. That's irony for you.'

Thackeray went to comfort her, but before he could, Harvey hailed them. 'I don't think we've got far to go before we find somewhere to hole up,' he said, motioning to the road sign he had just cleaned off.

It said: *Oxford.*

In his arctic survival clothes supplied by the quartermaster, Hal was almost unrecognisable as he trudged, head bowed, through the blizzard. Perhaps that was why Manning didn't notice him as she crossed the High Street on her way to the Cabinet offices.

It was a random moment that at any other time would have passed Hal by, but he was lost in thoughts of the Otherworld and its strange inhabitants and suddenly he was struck by a revelation. He'd always been suspicious of Manning's intentions, even before he had heard her talking to a seemingly invisible companion that night before the invasion had started. He'd dismissed the troubling event, sure he'd misheard, perhaps misinterpreted, had too much else on his mind. But now he knew there was something abnormal about her.

Even though she wore a fur coat and hat, they were scant protection against the cold, but when she passed Hal it was clear that the bitter temperatures weren't affecting her at all.

With the hairs on the back of his neck prickling, Hal made the decision to follow her. It was out of character for someone who paid little attention to instinct – he preferred things hard and fast – but he felt such an imperative that he knew he would regret it if he didn't.

Hal allowed Manning to reach the far end of the High Street before he turned and followed her, and that was when he noticed the second strange thing. He had been staring at her tracks in the fresh snow when he realised that there was not one set of footprints but two, intermingling so closely that if he had not been paying close attention he would have missed it.

With growing apprehension, Hal kept behind Manning until she disappeared into Oriel College. He anticipated that she would first be heading to her own complex of offices, which lay on the first floor of the building. Hal quickly hurried in through another entrance and made his way up a parallel flight of stairs so that he could approach from the opposite direction and, if discovered, it would not appear that he had followed her.

The building was quiet and he heard Manning moving around her office. There was a single set of footsteps at first, and then, eerily, there were two sets.

Hal edged cautiously along the corridor until he could peer in through the window in the door. The blind on the window was half-closed, impairing his view, but he could see Manning from the waist down. She was talking to someone just out of sight.

'Things are falling into place. Reid doesn't suspect a thing.'

'This is a strange alliance.' The voice was strong and resonant. Hal craned to see who was speaking

'That doesn't matter if it works to our mutual benefit. Now, timing is essential. Are you prepared?'

'I am. Are you? There will be great hardship for your kind.'

'I'm ready. Don't worry about me—'

Hal bumped against the door and rattled the blind in his attempt to see the mysterious visitor. Immediately, he sprinted quietly along the corridor and turned the corner on to the stairs just as the office door opened. He was sure Manning hadn't seen him, or if she had glimpsed him wouldn't be able to identify him, but he was angry with himself for alerting her before any action could be taken.

He slipped out of the building into the heart of the blizzard, relieved that it would cover his tracks.

At Queen's, Hal found Reid lounging in a chair, drinking a brandy in front of a blazing fire. He appeared at ease despite the impending crisis.

'Ms Manning,' Hal said breathlessly. 'I think she's a traitor. I think she's going to sell us all down the river.'

'Sit down. Have a drink.' Reid stood and thrust Hal into the chair by the fire, then stuffed a crystal glass of brandy into his hand. 'Now, tell me what you know.'

Hal blurted out what he had seen. Reid listened intently, then muttered, 'This changes everything.'

'Are you going to arrest her?'

'Of course. But if there's a conspiracy, I want to know who else is involved before I tip my hand.'

'She stressed that you didn't suspect anything. I'm sorry if I've made her suspicious now.'

'Don't worry about it.' Reid stared into the depths of the fire while he thought things through. Finally he said, 'The Void is coming soon. I've got new intelligence. The only chance we have to stop it is to get the Brothers and Sisters of Dragons together.' He turned to Hal. 'I believe Hunter to be one of them.'

Hal said nothing.

'The research carried out by Kirkham's team suggests that the Brothers and Sisters of Dragons become active – if that's the right word – in proximity to the crisis they're meant to deal with, or they are quickly drawn to that area. We'd already profiled a great many people in Oxford – that's why we've been carrying out a detailed census in recent weeks. Hunter was one of a very few who fit the profile.'

'How did you know Oxford was going to be the centre of the crisis?'

'The Government is here. It became obvious that this is where the last stand will be made.' Reid downed the rest of his brandy. 'I was ninety per cent sure about Hunter. When he disappeared with Mallory, I knew I was right.' Reid eyed Hal. 'Anything you want to say?'

Hal shook his head.

'You're his very best friend. I'm not stupid, you know. He must have told you.'

Hal remained silent, but Reid wasn't offended. He shrugged and said, 'I believe Hunter is getting his little band together. We need them here, now, if we are to stand a chance. Can you get word to him?'

'I don't think Hunter or any of the Brothers and Sisters of Dragons will work with the Government. They don't trust you . . . us.'

Reid nodded. 'Understandable, I suppose. In which case, I face a conundrum.'

'I don't know where they are, Mister Reid, and that's the truth.'

'Then all I'm asking of you, Hal – begging you – is that when Hunter does finally contact you, as he undoubtedly will, I want you to pass on to him the message that the last stand against the Void will be made here, and that he really needs to be with us. We're in the final stage of this game, Hal, and what may be the twilight days of the human race. None of us must falter.'

chapter fourteen

the secrets of god

'Mankind, when left to themselves, are unfit for their own government.'
George Washington

The screeching blast of the siren tore Hal from troubled dreams of betrayal and hatred. He scrambled out of his bed into the freezing cold room and ran to the window. Through the thick frost that lined the glass inside and out he could just discern frantic activity. Soldiers carrying rifles raced along the street. A few seconds later, a truck packed with more soldiers followed a snowplough down the centre of the road.

Hal's first thought was that either Manning had launched some kind of coup or that Reid had arranged for her arrest and some kind of disturbance had broken out. Still half-asleep, he stripped off the several layers of clothing he'd taken to wearing in bed, splashed some water on his face and quickly dressed.

He was barely out of his room when Samantha came running up the corridor in a state of distress.

'What's wrong?' he said, catching her in his arms.

She sobbed against his shoulder for a moment before she calmed enough to tell him. 'It's the prime minister – he's been assassinated.'

'What happened? Tell me.' Hal gently pushed Samantha away from him so that he could look in her face.

'I don't know.' She wiped her tears away with the back of one hand. 'No one's releasing any details. All we've heard is that it happened about half an hour ago. They're shutting down all buildings and instituting an immediate curfew while they search for the killer.'

Hal's jaw gaped in shock. Is that what Manning had been planning? If so, Reid must be devastated at not having acted immediately. But then no one could have foreseen it. Who would possibly kill their leader on the eve of a battle that would determine the survival of the human race? He decided not to tell Samantha anything about Manning and his conversation with Reid in case it put her in danger.

'If we're being confined to our quarters, I wanted to be here with you,' she said.

Hal took her back inside and quickly made up the fire. Once it was roaring, he brewed up and they sat warming themselves while they drank their herbal infusion.

'I don't know what's going to happen to us,' Samantha said desolately. 'I always had hope that things were going to turn out all right . . . they always do, don't they? Or did. Even at the Fall, when it seemed as if it was the end. We pulled through that. But now I'm not so sure.'

'Things will work out,' Hal said with as much optimism as he could muster. 'There are a lot of good people working on our behalf.'

Samantha didn't look convinced, so Hal changed the subject. 'I've been doing a bit more research on the mystery we found at Shugborough and I think I've made a breakthrough.' He fetched a pile of books and papers from his desk and spread them out around her.

'I don't know how you can think about that at a time like this,' Samantha muttered.

'Because it might be our only hope,' Hal said simply.

Reluctantly, she picked up a book of illustrations of one of the Grail romances. 'What's this? King Arthur?'

'The stone with the Poussin image inside was found at Cadbury Hill, one of the supposed locations of Camelot. There are lots of Arthurian links floating around this whole business. I'm starting to think that maybe the legend of King Arthur is a code, too, like the Poussin painting and the Shepherds' Monument – that the stories themselves and elements of them are meant to be symbolic. And that somehow they tie in to what we're looking for.'

'Sounds a bit tenuous,' Samantha said, unconvinced.

'Not really. Arthur's sword, Excalibur, was supposed to have come from the Otherworld. And that's where he went when he died. And the Poussin painting is of a tomb, and the mystery surrounding it points to T'ir n'a n'Og.'

'Arthur's Tomb?'

'Like I said, it's a code. We shouldn't take it at face value.'

'But the King Arthur legend goes back centuries before Poussin, even. How long has all this been weaving together?'

'Ah,' Hal said with a smile. 'That's the mystery.'

Before he could say any more, they were disturbed by the sound of numerous booted feet running along the corridor without. Doors were flung open, orders barked. Hal's door crashed wide and a grim-faced soldier stood there brandishing a rifle as if he was prepared to shoot Hal and Samantha on the spot.

'There's a curfew,' he said. 'No one's to leave their quarters.'

'We heard the news,' Hal said. 'Who's in charge?'

The soldier's cold eyes observed Hal with near-contempt for a moment before he replied, 'The General.' And then he was gone and Hal's many other questions were left unanswered: what about the rest of the Cabinet? Where was Reid? And what did the General plan to do now?

The journey from Glastonbury had been hard, over roads and fields that resembled the Arctic wastes in the face of a wind that raked at their flesh day and night. Mallory wished he could have turned his back on his responsibilities and stayed behind in the magical atmosphere of the sunlit Tor. When the summer gave way to winter as he passed the limit of the Culture's influence, he felt a palpable pang of despair and looked back repeatedly until the blizzard blocked the glowing uplands from view. The biting cold and the dark days felt more than just a physical hardship; they were signs of a world bereft of hope, winding down to die as the last candle guttered.

With his mood still tainted by the loss of Sophie, it would have been easy to give in to despair, but Shavi was there on the horse at his side with quiet words of encouragement. Mallory already felt that he could trust the young Asian man with his life. Shavi was the most spiritual person Mallory had ever met; the peace he radiated was almost contagious, filtering in through Mallory's pores, neutralising his blackest thoughts, shining a light into the dark areas of his soul. Mallory knew that over time the Brothers and Sisters of Dragons increasingly exhibited peculiar abilities, and this, he decided, was Shavi's: the magic of the soul, given strength and weight. That description had an uneasily religious tang for someone like Mallory, who had little time for God or gods, but even he instinctively felt the truth of it.

With the wind howling in their ears, Shavi told Mallory of how he had fled a repressive family in West London for a life of searching. He had hungrily devoured the teachings of every major religion and most of the minor ones, eventually turning to more esoteric knowledge as he quested for his own personal grail. But then he had experienced colourful dreams that drew him into contact with the other Brothers and Sisters of Dragons, much like the insistent pull that had dragged Mallory to Salisbury where he had first encountered Sophie.

'It's difficult to get your head around the fact that you're special,' Mallory said as he futilely attempted to warm himself beside a raging campfire.

'I do not consider myself special,' Shavi replied. 'I believe we have been given the tools to do a job on behalf of humanity. It is our duty to carry out our task to the best of our abilities. In truth, we are not special, we are servants. We act with humility, not arrogance. We accept sacrifice and suffering. That is our lot.'

Mallory jabbed a branch into the depths of the fire, watching the sparks fly up to meet the falling snow. 'And is that it? We have to accept misery? There's no cake when we get to the end of the road?'

Shavi smiled wryly. 'Happy endings, Mallory? You do not seem the type.'

'Yeah. Maybe you're right. I'm an old cynic. But I do have barely repressed romantic leanings.' Mallory pondered Shavi's words for a moment, then said, 'Not so long ago I was told that I come from another world that doesn't exist any more. Somehow reality changed. My world disappeared, and this world is what we have in its place. Do you think that's possible?'

'I think we live in a universe where anything is possible. The only reality that truly matters is the one inside here.' He gently tapped the position of his third eye, in the middle of his forehead. 'Something is troubling you. Would you like to talk about it?'

Mallory was surprised; he always guarded his true thoughts and feelings carefully, but Shavi had seen inside him effortlessly. Perhaps he shouldn't have been so taken aback. The initial elation when the gaps in his memory were filled had faded and the knowledge had developed a gravity that was gradually sucking all of his other thoughts into it.

Mallory told Shavi about the Fabulous Beast and Jenny, the woman who had been possessed by it, or had become its avatar, or some other relationship he couldn't quite understand. Shavi was both surprised and excited by Mallory's account.

'I feel this is very important,' he said. 'A bond established between human and Fabulous Beast. It could be a very good omen.'

'The girl told me that I died in the last world . . . blew my brains out.'

'I am sorry.' Shavi was not being glib; he looked truly upset by Mallory's bald statement.

'But I died, do you understand? And now I'm here, alive. This place doesn't look like heaven. It looks a lot like hell, but I don't think it's that, either. You visited the land of the dead on one of your transcendental super-jaunts, so tell me . . . what does it mean to die? Do you just carry on in some other place, like me? Or is all this some illusion playing out in my dying mind?'

'Perhaps this world is the Bardo Thodel of the Tibetan mystics, the place between death and birth.'

'They missed that bit out when I was doing my studies at Salisbury.'

'The Bardo is central to the Tibetan concept of the afterlife,' Shavi said. 'The word means "intermediate state". The Tibetan mystics believe that all of Existence is nothing but a series of transitional states, which they called Bardos. In the Bardo Thodel, there are three distinct stages between death and rebirth. The Chikai Bardo includes the process of dying and the break-up of the elements that make up the physical body. The Chonyid Bardo is next, with visions of gods, heaven, hell, judgment and so on.'

'That sounds familiar.' Mallory found Shavi's information disturbing in the light of his experience.

'Finally there is the Sidpa Bardo,' Shavi continued. 'During this, the consciousness chooses a new body into which to be born.'

'Do you believe that?'

'I believe there are many, many paths and that we must all be detectives, searching along them for any clues that might help us.'

'There's got to be some reason for all this misery,' Mallory said. 'If it's all just the result of some random chemical reactions at the dawn of time, it would be so crushing.'

'The search for meaning is the greatest quest of all.' Shavi's smile suggested that he knew much more than he was saying.

'When I was in Salisbury training to be a knight, I had to study a lot of Christian philosophy.' Mallory continued to prod the fire, watching the sparks leap heavenwards. 'There's a philosopher called Hicks – you've probably read him. He says that this world is basically a school for souls. All the struggles and hardships we go through, all the evils we face, are designed to challenge us and shape us until we develop our souls and become more like God.'

Shavi said nothing.

'There are a million explanations as to why we're here, putting up with all this shit.' Mallory was entranced by the fire, almost talking to himself. 'Where do we look for answers? Science or religion? Are there any answers? Or should we just stop wasting our time thinking about it and get on with it?'

'The answers are inside us,' Shavi said softly. 'We all know the truth instinctively. Many have forgotten how to listen to that part of themselves. We need to relearn.'

'If we don't know what's expected of us . . .' Mallory flailed around for the right words. 'How are we supposed to know whether what we're doing is right?'

Shavi could see the distress that lay behind Mallory's questions and moved quickly to calm him. In soft tones, he said, 'Consider, then, Hindu beliefs. To Hindus, the universe is a vast place filled with immeasurable numbers of thinking beings, gods and demons continually being born, dying and re-born. The time-scale is vast: three hundred billion years for the entire wheel of existence to turn. How can humans, so insignificant in this big picture, so powerless, make decisions about how to live? The Hindus find their answer in the Sanskrit word *dharma*. It is defined as each person's unique path in life, and the knowledge of how to find it. *Dharma* is always there to be discovered, and it is the answer when faced with something too immense to comprehend.'

'But how do you find *dharma*?'

Shavi smiled. 'That is the simplest path of all. To find *dharma*, you must be yourself, as fully as possible. All the information you need lies within you. Recognise that each human consciousness is unique, that each is an experiment in seeking the eternal truth.'

'Just be myself? I'm lucky to get across the room if I do that.'

This time Shavi laughed heartily. 'Mallory, your self-deprecation belies your true essence. I can see it. Allow yourself to see it.'

Mallory nodded, but the question he really wanted answered died on his lips. He wasn't concerned about himself. His desperate need to know the meaning of life and death, and whether death itself was an ending, was driven by Sophie. Was there hope for her, somewhere beyond the world? Would he ever meet her again?

They travelled for as long as they could, but the cold forced them to take regular breaks in any shelter they could find. At Barnsley House, Mallory searched for the Fabulous Beast and Jenny at Shavi's insistence, but they were gone. Yet there was still a faint echo of their presence in the air, like the intense atmosphere in a cathedral.

Somehow they made it across the freezing wastes without dying from the cold or starvation. They had come across many people frozen in their homes, their last fuel now ashes in the fireplace, their cupboards bare. After the Fall and the plague, humanity was barely clinging on; the new ice age was a crisis too far.

As they neared Oxford, they became distracted from the humanitarian crisis. Not far from the outskirts, Mallory reined in his horse on a ridge to survey a curious sight: a row of figures moving across a field in the wan, late-afternoon light. At first he thought they were residents of the nearby village, but their regimented actions made little sense.

'They are not human,' Shavi said quietly, as if he could read Mallory's thoughts. His head was back, his eyes closed so that he appeared to be either listening intently or smelling the air. 'I feel . . .

despair. It rises off them like smoke from a bonfire. They are all empty . . . shells given animation. Their humanity twisted, perverted.'

Shavi's words confirmed what Mallory thought he could see: weapons protruding from the bodies of the figures themselves as if they had been implanted by some horrific surgical technique. 'The enemy,' Mallory said, recalling his encounter with them at Cadbury Hill. He scanned the area. 'Advance troops.'

'They are encircling Oxford,' Shavi said. Mallory didn't think to ask how he could possibly know this. 'That is where the last stand will take place. And the enemy wants to make sure that no one will leave alive to drum up any further opposition.'

'Then the sensible option would be to stay outside town, mount some kind of guerrilla action behind enemy lines.'

'It would, if you think we could survive out here and maintain cover while their troops mass.'

Mallory considered what Hunter had told him about the vast and increasing numbers of the Lament-Brood in Scotland. 'What's the alternative? Suicide? If we go into Oxford, we'll never get out. They'll have us trapped. Then how will we find the Void and destroy it?'

'The Brothers and Sisters of Dragons should be united for the last stand. That is the will of Existence.'

'What if Hunter hasn't been able to get through enemy lines?' He paused, then answered the question himself. 'That's a risk we'll have to take. He'll be heading towards the meeting place, so that's where I ought to be.'

In the distance, purple mist drifted against the gleaming white background. Mallory knew it was more of the enemy, circling closer, drawing their lines together. 'Let's wait until night falls, then slip through between their patrols.'

In the depths of a copse now stripped of summer leaves by the biting cold, they watched the distant movement of dark figures against the snow, occasionally swathed in that eerie purple mist like soldiers on a First World War battlefield. Their numbers were increasing slowly, the space between patrols growing smaller. Night wasn't coming fast enough. The horses stamped restlessly on the edge of the stand of stark trees, snorts of hot breath billowing.

Twilight eventually came in fast and hard. Mallory and Shavi shook relentlessly with the cold, yearning for a fire or some movement to warm their blood. The dangers of exposure were readily apparent, and whenever Mallory saw Shavi's eyes begin to flutter shut, Mallory shook him awake with hands that could barely feel what they were touching.

Eventually, though, the cold proved the greater enemy and even Mallory began to succumb. His eyelids grew heavy and he fought to keep them open, pinching himself hard on the face, punching tree trunks, while watching for the last glimmer of light to fade.

The enemy moved across a field, ghostly against the growing gloom. Mallory's eyes dimmed momentarily, and when he forced them open again, the enemy were even nearer; Mallory could hear the crunch of their feet in the frosted snow. He pulled Shavi down, then eased them a few paces backwards so that they could more easily merge into the background vegetation.

Complete darkness was only a few minutes away.

Through branches and twigs, he watched the patrol's slow movement along the edge of the copse . . . and watched . . . and . . .

He woke with a start as activity exploded around him, cursing with the realisation that the vampire cold had sucked away his consciousness. It was dark, but the snow added an eerie luminescence to everything. Streams of purple mist floated amongst the trees.

Shavi's cry for help echoed from somewhere nearby. Mallory forced himself alert, then propelled his stiff, cold body forward in a lurching, drunken motion through the silver trees, his limbs too numb to feel any sensation. With a shock, he realised that the enemy were everywhere. Their ghostly figures loomed all around, sometimes standing motionless so that they appeared to be part of the copse itself, at other times stalking at a slow, measured pace. The oppressive atmosphere of despair made Mallory even more sluggish. There was whispering, too, so subtle it felt like the wind in the branches, urging him to give up, give in, die.

Another cry for help. The direction now clear, Mallory propelled himself forward once more. Two members of the Lament-Brood had Shavi pinned. Deep ruts marred the snow where he had been dragged. Blood ran down his face from a head wound that must have stunned him, and now one of the Lament-Brood was poised to complete the job with a spear protruding from its forearm.

Mallory drew Llyrwyn and the copse was suddenly flooded with sizzling blue light so strong that it shocked him motionless for a split second. Sapphire flames blazed around the edge of the blade, and the familiar smell of burned iron flooded the air.

Though the Lament-Brood appeared to be little more than machines, the two holding Shavi shied away from the burning sword. The spear hung mere inches from being plunged into Shavi's face.

Mallory bounded in, swinging Llyrwyn in an arc. It sliced through neck muscles and bone with a sizzle and the head flew into a snow drift where it stared at Mallory with wide eyes.

The other attacker, a more brutish and alien creature than his decapitated comrade, swung an arm with a fan of knives protruding from the wrist. His blood now hot and pulsing with adrenalin and the strange energy of the sword, Mallory ducked the attack, drove Llyrwyn hard into the creature's belly and then used all his strength to rip upwards. As it flopped backwards hanging in two halves, Mallory grabbed Shavi's arm and yanked him to his feet.

'Leave me here,' Shavi said. 'If you try to get me out they will have you, and that will be the end of all hope for humanity. You are the important one now, not me.'

Mallory looked around. The Lament-Brood were moving towards them from all directions through the ghostly trees. Shavi was right: if he ran, he could escape through the gaps to reach the horses. If he had to manhandle Shavi, he wouldn't have a chance.

He let Shavi sink gently back to the ground and headed for a clear path. But he'd only gone a few paces before he realised that he couldn't leave Shavi behind, whatever the cost. He ran back and before Shavi could speak, barked, 'Don't say anything! Just keep behind me!'

Shavi pressed against an ancient oak, continually wiping the blood from his eyes. Mallory gripped his sword tightly, set his legs apart and braced himself. It was too late to change his mind: the Lament-Brood had closed their ranks and were drawing nearer. In the dark, Mallory couldn't work out how many were approaching, but there were certainly more than he could destroy. But if this was to be his last stand, he would go out fighting.

For half an hour, Mallory battled fiercely, the air filled with the clash of steel and the hacking of flesh as brilliant blue light soared and fizzed and flashed as though they were at the centre of an electrical storm. The bodies of the Lament-Brood piled up all around, forcing Mallory to clamber on top of them, fighting for his footing so that he could strike again and again. And still the Lament-Brood came.

For Mallory, it was his finest hour. Blood seeped from a thousand cuts. His cloak was in ribbons, his shirt sliced open so that the cold bit into his bare chest. Every muscle was on fire, every ligament hurt and exhaustion always seemed but a hair's breadth away. But still he fought, scything and hacking, parrying, stabbing, chopping, with a skill that exceeded anything he thought he had within him.

Determination clouded his mind and weariness wrapped it in cotton wool until he had little idea how long he had been there or even what he was doing. There were only the constant shapes looming out of the night, the purple mist, the attack, the body in front of him falling, and then the next enemy approaching.

And then he found himself lashing the sword back and forth but no longer feeling the juddering impact of steel on bone. Yet still he continued to fight, blinded by the fury of battle, until he felt a hand on his shoulder and a calming voice just behind his right ear: 'Mallory, it is over.'

It felt as if a spell had been broken. His eyes cleared to reveal a mountain of bodies, parts scattered all around. Snow was falling softly on the still, motionless copse.

The exhaustion finally caught up with him and he staggered backwards into Shavi's arms. 'You proved yourself a Brother of Dragons tonight,' Shavi whispered. 'But you must not rest yet.' Shavi's face was covered with dried blood, but he was smiling. 'We must be away, Mallory. Escape, before more come.'

Mallory nodded and somehow found some last vestige of strength in his limbs. He forced his way through the trees to where the horses waited. Shavi helped Mallory into the saddle and pulled himself on to his own mount. They scanned the snow-covered countryside, saw that there were no further Lament-Brood in the immediate vicinity and then rode as fast as they could over the treacherous ground.

At first, Mallory barely had the strength to cling on, but when the lights of Oxford finally sparkled on the horizon, he raised himself up in his saddle and looked to Shavi. 'We did all right, didn't we? Not such a pair of losers after all. Maybe there is still hope.'

Shavi smiled. 'There is always hope,' the seer said.

When they entered the city's outskirts, Mallory and Shavi dismounted. They had hoped to sneak in quietly, but there was activity ahead. A makeshift barricade was being thrown up across the road from building to building: old vehicles, metal sheeting, household furniture piled high. Sparks from welding equipment arced in several places and the screech of metal goods being dragged around reverberated loudly, punctuated by barked orders.

Mallory was just about to urge Shavi that they should find another route into the city when they were caught in a powerful beam of light. Someone shouted threateningly, 'Who goes there?'

'Friend,' Mallory replied loudly. 'Two of us.'

A small group of heavily armed soldiers advanced from behind the barricade. Mallory's hand went to the hilt of his sword beneath the remains of his cloak. The captain of the guard led the way, his features obscured by the hood of his thermal uniform. He shone the light in Mallory's face, then illuminated his tattered clothes.

'You must be freezing,' the captain said. 'What happened to your clothes?' He indicated the cuts. 'You've been attacked?'

'These strange creatures set on us,' Shavi said, feigning ignorance of the situation. 'An army of them. We were lucky to get away with our lives.'

'How far away?' the captain said insistently.

'About five miles—'

'Jesus Christ.' The captain spun around on his heels and hollered at the men working on the defences. 'Get a move on! The enemy is almost here!'

He turned back to Shavi and Mallory, keeping the torch on their faces; he was still suspicious. 'You're lucky. We've had orders not to let anyone inside once the barricades are up.' He nodded to one of his men. 'Sergeant Priest here will take you to the gate office, where you'll be collected for debriefing. Leave your horses at the gate.'

'Can we find somewhere to rest and get a bite to eat?' Mallory asked.

'In a while. We're under martial law – no one is allowed to wander the streets without an escort. And I need all my men here.'

The captain turned brusquely away and hurried on ahead of them, while Priest led Mallory and Shavi through a small gap in the defences. The minute they were through, a large panel of rusted iron was hefted into the gap and men rushed forward with face-masks and canisters to weld it into place.

Mallory and Shavi exchanged a secret glance, but the place was swarming with soldiers and there was no way they would be able to make a run for it. The horses were led off to stabling and some much-needed food and warmth, while Mallory and Shavi were guided to a brightly lit makeshift office. Priest left them inside with a guard on the door and returned to his duties.

The warmth of the room was a fantastic relief to the two frozen men, but they barely had time to consider their options before there was an outcry at the barricade. Part of the defences had collapsed, pinning two soldiers beneath it. The guard at the door rushed to help.

Instantly, Mallory jumped to his feet and swung open the door. He glanced around to make sure no one was watching, but all the soldiers were involved in either rescuing the two men or patching up the barricade.

Motioning for Shavi to follow, Mallory glided into the shadows along the row of houses, keeping low. Within a minute, they were out of sight of the barricade and running as fast as they could manage in the heavy snow.

As they approached the city centre, they came to a sharp halt. The outline of the aged buildings against the night sky was indistinct, and there appeared to be another city shimmering over the top of it like a mirage, filled with a faint blue light.

'You see that?' Mallory asked.

'I do.'

'I've seen something like it before. In Salisbury,' Mallory said. 'For a time there was a warping effect that made the Cathedral stretch through into—'

'T'ir n'a n'Og,' Shavi finished for him, with a hint of awe.

286

Mallory shrugged. 'Whatever you want to call it. Why is it happening here?'

But Shavi was silent.

As they progressed cautiously into the heart of the still, silent city, entrancing events began to unfold around them: a tiny figure flying high over the street leaving a trail of gold sparkles behind it; a wolf with the body of a man rooting in bins down an alley at the side of a restaurant; ghostly figures fading in and out of focus, not quite human, all garishly dressed; and then in the distance, coming down somewhere in the city, what at first looked like a comet with a blue tail, but then became the Fabulous Beast Mallory had seen at Barnsley House.

Mallory began to point it out just as they were assailed by a rushing wind and the odour of burned iron. Blue lightning crashed all around and thunder rolled ominously close before a hole opened up in the air. Mallory and Shavi jumped back into the shadows of a building as a stream of figures poured out. They sprawled breathlessly on the frozen ground or turned to face the portal, instantly adopting a warlike stance. When the doorway finally clashed shut, there must have been about eighty of them, quickly forming a defensive posture back-to-back in the centre of the street. They all wore ornate, bizarre armour marked with a sun crest.

'The Tuatha Dé Danann,' Shavi said in amazement.

'You know them?' Mallory asked.

'They call themselves the Golden Ones and believe themselves to be gods.'

'Enemies or friends?'

'That has never been an easy question to answer.' Shavi shielded his eyes from the glare of the street lights reflecting off the snow and peered at the group. 'Is it . . . ? Yes, I think it is.' He marched forward from the shelter of the buildings, holding out his arms in a gesture of peace. 'Lugh!' he called out.

The leader of the group marched forward, proud and tall, the suspicion slowly falling from his face to be replaced by something that almost came close to awe. 'Great hero.' He bowed his head slightly. 'The *filid* of our court still sing songs of your exploits.'

Shavi took the compliment gracefully, then motioned to Mallory who was still surveying the group with caution.

'And a Brother of Dragons,' Lugh said with a bow. 'Surely, then, we have come to the right place.'

'Why are you here?' Shavi asked.

The tension that had turned Lugh's face to stone fell away to reveal deep emotion. Shavi was shocked by the grief he saw there. Lugh fought to control his voice, then said, 'The Court of Soul's Ease has been overrun by those who were once my brothers and sisters. But no longer. Now they are my enemies for all time. They wiped from Existence all those they encountered. The night turned golden with fluttering moths.' He gestured towards the rest of his group with a hand that trembled uncontrollably. 'These are all that remain.'

'The entire court was wiped out?' Shavi said, horrified.

Lugh struggled to contain his despair. 'If we had remained behind, we would have been extinguished, too. We retreated to the Watchtower, and then to here, to the Fixed Lands we love so much. That battle is lost, but the war will be rejoined once we have made contact with the Court of the Final Word.'

Mallory didn't like the note he heard in Lugh's voice. It was hard, uncompromising, and promised a brutal revenge.

'For the time being we have come here to help you with your struggle. For if this battle is lost, our war cannot be fought. Besides,' he added, 'we owe a great debt to your fellow Sister of Dragons and her associate, Sister no more.'

'Sister of Dragons?' Mallory said. 'Where is she?' He looked at Shavi eagerly. 'Then we've got another one.' He paused. 'Sister no more? What are you talking about?'

'You do not know them?' Lugh asked, puzzled. 'One of the Sisters has lost the fire that blazes inside. The Morrigan now rides her. The other Sister, a brave woman filled with power, came this way before us, through the Watchtower. In the names of your kind she is called Sophie—'

Lugh didn't have the chance to continue for Mallory turned to Shavi, passionate emotions running unchecked across his face. 'It can't be,' Mallory said; he was afraid that Lugh would reveal it to be a mistake or some cruel joke.

'The Brother of Dragons believed this Sister to be dead,' Shavi said to Lugh.

Lugh shook his head. 'She lives, though she was grievously

wounded when she came to the Far Lands. She was repaired in the Court of the Final Word, then—'

Ceridwen emerged from the group to join Lugh. 'Then I brought her to the Court of Soul's Ease. Sophie is brave and true, a fine addition to the ranks of the Brothers and Sisters of Dragons.'

Mallory was afraid he would cry with the heady mix of joy and relief. 'Where is she?' he asked, his voice breaking.

'The Sister of Dragons will be here,' Ceridwen replied, 'for the Watchtower always ensures that its occupants arrive where they are needed most.'

Mallory grabbed Shavi in a bear hug and lifted him off the ground. Shavi laughed. 'I am so pleased for you, Mallory,' he said. 'And for us all.'

Mallory dropped Shavi and looked around as if Sophie would miraculously appear before him. 'Come on! We have to find her!'

Shavi placed a hand on Mallory's shoulder, calm, assured. 'There will be time for a reunion, time for all the words you thought you would never have the chance to say. But that time is not now.' He motioned to the Tuatha Dé Danann, depleted in number but still strong. 'These are our allies. In the coming fight, we will need them at our side. But if they stay here, they will be taken away – or worse, attacked where they stand. We need shelter, Mallory. We must draw our forces together.'

Mallory's heart was thundering so hard that he could barely hear Shavi's words, but he knew the truth of them. Despite everything he felt, he accepted his duty. 'Tell your people to follow us,' he said to Lugh. 'We'll find a safe place for them until the time comes for the battle.'

Then he turned to Shavi, his face brighter and more hopeful than Shavi had ever seen it. 'We can do this. I really think we can.'

And with that, he was away along the street, leading the strange troupe with renewed energy.

In his room, huddled before the fire but still not warm, Hal sat surrounded by piles of books that would have seemed to the casual observer to have been arranged in such a way as to form a defence against the outside world. Samantha had been forced to return to her own quarters earlier. Left on his own, the assassination of the prime minister had haunted him for much of the day, his feelings exacerbated by his memories of his recent visit with the leader. The murder would cause despair at a time when they needed hope, chaos when they were desperate for an ordered defence.

During the previous few hours, his mind had found some solace in the mystery that had tested him for so many days. Burying himself in it was an attempt to regain some measure of control when he felt so powerless, but more importantly he was still convinced that it was the key to survival.

At first the puzzle had appeared intractable, but the more he allowed himself to sink into its depths, the more he began to discover subtle connecting strands. Hal was aware of the pitfalls: that mysteries have a seductive power to lull those trying to solve them into making great leaps that, however logical they seem, take them in the wrong direction. Even so, he was sure he was close to a breakthrough.

His thoughts were interrupted by footsteps pounding along the corridor without, then a desperate hammering on his door. Hal opened it to find Samantha in a distraught state.

'Why have you risked breaking the curfew?' Hal said, concerned, as she forced her way past him. 'Whatever it is, they won't be lenient if they catch you out there. I wouldn't be surprised—'

'Hal, shut up!' The sharpness in her tone silenced him instantly. 'What's wrong?'

Samantha listened intently. Through the open door, Hal could hear shouts, running feet, drawing closer. 'They're coming for you, Hal!'

'Me?'

'They're saying that you killed the prime minister—'

'But I was nowhere near him when it happened!'

'They're saying that he was killed by some secret weapon, something you planted on him when you met with him.'

'It's not true.' Hal took a deep breath. 'I'll explain it all when they get here. There's been some mistake.'

Samantha grabbed Hal by the shoulders and shook him roughly. 'Stop acting like a sensible clerk! They're after a scapegoat so that they can get everyone behind the new leader. And they're determined to pin it on you!' She swallowed. 'They're going to have you executed as a traitor . . . make an example of you.'

'But . . .' The thoughts wouldn't come quickly enough.

'Stop talking!' She grabbed him and thrust him out into the corridor. 'Run! Find somewhere to lie low until . . . until all this blows over!'

Oddly, the most overwhelming thought in Hal's head at that moment was the warmth he felt at the deep concern he could see in Samantha's face. 'What about you? If they catch you here—'

'They won't. Now, go!'

As she ran past him, she paused and gave him a kiss on the cheek, lingering just long enough to search his face before she was away and down the stairs. The sound of the guards was rapidly drawing closer.

Hal ran quickly along the corridor and down the far steps. More snow was falling, and he would be leaving footprints, but he had a head start. As he sprinted through the bitter cold and into the night, his alarm became intense. If they caught him, everything he had learned would be lost. But could he survive with everyone in the city looking for him? Suddenly lost and desperate, he ran as fast as he could to the only place he knew where he might be able to hide.

The barricades were up on every street into the city. Beyond them, purple mist was dimly visible away in the night. The Lament-Brood had arrived. Their forces encircled the city, thousands deep, an army that would never give up. There was no escape for anyone in Oxford.

The end had begun.

chapter fifteen

the light burns brightest

'The great mass of the people . . . will more easily fall victim to a big lie than a small one.' Adolf Hitler

In a bower of ivy and roses, Hunter and Laura lay in a post-coital glow that belied the freezing temperatures outside. Their refuge was well insulated, the ivy covering a layer of interlacing living hazelnut, encased in elder, then Russian creeper, and finally densely packed hawthorn at least two feet thick. The warmth of their bodies kept the interior temperature nicely balmy. Even the sound of the howling blizzard failed to penetrate.

Hunter plucked one of the blooms and examined it. 'Roses. Didn't quite picture you as the romantic type.'

Laura stretched like a cat. 'Actually, it masks your body odour. When was the last time you had a bath?'

'If you think I'm going to frolic around in water in sub-zero temperatures, you've got another thing coming. Even if I could crack the ice. No, I'm quite happy reeking, thank you very much.'

'For your information, I am romantic. It just has to be the right person, and you're not it. What we have here is sex, pure and simple. Of the moment and not to be considered the instant our bodies separate.'

'I'm in heaven.' Hunter put his hands behind his head and surreptitiously sniffed his armpits. 'I don't get how she became a hero.'

Laura knew exactly who he meant: Ruth had been on both their minds since they had left Lincoln. Laura had not been parted from her since the Fall, and for a while had thought she never would be; they had never really been the closest of friends, but they were kindred spirits, bound by the Pendragon Spirit, hope and sacrifice and struggle. Though she would never tell Hunter, Laura was feeling a loneliness she hadn't experienced for a long while.

'You don't know anything about her, so keep your trap shut,' she said.

'I know that she's supposed to be a champion of life or humanity or whatever you want to call it, and when it came to the crunch, she turned her back on her obligation.'

Laura hovered over him, eyes blazing. 'You have no right to judge her. Don't ever do that again.'

The chilling hardness of her expression made Hunter reconsider his approach. 'All right, I don't know her. But you must accept that her decision could mean the end for all of us.'

'And maybe it's all over because you lot fucked up. We've done our bit. We fought and sacrificed. Your Five were supposed to pick up where we left off. Now you've come crying back to us—'

'OK, back off. I wasn't trying to pick a fight—'

Laura wasn't about to let him off the hook. 'Ruth loved Church more than anything. She'd earned her right to be with him. But this life isn't fair, is it? We went through all we went through at the Fall and there's still no happy ending for her. They deserved to be together, just so that the rest of us could see what true love is really all about.'

Hunter grabbed her shoulders and gently pushed her back. He was a little disturbed at the way hawthorn shoots had started to burst out of the ground all around him as her anger increased.

'I'm not saying she hasn't had a raw deal—'

'Worse than that!'

'Whatever. But sometimes you have to rise above your own suffering. Duty, responsibility, call it what you will. Everybody's relying on us.'

'You're perfect for this job, aren't you?' she sneered, rolling away.

They lay separated by a gulf for ten minutes, until Hunter tenderly reached out to stroke her bare back. 'I'm sorry.'

'Forget it.'

'We're going to do our best. No blame. That's the job, too, isn't it?'

'Suppose.'

Hunter kissed her shoulder. 'So if you're all plant, how do you still get pleasure from this? Wouldn't you be happier photosynthesising or something?'

'I get pleasure from my clitoris, and yes, like all my other organs, I have one. I can, if I like, eat and drink, but I've given up on the periods.'

'Don't you miss being human?'

'Overrated. And I told you – I'll never be on the rag again. You tell me one woman who wouldn't rather be a nature spirit than have to go through that every month.'

Hunter watched her as she dressed. Her personality wasn't the easiest thing to like, but he admired her, and there weren't many people about whom he could say that.

He rolled over and propped up his head so that he could get a last look at her body. 'So was this plant thing written in the stars when you became a Sister of Dragons?'

'You ask a lot of questions. Can't you just go to sleep after sex like a normal bloke?'

'Stop avoiding.'

She sighed. 'Being a Brother or Sister of Dragons is about freeing the potential inside you. Didn't you get the manual? You run around, leading your day-to-day life, and then somewhere a switch gets thrown and you're activated. Over time, as you do your duty, you learn, you're changed by hardship and all the nightmarish things you face, and gradually all those hidden qualities you never dared believe you had are teased out into the open.'

'So you always had a bit of vegetation deep down inside.'

'With some work, you could almost be funny. I was an environmental campaigner, a member of a radical green group. Tree-huggers, the right-wing wankers called us. So it was there. And maybe Cernunnos saw that when he turned me into this. It was my potential, to be a champion of the green, living world.'

'And Ruth became the Uber-Witch.'

'Right. From pain in the arse to the most powerful woman on the planet. Shavi became a magician or a seer or whatever he used to call himself. He could contact spirits, see the other side, like that.'

She snapped her fingers. 'Veitch. Poor, pathetic, useless Veitch. He went from a jumped-up petty crook to some kind of Conan the Barbarian warrior. And Church . . .' Despite herself, her voice took on a hint of deep respect. 'He became the kind of leader you'd always want in a fight. And like the kings in the old stories, he sacrificed himself so that everyone could live again. End of fairy story.'

Hunter lay back, musing. 'Wonder what I'll become.'

Laura eyed him dismissively. 'Probably some kind of insect hybrid, if there's any justice.'

'You're just playing distant because you're secretly broken-hearted that we can never be together.' He sat up, scrubbed his hair and cracked his knuckles. 'Right. I've eaten as many vegetables and fruits as I can probably cope with. I've had sex. I think I'm ready for the rest of the journey.'

They hadn't seen a single soul on their travels south from Lincoln. Much of their route took them across the flat eastern lowlands, now a desolate frozen wasteland. Flurries of snow blew across it in little tornados and the wind cut through their thick clothes. There was no sign of any birds or wildlife. During the day, the sun blazed so brightly off the drifting snow that they had to keep their heads bowed to avoid blindness. At night it felt as if they'd been stranded on the surface of the moon.

They never spoke about what dangers lay ahead or whether they had any hope of survival. They lived for the moment, seeking what little pleasures they could, knowing full well they might be their last.

Ten miles from Oxford, just as Mallory was leading a strange group of gods through the deserted streets of the city, Hunter and Laura finally allowed their darkest thoughts to catch up with them. They looked out over a force that left them breathless with its size. The Lament-Brood numbered millions. Several miles deep, the enemy force now encircled Oxford completely, the purple mist streaming out from them in the darkness. The waves of despair that washed off them made Hunter sick to the pit of his stomach.

'Looks like we shouldn't have made that last pit-stop, big boy,' Laura said. 'Now who's the fuck-up?'

'Bloody hell. I never expected them to reach here so quickly.

Before I set off they were taking their time, wiping every population centre clean. They must have put on a spurt.'

'As if they knew that the Brothers and Sisters of Dragons were gathering. So they got straight to the source of the only opposition.'

'But how would they know about us?'

Laura pushed her hood away from her face; her shock of blonde hair glowed spectrally in the dark. 'Things like that, they can *smell* us. See us on some kind of level we don't understand. The Pendragon Spirit is like a beacon in the night to them.'

Hunter surveyed the extent of the Lament-Brood, his mind racing.

'Looking on the bright side, at least it means we're a threat,' Laura added.

'Why don't you divert your brain away from your mouth and come up with a way to get through them and into Oxford?' Hunter said humourlessly.

'Ask and you shall receive, little one.'

Hunter looked at her suspiciously, unsure whether her sarcastic sense of humour was at play again. She grinned, revelling in her position of strength, but gave nothing away. 'Just give me a while to prepare.'

'Take all the time you want. I'm going to scout around, see what other options we've got.' Hunter spurred his horse back down the road and rode for half an hour, hoping there would be some gap in the enemy lines, knowing in his heart that it was not to be. It was impossible for a human army to defeat this demonic force; any rational observer would have said that the situation was hopeless. But Hunter didn't feel that way at all. Since he had learned of his destiny as a Brother of Dragons, he had come to believe in the Pendragon Spirit and all that it represented with a faith he had not previously thought existed inside him. His life had made him cynical about human values. He had killed and seen killing, relentlessly. He had witnessed murders committed on a whim, or because someone was in a bad mood, or because of political ideology. If that was the norm, then human existence was pointless and the quicker the infestation was eradicated, the better, so that nature could get on with its benign job.

Yet the Pendragon Spirit had shown him that there was some essential structure underpinning all life, an intelligent plan, though he was loath to consider it in such a way because of all the baggage that concept carried with it. But he knew from his training that it was impossible to make judgments based on the small details – a death here, a defeat there. Only by viewing the vast, strategic plan could any decision be made about the value of what was happening. And for most soldiers on the ground, that grand plan was never visible; they simply had to trust.

He hoped Existence wouldn't let him down. That somehow a handful of flawed men and women burning with an inner fire could take a stand against the hordes of hell and win. That the source of their victory would be presented to them. That he – that all of them – were up to the job, with no weak links anywhere.

The alternative was unthinkable.

When he returned to Laura, she was sitting cross-legged in the snow, her head bowed. What little he could see of her skin was as white as the icy blanket that lay all around. At first he thought she was sick – or worse, had been killed by the enemy. But when she heard the crunch of his boots, she raised her head and forced a smile. Her face was filled with a debilitating exhaustion, as if her life had been sapped from her.

'Are you OK?' he asked, dropping to his knees to put an arm around her shoulders.

'It's not easy being the saviour of the moment. One thing you learn in this business, there's always a price to pay. For everything.'

Hunter could feel heat radiating off her, and when he pulled her closer a tingling sensation ran from her body into his, as though she was generating electricity. It was then that he noted the new green shoots breaking through the snow all around.

'You'd better stand back,' she said. 'I'm ready now.'

'What are you planning?'

'Wait and see.' As she bowed her head again, Hunter moved away from her to calm the horses, which had grown jumpy. He stroked their noses and whispered in their ears while he watched Laura. A tremble ran through her, then she bucked as though in the throes of a convulsion. A second later she pitched forward, slamming the palms of both hands down hard through the snow to the ground beneath. There was a discharge of blue light that slowly faded to green.

The horses' whinnying grew more insistent. A rumble like

thunder rolled across the land. The ground beneath Hunter's feet began to shake, gently at first, but then with more and more force. He held on to the horses' reins tightly, and watched waves roll out from Laura's epicentre.

The tremors built until the ground was rent open in a line running from Laura towards the Lament-Brood. From the churning soil sprouted shoots, rapidly growing into saplings, then soaring up into trees, rushing to meet the sky, leaves erupting from the branches. Thirty years of nature's growth condensed into a few seconds.

Laura bucked and writhed in a frenzy that could have been pain or ecstasy. Sparks, blue becoming green, fizzed around her fingers where they dug into the earth. Hunter was rooted in shock. He had been astounded by her abilities ever since they had met in Lincoln, but he had never guessed she was so powerful.

As the frozen soil tore apart, the noise was deafening, and the land rippled like water in all directions at the upheaval. The flourishing trees formed a densely walled avenue ten feet wide, the branches meeting high overhead to form a natural arch; the leaf cover was so thick that no sky could be seen through it.

The row of trees rushed out across the countryside through the ranks of the Lament-Brood. Though the detail was lost in the dark, Hunter imagined the trees tearing through the massive force, throwing those twisted, once-living bodies to either side as the avenue ploughed on towards Oxford. The sheer scale of what Laura had accomplished took his breath away, and left him a little uneasy at what she could have done to him if he'd pushed her temper a step too far.

After ten minutes, the sparks stopped arcing from her fingertips and she pitched forward into the snow. Hunter ran forward and lifted her up in his arms. Her eyelids fluttered; she was completely drained. 'Match that, soldier-boy,' she said hoarsely.

Hunter knew what had to be done. As Laura slipped into unconsciousness, he sat her on her horse and did his best to lash her to the saddle so that she wouldn't slip off. Setting her mount off ahead of his, he urged the horses into the dark avenue and then forced them to gallop as fast as they could manage. He didn't know whether the trees would soon start to wither and die or disappear as magically as they had grown. The last thing they needed was suddenly to find themselves stranded in the middle of the Lament-Brood army.

But Existence hadn't let him down yet. Oxford beckoned and the last stand was only hours away.

The Damask brothel on St Michael's Street was packed to the brim. In the ground-floor office space, in the sprawling first-floor lounge and the many bedrooms on the two floors above, the Tuatha Dé Danann moved like golden ghosts, aloof, introspective, silent as the night, while the girls gaped in awe or ran giggling to discuss the new arrivals in the confines of their changing rooms or the torture dungeon.

Mrs Damask wrung her hands, repeatedly dashing to the velvet-curtained windows to peek out into the deserted street. 'I would never have agreed to this if Jeffrey had told me what he was planning,' she wittered in her Scottish accent.

Mallory smirked. 'So Hunter has a first name.' He was sitting back in a plush armchair, boots up on an antique table, a crystal goblet of brandy in his hand. Washed, fed and dressed in clean clothes, he felt renewed.

'If the authorities investigate, they'll close me down for certain.'

'The authorities have more important things on their minds,' Shavi reassured her soothingly. He leaned on the mantelpiece next to the roaring fire, occasionally tipping back his head and closing his eyes as he smelled the perfume that wafted through the room.

'I'll expect to be well paid for this. Well paid,' she repeated, glaring at Mallory as she flounced out.

'Humanity's on the brink of extinction and only the privileged few know,' Mallory noted.

'What would it benefit the rest to know?' Shavi said. 'There is nothing they could do. Better they enjoy some normality in their final hours, if final hours they be.'

The ornate clock ticking away on the wall showed that it was just after one a.m. Mallory swigged back his brandy. 'I'm going out to look for Sophie.'

'This is a big city. I would think she has probably already sought shelter somewhere.'

'I know. But I need to see her again before everything blows up.'

Mallory acted blasé, but Shavi could see the emotion coursing through him. 'I understand,' Shavi said. 'But take care in those dark streets—'

The door swung open and Lugh and Ceridwen marched in, their mood intense. 'Brother of Dragons, please come with us,' Lugh said to Mallory. 'Time is short.'

'What's up?' Mallory looked from one god to the other.

It was Ceridwen who answered. 'There are many of our kind already here in the Fixed Lands. They can help us in the coming battle. Indeed, their presence may be vital, for they count amongst their number some of the most powerful of the Golden Ones. We must contact them. But we need your help.'

'How can we help?' Shavi asked.

'There is a ritual,' Lugh said, 'known only to our kind. It calls to the ties that bind us, however far apart we may be. Now that there are so few of us left . . .' He paused, letting the words sink into his own mind. 'Now that there are so few of us, those ties may be stronger. And our own brothers and sisters may be summoned to fight for the cause.'

'Why do you need me?' Mallory asked, with one eye on the clock.

'The fire that burns inside you will give strength to our call,' Ceridwen said.

'The Pendragon Spirit is the key,' Shavi said to Mallory. 'The Brothers and Sisters of Dragons are like batteries. Sometimes that power heals them; on other occasions, others may tap into it – if you so allow.'

'All right,' Mallory said, not attempting to mask his irritation. 'Get on with it.'

They collected the items they needed from Mrs Damask and then Lugh and Ceridwen led the way up a back staircase to a vast, dark attic room that had been knocked through into the houses on either side. Mallory shivered, pulling his cloak around him. Ceridwen marked a circle on the dusty wooden floor with a piece of dressmaker's chalk and then lit candles at the four cardinal points. Mallory was intrigued by how closely the gods' ritual resembled Sophie's work with the Craft.

'Is all this necessary?' he said to Shavi. 'They're gods. Can't they just snap their fingers or something?'

'Magic,' Shavi said with a strange smile, 'is the cheat code of reality. We are in a vast program of repeating patterns, a superstructure of encoded rules. Reality has been constructed, and once you know the code that underlies that construction you can change it.'

'And thereby change reality?'

'Reality is not fixed, Mallory, even here in what the gods call the Fixed Lands. It is less changeable than their home, but it is still possible to unpick the construction. Sound and symbol are the keys. Words of power. Arcane marks. In our literalist, rationalist society, we see those sounds and symbols only as what they are on the surface, but their true power to break through the inherent programming of reality is hidden behind them.'

Mallory shook his head dismissively. 'If reality can be altered, what's the point?'

'That is the point, exactly: that the world out there is not important. That it is what is inside us that truly matters. What we do. Who we are. The Chinese call it *chi*, spirit. It cannot be altered. It is the bedrock of everything.'

Ceridwen summoned Mallory and Shavi into the circle. They all sat cross-legged facing the centre, where another candle flickered. Lugh's face was determined, and Mallory had the strange impression that the god had altered his appearance, had somehow grown more heroic; something about his features, his bearing. Ceridwen, her dark hair falling about her beautiful face, forced a smile to put Shavi and Mallory at ease, but a deep sadness was etched into every aspect of her being at the devastation of her people.

'If only the Extinction Shears had not been lost,' Lugh said. 'They would have cut through the warp and the weft and the Devourer of All Things would have been destroyed.' He bowed his head in contemplation.

And then Lugh and Ceridwen began to speak quietly, the words passing back and forth, interweaving, overlaying, the rhythms and cadences gradually forming a complex chant-song.

Mallory couldn't understand any of what they said, but the words had a strange effect on him nonetheless; in that instant he understood exactly what Shavi had been saying.

Still chanting quietly, Ceridwen and Lugh put their heads back, their eyes rolling under the upper lids so that only the whites were visible. Within seconds, Mallory was disturbed to see a clasp at

Ceridwen's shoulder begin to move of its own accord, echoed by the shifting of an ornate dagger on Lugh's belt. The two items ran like water, becoming silvery, then white and finally forming into eggs, which then sprouted legs and scurried to the candle at the centre of the circle.

Mallory was fascinated but repulsed. Shavi saw his reaction and whispered, 'They are known as caraprix. All the gods have one. They are living creatures, but infinitely mutable.'

'Pets?'

'Much, much more than that. They appear to have some kind of symbiotic relationship with the gods.'

In the flickering glow of the candle, the caraprix altered shape once more, stretching and entwining, forming themselves into one object, a globe that slowly raised off the boards and began to spin.

Ceridwen's brow furrowed, her voice becoming more intense, and though Mallory still didn't recognise the language, this time he understood. 'I call to you, my brothers and sisters, here in the Fixed Lands. This is a time of crisis. You are needed to stand with us against a power that would wipe us all from Existence. Come now.'

In Mallory's mind, images began to appear, so richly textured that it was as if he was watching them on a movie screen, his emotions linked to what he was seeing. Before he was swallowed up by the evocative experience, he saw from Shavi's face that his friend was experiencing it, too. And then he was lost to the rush of visions and sensations as though carried along in the flow of a swollen river: he felt deep, abiding peace as he saw Cernunnos, his body a hybrid of flora and fauna, stag's horns protruding from his head. Mallory's emotions shifted to unease, then fear as the nature-god strode out from a grove of oak trees, altering his form as he moved, growing bony ridges on his head and greenish scales, becoming the Erl-King of myth. Somewhere a horn sounded eerily.

'The Wild Hunt has already been summoned by an ally,' he said. 'We, of all our brethren, are close enough to do battle.'

A black dog appeared from the undergrowth, accompanied by the sounds of horses and finally other hounds, smaller, red and white in colour. Mallory remembered the old stories of the Hunt tearing across lonely moors hunting lost souls and he hoped he would be nowhere near when the riders descended on the Lament-Brood.

There were other gods he didn't recognise – one that appeared to be made wholly of water, breaking through the ice of a deep, dark pool, another one soaring through the clouds with a face like a human hawk – but there weren't many of them and they all announced that they were too far away to be of help.

He was shocked out of his vision by a sudden sharp query from Lugh. 'He is here? In the Fixed Lands?'

Mallory had an image of a man in long red robes, his face half-covered by what appeared to be a surgeon's mask. With it came a spike of unease, perhaps fear.

'He resists,' Ceridwen said. Then: 'Gone.'

Any further discussion was disrupted by a sharp intake of breath from Lugh and Ceridwen together, at a vision of a thousand crows flying chaotically.

'She is here, too!' Ceridwen said. This time the note of dread was much stronger; so the gods were not equal, Mallory thought. Some were even feared by their own.

He had no idea what the birds meant, but then Shavi was tugging at his sleeve anxiously, his eyes rolled upwards, watching his inner visions.

'It is the Morrigan!' he hissed. 'And see . . . see! She hunts!'

Mallory slipped back into his own trance-state and saw more clearly: the birds were now transposed over a woman, somehow occupying the same space. The woman was carrying an axe and had another strapped on her back. She was rushing through a snowy street – Oxford, he guessed – pursuing three figures, a woman and two men.

The Morrigan, so dreaded by the others, was drawing closer to her prey, moving in for the kill. Mallory's attention was drawn to the hunted, instinctively concerned for their safety. He realised why a second later. The woman was Sophie.

Thackeray and Harvey were yelling something, but Sophie couldn't tell what it was. All she knew was that her lungs were filled with acid and her legs were on fire; her mind, pummelled by exhaustion, wandered back and forth, her vision snatching single images like a slow parade of still photographs: a piece of ornate stonework; a silhouetted tree, twisted like a praying mantis; a wide expanse of crisp snow bisected by a row of footprints. The part of her that still clutched on to consciousness didn't know how much longer she could keep going.

When they had first emerged through the portal from the Watchtower, she had thought that they would have some respite. But it wasn't long before Caitlin had burst through in their wake. Sophie recalled the chill she had felt when she had first heard those familiar footsteps crashing like hammer blows into the crisp snow somewhere behind them.

And so they had run, through bleak woods, across frozen fields, making their way towards Oxford. But the Morrigan never slowed, never deviated. And Sophie knew she never would. It was all simply a matter of time and the depth of the reserves Sophie had inside her.

It seemed so unfair. She wasn't the warrior; she wasn't supposed to engage in brutal hand-to-hand combat just to survive. Her skill was the Craft, manipulating from afar, perception, wisdom. She hadn't even done anything wrong. All she had tried to do was help, selflessly, and she had been punished again and again.

She skidded down a snowy bank and found herself on a hard surface. As she tried to run, her feet went from under her and she came down hard, stunning herself for a few seconds.

When she came round, her cheek was burning where it was pressed against ice. Sophie pushed herself up, slipping and sliding. Through her daze, she realised she was on a frozen river; that was why Thackeray and Harvey had been calling out to her. It was the Cherwell.

She couldn't go back, so she pressed forward across the ice, hoping to get to the other side where she could lose herself in the city centre, find a place to barricade herself in. Not that it would do any good.

In the centre of the frozen watercourse, she slipped again, and when she looked back a dark figure was coming down the bank. It slowed when it saw Sophie defenceless, but still advanced, now with measured, intense paces, an axe at its side.

It might have been an illusion in the gleam of the streetlights off the snow, but in that instant there was no sign of Caitlin at all. Sophie saw a woman of terrible beauty, long black hair streaming in the wind, white, white skin and lips as red as blood. Her eyes burned. They said: *I will hack and slash and drench myself in your blood and even then I will not be done with your body.*

Sophie had a shift of perception and it was Caitlin again, but this Caitlin still bore traits of the Morrigan, was still as terrible and elemental and filled with an insatiable lust for blood. The axe beat out a steady rhythm against her leg.

On the other bank, Thackeray and Harvey jumped up and down, urging Sophie to get up and run. Desperately, Harvey had begun to make snowballs to hurl at Caitlin, the only weapons he had left to drive her away.

Sophie dug in her heels, forcing herself backwards, away from Caitlin, with the last vestiges of her strength. She slid across the ice for a few feet, then came to a halt.

'Caitlin. Remember who you are,' Sophie said feebly. 'Why you're doing this.'

Caitlin marched forward, head bowed, eyes glowering.

'You're a good person, Caitlin. Don't let yourself be corrupted. This isn't you. This—' But Sophie didn't have the energy to continue. It was too late. The end. She lay back on the ice and looked at the vast sweep of stars in the dark vault of the sky. So beautiful. Warmth enveloped her at the knowledge that she could finally rest.

Caitlin loomed over her, blocking out the stars. She raised her axe high.

In a last act of defiance, Sophie closed her eyes.

In the dark of her head as she waited for the blow, somehow she sensed movement. A sudden jarring clang of metal on metal made her snap her eyes open. Caitlin was sprawling across the ice. A figure in black was moving with balletic grace and strength, swinging a sword that left a trail of blue flames searing through the icy air. It looked like some hero from myth, larger than life, filled with epic determination and uncanny bravery. It took a second or two before his real identity registered.

'Mallory?'

Caitlin rolled and sprang to her feet, attacking in a fluid movement so rapid she was almost a blur. The axe would have ripped open Mallory's chest if he hadn't bounded backwards, keeping his balance on the balls of his feet and plunging the sword past Caitlin's defences. A shower of golden sparks burst where the sword skidded off the axe-blade. It continued through, slicing into the top of Caitlin's shoulder.

She didn't cry out, didn't register any pain on her face at all, even though a spurt of blood shot out from the wound and splattered on the ice. Cold and determined, Caitlin attacked Mallory again.

They battled back and forth that way for several minutes, two jungle cats sparring with grace and savagery, neither gaining an upper hand. Sophie realised how much Mallory had advanced since their first meeting, from a novice with a sword to someone who could keep a goddess like the Morrigan at bay.

While the Morrigan-powered Caitlin could attack with never-ending ferocity, it was Mallory's human cunning that gave him his edge. Where Caitlin expected a thrust from Mallory's sword, instead he jammed the blade between her knees and used it as a pivot as he threw his full weight at her. She slammed down on the ice, wide open for Mallory's killing blow.

In that instant, Sophie saw clearly the Caitlin she had first met in the Court of Soul's Ease: sad, broken, hopeful, decent. 'Mallory! Don't hurt her!' she called out, pushing herself to her feet. Mallory stopped mid-blow, half-turned. But what surprised Sophie the most was the startled expression on Caitlin's face: it was almost human.

The crack that came from beneath Sophie was like a gunshot. Radial lines shot out across the ice from her feet. She didn't have time to think. A split second later she was falling into the bitterly cold water.

Mallory saw the ice break and Sophie plunge through the hole. He couldn't react. Half his attention was on Caitlin, knowing that she would kill him from behind if he went to Sophie's aid.

In the end, he couldn't help himself. He ran as close to the edge of the fractured, fragile ice as he dared, but Sophie was already gone. Falling to his knees, he tore at the hoarfrost until the ice was as clear as glass. Framed in the white window, he saw the horrific image of Sophie's pale face, her eyes wide, drifting slowly by, her cheeks inflated with her last breath, her hands scrabbling on the underside of the ice, unable to break through. Drowning. Freezing.

The blow to the side of his head made him see stars and he knew as he fell that Caitlin had recovered and attacked. But there was no blood. As he jumped to his feet, Caitlin had the axe over her head, and then brought it down with such force that she was obscured by the eruption of ice.

Before Mallory could move, she was on her knees. She raised one fist and smashed it through the remnants of the ice furiously. Somehow she latched on to Sophie's drifting hair, yanking her upwards, then hauled her through the hole she had made. Blood streamed down her wrist, spraying over Sophie's face.

Mallory grabbed hold of Sophie and helped to haul her out. She was shaking violently, but still conscious. Quickly, Mallory pulled her away from the dangerous ice to the bank where Thackeray jumped in to help, his face white with desperation.

Mallory threw his cloak at Thackeray to wrap Sophie in, and then turned back to Caitlin. She was herself again. Hot tears burning down her cheeks, she bared her throat. 'Kill me now!' she ordered. 'I can't control her!'

Thackeray stepped in and grabbed Mallory's sword hand. 'Don't hurt her!' he pleaded, with so much desperate love in his voice that Caitlin's eyes grew wide with realisation.

Mallory threw Thackeray off and swung his sword towards Caitlin, her eyes now closed, the long white line of her throat ready for the killing blow. Thackeray knew he would remember that image until his dying day: Caitlin looked like a saint preparing to make the ultimate sacrifice for the greater good.

Thackeray yanked his gaze away just as Mallory's sword made contact. Hot tears welled up in his eyes. But when they had cleared, he saw Caitlin lying on the frozen river and no blood staining the ice. A raw lump marked her temple where Mallory had struck her with the pommel.

'Pick her up,' Mallory barked. 'Let's get her back before she wakes.'

Next to the blazing fire of Mrs Damask's lounge, Mallory hunched over Sophie, rubbing her frozen hands gently. She looked like a little girl bundled in his thick cloak. Somewhere on the journey back she had lost consciousness and he feared the worst.

But as he watched intently for the slightest muscle tremor on her face, her eyes flickered open, dark and searching, and then a small smile crept to her lips.

'You saved me,' she said in a weak voice. 'My big hero.'

Mallory fought back the lump in his throat. 'I thought you were dead. I thought . . . I thought I'd never see you again.'

'You can't get rid of me that easily.' She was racked with a coughing fit and when it passed, a shadow briefly crossed her face before her smile returned.

'What's wrong?' he asked, concerned.

'When I was in T'ir n'a n'Og, I gave up something very valuable to help Caitlin. I thought I'd regret it till my dying day.'

'And?'

'It wasn't important after all.' She gently touched his cheek as she searched his face. 'This . . . here . . . is like meeting you for the first time all over again. How many couples get the chance to experience that same first moment again, with all its power?'

Mallory had no idea what she was talking about, but it wasn't important: she was alive; they were together. A single tear filled the corner of her eye and rolled down her cheek. Mallory wiped it away; he couldn't believe how happy she looked.

'It wasn't a punishment at all,' she said softly. 'It was a blessing.'

chapter sixteen

the lords of despair

*'When the people contend for their Liberty, they seldom get anything
by their Victory but new masters.'* George Savile, Marquis of Halifax

Hal sat in an alley just off the High Street and watched one of the
numerous patrols crawl slowly by. As the spotlight in the back of
the truck washed across the walls, he flattened himself into a
doorway as he had done several times already. Sometimes it was a
truck, occasionally a jeep or even a lone rider on horseback. Every
time he had finally screwed up the courage to move on, another
patrol passed, locking him in place for more long minutes.

His fingers and toes were already numb, and the lack of feeling
was creeping slowly along his limbs. More snow was falling, the
gale howling over the rooftops, raising whirlwinds of white along
the street. Hypothermia was a constant threat; freezing to death a
distinct possibility.

But the risk of getting caught was too great. In the current
climate of anger, fear and suspicion, it was more than likely that
some overzealous guard would save everyone the trouble of a trial.
A bullet in the back of the head. A foot on the windpipe. Or simply
locking him up without food or water in an unheated room. In the
looming crisis, who would even care? He would simply be one less
thing to worry about.

Beneath the cold was a sickness of spirit born of incomprehension. How had he become the chief and – from the way Samantha
had described it – sole suspect? He hadn't done anything that

might have hinted at his involvement. That left only one other possibility: that he was being set up. It was obvious that the Government had been a hotbed of plotting and counter-plotting in recent weeks, but he would never have suspected that any conspirator would go to such lengths. Clearly it had all been running slow and deep and dark, like the waters beneath the frozen river.

A rush of self-loathing swept through him. Why was he always so naïve, so self-obsessed, so consumed by his own petty emotions and intellectual games that he never saw the big picture?

Shouts rose above the wind: a large disturbance nearby. Afraid that he had been discovered, Hal ran to the other end of the alley only to be confronted by an iron gate topped with razor wire. His heart thundering, he huddled down, staring at the gleaming snow at the end of the alley in anticipation of a silhouette, the shadow of a gun, a barked order.

His attention was caught by a trail of golden light high overhead, seen briefly and then lost in the swirling snow. Slowly, a figure descended from the dark and the snowstorm. It was Petronus, the boy who was not a boy, still wearing his floppy nightcap mask and his romper-suit outfit. His hands were clasped nonchalantly behind his back and his feet crossed as he floated down.

'Brother of Dragons, why do you wait here in the cold and the dark?' Petronus asked, curiously.

'I'm hiding from the soldiers. Can you help me?' Hal said.

Petronus held out his hands. 'How can I refuse such a request after you saved the life of my companion? What do you require?'

'A diversion. Can you swoop around the patrols so they're distracted enough for me to slip by?'

Petronus nodded slowly, and under his mask Hal had the impression that he was smiling.

'But you must run fast, Brother of Dragons,' Petronus cautioned. 'Battle is about to be joined. The city is surrounded and soon it will be overrun.'

The news came as a shock, but Hal could only deal with one obstacle at a time. Petronus bowed theatrically, then swooped to the end of the alley where he paused for a second before darting out. As soon as Hal heard the sound of gunfire, he sprinted out of the alley and across the street as fast as the snow would allow.

Keeping to the backstreets and alleys as much as he could, he arrived at Mrs Damask's just as the sound of whinnying horses echoed across the approach route.

Hal dropped back to wait for the riders to pass, only to feel an almost overwhelming surge of relief when he saw that the first rider was Hunter. Behind him, a woman with pale skin slumped weakly in her saddle.

Hunter reined in his horse as Hal stepped out of the shadows, then jumped down in surprise to greet his friend raucously.

'I thought you wouldn't be coming back,' Hal said.

'Hal, this is me we're talking about.' Hunter held out his hands in a disbelieving gesture. 'I am unstoppable.'

'Unbearable, more like.'

'What are you doing out in the cold at this time of night?'

Hal's grin faded. 'The PM's been assassinated and they think I did it. Everyone's looking for me.'

Laura slid from her saddle and walked up to them wearily. 'Can we cut the male-bonding? I need to get inside to rest.'

'I didn't do it,' Hal protested.

'Course you didn't,' Hunter said. 'Let's face it, you're the most unlikely suspect for a political assassin I can imagine.' Hunter clapped a reassuring arm around Hal's shoulders and nodded towards the unfamiliar woman. 'She's a bossy witch but she's right – let's get inside. Time's running out and we've got a lot to do.'

As they walked to the door, Hal asked, 'Who's your friend?'

'Some kind of plant. Haven't quite decided the phylum, subphylum or class yet, but probably a distant relative of poison ivy.'

Hal gaped in incomprehension, while Laura eyed Hunter superciliously. Hunter smiled back at her. Then, as they passed through the door, Laura let it slam in Hunter's face.

The atmosphere in Mrs Damask's warm, fragrant lounge was subdued. Mallory, Shavi and Sophie talked intensely by the fire, while Lugh and Ceridwen pored over a map of the city at the table near the window. Sophie had already made a remarkable recovery.

When the new arrivals entered, Shavi strode quickly across the room and swept Laura into his arms with enthusiastic happiness.

'It has been a long time, Laura,' he said.

'Feels like years.' She put her head in close to his so that only he could hear. 'I've missed you. I've missed all of us, together. We made a good team, didn't we?'

'We did.'

'This new lot don't know what they've got.'

'Give them time. They need to draw closer to each other. Find their shared strengths. Overcome their weaknesses together.'

'Time is one thing they haven't got.'

Shavi ignored her last statement and looked to the door hopefully. 'Where is Ruth?'

Laura shook her head gravely.

While Laura and Shavi spoke quietly, Hunter and Hal gathered by the fire with Mallory and Sophie.

'You look very fit for someone who's supposed to be dead,' Hunter said to Sophie, with a hint of flirtation.

'You're wasting your time turning it on with me, Hunter. Mallory's already warned me about you,' she replied, in a not unfriendly manner.

Hunter feigned a hurt expression. 'Well, then. Down to business.'

'It's a bit late in the day to start talking,' Hal said.

'Who's this misery goat?' Sophie shucked off the cloak Mallory had wrapped her in; her skin, so pale and deathly less than an hour ago, now bloomed with vitality.

'Don't go saying anything against my chum.' Hunter clapped an arm around Hal's shoulders and crushed Hal to him. 'This is Hal Campbell, damned intellectual, the brains to my brawn, the brains to my beauty—' Hal fought his way free.

Sophie's eyes narrowed as if she was peering through skin and bone into Hal's very heart. 'There's something about you—'

'There's nothing about me!' Hal snapped.

'Stop picking on him.' Hunter edged Hal away from Sophie's probing stare. Hal wandered into a corner where he observed the proceedings sullenly.

'This is better than I thought,' Hunter continued. 'With Sabrina here back in the land of the living, we should be up to speed.' He glanced at Shavi and Laura, still locked in deep, quiet conversation. 'If you count our two substitutes.'

Quickly, they began to exchange information. Hunter explained

Ruth's absence – Sophie could barely hide her disappointment. 'I wouldn't be here today if not for the trail Ruth walked before me,' she said, before telling everyone how Caitlin had lost her Pendragon Spirit and become possessed by the Morrigan. Caitlin was locked up downstairs under the guard of Thackeray and Harvey in case the Morrigan reasserted herself.

'We stand a chance, then,' Mallory said. 'But I'd be happier if we had the true number instead of trying to pad it out with Laura and Shavi. Still, even if we had the proper number, five of us against a couple of million—'

Hal came forward and said passionately, 'You're missing the point.'

Hunter stepped in before Hal's brusque attitude could offend anyone in the tense atmosphere that lay across the gathering. 'Spit it out.'

'There's no point just lining up alongside the troops to fight the Lament-Brood. You can help, sure, but that's not what you're here for.'

'Go on,' Hunter said.

'You've been brought together to fight the Void, not its agents. That's what the Brothers and Sisters were designed for—'

'How would you know?' Mallory said sharply.

Hunter held up a silencing hand. 'Hal's got a brain the size of a planet. I trust him. Think about it – he's right. We need to focus on finding the real enemy, not waste our time fighting his pawns.'

'But we don't know where the Void is,' Mallory said. 'We can't just sit back and wait until we're overrun.'

'No, you can't,' Hal said, 'but sure as anything, the Void is going to be here. The Lament-Brood . . . his generals . . . will bring it into the city with them.' Hal felt uncomfortable when he noticed that everyone was now hanging on his words.

'I always thought it would be bigger than some physical presence,' Sophie said. 'Something that could be all around us.'

'Maybe it is. I don't know,' Hal back-tracked. 'But this is the place where the last battle will be fought. The Void is going to be here, and you need to be ready to face off against it. That's where whatever skills the Pendragon Spirit has given you will come into play.'

'See,' Hunter said, 'I told you he's not just an ugly face.'

'Then I say we do what we can on the front line,' Mallory said, 'to make sure that the city doesn't get swamped while we try to find out where the Void is.'

'Or what it is,' Sophie said. 'For all we know, it could be a little glass bottle of nothing. Or a ten-foot teddy bear.'

'I can help,' Shavi said. 'I can contact the spirits for more information. But it takes a great deal out of me, so I should not attempt it until I really need to.'

'Enough jawing,' Laura said. 'All you lot do is talk, talk, talk. It wasn't like that in our day.' She gave Shavi a wink. 'Let's hit that front line.'

As they trooped out, Hal called Hunter back. Hal had been fighting with what he had to say ever since they had entered the brothel. But when he saw the bravery the others were exhibiting by putting their lives on the line for a greater cause, the guilt consumed him. He had to speak out.

'That was smart talking there,' Hunter said. 'I'm proud of you.'

'You won't be in a minute,' Hal began. He steeled himself, then blurted, 'I'm a Brother of Dragons. I've known it for a long time, but I hid it away . . . I lied to you because . . . I was afraid.'

Hunter searched Hal's face. Hal couldn't read what was going on in his head, but knew that if Hunter condemned him, it would tear him apart.

'You know, now that you say it, I can see it,' Hunter mused.

It certainly wasn't the reaction Hal had expected. 'Aren't you angry with me?'

'Everybody does what they have to. You don't need to be fighting at the front to play your part – that's not why you were chosen. I'm betting you're doing your own thing, secretly, away from the limelight, which is just so very Hal.'

Hal was deeply moved by Hunter's complete belief in him. For the first time, he realised the true depth of their friendship and how much it meant to him.

Hunter clasped Hal's arm in a powerful gesture of support. 'You decide where you need to be, and what you have to do. If you don't want to come to the front line, that's fine.'

'Don't let me off the hook,' Hal said. 'Make me come! I'm a coward!'

'No, you're not.' Hunter glanced towards the open door: he had to go. 'I bet you haven't been hiding out in a bunker since you found out what you are. You've been doing something to help, haven't you?'

'Well . . .'

'See? You're playing your part, Hal. You'll be where you need to be. I trust you.'

'How can you say that? I've betrayed you, and what it means to be a Brother of Dragons. I'm not up to it.'

'Stop talking such bollocks. Now, I need to go before someone nicks my horse, but I'll see you again soon, all right?'

Hal nodded reluctantly. 'Come back. For Samantha. I think she's in love with you.'

Hunter gave him a curious look, then one more smile and he was gone, to death or glory. Hal wanted to hate himself, but Hunter's words were still flying around in his head: perhaps he hadn't been fooling himself that his investigation into the mystery of the Wish Stone was vital. Was that really his role as a Brother of Dragons? If so, he had to find the solution quickly.

Hunter reined in his mount next to Mallory, who was just climbing into the saddle of Laura's horse. Sophie, Shavi and Laura waited next to one of the patrol jeeps that had been fitted with a snow plough; Laura claimed that she had 'found it' in the next street.

'There'll be hotspots at three main barricades,' Hunter began. 'On Saint Giles, Saint Aldate's beyond Thames Street and the High Street beyond Magdalen. There'll be another couple of barricades to the west, and on the smaller roads to the north-east, but those routes won't present easy attack routes, so I'm betting that the main forces will come in from the north, south and east.'

'We can't be everywhere,' Mallory said. 'What are you suggesting?'

'I'll take the High Street, you head south down Saint Aldate's.' Hunter turned to Laura. 'Think you can grow something strong enough to form a barrier across Saint Giles? It's a big road.'

'No problem.' Her smile unnerved Sophie, who hadn't taken to Laura at all. 'Looking forward to it.'

'Sophie, you need to stay in the jeep with Shavi,' Hunter went on. 'Move back and forth between the main battle areas and do what you can with your thing. Storms, rats . . . ferocious rabbits, if you've got any hats you can pull them out of.'

Sophie felt excited at the prospect of using her Craft to the extent of her abilities. It would be a massive release after all the stress and suffering of the preceding weeks.

'Shavi, we're counting on you to find our primary target,' Hunter continued. 'Do whatever you have to do. If Sophie stays by your side, she can protect you if you get into a weakened state.'

Shavi smiled enigmatically.

'What?' Hunter said.

'You remind me of my good friend, Church.'

Silenced by the comment, Hunter urged the others to leave. They didn't say goodbye, didn't consider the future for a second. Surviving the present situation was the only thing that mattered.

Alone in the room, Hal watched the crackling flames as he sank deep into thoughts of King Arthur, a raging Blue Fire and the secret language of symbols. The solution was so close that he could almost touch it, and this time he was going to succeed.

Carefully, he laid out the evidence in his mind. It was complex, but he was sure he had all the information he required; the only thing he needed was the key that would unlock the code.

The underlying pattern of the mystery was the legend of King Arthur. From everything Hal had learned, it was clear that the story had been devised at some point in ancient times as a symbolic means of passing information down the years. That was a standard way of operating for cultures without the written word. In the distant past, memory skills had been developed far beyond what modern man was used to. Greek storytellers could recite by heart every word of Homer's *Iliad*. The Celtic bards had vast, detailed story banks recorded in their heads, passed down from father to son. Those stories were a secret language: locked in their accounts of gods and heroes and men were rules for living life, as well as tracts of knowledge about the stars and animals and plants. Most importantly, the stories preserved for all eternity the vast mysteries held by the wise men and women in the only way their culture knew.

It was an elegant solution. Lists of facts and figures, rules and regulations, could be corrupted by memory or easily forgotten. But stories went on for ever. With the vital information stitched into the fabric of a tale, it would always be there to be discovered by anyone who understood the secret language of symbolism.

The true story, the important story, was not the one on the surface; it was the one hidden beneath. And that's what Hal knew he had to do: cut through the surface story to find the real message.

The Arthurian legends spoke of places where the power of the king was concentrated, of Camelot and Avalon and the lake where Excalibur was found. Many of these places, the stories said, were pathways to another world. But Hal knew that the power of the king in the legends was not meant to be the temporal power of an earthly ruler. It was real power: the Blue Fire, the energy that coursed through the Earth and every living thing upon it. That was the first, and greatest, of the hidden messages.

Ley lines, spirit paths, the dragon lines of the Chinese. King Arthur, who was a force for good against evil and the defender of the land against the darkness, was a code for this power. Any place linked to Arthur was a spot where the Earth Power was strongest. And these power nodes could be used to cross over to the Otherworld, the place he had witnessed with awe when he had gazed through the reversed monument at Shugborough.

As Hal turned these things over in his mind, he found himself becoming increasingly excited, for instinctively he knew that he was nearing some point of revelation. When a log crackled and spat, another connection leaped forward: he suddenly realised that like the Shugborough monument, the symbols coded into the stories had two faces, dual strands of information operating one on top of the other. In fact, the more he considered it, the more he knew this to be true. Duality was everywhere. Two worlds, side by side, reflecting each other yet different, both influencing the other. Good and evil. Humans and gods. Life and Anti-Life.

So if there were double meanings in the legends, what did that suggest? Certainly, on one level, that King Arthur was a symbol of the Blue Fire.

But on another, also that there was a king. A king who embodied the Earth Power. A defender waiting to be called back in Britain's darkest hour – that was what the legends said. And surely this was the darkest hour of all, when life was about to be subsumed by Anti-Life.

His heart beat faster.

Et in Arcadia Ego. And in Arcadia – the Otherworld – I wait. But 'I' was not death. It was the king, and the tomb in Poussin's painting was where he lay, waiting to be awoken.

And the flipside of that was the anagram of the inscription on the tomb: *I Tego Arcana Dei*. Begone! I conceal the secrets of God. The king was infused with the power of God, the Blue Fire. The power of life that could throw back the Void.

That was why the secrets had been waiting until this moment to be revealed, to be discovered by Hal: so that he could bring the defender back. Hal felt a frisson as the pattern surfaced. It suggested the influence of a hidden intelligence, and a vast, unimaginable master plan with connections stretching across millennia.

Almost there now. One final question: who was the king?

The plan had clearly been put in motion at some point in the ancient history of Cadbury Hill when the Wish Stone had been buried. But not just anyone could have found it.

Another connection.

Not just anyone: only a Brother or Sister of Dragons. That was the key: the Pendragon Spirit was integral to this grand scheme.

And then he had it. 'Jack Churchill,' he said out loud. The symbolic 'King' of the last group of Five. Ryan Veitch was definitely dead and buried after the devastation of the Battle of London, but Jack Churchill was only *presumed* dead. There hadn't been a body, that much was clear from the intelligence briefing Samantha had recovered from the files.

What if, during the final cataclysmic struggle, Jack Churchill had somehow been thrown into T'ir n'a n'Og? Perhaps amnesiac, perhaps in a coma. Hal's mind raced. What if he was such a powerful avatar of the Pendragon Spirit that he could defeat the Void's Anti-Life? A secret weapon, waiting to be found, and brought back, and used. The ultimate weapon that would tip the balance in the war.

Hal couldn't be sure that he was right, not completely, but the symbolism and the facts fitted together nicely; and instinctively he *was* convinced.

He had to tell Hunter immediately. Perhaps there was still time for the Brothers and Sisters of Dragons to cross the barrier between the worlds somehow and bring Jack Churchill back from his exile. The stories said that time operated differently in the Otherworld. Hunter and the others could be there and back in the blink of an eye.

Hal felt a rush of excitement mingled with relief. He had played his part, and he'd done so without leaving his armchair. With a whoop, he jumped up, ready to rush out to the High Street to find Hunter.

Only he was no longer alone. Two armed soldiers stood just inside the door, and between them was Reid.

'Time to go, Hal,' he said, with a cold smile.

As he made his way along the High Street towards the barricade, Hunter heard his name called anxiously. He turned to see Samantha running through the snow, looking desperate.

Jumping down, he ran to her and they embraced passionately. 'How did you find me?' he said softly when they pulled apart.

'There was a giant ... all surrounded by blue light ...' Samantha appeared dazed after her meeting with the Caretaker. 'He told me where you were, said I had to take his lantern back to him.'

Hunter fetched the Wayfinder from the horse, where it had been hanging from the saddle. 'Tell him thanks for the loan,' Hunter said, handing it over.

Touching the lantern had an effect on Samantha: her pupils grew less dilated, her mind cleared. 'Hal's in trouble,' she said suddenly.

'I know.'

'He's—'

Hunter took her by the shoulders to calm her. 'He's safe. Don't worry.'

She leaned forward to kiss him strongly, and Hunter felt a surge of love so deep and powerful that it shook him to the core. As he pulled away, he could see that Samantha felt it, too. 'Don't get killed, Hunter.' She caught herself, then added, 'You and I—'

'You know Hal loves you,' Hunter interrupted. It was a truth that he had only come to realise in the last hour, but once he had recognised it, it was obvious.

Samantha was taken aback by his response. 'I know he likes me—'

'You should go to him. You'll make a good couple. If all this pans out right.'

Samantha took a step back, struggling to find solid ground. 'I thought . . . we could . . .'

'A betting man would say I probably won't come out of this alive. And even if I do, there are lots of places to go, people to see. Women . . .' His voice trailed off; he couldn't keep it up any longer, but he could see from the hardening of Samantha's face that he had done enough. 'Go to Hal. He's at Mrs Damask's,' he said. 'He needs you.'

She backed away, still unsure what to make of his words, but her pride would not allow her to say any more. 'Don't worry, I will.'

When Hunter was a short way down the road, he allowed himself one quick glance back at the tiny departing figure, the blue light from the Wayfinder washing out across the snow. The sight was heartbreaking.

Then he turned towards the sounds of battle rising up from all sides and spurred his horse onwards, his mind locked on conflict and victory.

The snow was falling heavily when Mallory arrived at the southern barricade. It added an incongruously ethereal atmosphere to the street scene, dampening sounds, blanketing the flaws of human living. But as he neared the hastily erected metal wall, the sounds of battle rose up. There were no cries of pain or anger from the Lament-Brood beyond; they remained eerily silent, washing against the barricade like a summer swell in a harbour.

But the soldiers lined up along the walls made up for it with a cacophony of defiance. It was all an act; Mallory could see that their faces were etched white with fear. Beyond the barricade, the hellish invading army stretched as far as the eye could see.

They fired SA80s, hand pistols, rifles, from the walls and from all vantage points on the nearby buildings. Brass cartridges rained through the air, glittering in the arc lamps, and the sound was like a Caribbean rainstorm. Further back from the barricade, the big guns waited for any enemy breakthrough of the front line.

Mallory reined in his horse and waited; it was only a matter of time before the defences were swept aside by the massive, unfeeling force pressing against them. Yet it happened even more quickly than he had anticipated. Within fifteen minutes, there was a sound like the howl of a dying animal as the metal plates began to buckle under the weight of bodies crushed against them.

One of the soldiers firing from the top of the wall lowered his weapon, his mouth gaping. 'Jesus Christ. What's that?'

On the other side of the barricade, the purple mist was rising as the Lament-Brood clambered on top of each other to allow those behind to gain purchase. They reminded Mallory of ants. But riding the crest of the twisted bodies was a gleaming yellow-white figure that Mallory recognised from Hunter's description as the Lord of Bones. It had grown in size, now almost twice the height of a man, its bulk increasing a little with every skeleton sucked into its voracious mass. There was a hunger to it, in the avid gleam of its eyes and the way it reached out with clacking-bone hands, desperate to snatch anything that fell within its reach.

Most of the soldiers leaped from the wall as it fell apart, but one remained in position a second too long, firing his pistol futilely into the seething mass. The Lord of Bones' eyes swivelled towards the soldier, fixed on its target and then moved towards it with alarming speed. Crushing hands shattered the soldier's wrist and yanked him forwards.

The Lord of Bones stood erect on the roiling Lament-Brood beneath it and pressed the yelling, squirming soldier against its chest. Mallory was sickened as he watched the victim's skeleton sucked out of his body, leaving a flopping sack of skin and organs that was tossed to one side to splatter into the snow.

And then the Lord of Bones threw its head back, opened its mouth and released a sound that was not a sound. It made Mallory's stomach turn and his brain fizz. It was the creature's roar of victory.

Mallory lost sight of the Lord of Bones in the confusion as the barricade burst apart and the Lament-Brood flooded through into the city. For a brief moment, he was rooted as the Lament-Brood caught hold of fleeing soldiers, broke necks, ran swords through stomachs, gouged out eyes. And then, mere seconds later, repossessed the dead, twisting their bodies, forcing weapons to meld with bone and flesh, the re-animated corpses joining the ranks of those who had slain them to turn on their former comrades.

The big guns released a hail of massive fire power. Mallory fought to control his horse, glad that something had torn his gaze away from the hellish vision. Smoke swept across the street. When it cleared, scores of the Lament-Brood had been ripped to pieces, but hundreds more surged in to take their place. The gun positions were overrun in seconds, the remaining soldiers fleeing, powerless.

Mallory drew Llyrwyn and suddenly the street was flooded with brilliant blue light; even the falling snow appeared to be sapphire flakes. Mallory had never seen such a powerful display: the flames raged so forcefully along the blade that it vibrated in his hand, rang up his arm and into his heart.

Digging in his spurs, he propelled his horse into the fray. Lament-Brood fell beneath the trampling hooves, skulls split, torsos crushed. The air itself singed as Mallory swung his sword. The Lament-Brood fell before him like grass before a scythe. None could touch him, and soon the ground was covered with corpses and his horse was trampling them into the snow.

In Mallory's mind, all sound disappeared, the hacking of bone, the ringing of steel, the thunder of hooves, until a deep silence swaddled him. He couldn't smell, taste, touch, and a blue sheen lay across his mind. In that instant, he was the sword and the sword was him, each possessing and being possessed by the other.

Finally the Lament-Brood fell back at some silent summons. Their ranks parted and the Lord of Bones marched through. It towered over Mallory even on horseback, its bones splattered with red human blood.

It surveyed Mallory for a moment, a cold intelligence that insinuated through the blue into Mallory's mind, unbearably alien, betraying no recognisable emotion. And then, when it was satisfied that it understood what lay before it, it drove forward with a speed belied by its size.

Mallory forced his horse to dance out of the creature's path, but it only just evaded the charge. The Lord of Bones' talons ripped through Mallory's trousers and into the flesh beneath. And as the fingers scythed across his flesh, Mallory felt a tugging in his bones, as if they were on the verge of being sucked out of his body.

Mallory guided the horse to circle and then drive in. Llyrwyn blazed through the air to smash against the bone-creature's shoulder blade. The impact almost threw Mallory out of the saddle. Bone erupted outwards and parts of the creature's form began to fall away. But it clearly felt no pain and immediately launched another attack that Mallory only just avoided.

They continued that way for nearly half an hour, with no sign of the creature weakening. Every now and then, the Lord would draw blood with its razor-sharp fingers and Mallory's clothes were now wet and sticky in many places. Mallory had a vision of losing the battle, of the thing pulling his skeleton clean out of his skin. He wondered with a sickening fascination what his final thoughts would be.

The horse's breath and his own mingled in a hot, white cloud in the freezing air. But while Mallory tirelessly sustained his attack, his horse was growing sluggish. Finally, as Mallory brought his searing sword down in a hissing strike that shattered a portion of the Lord of Bones' skull, his mount failed to retreat quickly enough.

The Lord of Bones seized its moment. Like a striking snake, it grabbed Mallory and ripped him from the saddle, pressing him close to its hard body. It smelled incongruously of milk.

Mallory fought to free himself, but a powerful sucking sensation had already manifested deep inside him. It felt as though hooks had been attached to his bones and were pulling them out through his muscle and skin. The agonising pain drove him to the edge of unconsciousness, but he continued to fight to the last.

The hurricane wind came from nowhere. Mallory and the Lord of Bones were thrown through the air against a building on the far side of the road. The Lord of Bones took the brunt of the impact, but Mallory was knocked unconsciousness by the shock.

When he came round, he was lying in the snow, his entire body on fire with pain from the sucking power of the Lord of Bones. But it was fading. The creature was staggering around, its right arm shattered into pieces and a section of its torso falling away.

The wind had died down a little, but the snow still blasted against Mallory's skin like hot pins. Dazed, he staggered to his feet, searching for his sword. It lay half-buried in a drift nearby. But the Lord of Bones had seen him again and was rapidly stalking his way.

Before it could reach him, there was a deafening clap of thunder. Lightning crashed down in a direct hit on the Lord of Bones. In the flash of blinding light, Mallory was hurled backwards, but this time he fought to stay conscious.

The air reeked of burned iron. What remained of the Lord of Bones still stalked around, smoke rising from the shattered bones. Drunkenly, Mallory retrieved his sword. The moment the weapon was in his hands and the blue flames were roaring, his mind became sharp and focused. He attacked the Lord of Bones with venom, not stopping his hacking and slashing until only a few bone shards remained and a faint purple mist was drifting in the now-subsiding gale.

Mallory looked around eagerly. He knew who he had to thank for his survival. Sophie stood in the driver's seat of the jeep, arms raised in supplication to the sky. Gradually, she sagged as the power faded. She managed a wave and a smile before Shavi urged her to drive to another location.

The Lament-Brood appeared disoriented by the Lord of Bones' destruction, but Mallory could see that they were slowly re-forming their ranks to prepare for their next advance. All the surviving soldiers had fled to another fall-back position. There was nothing else he could do. Reclaiming his weary horse, he turned back into the city, following the tracks of Sophie's jeep.

The row of mighty oaks soared more than thirty feet above Laura's head, and the barrier was at least the same distance thick. Almost all her reserves had gone into constructing it, but she knew it would not keep the Lament-Brood out for long. Already she could hear the hacking of their weapons against the trunks. They would not tire, would not defer to serious injury; they would just keep going until they crushed everything in their path.

Laura walked away in search of shelter to recover, only to be halted in her tracks by gunfire coming from the buildings on either side of the wall of trees. Knowing instantly that it signalled a change in tactics, she angrily stormed into the nearest building and climbed the stairs to the second floor where two soldiers were pumping rounds wildly into the swarming Lament-Brood on the other side of the defence.

They were so preoccupied with their task that Laura could creep close enough to see past them. The Lament-Brood were clambering up the side of the building to get access to the windows so that they could bypass the trees. Some were smashing their weapons into the brickwork to gain foot- and handholds; others were simply clambering up on top of compacted bodies. But at the head of the climbing ranks was the Lord of Lizards. The glow from the street lights glistened on its skin, its entire body writhing with the packed combination of snakes, toads and newts. Its appearance revolted her, but what made her feel worse was the hunger that gleamed in its reptilian eyes.

The soldiers' slugs ripped through it with little effect and the two men were growing increasingly scared as the beast drew nearer to them. Soon it would be in a position to pull itself through the window.

Laura leaned against a wall and closed her eyes. In her mind, she could see one final blue spark of power burning in the depths of her. Would it be it enough? She coaxed the spark higher and focused.

Just beyond the window, the Lord of Lizards paused as an odd sensation moved through its body. Deep in the stomachs of the many creatures that made up its form, biological matter was starting to move, change, grow.

Laura concentrated. She had all but exhausted her abilities; one last drop remained, one minute amount left to be squeezed out.

The pressure inside the Lord of Lizards grew. Laura gave it her last burst of energy. A holly bush, a rowan tree, a hawthorn and several other small shrubs and plants grew within the Lord at once, ripping through weak flesh in an instant. The amalgamation of lizards exploded in a puff of purple smoke and a sudden shower of red roses. Laura thought that was a nice touch.

Too weak to be any more use, she lurched back down the stairs to the street. Her actions had bought them a little time to find the Void, that was all. But as she headed back towards the city centre humming an old Basement Jaxx song, she reflected that she'd at least got a little pleasure from her last wanton act of violence.

Sophie brought the jeep to a sharp stop, the wheels skidding in the snow.

'Anything?' she asked.

Shavi shook his head, the strain on his face starting to show. 'It used to take an intensive ritual to contact the spirits, but recently I have been able to do it easily. Often they felt as if they were always around, so that I could talk to them at any moment. But now . . .' A shiver ran through him. 'They are not answering my call.'

'Come on, Shavi, we have to find the Void. It's all down to us.'

'You mean it is all down to me. I know. I will not fail you.' He looked around, then said, 'Get me inside one of the buildings. Away from this cold, I can concentrate, set up a ritual . . .' There was a faint note of desperation in his voice that to Sophie sounded out of character. They clambered out of the jeep and struggled through the snowstorm towards the nearest buildings.

Hunter was aware of Mallory's arrival, but he couldn't take his eyes off the Lord of Flesh. The scores of snapping animal mouths threatened to tear at his flesh whenever he came close. He'd already discarded his gun as useless. After that, he'd wrenched a spear from one of the Lament-Brood's limbs in the hope that it would allow him an arm's length attack, but it had simply passed through the churning furry bodies without inflicting any serious harm. Now he was left with a rusted sword, the jagged forearm of one of the Lament-Brood still hanging from the hilt.

'I've taken one of these things down already,' Mallory yelled, as he guided his horse in a circle around Hunter and the Lord of Flesh.

'Aren't you the big-shot?' Hunter replied through gritted teeth. He attempted another flailing lunge that resulted in a ferocious snapping of jaws.

'You need a hand?' Mallory swung Llyrwyn and sheared through several of the Lament-Brood who were drawing too close for comfort. The brilliant light from the sword made the others shy away.

'What do you think?' Hunter snapped.

Mallory directed his horse to the opposite side of the Lord. The creature ranged back and forth, attempting to strike at one, then the other.

'I prefer my weapons a bit more on the modern side,' Hunter said.

Mallory grunted. 'A poor workman always blames his tools.'

'There's only one tool around here.' Hunter relished landing a blow that took the head off a badger. 'And it's not me.'

As the Lord of Flesh responded furiously to Hunter's attack, Mallory seized his moment, driving in to hack at the creature's head from behind. A mass of furry bodies rained across the area. Before the Lord could recover from Mallory's blow, Hunter had leaped from his horse and was slashing at its legs. Bloody chunks fell all around and within seconds the Lord had crashed down into the snow.

Together, Mallory and Hunter jumped in to finish the thing off. They didn't stop chopping until there was no recognisable shape left amongst any of the animals that had made up the Lord's form. Mallory held Hunter back as purple mist drifted up. 'All right,' he said, 'he's done for.'

They ran to their horses and mounted them quickly. 'We'll regroup further down the street,' Hunter yelled above the wind. 'I wonder if these things burn?'

'Got a plan?'

'I wouldn't quite call it that yet—' Hunter reined in his horse and looked around. 'Can you hear that?'

At first, Mallory couldn't. But then a low drone began to float in from the darkness beyond the city, growing louder, gradually becoming even louder still. The wind suddenly and mysteriously dropped.

'Look,' Hunter said.

The Lament-Brood had stopped moving. It was an eerie sight to see them all standing stock-still like statues. They were waiting for something.

'What's that noise?' Mallory said, rubbing his ears. The rising sound felt as if it was drilling deep into his brain.

Hunter knew: he'd heard it before and the memory brought a strong, queasy response. 'I think,' he said, 'that the king is about to enter the building.'

chapter seventeen

twilight of the gods

'I leave you, hoping that the lamp of liberty will burn in your bosoms, until there shall no longer be a doubt that all men are created free and equal.' Abraham Lincoln

Blood stained the front of Hal's shirt and crusted his top lip where he had been punched repeatedly in the face by members of the arresting party. His jaw ached and one eye was so swollen that he could barely see out of it. The guards had made it quite plain that there would be no trial, judge or jury: it had already been decided that he was guilty of the assassination plot.

He'd lost consciousness at some point during the beating, but now, as he looked around, he saw that he was in one of the cells in the high-security area in the Brasenose/Lincoln complex. Through the walls, he could hear the dim cries of the supernatural creatures that had been imprisoned down there; they all sounded distressed, frightened.

Dull panic battled with guilt. Everyone was relying on him and he'd allowed himself to be taken; he should have guessed that Reid and the others would know where he'd be hiding out. Hunter wouldn't have made that mistake, nor would any of the others. Why was he so useless? He fought down his contempt for his own abilities and forced his mind to focus on a way of getting out. The alternative was unthinkable.

As Hal racked his brains for some kind of strategy, the door swung open and Reid slipped in.

'Mister Reid, I didn't do anything—' Hal's protestations died on his lips when he saw Reid's slight smile.

'Of course you didn't.' Reid leaned against the door and folded his arms. He was completely assured, displaying just a hint of the arrogance that he had kept in check in recent weeks. Hal could see Reid's complicity writ large in his features.

'You set me up. You're responsible for this whole plot.'

'Yes and no. I'm just a loyal servant, doing what I'm told, going where I'm ordered.'

'Then who do you report to? The General?'

Reid laughed. 'The General is a simple man. Soldiers do not normally make good politicians. He's even more of a lick-spittle than me, though I'm sure he would never characterise himself in that way. Just following orders, that's the General. The dignity and honour of being a public servant.'

Reid watched the thought processes rush across Hal's face and shook his head, laughing. 'You're too simple a person, Mister Campbell. Uncomplicated, I think is the polite phrase. Not cynical. Very, very innocent.' Reid made it sound like an insult. 'The conspiracy extends much more widely than you could possibly guess. Everyone in the Government is involved. Certainly everyone in the upper echelons.'

'The Cabinet—'

'The Cabinet, the senior advisors, spies, policemen, business leaders, aristocrats – all the people who made up the great and the good before the Fall and who now keep the country running.'

Hal was dumbfounded. 'All of them? Why? What could you possibly gain by killing the PM now, when everything is falling apart and we need a strong leader?'

'Exactly. The PM was being particularly obstructive to the route that everyone else felt was best to preserve traditional values and our way of life. And time was running out.'

'So you killed him.'

'No, you killed him.'

'There's no evidence of that,' Hal protested.

'Ah, but there is. A great deal of evidence, in fact.' Reid pulled out a digital photo of a strange star-shaped object. Hal recognised it instantly: Reid had handed it to him when he had taken Hal into the secure storeroom to give him the Wish Stone mystery to investigate. 'Odd thing, this,' Reid continued. 'We still haven't discerned if there's a biological element to it. But one of our scientists discovered early on, to his great misfortune, that when activated it pumps ever-expanding tendrils into the body and tears it apart from within. And this innocuous-looking object was by the side of the PM's body when it was found, with your fingerprints all over it.'

'So you didn't want the Stone investigated at all. It was just a ploy to fit me up.' Hal put his head in his hands, sickened by the machinations. 'What was the point in framing me? If there were so many people involved in the conspiracy, why didn't you just bump the PM off and have done with it?'

Reid grew uncomfortable; he was still hiding something. 'The majority of our soldiers and employees . . . the people generally . . . needed a culprit to focus their minds and keep them fully behind the project.'

'But why me? Was I simply in the wrong place at the wrong time?'

Reid didn't answer.

'And what was happening with Manning? All the weird things I saw—'

'Ah, Ms Manning. A very puzzling woman. She appeared to be on board at first, but recently . . .' He shrugged, shook his head. 'There's an order out for her arrest.'

'You think you've got everything covered, but it's all a waste of time. The Void is still going to wipe everything out.'

Reid nodded. 'Indeed.'

'You want that?' Hal jumped to his feet in disbelief.

Reid raised one warning finger; he remained calm, but there was a deep threat implicit in that simple motion. 'You can't escape, Hal. You can't run. Every single person in authority out in the city has your description. Orders have now gone out for you to be shot on sight. You're safer here.'

'Why don't you just kill me now?' Hal flopped on to the bed and covered his face again; nothing made any sense.

'Oh, I will. Your execution is imminent. We can't have you blurting all this out and ruining things. But first you have one more little part to play.'

It took a second for Reid's words to register, and by then the spy was slipping out of the door with a cruelly triumphant smile directed at Hal. The door closed with a click; the locks slipped back into place.

'You can set me free. I'm not going to hurt anyone.'

Caitlin's pleading voice cut to Thackeray's heart. He could barely look at her, tied to an old wooden chair, her wrists bound behind her back and roped to her ankles, the knots pulled so tightly that they had brought droplets of blood to the surface of her pale, chafed skin. Her face looked so innocent, the Caitlin he had met all those weeks ago in the devastation of Birmingham, when he'd cared for her and first realised he had fallen in love. But with the Morrigan still inside her, they couldn't take any chances. He'd seen what the goddess could do: one flick of a wrist could snap his neck and she'd move on without giving it a second thought.

'You know I can't do that,' he said.

'But there's been some kind of change. I can feel it! The Morrigan isn't controlling me any more.'

Her eyes were wide and hopeful; a faint smile played on her lips. Thackeray looked away, hating himself that he couldn't trust her any more. Part of him wished he hadn't been dragged into this senseless world of gods and magic, but then he would never have met Caitlin and his life would have been immeasurably diminished.

Yet when he glanced back at her, he felt that there *was* something subtly different about her, though he couldn't quite put his finger on what it was.

Caitlin put her head back, her eyes flickering. 'It feels as if she's . . . waiting,' she muttered to herself.

The door was thrown open abruptly and Harvey launched himself into the room. He'd been keeping watch from the first floor for any developments. 'We've got to get out of here. They're evacuating the street.' He rubbed a hand over a thin wrist for warmth. 'Moving everybody to some buildings down in the centre. Like that's going to do any bloody good,' he added dismally.

Thackeray glanced at Caitlin, her head framed against the window where the snow fell heavily. Harvey was one step ahead. 'What are we going to do with her?'

'We can't leave her here.'

'It's too dangerous to take her with us.' Harvey's Birmingham accent grew thicker in times of stress. 'Bloody hell, Thackeray. You've got us into a right old mess. Why couldn't you have fallen for a normal girl?'

Torn, Thackeray wandered past Caitlin to look out of the window. There was frantic activity in the street, people running, others tumbling out of doorways, laden with possessions. Unconsciously, he reached out a hand to touch Caitlin's hair.

The snapping of ropes caught him by surprise. His wrist was snatched, gently, as Caitlin rose up and turned towards him. Across the room, Harvey flung himself back against the wall, whimpering. 'Don't hurt him,' he pleaded.

But after the initial shock, Thackeray wasn't scared. The cold, terrifying fury of the Morrigan was no longer visible in Caitlin's face. Thackeray pulled her to him and held her tightly, her heart thundering against his chest.

When she pulled back, tears gleamed in her eyes. 'It's come back.' A transcendental smile leaped to her lips. 'I felt it enter me . . . blue . . . so very blue. It's back, Thackeray. I'm one of them again.'

Corpus Christi was filled with long shadows as Shavi and Sophie made their way along empty corridors where the only sound was their footsteps. Finally, they found an unlocked office and slipped inside.

Sophie battened down her anxiety and said, 'Do you think you can make contact here?'

'I will try.' Shavi cleared a desk to one side to make a space on the floor for him to sit. 'Something is amiss. There is what I could only characterise as background interference, which is impeding my attempts to reach the spirits on the other side.'

'Interference? Is it being caused by the Void?'

'Perhaps.'

Sophie stood quietly in one corner while Shavi sat cross-legged in the centre of the room. Slowly, he lowered his chin on to his chest, his long hair falling across his face. His breathing grew slower, more measured, until he began to make a faint *soooo* sound on each exhalation. It was a ritual chant of some kind, Sophie knew, designed to attract the attention of the spirits with which Shavi communed.

After five long, tense minutes, Sophie began to believe that it wasn't going to work. But then Shavi's head snapped back as if he had been punched on the chin. His eyes were open, but all that was visible were the whites. His breathing had become laboured, and from the twitching of his facial muscles it was clear that he was in some distress. Sophie wasn't sure if it was part of the ritual, but was afraid that if she disturbed him, Shavi might come to harm.

Her paralysis was broken when blood gouted from Shavi's nose, mouth and ears, and in scarlet teardrops from the corners of his eyes. She ran to his side and put her arms around him, gently urging him to break the trance.

He came round with a convulsion that threw him halfway across the room, as if he had been hit.

When his eyes finally flickered back to normal, she began to ask what had happened. His response was so violent, it shocked her. 'It is here!' he yelled, still in the final grip of the trance. 'It has been here for a long time!'

Sophie gradually managed to calm him. Sitting up, with his head in his hands, he said with a shudder, 'My consciousness touched it. I felt . . .' He swallowed. 'Nothing. A bleak emptiness of the soul. It was horrible.'

'Are you OK?'

'I will recover.' Another shudder. 'It is as I feared: it is protecting itself, hiding its location.'

'That's interesting,' Sophie mused. 'Why would something so powerful feel the need to hide?'

Shavi forced a weak smile. 'Because the Brothers and Sisters of Dragons can stop it. It is remaining hidden until it is too late for us to do anything.'

'We have to tell the others.' Sophie helped Shavi to his feet. 'But if you can't find it, how are we going to pin it down?'

The door swung open before Shavi could respond. The silhouette framed in the doorway at first gave the impression of two people standing one just behind the other. But as the figure moved into the room, Sophie and Shavi saw that it was just one woman, her hard, pale face framed by black hair, her body swathed in expensive furs.

'My name is Catherine Manning. I know who you are, I know

what you're doing and I'm on your side,' she said in sharp, clipped tones. 'You need to come with me.'

Anticipating a weapon, Sophie pulled Shavi back towards the far wall. Even when she saw that Manning didn't appear to be armed, she still maintained her guard. 'What do you want?'

'We're in the last hour of the human race.' Manning's eyes shone glassily. 'Everything's coming to an end. The enemy have broken through our defences, and you're sitting here getting nowhere.'

'Leave us alone,' Sophie said. 'We know what we're doing.'

'Really?' Manning couldn't restrain the snide tone that came too easily to her voice. 'Do you realise what little time you have? You know nothing, do you?'

Sophie made to respond angrily, but Shavi held her back with an arm across her chest. 'And you know something?'

She nodded. 'I know the only information you need. I know where the Void is.'

Sophie turned to Shavi. 'We can't trust her. We ought to find the others.'

'We have no choice,' Shavi said. 'I have failed.' He turned to Manning. 'Where is the Void?'

'I have to take you there.'

'Shavi . . .' Sophie cautioned, but she knew he was right: if there was even the slightest chance that Manning knew the location of the Void, they had to seize it. 'All right. Take us there quickly,' Sophie said. 'But I'll be watching you.'

'Stop whining and get a move on. We may already be too late.' Manning stood back to let Shavi and Sophie pass through the door. Neither of them saw the faint outline of another figure behind her, shimmering as if fighting to gain weight and form.

The drone reverberated off buildings, setting Mallory and Hunter's teeth on edge; it sounded as if a wasp's nest as a big as a house had been disturbed. The whole of the High Street was filled from wall to wall with Lament-Brood. They lapped around on either side, their measured, relentless pace driving them on, eyes dead, weapons scraping against brickwork. An echo of the buzzing hummed in Mallory and Hunter's heads, but that was the collective voice of the Lament-Brood, whispering, cajoling, spreading its message of despair. Mallory and Hunter fought back, but it felt as though a tidal wave of depression was about to break over their spirits and consume them.

Mallory clutched his sword tightly as he urged his horse back a few paces; even the blue flames that danced along the blade were dampened. He glanced at Hunter, who looked back at him before they both fixed their eyes on the darkness looming over the heads of the marching monstrous army.

They moved their horses a few more yards away from the enemy, and when they turned back, it was there. Towering a good ten feet off the ground was the King of Insects, its body a swarming mass of wasps, bees, flies, dragonflies, every tiny scurrying creature that had been sucked into its orbit. The gravity of the being far exceeded its physical dimensions. Hunter remembered when his mind had briefly touched it on the killing fields of Scotland, but now it was more powerful, stronger, more intelligent and more savage than any of the Lords, the force of its monstrous will radiating off it like the heat from a furnace. The Lament-Brood parted in small eddies as it moved amongst them, but when its ranging eyes fell on Mallory and Hunter, both of them were stunned by the voracious glee they sensed. It wanted them; it desired to rip them apart and crush both their bodies and their souls, and they knew this as completely as if it had spoken to them.

'I'm going to need a bigger sword,' Mallory said with flat humour.

'We're going to need something,' Hunter replied. 'Let's find the others.'

They turned their horses and sped away, the weight of the King of Insects' stare hard on their backs. It was speaking to them: *I can bide my time. You cannot run. You cannot hide. Your end is near.*

They found Laura where the High Street met Cornmarket Street. She was recovering from her exertions. 'I killed the Lord of Lizards,' she said with untoward glee, 'but the Lament-Brood broke through. They're on their way here.'

'They're coming from three directions.' Hunter glanced around quickly; Laura and Mallory both knew that he was looking for a place to make a final stand. 'Have you seen Sophie and Shavi? If we can find the Void before the rest of the Lament-Brood get here, we might actually be able to achieve something.'

'Sophie helped me out earlier,' Mallory said. 'Then she drove off in the jeep with Shavi.'

'Not seen either of them since they dropped me off,' Laura said.

'Where the hell are they?' Hunter cracked his knuckles irritably, before adding to himself, 'And where's Hal?'

Rapid gunfire interrupted them as a small group of soldiers hurried past from the south. The leader saw Hunter and yelled, 'Fall back! They're coming!' The men disappeared along Cornmarket Street. The steady tramp of thousands of feet could be heard approaching up St Aldate's.

'We're going to get boxed in if we follow them,' Mallory said.

'I don't think we have a choice,' Hunter replied.

'Shame. And it's such a beautiful night,' Laura said. She raised her face so that the big white flakes could settle gently on it.

Laura climbed on to Hunter's horse and they caught up with the soldiers as they veered right into Market Street. Further along Cornmarket Street, a wall of Lament-Brood moved towards them. Mallory, Hunter and Laura galloped into Market Street, where Government workers were congregating in Jesus College and the other buildings surrounding it in a futile bid for safety.

Ahead, Hunter caught a glimpse of gold amongst the falling snow. As he neared, he saw that it was the Tuatha Dé Danann, their battle armour gleaming as they waited, bristling with arms. Lugh hailed them.

'This is where we make our stand,' Lugh said as Hunter jumped down to greet him. 'The street is narrow enough for us to hold back the main flow of the enemy.' He motioned behind him to the Divinity School. 'And if we fall, you Brothers and Sisters of Dragons may retreat in there. It is defensible. You may be able to hold it for a while.' There was little hope in Lugh's voice, but oddly little despair, either; he acted as if impending doom was just another twist in life's plan.

Hunter surveyed the Divinity School. It was easily the most beautiful medieval building in Oxford; he couldn't have imagined anywhere better for a last stand. For hundreds of years, the walls had rung with the lectures and disputations of the Theology Faculty, with talk of higher purpose, of meaning. It would be a fitting context for their defeat.

Mallory gripped Llyrwyn when he saw Caitlin marching towards them from the shadows of the ancient building. Lugh held up his hand. 'Hold your sword, Brother of Dragons. She is one of you once more. A Sister of Dragons.'

'I'm sorry,' Caitlin said when she stood before them. 'I made a mess of things. But I'm all right now. I can help.'

'How did that happen?' Mallory asked suspiciously. He couldn't forget the unbridled ferocity he had seen inside her on the frozen river.

'I think saving Sophie was the key,' Caitlin replied hesitantly. 'I don't know ... It might have been some kind of test.' She shrugged, smiled. 'Whatever, I passed. The Pendragon Spirit came back into me.' She closed her eyes beatifically, revelling in the surging energy she could feel inside her. 'I'm a Sister of Dragons again ... and I've still got the Morrigan inside me. But I can control her now.'

'Nearly a full complement of the true Five,' Mallory said.

'Nearly.' Hunter's jaw was set. He wondered if Hal was really going to let them all down when they needed him the most.

The teeth-jarring drone of the King of Insects rose up once more, the noise echoing even more loudly off the closely packed buildings. Lugh gave an order in a language that Hunter couldn't understand, and the gods fanned out across the street.

'We should be standing with you!' Mallory yelled to Lugh.

'You will get your chance to fight, Brother of Dragons,' the sun god said. 'You form the second rank. Any of the Lament-Brood who break through must be dispatched by you.'

Hunter, Mallory, Caitlin and Laura exchanged silent glances. They all knew that it was too late to consider tactics, too late to give in to despair at their diminishing chances of survival. They were in the twilight hours and the light was fading fast. All that was left to them was to immerse themselves in the moment, to fight the battle before them, and to hope that others would save the day.

The Lament-Brood came first, a purple-tinged wave breaking against the golden shore. Hunter speculated that the King of Insects had sent them ahead to test the defences. The monstrous being hovered back, watching intensely, wasps swarming around its head. The Lament-Brood slashed and hacked with the weapons embedded in their limbs, not caring whether they lived or died. The first wave fell like corn at harvest time, but their ranks were replenished in seconds. They would not be repelled, they would not be beaten.

Even so, the Tuatha Dé Danann fought with breathtaking skill and fury. Hunter, a dedicated student of the art of war, had never heard of anything like it in the annals of human history. The fluid movements of the gods' swords became a golden blur flashing back and forth, lightning strikes that sent heads and limbs flying and made a growing mountain of the desiccated, soulless bodies of the Lament-Brood. In that moment, Hunter saw clearly why the Celts had considered them gods. The Tuatha Dé Danann were glorious; their human form made them appear commonplace and understandable, but they were far, far beyond human, refined power like electricity briefly taking a shape humans could recognise.

Lugh was in the forefront of the battle, one foot braced against the bodies of the Lament-Brood as he cut down all who came at him, seemingly with no need for rest. To Hunter, he looked like the sun itself, for a powerful light shone off him the more invigorated he became; and seeing the dedication with which the Tuatha Dé Danann threw themselves into the defence of Fragile Creatures, Hunter wondered if there was a chance they could win, despite the odds.

Like the others, he was gripped by the battle and the clashing of steel, but his attention was disturbed by a presence beside him. It was Ceridwen, floating like a ghost from the Divinity School. 'You are seeing the twilight of a race,' she said. Tears glistened in her eyes.

And as if in answer to her words, the first of the Tuatha Dé Danann fell. A flurrying cloud of golden moths soared up to meet the falling snow from the place where his body had been sundered by a Lament-Brood axe. In that instant, Hunter knew that he had been fooling himself. However great the Tuatha Dé Danann were, they were just a handful against a multitude, and like the rocks on a beach they would slowly be eroded by the pounding waves.

Laura darted forward and retrieved the sword dropped by the departed god. She offered it to Hunter. 'A going-away present,' she said with a wry smile. 'Use it wisely.'

Hunter gripped it tightly, enjoying the way it appeared to sing in his hands. 'Get set,' he shouted.

'There's just too damn many of them,' Mallory said bitterly.

Another of the gods fell in a burst of golden wings. Caitlin removed one of the axes fastened to her back. A chill ran through Hunter as he saw the odd cast of her face: the Morrigan was preparing for battle.

'Since the first glimmer of light in the universe, my people have been bound into the heart of Existence,' Ceridwen continued in a low, mournful tone that oddly rose above the sound of battle. 'We thought we would always be here, always standing proud with a view across the many lands. But now our age is coming to an end.'

'You don't have to die here,' Hunter said.

Ceridwen shook her head. 'We have chosen to make a stand with the Fragile Creatures, our kindred now. We will not let you down, whatever is to become of us. The Golden Ones will fight to the last.'

She bowed her head slightly, then returned to the Divinity School as if the battle had already ended.

At the far end of the street, beyond the looming bulk of the King of Insects, Hunter could just make out a disturbance, rapid movement, the flash of steel.

'The Wild Hunt,' Mallory said in awe.

Otherworldly horses, filled with power and ferocity, cut a swathe through the Lament-Brood. Their riders brought down scores of the enemy with long pikes affixed with sickle-shaped blades. Every now and then, strange red and white dogs ran up sheer walls before descending on the Lament-Brood with snapping jaws.

Though the Hunt fought ferociously in and out of the surging currents of the Lament-Brood, there were not enough of them to make any significant impact. Hunter felt his mouth grow dry, his palms sweaty, familiar signs that told him instinctively that battle was not far away.

Four more of the Tuatha Dé Danann fell on one edge of their defensive line, leaving a gap through which the Lament-Brood surged. Caitlin bounded forward in an instant with a blood-curdling yell and a flash of an axe, and the first of the Lament-Brood dropped to its knees, its head cleaved in two at the level of the top of its ears. Caitlin followed through with a backhand slash that took down another. And then she was fighting wildly, using not just the axe, but tearing at throats with nails and teeth if her strokes were constricted. Eyes were torn out, ribs dug open and snapped, jaws ripped off.

And then Mallory was at her side, the blazing blue flames of Llyrwyn adding a majestic counterpoint to the Morrigan's horror of blood and death. Together they plugged the gap.

Yet there was only the briefest lull, for more gods fell at the other end of the line and Hunter threw himself into the fray to fight alongside Laura, who was using both a short sword and her own abilities to send nature rampant in the vicinity, bursting bodies with suddenly sprouting trees or tying others up in constricting ivy.

In the thick of it, there was no room for distraction; every iota of concentration and energy was given over to staying alive. Each opponent was only inches away from Hunter's face, their eyes glassy, their flesh peeling back to reveal the bone beneath. And as each one fell, another took their place. Wounds multiplied across Hunter's body.

Then an axe came crashing down towards him. Hunter barely avoided it, but the blow continued to fall and sheared Laura's sword hand off at the wrist.

'Don't worry!' she cried. 'Don't worry!' She staggered back, clutching at the stump, her face drawn. But there was no blood.

Hunter had no chance to check whether she had crawled back to safety, for the Lament-Brood were instantly forcing their way through the gap in the line, driving the other defenders back.

'Retreat! Regroup!' Lugh yelled.

Hunter ran into the shadow of the Divinity School and only then did he see with dismay that a mere seven of the Tuatha Dé Danann remained. Lugh stood amongst them, heroically organising his dwindling band for their final stand, and though his face remained stoic and committed, Hunter knew what desperate thoughts must be raging through his head at the impending destruction of his race.

Lugh saw Hunter staring and said, 'We stand and fall as brothers, our two peoples joined for all time. Equals. What do you say, Brother of Dragons?'

'I say we're proud to have you at our side, Lugh.' Hunter's attention was caught by Laura sitting against a wall.

'Keep your eyes on the battle,' she snapped. 'I can look after myself.'

340

Though he couldn't be sure, it appeared to Hunter that where her stump had been, something was growing.

Mallory was suddenly at his side. 'This is madness. We've barely made a dent in the Lament-Brood and that big bastard is still waiting there, untouched. If he's directing them, we should try to take him out.'

'I agree,' Hunter said. 'But how do you propose we get through that lot?'

The next wave of Lament-Brood reached them a second later. The defenders fought furiously, but their numbers were too few. They were driven back and back, until they were pressed against the ancient brick walls. Hunter knew the signs: they were minutes from being overrun.

Another of the Tuatha Dé Danann fell, and then another, as Hunter yelled, 'We can't hold the position! Get inside the building and barricade the doors!'

But they were already too hemmed in to escape to the Divinity School's entrance. While striking out with his sword, Lugh turned to Hunter and said, 'Get set, Brother of Dragons. The Golden Ones will buy you time.'

Hunter knew what he meant, and felt a wave of sadness wash over him. But there was no time to consider it or even to acknowledge Lugh's final act of sacrifice. While Hunter fought for his life against two of the Lament-Brood, Lugh drove forward with his remaining men, apparently towards the King of Insects. The Lament-Brood instantly turned all their attention on the gods.

Lugh led his men into the heart of the surging mass. There was no possible escape; blows were raining in from every side.

With Caitlin fighting a frenzied rearguard action, Hunter led Mallory and Laura through the open door of the Divinity School. Once inside, Hunter turned to look back. Golden moths were glowing amongst the snowflakes.

But Lugh fought on alone, not relenting in his determination to repel the attackers, until there was a bright flash like the sun coming up on a glorious day. When the light cleared, he was gone.

chapter eighteen

the king of insects

'The next greatest misfortune to losing a battle is to gain such a victory as this.' Arthur Wellesley, Duke of Wellington

Hal refused to give in to despair. While the cries of the supernatural beings that filled the cells around him grew more frenzied with each passing hour, he had reached a Zen-like state where he had just about managed to prevent the guilt and the powerlessness from eating away at him. All his hope was placed in Hunter and the others. They would discover where he was, and then overcome all odds to free him. That was the kind of thing the Brothers and Sisters of Dragons did.

The door swung open and two armed guards stood there. 'It's time, traitor,' one of them said with an underlying note of contempt. 'We're to take you to your place of execution.'

The hammering at the doors sounded like the end of the world. Deafening echoes reverberated so loudly throughout the Divinity School that Mallory had to yell to be heard above the din.

'What's the point of this?' he shouted. 'All we're gaining is a few more minutes. Sooner or later they're going to break in and this place will be a slaughter house.'

Hunter remained unaccountably · calm. Though the others couldn't see the signs in his face, Lugh's sacrifice had affected him deeply – a higher being giving up its existence for a lesser life form;

342

it brought sharply into relief the responsibilities that he had already accepted.

'We're not giving up,' he said calmly.

The Divinity School was a long hall with a flagged stone floor and rows of tall windows on opposing walls that flooded the place with sunlight during the day. Overhead, a carved, vaulted ceiling added to the atmosphere of majesty, which coexisted uncomfortably with the chaotic sound of the Lament-Brood attempting to smash down the doors with their weapons and fists.

A group of around forty people cowered in one corner of the room. Thackeray and Harvey were doing their best to calm them, and were looked upon with a touch of awe, as if they were emissaries between the heroic, almost god-like defenders and the ordinary people.

Hunter observed them and felt a touch of humility at the task that had been presented to him. For the first time in his life he was in a fight that felt completely just, where death was not simply a matter of political expediency. 'There's a second storey housing the library,' he said. 'Let's get up there. And bring Ceridwen.'

As they crossed the floor, Thackeray grabbed Caitlin. 'You're not going out there, surely?' he asked.

She nodded. 'I've got a big responsibility invested in me, Thackeray. I can't turn away from it.'

A huge weight of emotion lay behind his quiet sigh. 'I followed you from this world to T'ir n'a n'Og, put my life on the line . . . bloody hell, put Harvey's life on the line, which he'll never let me forget. You're a very special person, Caitlin. I've never met . . .' His words faltered. 'Look, I'm a soft old romantic and I don't want you holding that against me. I just wanted to say that I love you. I've never loved anybody the way I love you.' He let out another sigh. 'There. No going back now.'

Caitlin leaned forward and kissed him gently on the lips. 'I know.' She smiled, turned to leave, then paused. When she looked back, her eyes were bright and free of the Morrigan's coldness. 'I love you, too, Thackeray. And given time . . . when my husband's death isn't so raw . . . I'm sure that love would grow. I know it would.'

'That's a relief,' he said with faux-lightness. 'Then you'd better make sure we get the time together that we need.'

His eyes never left her as she joined the others and then disappeared in search of the stairs. Even then, he concentrated on the ghost-image she had left in his mind, until Harvey urged him to return to help the frightened group of survivors.

From the first-floor window, Mallory and Hunter looked out on a street where purple mist almost obscured the packed bodies of the Lament-Brood pressing against the Divinity School. The sheer weight of their bodies would soon break down the doors. Further along, the King of Insects rose up above the seething mass. Whatever power lay within it disrupted Mallory and Hunter's thoughts with mind-images of a world swarming with nothing but cockroaches.

'We're mad, aren't we?' Mallory said quietly.

'Not mad,' Hunter replied. 'We simply don't have a choice. This is what we do.' Hunter glanced at Mallory, reading his secret thoughts easily. 'She'll be all right.'

'I'm glad you're so confident.'

'She's as tough as us and probably significantly smarter. She'll be hiding out somewhere.'

Mallory nodded, but didn't meet Hunter's eye. Caitlin led Ceridwen up to the window; the goddess was broken, barely able to cope with the devastation that had been inflicted on her people.

'We need your help,' Hunter said bluntly. 'There aren't many of your kind left out there, but we need the ones that are. Specifically, we need the Wild Hunt. Can you contact them?'

Dazed, Ceridwen nodded slowly. Hunter explained to her exactly what he required, then sent her off to perform whatever ritual she needed to carry out to reach the Hunt.

Before she left, she paused and turned back. 'Watch the dogs carefully,' she said.

'The Hunt's dogs? Those weird red and white things?' Mallory said.

'Your kind used to call them the Hounds of Annwn, but they are also known as the Hounds of Avalon. Though they appear as hunting dogs to you, that is not what they are. Like many things from the Far Lands, your limited perception gives them a form you can understand.'

Mallory opened his mouth to ask a question about the dogs' true nature, but Hunter interrupted him. 'Why should we watch them carefully?' he asked simply.

'They know when everything is coming to an end. When all of this –' she made a broad gesture '– is falling apart. When the time comes, they will band together and their multiplicity of howls will become one – a sound of sadness that will rip into your hearts. It is the cry of dying.'

Ceridwen left and the others returned to the window. 'I don't like it that we're weakened,' Mallory said. 'The Five who fought at the Fall clearly have some of the Pendragon Spirit left in them, but it's not enough. We need the Five who are supposed to be here, standing shoulder to shoulder.'

'There's still time,' Caitlin replied. 'We need to be united to defeat the Void and we still have no idea where it is.'

'I wonder who the fifth is,' Mallory mused. 'When I was on the road, I met a woman who was in tune with the original Fabulous Beast. She told me that Existence, or whatever you want to call it, had been a bit cannier this time in bringing the latest Five together.'

'How so?' Hunter asked, intrigued.

'Three of us are different this time.' Mallory peered into the distance through the falling snow, waiting for the Wild Hunt to appear. 'It was an attempt to mask us from the Void, so that we would have a chance to get together before it wiped us out. Me,' he looked at Hunter, 'I'm dead. Died in another world, then was resurrected here. I can't begin to get my head around that. It's too big. But the Void still picked up on me pretty quickly. Then there's one called the Broken Woman . . .' He glanced at Caitlin; she nodded.

'I went over the edge for a while.' She smiled tightly. 'Some might say I never came back.' She tapped her head. 'Different personalities in here. But the Void sniffed me out quickly as well.'

'The other one was described to me as the Shadow Mage,' Mallory continued. 'I don't know what that means, but if he or she is still below our radar, maybe that bodes well.'

'Who could it be?' Caitlin said. 'They must have been drawn here. Thackeray? Harvey?' She shook her head, knowing it was neither of them.

They had no more time to ponder the conundrum, for the Wild Hunt suddenly burst into view, tearing their way through the

Lament-Brood like a hurricane of knives. In a matter of seconds, they had cut their way past the King of Insects and reached the Divinity School.

'No more talking,' Hunter said. 'Time to do the business.'

The chaos the Wild Hunt had caused in the ranks of the Lament-Brood prompted the King of Insects into violent activity. The towering creature lurched forward, surrounded by a cloud of wasps and flies that surged out in all directions.

Hunter was the first to drop from the window into the mêlée, followed swiftly by Mallory and Caitlin. The instant they hit the ground, they struck out for the King of Insects, ruthlessly chopping down any Lament-Brood that fell in their way. Mallory's sword was a blaze of Blue Fire, lighting the way for the others. Caitlin hacked savagely with her twin axes, while Hunter darted and thrust with power and grace.

In the thick of the transformed warriors, the air of despair was palpable, but Hunter, Mallory and Caitlin kept the sour emotions at bay by sheer force of will.

Within minutes, it became apparent that they would not succeed. Even with the Wild Hunt carving a path for them towards the King of Insects, the Lament-Brood were so numerous that Hunter realized that the three of them would not be able to get back to a position of safety even if they did kill it. They would fall and die there, in the middle of the walking-dead army.

It was not something they had time to consider; their world was confined to inches around their bodies and their lives were counted in seconds as they survived one attack and prepared for the next.

By the time they reached the King of Insects, the creature was in a frenzy. Its massive droning arms thundered, crushing the heads and spines of its own troops as it drove towards the Brothers and Sister of Dragons.

Caitlin was just emerging from the dismembered bodies of two of the Lament-Brood when one of the King's fists smashed against the side of her head, flinging her yards away. In his peripheral vision, Hunter was convinced that she had been killed by the force of the blow. But a second later she was on her feet, shaking the echoes from her head as she launched herself at the King of Insects in a berserker rage; the Morrigan had come to the fore, raining axe-blows, hacking viciously into the King of Insects' form.

Hunter lost sight of her as he fought his way around a knot of Lament-Brood. When he surfaced, it was into the path of one of the King of Insects' gigantic hands. It closed rapidly around his head, hauling him off his feet and high into the air. The memories of the torment he had suffered in Scotland came flooding back. Dry insect bodies squirmed against his face and flies forced their way up his nostrils and into his mouth, the pressure of them increasing inexorably, their buzzing so loud that he thought his head would explode.

And just when he thought his skull would shatter, he was falling. He came down in front of Mallory, whose fiery sword had hacked through the King of Insects' wrist.

Hunter choked and spat out a mouthful of dead flies. 'Thanks,' he croaked, but Mallory was already throwing himself into another furious attack.

The three of them fought for long minutes, circling the King of Insects rapidly. They attacked whenever its defences dropped, while at the same time fighting the Lament-Brood, which not even the Wild Hunt could keep at bay.

With exhaustion creeping up on him, Hunter knew that the end was near. Steeling himself for a final burst of effort, he caught sight of a white flash, like sheet lightning, that appeared to emanate from a street away.

He fought on, wondering if it was some optical illusion caused by the patterns left on his retina by Mallory's flaming sword, or a sign of even more bizarre weather on the way.

Another flash burst brightly at the end of the street, this time unmistakably lightning. Caitlin launched herself on to the King of Insects' back, ignoring the stings and bites as she clung on with one hand, chopping relentlessly with her remaining axe. Hunter saw her pause mid-strike, drawn by whatever was taking place further down the street.

Another bolt of lightning seared down from the heavens mere yards away. Hunter was blinded by the flash for a split second, and when his eyes cleared there was a heap of charred Lament-Brood corpses all around. It was a miracle it had missed him.

Then events happened in rapid succession. As he fought, Hunter became aware of Lament-Brood bodies churned up into the air as if struck by a powerful machine. They crashed against walls, rained down into the mass all around, taking more down with them.

Something was coming, tearing through the army like a whirlwind. The King of Insects' bludgeoning attack kept Hunter fully occupied – swarms of insects engulfed him repeatedly before returning to the central form, and those powerful fists swung down like sledgehammers – but his mind raced with one question: friend or foe? Friend or foe? He was exhausted. They couldn't fight on three fronts.

Caitlin's frenzied axe-attacks on the King of Insects started to have results. In several sections, though small, its basic form appeared to be ruptured; insects sprayed out into the freezing air like steam escaping from a pipe.

Mallory's sword blazed as it took off part of the King of Insects' ribcage, and in that sapphire illumination, Hunter saw Mallory's puzzled expression as he glanced once again at what was approaching.

The rain of dismembered Lament-Brood grew more intense and Hunter had to dive out of the way of several falling bodies. His final leap somehow brought him into a position that gave him a good view down the street, and in that instant, he froze, oblivious to the peril all around him, at first not quite believing what he was seeing.

Walking slowly along the street was a single figure: a woman, her face as pale as the snow and terrible in the power and fury it contained. Her dark hair flew all around her head as if caught in a great wind, but her body was untouched by the buffeting. Lightning crashed all around her, and the hurricane-force gales whisked up any member of the Lament-Brood in the vicinity to dash them violently this way and that. She was glorious and untouchable. It was Ruth Gallagher.

Hunter recalled the last time he had seen her in her private ice cavern in Lincoln, devastated, frozen, and wondered what had driven her to cross the barren wastes. Her power stunned him; it was greater than anything he had ever thought could possibly exist in a human.

The King of Insects leaned forward and blasted Hunter with a stream of bees that roared from its mouth like bullets. He dived out of the way, but the few that hit him brought up red welts on his neck.

As he danced backwards and forwards, looking for a way past the King of Insects' defences, he heard his name called in an insistent, frightened voice. He turned to see Samantha sprinting towards him from the cover of one of the buildings.

'Go back!' he yelled, but she wasn't about to be deterred. He abandoned his attack on the King of Insects and ran towards her. Another of the Lament-Brood broke past the Wild Hunt into Samantha's path. Hunter reached it just in time, taking off its head with one blow, then hacking through its chest for good measure.

But as he turned back to Samantha to protect her, he just caught a fleeting glimpse of another of the Lament-Brood coming up behind her. He started to call a warning, but it was too late. A spear-head burst out of her chest and her face took on a startled, not-quite-comprehending expression.

Fury and desperate grief fighting for control, Hunter charged forward and dispatched the attacker with brutal ease. He hacked off the spear shaft and Samantha slumped on to her back in the churned-up grey snow. She coughed, and a bubble of blood trickled down her chin.

Hunter's heart hammered so loudly in his chest that it drowned out all sound of the battle. Ignoring his own safety, he cradled her head. He had seen enough deaths to know that she had little time left, but this was the first one that had affected him so profoundly.

'You've got to get to Hal,' she said. Her eyes were wide and staring, still not understanding what had happened to her. The shock had eliminated all her pain.

'Don't talk,' he said, though he was really saying it to himself. *Don't talk, don't think, don't see what you're seeing.*

'No,' she croaked, 'you don't understand. Hal's been arrested ...' Another cough, another bubble of blood. 'Reid's got him ... trying to frame him. Hunter, they're going to execute him—'

'When?'

'Don't know. Probably soon—'

'Is he being held under Brasenose?'

But she was already gone. Hunter scooped her up in his arms and ran to the edge of the street, where he placed her gently in a doorway. He allowed himself one last look at her, but no emotion. Then he bounded back into the fray as if nothing had happened. 'We have to wrap this up quickly,' he yelled to Mallory.

The King of Insects was sagging now. Mallory took out another chunk of torso, releasing a further cloud of flies and wasps. They buzzed briefly before dying in the cold.

'Why?' Mallory gasped. 'You just want to spoil the fun.'

'We've got to stop them from killing Hal. If they do, it's all over.'

Mallory eyed him curiously. 'Is he the fifth?'

Hunter said nothing, but his silence was answer enough.

Just beyond the King of Insects, Ruth directed the lightning and wind like a goddess come down to earth. Her face registered no emotion, but her eyes would have broken anyone's heart.

Finally the King of Insects expired in a gush of flying creatures and a burst of purple mist. Even then Caitlin didn't stop; she crushed carapaces underfoot and chopped at what remained of the thing's form until there was nothing left but an ugly smear in the snow. Finally, the frighteningly intense cast of her face lifted to reveal the gentle, hopeful Caitlin who had been waiting within.

There were no more standing Lament-Brood in the street, though others were beginning to arrive at the far end. The Wild Hunt charged down to meet them head on.

While Mallory gathered his strength, Hunter ran over to Ruth. The winds dropped and the lightning faded away.

'Why?' was all he said.

'There's no escape from responsibility,' she said bitterly. And this time Hunter knew exactly what she meant.

'Church would have been proud of you,' he said.

'If he was still alive, I would have thought that worthwhile.'

Knowing there was nothing else to say, Hunter returned to the others, not realising the desperate pain that Ruth had suffered in the silence of her sanctuary after he and Laura had left her alone in Lincoln, not comprehending her grief at the memories of the man she had loved and lost, and what that man would think of her for ignoring such a call. As she had left Lincoln on horseback, a part of her had even hoped that she would die so that she could be with her love again. No one would ever understand the depth of her despair that she still lived on, to suffer more. Icily, she set off to seek out more Lament-Brood. She wouldn't rest until they were all driven back to the darkness or torn asunder. And even then there would be no peace. If only she could see Church again, she thought. If only she could feel his strength, and his wisdom, and his sensitivity. But wishing achieved nothing.

In the complex deep beneath the echoing, empty corridors of Brasenose and Lincoln, the General sat in a bleak room, struggling with a half-remembered notion of a similar occasion when he had been surrounded by other hard men. The memory was elusive, and could well have been a dream, but it only added to his sense of desperation.

On the table before him was an ivory-handled pistol that had once belonged to his father. The knowledge that he had been called on in Britain's darkest hour and found lacking was almost impossible to bear. He'd wrestled with his terrible failure for too long. The honourable thing would be to pay the ultimate price for losing the country to the invading force, yet he'd even failed there. He wished he was in his comfortable office in Magdalen, with its atmosphere of tradition and history, the wall of war art that spoke of his responsibilities; it would have been easier to make the decision there.

He thought of his family and wondered where they were. Still alive? He'd failed them, too, in so many ways.

All he wanted to do was to make amends, but the only option left to him would change nothing. No one would even know he had pulled the trigger.

Absently, he flicked through the very latest intelligence report that Reid's department had prepared for him. It was about the gang of thugs who wore black T-shirts marked with a red 'V'. They'd terrorised the country for months, growing in number with each passing week. All of them had now gathered in Hampstead to carry out some kind of crazed ritual in the belief that they could bring Ryan Veitch back from the dead. The population was dying in their millions and a bunch of nutters had decided to turn some rotting Brother of Dragons into a messiah. The whole world had gone insane, the General thought. What was the point in any of them carrying on?

Reid breezed in. He glanced at the gun and then at the General, but if he had any understanding of the situation he didn't show it; he probably didn't care, the General reflected.

'The men need a pep talk,' Reid said.

'What's the point?'

'It's not over yet.'

The General fixed a cold gaze on the spy. 'Have you got something planned?'

'Come on.' Reid marched out, ignoring the question.

The General sat for a second in thought, then pocketed his pistol and followed. There would be time for honour later.

In the Divinity School, the survivors chatted with incipient hope that victory had been achieved. Thackeray, who knew the worst was yet to come, did nothing to dash their optimism – after all they had been through, these people deserved at least that. Instead, he quietly found Caitlin, who was squatting in one corner, catching her breath. When she saw him coming, she stood up and they hugged each other, and then they kissed passionately, which was a shock to both of them.

'They're already talking about you in the same breath as the Five who fought at the Fall. They're going to put your name up in lights,' Thackeray said.

'Only if we win.'

'You will. I have every faith in you.'

His words filled her with a powerful sense of the responsibility that had been bestowed on her.

They were interrupted by Hunter, who urged her to come with him and Mallory to the high-security wing under Brasenose. Laura approached, her hand now fully healed. 'I'm coming, too,' she said.

Hunter bluntly refused. 'You have to find Sophie. We need her. Tell her she has to come to Brasenose immediately – she can't waste a second. All five of us have got to get together to prepare for the Void.' He turned to go, then added, 'And when you've done that, go and help Ruth. She needs you.'

Laura nodded once in agreement, and departed without another word.

'When are you going to fill us in on who the fifth Brother or Sister is?' Caitlin asked as she ran alongside Hunter and Mallory through the frozen night.

'When I'm sure that information isn't going to prejudice our survival,' Hunter replied.

★

352

On the journey through the cold night from Corpus Christi, Sophie had never let her attention waver from Manning. Sophie didn't trust her at all, despite what Shavi had said about them having no other choice. The woman's contemptuous nature made Sophie's hackles rise, but there was some other troubling quality about Manning that Sophie couldn't quite define.

The corridors they were now walking along were dark and quiet. Sophie didn't know Oxford well enough to be able to work out where they were and Manning had refused to offer any guidance. Shavi wasn't any help, either. Since they had left Corpus Christi he had been slipping in and out of a trance state, as if the ritual he had conducted earlier refused to let him go.

Manning suddenly stopped short, as though sensing something beyond Sophie's range of perception. 'There'll be things coming down here soon,' she hissed. She chose a door at random, then ushered Sophie and Shavi in.

Shavi slumped into a corner, barely conscious. Sophie turned on Manning, her patience gone. 'You said you were taking us to the Void.'

'I lied.'

The baldness of Manning's response brought Sophie up sharp, but within a second she was preparing to summon up the power that the Craft put at her disposal.

'Don't try any of your witchy stuff on me. Really, it won't do any good,' Manning cautioned. 'Let me rephrase: I lied about taking you to the Void, but that wouldn't help you anyway. You'd be destroyed in a second. But I have brought you here for a reason.'

'You'd better explain yourself quickly. I'm not going to be pushed around any more.'

'All right. Now's as good a time as any. You need to be here—'

'Why?'

'Because here is where everything's going to end. And if you're not here it would ruin my plans.'

'A trap, then.' Sophie's eyes narrowed. She steeled herself, ready to attack.

'Really, there's no hope of winning this battle,' Manning said. 'But just to show you what a good sport I am, let me tell you how it all *is* going to end. I'll tell you the truth. About everything. I'm sorry to say you're not going to like it. Even worse, you're not going to be able to tell a soul.'

The guards led Hal through the maze of corridors, then up a flight of stairs and out into a small courtyard that smelled of rotting refuse. Walls rose up on either side, making it oppressively dark.

'Kneel,' one guard barked. He motioned with a handgun to the centre of the courtyard.

The realisation that this was the place where he was going to die hit Hal hard. A shudder ran through him, closely followed by the absurd acknowledgement that the location was so mundane. He'd end his life, unmourned and forgotten, in a place where rubbish was disposed of.

As he knelt in the thick snow, the blood thundering in his head, every sensation was heightened: the stink of old cabbages; the bitter cold making his skin ache; the distant, undefined noises of the city; snow crystals glimmering like jewels in the thin light that filtered into the courtyard; the bitter taste of bile in his mouth.

The hard muzzle of a gun pressed against the back of his head. For a second, Hal thought he was going to be sick.

And in that instant, remembrance surged through him like a shock of electricity. His hand shot into his pocket and his fingers closed around the Bloodeye for the final time. Words sprang to his lips unbidden: 'Far and away and here.' Just a rustle in the stillness of the courtyard, but they were heard a universe away.

A shadow like a giant spider fell across the snow. One of the guards choked on an exclamation of horror in his throat.

The gun fell into the snow and hot, sticky liquid splattered over the back of Hal's head. The other guard was shouting into his radio: 'The prisoner is escaping. Repeat, the prisoner is—'

There was a tearing sound, a gurgling and then silence. Still shaking, Hal raised his head to see the bodies of the guards lying nearby, broken and bloody.

'Come, Brother of Dragons.' The voice sounded like fingernails on glass. Hal looked around to see Shadow John from The Hunter's Moon lurking in the twilight area between the shadows and the snow, his seven-foot-tall, painfully thin figure given extra height by his stovepipe hat. Yet there was something different about him. In the pub, he had appeared jovial and elegant, but in the cold, hard night of the real world there was a menacing air about him. He was hunched slightly, one gimlet eye darting hungrily back and forth, those stretched-toffee fingers now sharp as razors and stained with blood.

Hal stood up, fighting to steady himself. 'I don't know what to do,' he ventured.

'Do? You must run, Brother of Dragons. Run!' Shadow John waved a skeletal arm wildly. 'And hide! Your enemies here will kill you if they find you! Run! And we shall protect you!'

There was a frightening insistence in Shadow John's voice, verging on madness. Hal didn't wait a second longer. He turned and bolted back the way he had been brought.

In the first corridor, he came across Mother Mary, the cackling old crone, who had seemed almost senile the last time he'd seen her. She sat cross-legged in a pool of gore, white cap stained scarlet, while her black cat played with the remains of a guard. As Hal ran past her, she eyed him coldly, like a lion ready to pounce. Hal didn't look back.

Two minutes later, he came across another familiar figure. The attractive but unbalanced woman with the long blonde hair that moved like snakes had another guard pinned against a wall; it was impossible to tell if she was attacking him or seducing him. His trousers were open, his erect penis gripped tightly in her hand, but his eyes had rolled upwards to show the whites and a string of drool was falling from one corner of his mouth.

She looked at Hal seductively. 'Run, Brother of Dragons,' she whispered sibilantly.

Hal ran, scared now that what he had unleashed might prove worse than the threat he had sought to eliminate. The man who resembled a devil, with horns and cloven hooves, stalked past, completely oblivious to Hal; there was murder in his eyes and a smell of brimstone about him. Further on, Bearskin hunched over a bundle of bloody rags, feeding.

Finally, Hal came to a dark, deserted room and flung himself inside. He slammed the door shut and slipped down to the floor, listening to the constant padding of feet without, and the sounds of rending, and the running, and the screams, until he covered his ears and bowed his head and wished he was a boy again.

chapter nineteen

the cold at the end of the world

'Those who cannot perform great things themselves may yet have a satisfaction in doing justice to those who can.' Horace Walpole

Oxford felt like Christmas Eve as Hunter, Mallory and Caitlin ran through the deserted streets. Preternaturally quiet, with the snow lying heavy on the rooftops and roads, there was something uncannily magical about the city. Occasionally, they glimpsed shimmering buildings, ghostly in blue, hovering just behind the familiar ancient landmarks. Just a trick of the light, they told themselves.

Somewhere, Ruth Gallagher was harrying the remnants of the Lament-Brood to destruction. It was in all their minds: once she had been like them, someone struggling to do the right thing against impossible odds, and now she had risen to the status of legend. A human become god. And so it was for all the Five who had fought at the Fall: gods and demi-gods, angels – and even, in Veitch, a devil to haunt the nightmares of the people. Great, greater, greatest.

Yet this time it was down to the three of them, and Sophie wherever she was, and the mysterious fifth, to defeat something of such magnitude that it was defined as the opposite of life. It didn't seem right; it certainly wasn't fair.

Only Hunter had reached any kind of accommodation with the dilemma. For him, it was simply a matter of acceptance. Samantha's death had removed any link he had with the rest of the world.

He had no need of softness or any care for his own survival. Now it was simply death or glory.

And so they arrived at Brasenose. At first glance it appeared deserted, though lights glared from the windows. No sounds of life greeted them as they ventured into the echoing corridors.

'Maybe they all evacuated when the Lament-Brood came,' Mallory hissed.

Hunter shook his head. 'When the Government first moved here, they restructured this place for high security. It wouldn't make sense for them to leave – they'd be safer here than anywhere else.'

Caitlin stopped moving and sniffed the air. 'There are people here. Down below.'

'You can smell them?' Mallory said incredulously. 'You know what, sometimes you are an extremely creepy woman.'

Her smile was a challenge. 'You don't know the half of it.'

'Then we should proceed with extreme caution,' Hunter said. 'Either they're gathered for the execution, or they're barricaded in waiting to blow the heads off anyone who turns up.' He crept stealthily to the end of the corridor and sneaked a glimpse around the corner.

'You've done this kind of thing before, haven't you?' Mallory said wearily.

'Once or twice. Luckily for you.'

'Me, I'd just charge in with sword swinging.'

'Like I said, luckily for you one of us knows what they're doing.'

Hunter led the way down a short flight of stairs to the lower level. At the bottom step, Caitlin caught his arm. 'Someone's nearby,' she mouthed. She paused, raised her head slightly. 'It's—'

'Over here.' Sophie beckoned them urgently. At the end of the corridor, she was staggering under Shavi's weight, who was pale and a little delirious. The others ran up to relieve her.

Mallory grabbed her by the shoulders, unable to restrain his joy. 'Are you all right?'

'Fine.' She forced a smile, but Mallory could see that she was lying.

'What's wrong?'

'Nothing.'

'You don't fool me. Spit it out.'

She pulled him towards her and kissed him with a surprising passion that spoke of desperation and loss. When she broke off, she said quietly, 'Don't ask me any more. I can't tell you. Not now.'

'Later?'

She nodded, but there was a deep sadness shadowing her smile that Mallory didn't notice. He was distracted by Hunter gently slapping Shavi's cheeks to bring him round.

'He's been in a trance,' Sophie said. 'There were some things he needed to find out. But then he started raving, as if . . . as if what he saw was too terrible to believe. And then he ended up like this.'

'Have you found anyone down here?' Hunter asked her as he continued to try to bring Shavi back to consciousness.

'There was a lot of commotion along that way.' She motioned in the direction of the high-security wing. 'We found some guards dead . . . butchered. That's when we decided to come back to look for you. If there's anyone left alive, they must have locked themselves in somewhere secure.'

Caitlin nodded. 'That's what we thought, too.'

'Then maybe they haven't had time to carry out the execution,' Hunter said with some relief.

Hunter's insistent efforts finally brought Shavi round, his eyes gradually focusing. He tried to support his own weight, staggered, then succeeded in propping himself against the wall.

'The things I saw,' he said, shuddering at the memory. The horror in his voice chilled them all.

'What's up, Shavi?' Mallory clapped the arm of the man he had come to consider a good friend.

Shavi managed a wan smile. 'I saw the Cailleach Bheur filling the universe with ice and snow. The White Walker has failed. The Fimbulwinter . . .' He gasped, took a deep breath. 'The prophecy of the Fimbulwinter at the end of the world, the coming of the Void – both are linked. The End-Winter comes because the final days are near . . . and the final days are near because the Void has come. But the Void needs the extreme cold to exist. It can't abide heat. It comes from beyond the edge of the universe where there is no light or warmth. It has been here, gestating in the cold, waiting until the moment is right—'

'Here?' Hunter grabbed Shavi's arm. 'Where?'

Shavi shook his head. 'I saw so many things . . . I saw the

followers of Veitch prepare a ritual of such magnitude that it sent ripples through the world. Black T-shirts, red V, faces like rainy city nights.' His eyes were glazing over again as the images paraded across his mind. 'They were drawing on the dark energy the Void brought in its wake, trying to bring him back, calling to his wandering spirit, corrupting it with the blackness, sucking all hope and chance of redemption from it.'

'Veitch is coming back?' Mallory asked. 'Are you saying he's becoming part of the Void?'

'I don't know, I don't know . . .' Shavi was slipping away again.

Hunter shook him roughly. 'Come on. Focus. We need to know what's going on.'

'And I saw . . . I saw . . .' Shavi looked at Sophie and fell silent at the expression in her eyes. 'There is no more I can tell you. The Void is here. It is ready to do what its nature has prepared it to do. The rest is not important.'

Hunter turned to the others, his face grim. 'We need to find the fifth quickly. Then get out of here and locate the Void . . . before it gets us first.'

'Bloody hell! Can't you say the name yet?' Mallory said.

'No!' Sophie gripped his wrist so tightly that her nails raised blood.

It was clear to Mallory that she knew more than she was saying; he accepted her plea with a silent nod.

'Leave me here,' Shavi insisted. 'This is no longer my business. It is the time of the new Five now. Only you can save . . . everything.'

'In case you haven't noticed,' Mallory said, unable to hide the bitterness in his voice, 'there's only four of us.'

Shavi slumped into a cross-legged position, his back against the wall, and lapsed into unconsciousness once more. That was the way they left him, a faint transcendental smile on his face, like a saint about to be led to his death.

The four of them made their way towards the high-security wing. All the cells were silent, their once-noisy occupants either dead or stilled in the gloom. They came across the corpses of many guards in various states of butchery, but whatever had slaughtered them appeared long gone.

'Is it me or is it colder in here?' Mallory said.

Caitlin exhaled heavily; a white cloud bloomed from her lips. 'It's colder,' she said.

Hunter drew his sword; Mallory followed suit, the flames of Llyrwyn painting the walls and ceiling a brilliant blue. Caitlin balanced an axe carefully in each hand; the light of the Morrigan began to come on in her eyes. Sophie followed behind, head slightly bowed, her hands at her sides.

They turned into another corridor and were shocked to see the walls glistening with a rime of frost; it was as if they'd stepped into a butcher's meat locker. The lights here were eerily dimmer, and further on the corridor progressed into darkness.

'Looks like this is it,' Hunter said redundantly.

The words had barely left his lips when a security door crashed shut behind them. They started in shock, but it was too late: their exit had been cut off. As they turned back, another security door, this time barred like a jail cell, slid into place ahead of them.

Hunter took point as doors further along the corridor opened slowly. Reid was one of the first to emerge, but behind him Hunter could just make out the shadowy figures of Government officials, the Cabinet, senior advisors who had once been the captains of industry, the aristocrats, the financial sector's biggest players.

'Open the doors,' Hunter said. 'We're here to protect you.'

Reid stood before them, carefully surveying Mallory, Caitlin and Sophie before moving his attention to Hunter. 'Still only four of you?'

'Reid, time is running out.' Hunter attempted to moderate his voice against the urgency that was straining every fibre of his being. 'The thing that's behind the invasion is already here. We need to find it – destroy it – before it wipes everything out.'

'I know exactly where it is.'

Hunter was struck dumb by the quiet confidence in Reid's voice.

Reid motioned further down the corridor. On the edge of the crepuscular zone, Hunter saw the frozen door that he had noticed when freeing Mallory. 'It's been here for a long time, Mister Hunter.'

Realisation crept up on Hunter, but not comprehension or acceptance.

Mallory, a man who mistrusted all authority, grasped the

situation instantly. 'You're working for it.' His eyes blazed as brightly as his sword.

'In a way.'

'It's controlling you,' Caitlin ventured. 'It's a very seductive power—'

Reid silenced her with a simple shake of his head. 'People who deal with power on a daily basis are pragmatic. That is the most vital quality for any political leader—'

'What about honour?' Mallory interrupted, his voice cold and hard. 'Integrity, ethics?'

'Unnecessary,' Reid replied. 'Oh, lovely, lovely qualities, of course. No one would disagree with that. But completely useless for the job of leadership. The traits you mentioned are useful for winning one great battle. But then you have to retire. Politics is about winning battles every day, little ones, mundane ones. You need to be pragmatic to retain power so that you can continue to do that.'

'Politics,' Mallory sneered. Behind him, Caitlin was checking the security door for a way out.

'Oh, politics is the most important thing of all, because it's about the way we live our lives. Every decision is a political decision. Most of us who work to keep things running can't afford the luxury of fighting for a cause, like you, however worthy that cause might be. We need to make sure that we stay in power so that we continue to live our lives the right way.'

'Which implies that *your* way is the right way.' Hunter was trying to buy the others time to find a way to break free; it was a clumsy attempt, but Reid didn't appear to mind.

'It *is* the right way. It's been proven by time. It's been accepted by the majority of the people, and consequently it is, by definition, normal. Any opposing view is therefore aberrant, and something to be resisted.' The most chilling aspect about Reid was his calm expression of his views. There was no hatred there, no contempt or anger, not even any superiority. He was like someone patiently explaining a scientific fact to the uneducated.

In a display of impotent anger, Mallory crashed his sword against the bars. The flames surged at the impact, but the blade left no mark. 'You're thinking you can use the Void to maintain power?' he raged. 'You're insane! It's Anti-Life. You can't control it. It wants to wipe out us, the world, the universe!'

'Not in the way you suggest.' Reid summoned two guards and motioned for them to train their guns on Caitlin, who was clearly considering throwing one of her axes through the bars. She reluctantly lowered her weapon. 'The Anti-Life it represents is not an absence of life. It's more abstract than that. I suppose I could wallow in the depths of philosophy, but to put it simply, you have to consider what *life* actually means. As a concept. This is all profoundly pretentious, is it not?' He gave a small laugh.

'You've communicated with it?' Hunter said incredulously.

'I wouldn't say we exactly sat down over beer and sandwiches, but yes, after it sent its advance guard to prepare the way, we found it a place to wait. And then we entered into negotiations.' He shook his head. 'If you knew what we went through, you would find that almost laughable. Negotiations. The Void, as you call it, is not a *thing*. It's not a life form. It doesn't exist in any physical way you or I could comprehend. But even so, it connected with us, and we with it. And . . . ' He held out his hands and gave a small shrug that made Mallory even angrier.

'So you gave in to it?' Caitlin said.

'You have to understand, we couldn't win. That was never on the agenda. It's too powerful. It's like trying . . .' He searched for the words to describe the magnitude of what he was attempting to say. 'Like trying to punch the universe. No point even beginning to fight. So . . . pragmatism, you see. We found out that what it wanted wasn't actually very far from what we wanted. Certainly it was something we could live with. And that's when we decided on the most beneficial course of action. If you can't win everything, you should at least try to win something.'

Hunter looked past Reid to the shadowy figures hovering in the background. 'You betrayed the whole of humanity just to save yourselves?'

'You're missing the point,' Reid said. 'Our aims are the aims of society. What's best for us is best for you. It's the same. We did the right thing.'

Hunter could see that Reid completely believed what he was saying, and that all those waiting behind him believed it, too. Flickers of dread rose in his heart. They'd lost the fight the minute they started; the seeds of that defeat were buried in the heart of what they were fighting to save. The enemy – the true enemy – was all around them. But they didn't look like the enemy, and didn't believe they were the enemy. How could anyone fight that?

'We went to the PM with our plan,' Reid continued, 'but he refused to reach an accommodation. He had to be . . . removed.' He saw the looks on Hunter and Mallory's faces and added with annoyance, 'If he'd been allowed to do what he wanted, the human race would have been extinct. How could that be right?' He loosened his tie, took a deep breath. 'You were the only real threat to everything. You Brothers and Sisters of Dragons.'

'There's no logic in what you're saying,' Hunter stated. 'If we defeat the Void, you won't have to reach any *accommodation*.'

'We weighed up that option, and for a while it was certainly a possibility. But in the end we decided that the risks were too great. The chances of outright victory seemed extremely thin, and anything less would likely result in complete eradication. So—'

'So you decided to get us out of the way.' Hunter tried to ignore Mallory, who was pacing the confines of their prison like a tiger, occasionally rattling the bars or attempting to prise open the security gates with his sword.

'There was no attempt at violence.' Reid looked horrified at Hunter's implication, completely ignoring the irony that he was complicit in the assassination of the country's leader. 'Your young friend, Mister Campbell – Hal, wasn't that his first name? I feel quite sorry for the way we had to use him. He's a rather naïve chap. Not cut out for any of this business.'

Hunter's temper flared. 'What have you done with him?'

Reid chewed his lip for a second, and it appeared that he wasn't going to answer. Then he changed his mind. 'Once we realised you were a Brother of Dragons, our route to controlling you was easy. Your long friendship with young Hal was obvious. We were able to use him to direct you to where we needed you to be.'

'Here,' Hunter said. 'So you could trap us.'

'Exactly. We framed him for the assassination in a very clumsy way, knowing that he would realise I had organised the plot. When we allowed him to escape from custody, we knew he'd go directly to your hiding place, and that once he met up with you, he would identify me or someone in the Government as the chief suspect.

Then when we let his young female friend *accidentally* discover information about his impending execution, we knew you'd realise that I would do anything to hide my complicity. Kill him even sooner to silence him. And so you would rush here to save him, even though all sense would tell you to stay away from my base of power and concentrate on the more pressing task of locating the Void. You're very easy to manipulate, Mister Hunter.'

'Not as easy as you think.' Hunter was relieved to discover that Reid still hadn't found out that Hal was the fifth, the real reason all of them had rushed to Brasenose. 'Is Hal dead?'

'The execution was set to take place half an hour ago.'

'Have you seen the body?'

'Two men with guns. One young, frightened, bookish man. Do I really need to?'

Hunter turned to the others and said quietly, 'There's still hope. Don't give up.'

Reid must have guessed what Hunter was saying, for he added, 'I'm sorry, but you really mustn't think you stand a chance. I don't know what it is about the Pendragon Spirit that makes you a threat to such a vast, unknowable force as the Void, but here you are close enough for it to work its ways on you, yet, unfortunately for you, not close enough to harm it.'

'That was always the plan,' Hunter noted.

'That was always the plan,' Reid confirmed.

Kirkham emerged from the grey background. With a cough to gain Reid's attention, the chief scientist said, 'It's time.'

Reid nodded to him. Pulling a torch from his pocket and shining it ahead of him, Kirkham proceeded towards the growing gloom emanating from the door behind which the Void existed. As he drew closer, he began to shake from the extreme cold. Frost began to form down his front.

'What are you expecting to get out of this?' Mallory shouted. 'What do you think the Void's going to give you?'

'A new world,' Reid said. 'The Void's world.'

'A world ruled by the opposite of life?' Mallory was incredulous. 'How could anyone exist in that?'

'You think this one is any better?' Reid said. 'The country's falling apart—'

'People still have their lives, their freedom,' Mallory replied, urging Reid to change his mind.

'There's magic everywhere,' Caitlin continued. 'Wonder. Endless possibilities. All the things people hoped for before the Fall—'

Reid cut her dead with a cold stare. 'It's unpredictable, uncontrollable. We can't govern. None of the things we had before the Fall can thrive here. You can't work hard to better yourself. You can't have rules and regulations. You can't have a strong society producing for the common good. No one's going to get rich here, or fat, or live out their lives in luxury. This isn't the world we spent thousands of years of human civilisation trying to form.'

'What's the Void's world going to be like?' Mallory shouted. 'Constant night? Blood? War? Death? Hopelessness?'

Reid merely gave a faint smile, then a shrug. 'Do it,' he said to Kirkham.

'There's still hope,' Hunter said to the others.

From the back of the faceless crowd of politicians and civil servants, the General made his way forward. He had a gun. 'Time to stop this,' he said.

Reid turned just as the General raised the pistol and fired. The bullet hit Reid directly between the eyes. His body slammed against the bars and then slumped down in an awkward jumble of limbs.

'Come on,' Hunter said under his breath.

'I'm in charge now,' the General said to the others. 'Stop this nonsense immediately. Free these people.'

Hunter, Caitlin and Mallory watched, silently urging the crowd to obey the General. No one moved.

The General brandished his gun at the crowd. 'I said—'

'Kill him.' The voice may have come from the deputy prime minister, or one of the Cabinet members, but it didn't really matter which. The guards responded instantly, turning their weapons on the General and cutting him down.

'Look at them,' Mallory said sickened. 'Like animals, fighting amongst themselves.' The General's blood flowed into Reid's, mingled with it, formed an ocean that separated the Brothers and Sisters of Dragons from the small crowd huddled together against the gloom.

Mallory glanced at Hunter. 'That's it, isn't it? All over.'

Shaking violently, Kirkham continued towards the frozen door that was now leaking darkness rapidly.

Hunter repeated his mantra, now a wish, a prayer: 'There's still hope.'

Kirkham's palsied hand grasped the handle. Hunter guessed that the ice must be burning his flesh, but the scientist didn't flinch; he almost appeared to be in a trance.

From somewhere that could have been far, far away or in the next corridor, an awful sound rose up that made all of them feel sick to their stomachs. It resonated deep into their bones, stabbing into their brains. They wanted to scratch at their ears, make themselves deaf. The howls of dogs joining together to form one note, one ringing chime of despair.

The blood drained from Caitlin's face. 'The Hounds of Avalon,' she whispered.

For all the time they had been imprisoned, Sophie had stood silently, observing. Mallory stepped back to take her in his arms and when he saw her face, he realised the truth. 'You knew. Why didn't you say something?'

'I couldn't take the risk that the Void might discover the fifth.' There were tears in her eyes, but no despair. She smiled. Mallory pulled her to him and they held each other tightly.

Caitlin closed her eyes and bowed her head, resting it gently against the bars.

Hunter couldn't believe it. He'd put his trust in Existence and he'd been wrong. They'd failed in the worst way possible. There was no hope.

Kirkham opened the door. The obscene howling grew deafening, subsuming every other sound. Between one tick of a clock and the next, the moment appeared to drag on for ever as all eyes focused on the gaping door. Kirkham stared into its depths, frozen. And then darkness began to seep out, slowly at first, then faster, rapidly becoming a torrent. Everything it touched became fluid, began to alter, twist out of shape, the very molecules of the fabric becoming something else. With it came an awful wave of despair, a million times more potent than anything sent out by the Lament-Brood, and everyone it touched fell to their knees, devastated at what was to come.

Hunter gripped the bars, tears burning the corners of his eyes, still unable to accept that humanity had betrayed itself, that the basest elements had won out over all that was noble in mankind.

Reality began to warp and as it rushed towards him, he had a glimmer of what it was becoming. It looked very much like the worst of all possible worlds. It looked very much like hell.

Jagged static jumped across Sophie Tallent's mind. It startled her so badly that she almost knocked her polystyrene cup of coffee across the keyboard. She guessed she had been daydreaming. It must have been a particularly deep one, for it took her a moment to orient herself, and though she couldn't recall the details, it must have been satisfying, for she felt a great wistfulness at having left it behind.

She was sitting at her desk at Steelguard Securities, the screen in front of her flickering with the constant updating of currency information from all over the world. Beyond her was the window, offering views from high over Canary Wharf across London's financial district, sitting smug and bloated beneath the thick blanket of pollution from car exhausts and the jets flying into Heathrow or London City Airport every few seconds.

Something hit her across the back of the head and this time she did spill her coffee. It was Kane, his chubby face looking like a side of ham above his salmon pinstriped shirt, and he was clutching the file with which he had clipped her. 'You're useless, Tallent. How do you expect to get any bonuses? Watch the screen.' He tapped it with a fat forefinger. 'Never take your eyes off it. If anything interesting happens, get on the phone.' He snorted with disgust. 'You're a waste of space. You know they only keep you on here because you're decorative? Mister Rowe likes to look at your tits in that nice white blouse. So if you want to hang on to your job, take your jacket off.' He stalked off to abuse some other unfortunate labouring for ten to twelve hours a day in front of one of the rows and rows of screens on the Steelguard floor.

In the corner, the TV came alive as someone turned up the sound for the morning news. More deaths after the rebels shelled a market in Najaf in Iraq. A Western businessman had been taken hostage somewhere else in the Middle East. His captors had released a video of him, staring beaten and humiliated at the camera, a knife at his throat. The prime minister and the president of the United States shook hands; another successful summit, another announcement of millions poured into a new joint weapons project. Inflation holding steady. (A cheer ran around the room.) The poverty gap had widened again. (Another cheer.)

Sophie's attention was caught by a cleaner making his way slowly across the floor, unnoticed by anyone else. He had a handsome face, though he occasionally let his long hair fall across it, as if embarrassed. He looked beaten and dejected, like a badly fitting shoe.

Mallory briefly met Sophie's gaze. Somewhere in the dark recesses of his subconscious, something stirred: a hint of recognition so vague that it was almost a shiver across his synapses, there then gone. Crazy, he thought. No details surfaced because there weren't any. His kind and hers would never meet. It just wasn't done; better keep his mind on the work if he wanted to hold on to his job. There were the toilets on this floor to clean, then the two floors above, then back to this floor. An endless cycle, never to be broken.

The dying part of Mallory knew that he would see Sophie every day as he crossed that room; their eyes would meet in vague, uncomfortable recognition, but it would never be reconciled. They would never meet. They would never speak.

Five burgers sizzled in pools of grease. Laura DuSantiago watched them, oddly captivated by something she didn't quite comprehend. How many had she cooked that day in the fast-food joint stinking of stale fat down a dingy side street not far from Northampton's main drag? How many tomorrow and the endless days after? Why was she so unaccountably queasy? It was a job; she should be thankful.

On the other side of the counter, a queue of dead-eyed people shuffled and waited, most of them overweight, heading for a heart attack sooner rather than later, clad in ugly, cheap leisurewear and knock-off trainers from the market.

Laura flipped the burgers. Five, she thought. Why was she so ill at ease? Get a grip. This is it, this is your life.

Caitlin sat in a traffic jam, listening to a Radio 1 DJ trying to get listeners excited about some kind of *event* that weekend. The cars snaked on for eight miles ahead of her and another four behind. They hadn't moved for the last five minutes; she knew because she'd watched the clock tick around on the dashboard.

She should have been at the beautician's in Gateshead fifteen minutes ago. In the boot, the boxes of samples sat, pretty pinks and russets, hair products that had been 'scientifically tested', that could make you into someone else. Really. Truly.

And of course, if she was late for the Gateshead appointment, how was she supposed to get down to Middlesbrough on time?

She thought about this for a second, then shrugged. Who cared? Who cared about anything, really? The thought made a lot of sense to her, but she still couldn't explain the grating feeling of unease in the pit of her stomach. She turned up the radio so that she didn't have to think.

Shavi sat at his desk in the accountancy office of Gibson and Layton and wondered why he'd absently doodled the number five on his pad. He didn't have time to spend daydreaming. Mr Gibson had just brought in the file for some property developer, 'a personal friend', and Shavi had a few hours to locate every possible loophole and find every creative way to lie, cheat and deceive so that the income-tax liability was as close to zero as possible.

As Shavi opened the box file, he wondered why he felt such an abiding sense of despair.

Ruth Gallagher broke off from her shift in the old people's home to sneak outside for a little cry. The owners salted away most of the vast amounts of cash paid by the loving relatives and left the poor occupants to survive – or not – on a subsistence diet, drugged up with Valium, staring vacantly at daytime TV.

Another one had died that morning, and it had been Ruth's job to clean the bedroom. She was always cleaning bedrooms. They came and went with remarkable regularity, a production line shipping them to the afterlife. No point getting to know them; they were too drugged for any conversation. The relatives didn't really care; it made the visits so much easier.

Ruth dried her eyes. No point being miserable. It was a life, wasn't it?

★

And Hunter sat in the briefing, overcome with a strange feeling of déjà vu. The map on the wall showed the former Yugoslavia, little flags signifying the rebel forces threatening to break the fragile peace.

'OK,' he said wearily, 'who do you want me to kill this time?' while entertaining an odd thought of a world where he was a force for life, not death.

In a quiet, dusty room in Brasenose, Hal huddled against a door, wondering why he was such a failure. He grew tense as footsteps echoed in the corridor outside, then rigid when they stopped at the door.

'Open up.' A familiar woman's voice.

Hal flinched. He could pretend that the room was empty, but what good would it do? She'd come in anyway. He'd been caught, might as well own up. After all, there was nowhere left to run.

When he opened the door, Catherine Manning stood there, swathed in her expensive furs. 'Ms Manning,' Hal stuttered. 'Were you looking for me?' He caught himself when he saw Manning's glassy eyes and the disturbing waxy sheen across her face; she looked oddly like a marionette.

Her mouth opened and closed, opened and closed, and when a sound finally did come out it was no longer her voice. 'The strain has been too much for this form. It cannot hold.'

Hal took a step backwards at the eeriness of a man's voice emanating from Manning's full, feminine lips.

Suddenly Manning collapsed, and as she fell to the floor she wasn't like a flesh and blood woman at all. Her body appeared to be made of paper, or perhaps just skin, folding up on itself. What was left of her lay on the floor, flat and wrinkled and twisted, like a discarded set of clothes.

And where she had been, someone else now stood. At first, the face appeared to swim before Hal's eyes and he had fleeting images of people he thought he knew and probably disliked, before the visage settled down to that of a stern-faced man dressed in flowing scarlet robes.

'Who are you?' Hal gasped.

'In the time of the tribes, I was known as Dian Cecht of the

Court of the Final Word, wise man, healer, now the last of the Tuatha Dé Danann.' The bitterness in his voice made Hal wince.

'Ms Manning—'

'She thought she could use me for her ends. I was using her for mine. I rode her body and her mind through these Fixed Lands, avoiding the notice of the Devourer of All Things, preparing for this moment.'

'I don't understand.' Hal knew that he sounded like an idiot, but he didn't know what else to say.

'Your kind have long been an interest of mine,' Dian Cecht said in a manner that on the surface appeared quite unassuming, but Hal found distinctly menacing. 'I know how you work. Inside and out. Down to the smallest particle. Though many of my kind had a strange affection for Fragile Creatures, I was not one of them. I saw in you something else: a chance for the Golden Ones to survive in a place that had grown tired of them.'

'I don't understand what you're saying,' Hal said weakly.

'In you lies the last hope of my people, and the last hope of your own. Are you ready for the task that lies before you?'

Hal stared blankly at Dian Cecht for a moment, then nodded.

'Then come.' Dian Cecht led Hal out into the corridor. 'You are a strange people,' Dian Cecht continued. 'I told a Sister of Dragons what was planned. I needed her to be there, at the end, so that the Devourer of All Things would not suspect. And she kept the secret well, even though it meant her suffering.' Dian Cecht clearly could not understand Sophie's sacrifice.

Several feet away, a shimmering wall of blue ran from wall to wall.

'What's that?' Hal asked.

'Though it took all my abilities, I have closed this small space off from Existence. It lies beyond the world on the other side of the wall, yet is still a part of it. But only for a short while. And here the Devourer of All Things has no power to see.' Dian Cecht strode ahead, so that Hal had to skip to keep up.

The god led Hal to the research rooms where Kirkham had carried out most of his experiments into finding a way to cross over to T'ir n'a n'Og. They came to the Plexiglas window that looked on to the lab where Glenning had turned to a pile of dust after returning from his trip to the other side, and Hal was surprised to see it awash with a brilliant blue light. The stately bluestone that had been brutally ripped from Stonehenge was glowing with the sapphire radiance.

'It never stopped working,' Hal said in amazement. After Glenning's death, no one had felt the need to return to the labs down here. It was considered a failed experiment and everyone had more important things on their minds.

The sheer power coming off the megalith gave Hal pause. 'That's why,' he said to himself. Then to Dian Cecht: 'Oxford was flitting in and out of the Otherworld because of this stone! The power must have been infusing the whole city!'

The door opened of its own accord and Dian Cecht stepped into the blue world. Hal followed.

'He is here,' Dian Cecht said. 'He is in your hands now.'

Standing nearby was the giant who had appeared to Hal in the Grove behind Magdalen what seemed like so long ago. The Caretaker held the Wayfinder lantern aloft, and when he smiled warmly, Hal felt all the tension leave his muscles. 'I knew you would be here, now, Brother of Dragons,' the Caretaker said warmly. 'This lantern will light your way, as it has done for many of your kind before you.'

As Hal's eyes adjusted to the megalith's flooding light, he realised that there was something else in the room. Coiled around the walls was an enormous Fabulous Beast that appeared to be made of the blue energy, yet which had solidity and weight. Its sapphire eyes were fixed firmly on him, and to Hal they appeared not like those of a beast at all, but wise and calm and wonderful. Hal had no idea how it could have entered that enclosed space.

And standing in the sinuous loops of its tail was a woman, her own eyes as blue as the Fabulous Beast's; skin pale, hair black. 'This is your time, Brother of Dragons.' It was the woman who had spoken, but the voice was deep, male and slightly sibilant.

All eyes were on him. Hal looked from one to the other and realised that he was being asked something of great importance.

'Do you understand your responsibilities, Brother of Dragons?' the Caretaker asked.

'Yes. I haven't lived up to them,' Hal admitted. 'I'm sorry . . .' He caught himself and then added honestly, 'I think I'm too much of a coward for this job.'

'Everyone has a different strength,' the woman said. 'You have used yours effectively.'

Energy arced across the room. The power emanating from the bluestone was growing more intense. Hal stood entranced by the light show for a moment before adding, 'You're talking about the code, in the painting.' He sighed. 'I know who the king is now. But it's too late.'

'It is never too late,' the Caretaker said firmly. 'The signs were left for you, and you alone, to prepare you for this moment.'

'Me?' Hal said, puzzled.

'You have a choice,' the woman added. 'You may turn away now and give all of Existence up to the Devourer of All Things. Or you must find the king and bring him back here, but the sacrifice you make will be great indeed.'

'You're saying I have to die,' Hal said. Not far from the megalith, the Blue Fire had begun to take on some kind of shape.

The Caretaker stepped forward and, for a second, Hal felt as if he was in the presence of his father. 'Nothing dies. Nothing new is created, nothing is destroyed. It is simply transformed.'

'And he's not dead? The king?'

The Caretaker smiled once more, reassuringly. 'Nothing dies.'

'He is lost,' the woman said, as if she could read Hal's mind. 'In distant times, in a faraway place, his memory fading. He will not find his way home without your guidance.'

'How can I do that?'

The Blue Fire had now formed itself into a rectangle, like a burning doorway in the air. The Caretaker stood next to it, holding the Wayfinder as if to light the way through; the lantern's flame surged and flickered and tugged towards the door.

'You must give up your mortal form,' the woman answered. 'Become one with the Pendragon Spirit.'

'In that way,' the Caretaker continued, 'you may pass through this door to the source of all things. You will become a part of Existence. You will reach through all time, all space. And for the briefest of moments you will have subtle influence. A mere tug, but it may be enough to direct the king towards this place.'

'You're saying it's like becoming . . . part of God?' Hal's mind spun.

'Everything rests with you, Brother of Dragons.' Dian Cecht was grim-faced. 'Only the king can defeat the Devourer of All Things Only he can save my people and guide your own race back to the upward path. And only you can call him.'

In a moment of utter clarity, Hal understood exactly what his sacrifice would mean: he would be converted into energy, a wavelength, a thought, a message to the past and the future. And then he would be gone, absorbed into the background energy of the universe. It was the ultimate sacrifice. Yet for the briefest time, he would be a conscious part of the underlying intelligence of Existence, and he would be able to search the twists and turns of reality for the man who would be the ultimate representation of the Pendragon Spirit. The Champion of Life, the only one who could defeat the embodiment of Anti-Life. And Hal would be a part of that champion, and a part of all the Brothers and Sisters of Dragons who had ever existed across the millennia.

After all his failures and his weaknesses, here was his chance to redeem himself, the once-in-a-lifetime opportunity to find the true strength inside him. Briefly, he had a vision of himself flashing back across time, appearing to Poussin to plant the message that he would eventually find in his real life, manifesting to the Dilettante Society and all the others he would guide so that at this point in time he would have already assimilated the information he needed to make his choice.

In truth, he had made the decision long ago.

The doorway was crystal clear now, manifested and held in place by the combined power of the Caretaker and the Fabulous Beast.

'Will you accept this quest, Brother of Dragons?' the Caretaker asked.

Hal smiled and stepped towards the light.

'We are caught in an inescapable network of mutuality, tied in a single garment of destiny. Whatever affects one directly, affects all indirectly.' Martin Luther King, Jr.